Praise for #1 *New York Times* bestselling author

NORA ROBERTS

"Nora Roberts is among the best." —*Washington Post*

"With clear-eyed, concise vision and a sure pen, Roberts nails her characters and settings with awesome precision, drawing readers into a vividly rendered world of family-centered warmth and unquestionable magic."
—*Library Journal*

"Roberts...is at the top of her game." —*People* magazine

"When Roberts puts her expert fingers on the pulse of romance, legions of fans feel the heartbeat."
—*Publishers Weekly*

"You can't bottle wish fulfillment, but Nora Roberts certainly knows how to put it on the page."
—*New York Times*

"America's favorite writer." —*New Yorker*

D0011777

**Also available from Silhouette Books
and Harlequin Books by**

NORA ROBERTS

SECRET GETAWAY
Diamonds can be a girl's best friend—or her worst enemy

WRITTEN IN THE STARS
Fairy-tale magic can charm the most stubborn heart

THE MacGREGOR BRIDES: Engaged for the Holidays
These unsuspecting MacGregor bachelorettes
will be engaged by Christmas

IMAGINE US
Sisters, secrets and sweet romance

MIDNIGHT SHADOWS
Sometimes the last person you trust is your only ally

FROM DUSK TO DAWN
Danger, secrets and romance lurk under the cover of darkness

For a full list of titles by Nora Roberts,
please visit www.noraroberts.com.

If you purchased this book without a cover you should be aware
that this book is stolen property. It was reported as "unsold and
destroyed" to the publisher, and neither the author nor the
publisher has received any payment for this "stripped book."

SILHOUETTE ™

MacGregor Ever After

ISBN-13: 978-1-335-42600-0

Recycling programs
for this product may
not exist in your area.

Copyright © 2023 by Harlequin Enterprises ULC

The Winning Hand
First published in 1998. This edition published in 2023.
Copyright © 1998 by Nora Roberts

The Perfect Neighbor
First published in 1999. This edition published in 2023.
Copyright © 1999 by Nora Roberts

All rights reserved. No part of this book may be used or reproduced in any manner
whatsoever without written permission except in the case of brief quotations
embodied in critical articles and reviews.

This is a work of fiction. Names, characters, places and incidents are either the
product of the author's imagination or are used fictitiously. Any resemblance to
actual persons, living or dead, businesses, companies, events or locales is entirely
coincidental.

For questions and comments about the quality of this book, please contact us
at CustomerService@Harlequin.com.

Silhouette
22 Adelaide St. West, 41st Floor
Toronto, Ontario M5H 4E3, Canada
www.Harlequin.com

Printed and bound in Barcelona, Spain by CPI Black Print

NORA ROBERTS

MacGregor EVER AFTER

Includes *The Winning Hand* & *The Perfect Neighbor*

 *Silhouette Books*

CONTENTS

THE WINNING HAND

To the Vegas Queens, with thanks.

Chapter 1

When her car sputtered and died a mile outside of
Las Vegas, Darcy Wallace seriously considered staying where she was and baking to death under the brutal
desert sun. She had $9.37 left in her pocket and a long
stretch of road behind her that led to nowhere.

She was lucky to have even that pitiful amount of
cash on her, as her purse had been stolen outside a diner
in Utah the night before. The rubbery chicken sandwich
was the last meal she'd had, and she figured the stray
ten she'd found in her pocket was the last miracle she
could expect.

Both her job and her home in Kansas were gone. She
had no family and no one to go back to. She felt she'd
had every reason for tossing her clothes into a suitcase
and driving away from what had been, and what would
have been, had she remained.

She'd driven west simply because her car had been pointing in that direction and she'd taken it as a sign. She'd promised herself an adventure, a personal odyssey and a new, improved life.

Reading about plucky young women who braved the world, carved a path, took risks and blithely accepted challenges was no longer enough. Or so she'd told herself as the miles had clicked away on the odometer of her ancient and sickly sedan. It was time to take something for herself, or at least to try.

If she had stayed, she would have fallen in line. Again. Done what she was told. Again. And spent her life haunted by dreams and regrets.

But now, one long week after sneaking out of town in the middle of the night like a thief, she wondered if she was destined for the ordinary. Perhaps she'd been born to follow all the rules. Maybe she should have been content with what life offered and kept her eyes cast down, instead of constantly trying to peek around the next corner.

Gerald would have given her a good life, a life she knew many women would envy. With him, she could have had a lovely home tidily kept by a loyal staff, closets bursting with conventionally stylish wife-of-the-executive clothes, a summer place in Bar Harbor, winter getaways to tropical climes. She would never be hungry, never do without.

All it required was for her to do exactly as she was told, exactly when she was told. All it required was for her to keep buried every dream, every longing, every private wish.

It shouldn't have been hard. She'd been doing it all of her life.

But it was.

Closing her eyes, she rested her forehead on the steering wheel. Why did Gerald want her so much? she wondered. There was nothing special about her. She had a good mind and an average face. Her own mother had described her just that way often enough. She didn't believe it was so much a physical attraction on Gerald's side, though she suspected he liked the fact she was a small woman of slight build. Easily dominated.

God, he frightened her.

She remembered how furious he'd been when she'd cut off her shoulder-length hair, snipping away until it was as short as a boy's.

Well, she liked it, she thought with a little spurt of defiance. And it was her hair, damn it, she added, pushing her fingers through choppily cut, toffee-colored locks.

They weren't married yet, thank the Lord. He had no right to tell her how to look, how to dress, how to behave. And now, if she could just hold on, he never would have that right.

She should never have agreed to marry him in the first place. She'd just been so tired, so afraid, so confused. Even though the regrets and the doubts had set in almost immediately, even though she'd given him back the ring and apologized, she might have gone through with it rather than stand up under his anger and live through the gossip of a broken engagement. But she'd discovered he'd manipulated her, that he was responsible for her losing her job, for the threat of eviction from her apartment.

He'd wanted her to buckle. And she'd nearly obliged him, she thought now as she wiped sweat from her face with the back of her hand.

The hell with it, she decided and pushed herself out of the car. So she had less than ten dollars, no transportation and a mile hike ahead of her. She was out from under Gerald's thumb. She was finally, at twenty-three, on her own.

Leaving her suitcase in the trunk, she grabbed the weighty tote that contained all that really mattered to her, then headed off on foot. She'd burned her bridges. Now it was time to see what was around that next corner.

It took her an hour to reach her destination. She couldn't have explained why she kept walking along Route 15, away from the scatter of motels, gas stations, and toward that shimmering Oz-like skyline of Vegas in the distance. She only knew she wanted to be there, inside that globe of exotic buildings and shapes where lights were twinkling like a carnival.

The sun was tipping down below the western peaks of the red mountains that ringed that glittering oasis. Her hunger had gone from grinding distress to a dull ache. She considered stopping for food, to rest, to drink, but there was something therapeutic about simply putting one foot in front of the other, her eyes on the tall, spectacular hotels glimmering in the distance.

What were they like inside? she wondered. Would everything be glossy and polished, colorful to the point of gaudy? She imagined an atmosphere of sex and gambling, desperation and triumph, with an underlying snicker of naughtiness. There would be men with hard eyes, women with wild laughs. She'd get a job in one of those opulent dens of indulgence and have a front row seat for every show.

Oh, how she wanted to live and see and experience.

She wanted the crowds and the noise, the hot blood and the cold nerves. Everything, everything that was the opposite of what she'd had before. Most of all she wanted to feel—strong, ripping emotions, towering joys, vivid excitement. And she would write about it all, she determined, shifting the tote which, filled with her notebooks and manuscript pages, weighed like stone. She would write, tucked in some little room looking out at it all.

Stumbling with exhaustion, she tripped on a curb, then righted herself. The streets were crowded, everyone seemed to have somewhere to go. Even at dusk, the lights of the city winked and gleamed and beckoned: *Come in, take a chance, roll the dice.*

She saw families of tourists—fathers in shorts with legs pink from the unforgiving sun, children with wide eyes, mothers with the frantic look of sensory overload.

Her own eyes were wide, the golden brown glazed with fatigue. The man-made volcano erupted in the distance, drawing screams and cheers from the crowd who'd gathered to watch and making Darcy gape with glassy-eyed wonder. The noise smothered the odd buzzing in her ears as she was jostled by the crowd.

Dazed and dazzled, she wandered aimlessly, gawking at the huge Roman statues, blinking at the neon, passing by the spurting fountains that gushed with shifting colors. It was a wonderland, loud and gaudy and unapologetically adult, and she was as lost and as fascinated as Alice.

She found herself standing in front of twin towers as white as the moon and joined together by a wide, curved bridge with hundreds of windows. Surrounding the building were seas of flowers, both wild and exotic, and pools of mirror-bright water fed by the rush of a terraced waterfall that tumbled from the topmost spear of a mountain.

Guarding the entrance to the bridge was an enormous—five times larger than life—Native chief astride a gold stallion. His face and bare chest were gleaming copper. His headdress flowed with winking stones of rich reds and blues and greens. In his hand he carried a lance with a diamond-bright tip that winked fire.

He's so beautiful, was all she could think, so proud and defiant.

She would have sworn the statue's dark eyes were alive, fixed on hers. Daring her to come closer, to go inside, to take her chances.

Darcy stepped into The Comanche on watery legs and swayed against the sudden rush of cool air.

The lobby was immense, the tile floors a bold geometric pattern of emerald and sapphire that made her head spin. Cacti and palms grew regally out of copper or pottery urns. Brilliant floral displays graced huge tables, the scent of the lilies so sweet it brought tears to her eyes.

She walked on, amazed by the waterfall that rushed down a stone wall into a pond filled with bright fish, the sparkling light that shimmered from huge crystal-and-gold chandeliers. The place was a maze of color and flash, brighter and more brilliant than any reality she'd known or any dream she'd imagined.

There were shops, the offerings in the windows as glittery as the chandeliers. She watched an elegant blonde debate between two diamond necklaces the way another might consider her choice of tomatoes.

A laugh bubbled up in Darcy's throat, forcing her to press a hand to her mouth to hold it in. It wasn't the time or place to be noticed, she warned herself. She didn't belong in such glamorous surroundings.

She turned the corner and felt her head reel at the sudden brassy sound of the casino. Bells and voices, the metallic rat-a-tat of coins falling on coins. Whirls and buzzes and hoots. The wave of energy pouring out brought a rush to her blood.

Machines were everywhere, shoulder to shoulder with their faces spinning with colors and shapes. People crowded around them, standing, sitting on stools, pulling coins from white plastic buckets and feeding the busy machines. She watched a woman press a red button, wait for the spin to end, then scream with delight as triple black bars lined up in the center. Money poured out into a silver bowl in a musical rush.

It made Darcy grin.

Here was fun, reckless and impulsive. Here were possibilities both grand and small. And life, loud, messy and hot.

She'd never gambled in her life, not with money. Money was something to be earned, saved and carefully watched. But her fingers slipped into her pocket where the last of her crumpled bills seemed to pulse with heat against her skin.

If not now, when? she asked herself with another bubbling giggle she could no longer quite control. What good was $9.37? It would buy her a meal, she told herself, gnawing on her lip. But then what?

Light-headed, her ears ringing oddly, she roamed the aisles, blinking owlishly at people and machines.

They were willing to take a chance, she thought. That's why they were here.

Wasn't that why she was here?

Then she saw it. It stood alone, big and bright and fascinating. It stood taller than she, its wide face made up of stylized stars and moons. The handle was nearly as thick as her arm and topped with a shiny red ball.

It called itself Comanche Magic.

JACKPOT! it proclaimed in diamond-white lights that flashed on and off and made her dizzy. Ruby red dots flowed along a black strip. She stared, fascinated at the number showing within the blinking lights.

1,800,079.37

What an odd amount. Nine dollars and thirty-seven cents, she thought again, fingering the money in her pocket. Maybe it was a sign.

How much did it cost? she wondered. She stepped closer, blinked to clear her wavering vision and struggled to read the rules. It was a progressive machine, so the numbers would change and grow as players pumped in their money.

She could play for a dollar, she read, but that wouldn't get the jackpot even if she lined up the stars and moons on all three lines. To really play, she'd have to put in one dollar times three. Nearly all the money she had left in the world.

Take a chance, a voice seemed to whisper slyly in her ear.

Don't be foolish. This voice was prim, disapproving, and all too familiar. *You can't throw your money away.*

Live a little. There was excitement in the whisper, and seduction. *What are you waiting for?*

"I don't know," she muttered. "And I'm tired of waiting."

Slowly, her eyes on the challenging face of the machine, Darcy dug into her pocket.

With his gaze scanning the tables, Robert MacGregor Blade scrawled his initials on a chit. The man in chair three on the hundred-dollar table wasn't taking his losses in stride, he noted. Mac lifted a brow as the man held on fifteen with the dealer showing a king. If you're going to play for a hundred a hand, he mused as the dealer turned up a seven, you ought to know how to play.

In a casual gesture, Mac lifted a hand to call over one of the tuxedoed security men. "Keep an eye on him," Mac murmured. "He's thinking about making trouble."

"Yes, sir."

Spotting trouble and dealing with it was second nature for Mac. He was a third-generation gambler, and his instincts were well honed. His grandfather, Daniel MacGregor, had made a fortune taking chances. Real estate was Daniel's first love, and he continued to buy and sell property, to develop and preserve, to wheel and deal, though he was into his nineties.

Mac's parents had met in a casino aboard ship. His mother had been dealing blackjack, and his father had always been a player. They'd clashed and they'd clicked, both initially unaware that Daniel had maneuvered their meeting with marriage and the continuation of the MacGregor line in mind.

Justin Blade had already owned The Comanche in Vegas, and another in Atlantic City. Serena MacGregor had become his partner, then his wife.

Their eldest son had been born knowing how to roll the dice.

Now, just shy of his thirtieth birthday, Comanche Vegas was his baby. His parents trusted him enough to leave it in his hands, and he made very certain they wouldn't regret it.

It ran smoothly because he made certain it ran smoothly. It ran honest because it always had. It ran profitably because it was a Blade-MacGregor enterprise.

He believed, absolutely, in winning—and always in winning clean.

His lips twitched as a woman at one of the five-dollar tables hit twenty-one and applauded herself. Some would walk away winners, Mac mused, most wouldn't. Life was a gamble, and the house always had the edge.

A tall man, he moved through the tables easily, in a beautifully tailored dark suit that draped elegance over tough and ready muscle. The legacy from his Comanche heritage showed in the gold-dust skin pulled tight over his cheekbones, in the rich black hair that framed a lean, watchful face and flowed to the collar of his formal jacket.

But his eyes were Scot blue, deep as a loch and just as unfathomable.

His smile was quick and charming when a regular hailed him. But he kept moving, barely pausing. He had work waiting in his office high above the action.

"Mr. Blade?"

He glanced over, stopping now as one of the roving cocktail waitress moved to him. "Yes?"

"I just came over from the slots." The waitress shifted her tray and tried not to sigh as Mac gave her the full benefit of those dark blue eyes. "There's a woman over at the big progressive. She's a mess, Mr. Blade. Not too clean, pretty shaky. She might be on something. She's just staring at it, you know? Muttering to herself. I thought maybe I should call security."

"I'll take a look."

"She's, well, she's kind of pathetic. Not a working girl," the waitress added. "But she's either sick or stoned."

"Thanks, I'll take care of it."

Mac shifted directions, moving into the forest of slots rather than his private elevator. Security could handle any trouble that threatened the smooth operation of the casino. But it was his place, and he handled his own.

A few feet away, Darcy fed her last three dollars into the slot. *You're insane,* she told herself, carefully babying the last bill when the machine spit it back at her. *You've lost your mind,* her pounding heart seemed to scream even as she smoothed the bill and slid it back in. But God, it felt so good to do something outrageous.

She closed her eyes a moment, breathing deeply three times, then opening them again, grabbed the shiny red ball of the arm with a trembling hand.

And pulled.

Stars and moons revolved in front of her eyes, colors blurred, a calliope tune began to jingle. She found herself smiling at the absurdity of it, almost dreaming as the shapes spun and spun and spun.

That was her life right now, she thought absently. Spinning and spinning. Where will it stop? Where will it go?

Her smile only broadened as stars and moons began to click into place. They were so pretty. It had been worth the price just to watch, to know at least she'd pulled the handle.

Click, click, click, shining stars, glowing moons. When they blurred, she blinked furiously. She wanted to see every movement, to hear every sound. Wasn't it pretty how neatly they all lined up? she thought and braced a hand against the machine when she felt herself begin to tip.

And as she touched it, as her hand made contact with the cool metal, the movement stopped. The world exploded.

Sirens shrieked, making her stagger back in shock. Colored lights went into a mad dance atop the machine, and a drum began to beat. Whistles shrilled, bells clanged. All around her people began to shout and shove.

What had she done? Oh, God, what had she done?

"Holy cow, you hit the big one!" Someone grabbed her, danced with her. She couldn't breathe, flailed weakly to try to escape.

Everyone was pushing, pulling at her, shouting words she couldn't understand. Faces swam in front of hers, bodies pressed until she was trapped against the machine.

An ocean was roaring in her head, a jackhammer pounded in her chest.

Mac moved through the celebratory crowd, nudging well-wishers aside. He saw her, a slip of a woman who looked barely old enough to be inside the casino. Her dark blond hair was short and messily cut, bangs flopping down into enormous fawn-colored eyes. Her face was angular as a pixie's and pale as wax.

Her cotton shirt and slacks looked as though she'd

slept in them, and as if she'd spent her sleeping hours curled up in the desert.

Not stoned, he decided when he took her arm and felt the tremble. Terrified.

Darcy cringed, shifted her gaze to his. She saw the chief, the power and the challenge and the romance of him. He'd either save her, she thought dizzily, or finish her.

"I didn't mean—I only…what did I do?"

Mac angled his head, smiled a little. A dim bulb, perhaps, he mused, but harmless. "You hit the jackpot," he told her.

"Oh, well, then."

She fainted.

There was something wonderfully smooth under her cheek. Silk, satin, Darcy thought dimly. She'd always loved the feel of silk. Once she'd spent nearly her entire paycheck on a silk blouse, creamy white with tiny gold buttons, heart-shaped buttons. She'd had to skip lunch for two weeks, but it had been worth it every time she slipped that silk over her skin.

She sighed, remembering it.

"Come on, all the way out."

"What?" She blinked her eyes open, focused on a slant of light from a jeweled lamp.

"Here, try this." Mac slipped a hand under her head, lifted it and put a glass of water to her lips.

"What?"

"You're repeating yourself. Drink some water."

"Okay." She sipped obediently, studying the tanned, long-fingered hand that held the glass. She was on a bed, she realized now, a huge bed with a silky cover.

There was a mirrored ceiling over her head. "Oh, my." Warily she shifted her gaze until she saw his face. "I thought you were the chief."

"Close." He set the glass aside, then sat on the edge of the bed, noting with amusement that she scooted over slightly to keep more distance between them. "Mac Blade. I run the place."

"Darcy. I'm Darcy Wallace. Why am I here?"

"It seemed better than leaving you sprawled on the floor of the casino. You fainted."

"I did?" Mortified, she closed her eyes again. "Yes, I guess I did. I'm sorry."

"It's not an atypical reaction to winning close to two million dollars."

Her eyes popped open, her hand grabbed at her throat. "I'm sorry, I'm still a little confused. Did you say I won almost two million dollars?"

"You put the money in, you pulled the lever, you hit." There wasn't an ounce of color in her cheeks, he noted, and thought she looked like a bruised fairy. "We'll deal with the paperwork when you're feeling a little steadier. Do you want to see a doctor?"

"No, I'm just… I'm okay. I can't think. My head's spinning."

"Take your time." Instinctively he plumped up the pillows behind her and eased her back. "Is there someone I can call to help you out?"

"No! Don't call anyone."

His brow lifted at her quick and violent refusal, but he only nodded. "All right."

"There isn't anyone," she said more calmly. "I'm traveling. I—my purse was stolen yesterday in Utah.

My car broke down a mile or so out of town. I think it's the fuel pump this time."

"Could be," he murmured, tongue in cheek. "How did you get here?"

"I walked in. I just got here." Or she thought she had. It was hard to remember how long she'd walked around, goggling at everything. "I had nine dollars and thirty-seven cents."

"I see." He wasn't sure if she was a lunatic or a first-class gambler. "Well, now you have approximately one million, eight hundred thousand, eighty-nine dollars and thirty-seven cents."

"Oh…oh." Shattered, she put her hands over her face and burst into tears.

There were too many women in his life for Mac to be uncomfortable with female tears. He sat where he was, let her sob it out.

An odd little package, he thought. When she'd slid unconscious into his arms she'd been limp as water and had weighed no more than a child. Now she'd told him she'd hiked over a mile in the stunning late spring heat, then risked what little money she'd had on a yank of a slot.

That required either steel or insanity.

Whichever it was, she'd beaten the odds. And now she was rich—and for a while at least, his responsibility.

"I'm sorry." She wiped at her somehow charmingly dirty face with her hands. "I'm not like this. Really. I can't take it in." She accepted the handkerchief he offered and blew her nose. "I don't know what to do."

"Let's start with the basics. When's the last time you ate?"

"Last night—well, I bought a candy bar this morning, but it melted before I could finish it. So it doesn't really count."

"I'll order you some food." He rose, looking down at her. "I'll have them set it up down in the parlor. Why don't you take a hot bath, try to relax, get your bearings."

She gnawed her lip. "I don't have any clothes. I left my suitcase in my car. Oh! My bag. I had my bag."

"I have it." Because she'd gone pale again, he reached down beside the bed and lifted the plain brown tote. "This one?"

"Yes. Yes, thank you." Relief had her closing her eyes and struggling to calm herself again. "I thought I'd lost it. It's not clothes," she added, letting out a long sigh. "It's my work."

"It's safe, and there's a robe in the closet."

She cleared her throat. However kind he was being, she was still alone with him, a perfect stranger, in a very opulent and sensual bedroom. "I appreciate it. But I should get a room. If I could have a small advance on the money, I can find a hotel."

"Something wrong with this one?"

"This what?"

"This hotel," he said with what he considered admirable patience. "This room."

"No, nothing. It's beautiful."

"Then make yourself comfortable. Your room's comped for the duration of your stay—"

"What? Excuse me?" She sat up a little straighter. "I can have this room? I can just…stay here?"

"It's the usual procedure for high rollers." He smiled again, making her heart bump. "You qualify."

"I do?"

"The management hopes you'll put some of those winnings back into the pot. At the tables, the shops. Your room and meals, your bar bills, are on us."

She eased off the bed. "I get all this for free, because I won money from you?"

This time his grin was quick, and just a little wolfish. "I want the chance to win some of it back."

Lord, he was beautiful. Like the hero in a novel. That thought rolled around in her jumbled brain. "That seems only fair. Thank you so much, Mr. McBlade."

"Not McBlade," he corrected, taking the hand she offered. "Mac. Mac Blade."

"Oh. I'm afraid I haven't been very coherent."

"You'll feel better after you've eaten, gotten some rest."

"I'm sure you're right."

"Why don't we talk in the morning, say ten o'clock. My office."

"Yes, in the morning."

"Welcome to Las Vegas, Ms. Wallace," he said, and turned toward a sweep of open stairs that led to the living area.

"Thank you." She ordered her shaky legs to carry her to the rail, then lost her breath when she looked down at the sprawling space done in sapphires and emeralds, accented with ebony wood and lush arrangements of tropical flowers. She watched him cross an ocean of Oriental carpet. "Mr. Blade?"

"Yes?" He turned, glanced up, and thought she looked about twelve years old and as lost as a lamb.

"What will I do with all that money?"

He flashed that grin again. "You'll think of something. I'd make book on it." Then pressing a button, he stepped through the brass doors that slid open, into what surely was a private elevator.

When the doors closed again, Darcy gave in to her buckling knees and sat on the floor. She hugged herself hard, rocked. If this was some dream, some hallucination brought on by stress or sunstroke, she hoped it never cleared away.

She hadn't just escaped, she realized. She'd been liberated.

Chapter 2

The bubble didn't burst in the morning. She shot awake at six o'clock and stared, startled, at her reflection in the mirror overhead. Testing, she lifted a hand, watched herself touch her cheek. She felt her fingers, saw them slide up over her forehead and down the other side of her face.

However odd, it had to be real. She'd never seen herself horizontal before. She looked so…different, she decided, sprawled in the huge, rumpled bed surrounded by a mountain of pillows. She felt so different. How many years had she awakened each morning in the practical twin bed that had been her nesting place since childhood?

She never had to go back to that.

Somehow that single thought, the simple fact that she would never again have to adjust her body to the stingy mattress of the ancient bed sent a rush of joy through her so wild, so bright she burst into giddy laughter, unable to stop until she was gasping for air.

She rolled from one end of the bed to the other, kicked her feet in the air, hugged pillows, and when that wasn't enough, leaped up to dance on the mattress.

When she was thoroughly winded, she dropped down again and wrapped her arms tight around her knees. She was wearing a silk sleep shirt in candy pink—one of several articles of basic wardrobe that had arrived just after her dinner. Everything had been from the boutique downstairs and had been presented to her courtesy of The Comanche.

She wasn't even going to worry about the fact that the gorgeous Mac Blade had bought her underwear. Not when it was such fabulous underwear.

She jumped up, wanting to explore the suite again. The night before, she'd been so punchy she'd just wandered around gawking. Now it was time to play.

She snatched up a remote and began punching buttons. The shimmering blue drapes over the floor-to-ceiling windows opened and closed, making her grin like a fool. Opening them again, she saw she had a wide window on the world that was Vegas.

It was all muted grays and blues now, she noted, with a soft desert dawn breaking. She wondered how many floors up she was. Twenty? Thirty? It hardly mattered. She was on top of a brave and very new world.

Choosing another button, she opened a wall panel that revealed a big-screen television screen, a VCR and a complicated-looking stereo system. She fiddled until she filled the room with music, then raced downstairs.

She opened all the drapes, smelled the flowers, sat

on every cushion of the two sofas and six chairs. She marveled at the arched fireplace, at the grand piano of showy white. And because there was no one to tell her not to touch, she sat down and played the first thing that came into her mind.

The celebratory, arrogant notes of "Everything's Coming Up Roses" made her laugh like a loon.

Behind a glossy black wet bar she found a small refrigerator, then giggled like a girl when she saw it contained two bottles of champagne. With the music blaring, she waltzed into the bath off the living area and grinned at the bidet, the phone, the wall-mounted TV and all the pretty toiletries arranged in a china basket.

Humming to herself, she climbed the curving chrome steps back to the bedroom. The master bath was a symphony of pure sensory indulgence from the lake-sized motorized tub in sensuous black to the acre of counter under a wall-sized lighted mirror. The room was bigger than her entire apartment back home.

Tuck in a bed, she thought, and she could live happily right here. Lush green plants lined the tiled shelf beside the tub. A separate rippled glass shower stall offered crisscrossing sprays. Lovely clear jars were arranged on glass shelves and held bath salts, oils, creams with scents so lush she moaned in pleasure at every sniff.

The adjoining dressing room boasted a walk-in closet that contained a robe and a pair of brushed cotton slippers with The Comanche logo, a triple-glass, full-length mirror, two elegant chairs and a table where fragrant flowers spilled out of a crystal vase.

It was the kind of indulgence she'd only read about or seen in movies. Plush, sleek, shimmering with wealth.

Now that her initial rush of adrenaline was leveling, she began to wonder if there hadn't been some mistake.

How could this have happened? The time and circumstances after she'd begun her long hike into town were all blurry around the edges in her mind now. Snatches of it came clear, the whirling lights on the machine, her own thumping heart, Mac Blade's impossibly handsome face.

"Don't question it," she whispered. "Don't ruin it. Even if it all goes away in an hour, you have it now."

Biting her lip, she picked up the phone and punched in the button for room service.

"Room service. Good morning, Ms. Wallace."

"Oh." She blinked, looking guiltily over her shoulder as if someone had sneaked up behind her. "I was wondering if I could order some coffee."

"Of course. And breakfast?"

"Well." She didn't want to take advantage. "Perhaps a muffin."

"Will that be all?"

"Yes, that would be fine."

"We'll have that up to you within fifteen minutes. Thank you, Ms. Wallace."

"You're welcome, um, thank you."

After she hung up, Darcy hurried into the bedroom to turn off the stereo, switch the TV on and check the news to see if there were any reports of mass hallucinations.

In his office above the carnival world of the casino, Mac flicked his gaze over the security screens where people played the slots, bet on red or waited for their dealer to bust. There were more than a few diehards who'd started the night before and were still going at it. Slinky evening dresses sat hip to hip with jeans.

Ten o'clock at night, ten in the morning, it made no difference. There was no real time in Vegas, no dress code and, for some, no reality beyond the next spin of the wheel. Mac ignored the whine of an incoming fax, sipped his coffee and paced the room as he spoke to his father on the phone.

He imagined his father was doing virtually the same thing in the office in Reno.

"I'm going to talk to her in a few minutes," Mac continued. "I wanted to let her smooth out a little."

"Tell me about her," Justin requested, knowing his son's instincts for people would give him a clear picture.

"I don't know a lot yet. She's young." He kept moving as he talked, watching the screens, checking on the placement of his security people, the attitude of the dealers. "Skittish," he added. "Looked like a woman on the move to me. Trouble somewhere. She's out of her element here."

He cast his mind back, bringing the image of Darcy into focus, letting himself hear her voice again. "Small-town, Midwest, I'd say. Makes me think of a kindergarten teacher—the kind the kids would love and take merciless advantage of. She was broke and running on fumes when she hit."

"Sounds like it was her lucky day. If someone's going to hit, it might as well be a broke, small-town kindergarten teacher."

Mac grinned. "She apologizes all over herself. Nervous as a mouse at a feline convention. She's cute," he said finally, thinking of those big, dark gold eyes. "And I'd have to guess naive. The wolves are going to tear off pieces of her in short order if she doesn't have some protection."

There was a short pause. "You planning on standing between her and the wolves, Mac?"

"Just steering her in the right direction," Mac muttered, rolling his shoulders. His reputation in the family for siding with the underdog was inescapable. "The press is already hammering at the door. The kid needs a lawyer, and some straight talk, because the vultures circle right after the wolves."

He imagined the barrage of requests and demands that would come, begging for contributions, offering investments. A smattering of them would be genuine, and the rest would be playing one of the oldest games. Get the money and run.

"Keep me up to date."

"I will. How's Mom?"

"She's good. Hosting some big charity fashion show here today. And she's making noises about dropping in on you before we head back East. A quick visit," Justin added. "She misses the baby."

"Uh-huh." Mac had to grin. He knew very well his father would crawl over broken glass for a chance to visit his grandchild in Boston. "So how is little Anna?"

"Great. Just great. She's teething. Gwen and Bran aren't getting a lot of sleep right now."

"The price you pay for parenthood."

"I had plenty of all-nighters with you, pal."

"Like I said..." Mac's grin widened. "You pay your money, you make your choice." He glanced up at the quiet knock on his door. "That must be the nervous fairy now."

"Who?"

"Our newest millionaire. Come in," he called out, then curled a finger when Darcy hesitated on the threshold. "I'll keep you posted. Tell Mom I said hi."

"I've got a feeling you can tell her face-to-face in a few days."

"Good. Talk to you later."

The minute he hung up, Darcy launched into an apology. "I'm sorry. I didn't realize you were on the phone. Your assistant, secretary, whatever, came to bring me up, and she said I should just come in. But I can come back. If you're busy... I can come back."

Patient, Mac waited until she'd run down. It gave him the opportunity to see what a meal and a good night's sleep had done for her. She looked a little less fragile, incredibly...tidy, he decided, in the simple blouse and slacks he'd had the boutique send to her suite. And no less nervous than the evening before.

"Why don't you sit down?"

"All right." She linked her fingers together, twisted them, then stepped to a high-backed deep-cushioned chair in hunter green leather. "I was wondering—thinking...has there been a mistake?"

The chair dwarfed her, and made him think of fairies again, perched on colorful toadstools. "Hmm? About what?"

"About me, the money. I realized this morning, when I could think a bit more clearly, that things like this just don't happen."

"They do here." Hoping to put her at ease, he leaned a hip on the corner of his desk. "You are twenty-one, aren't you?"

"Twenty-three. I'll be twenty-four in September. Oh, I forgot to thank you for the clothes." She ordered herself not to think about the underwear, not to so much as consider that *he* was thinking of it. But color rose into her cheeks. "It was very kind of you."

"Everything fit all right?"

"Yes." Her color deepened. The bra was a lovely champagne color with edgings of lace, and was precisely her size. She didn't want to speculate how he could have been quite so accurate. "Perfectly."

"How'd you sleep?"

"Like someone put me under a spell." She smiled a little now. "I suppose I haven't been sleeping well lately. I'm not used to traveling."

There was a dusting of freckles over her pert little nose, he noted, a paler gold than her extraordinary eyes. She smelled lightly of vanilla. "Where are you from?"

"A little town, Trader's Corners, in Kansas."

Midwest, Mac thought. Hit number one.

"What do you do in Trader's Corners, Kansas?"

"I'm—I was a librarian."

Close enough for hit number two, he decided. "Really? Why'd you leave?"

"I ran away." She blurted it out before thinking. He had such a beautiful smile, and he'd been looking at her as if he were really interested. Somehow he had lulled her into the admission.

He pushed away from the desk, then sat on the arm of the chair beside hers so that their faces were closer, their eyes more level. He spoke gently, as he might to a cornered puppy. "What kind of trouble are you in, Darcy?"

"I'm not, I would have been if I'd stayed, but…" Then her eyes widened. "Oh, I didn't do anything. I mean I'm not running away from the police."

Because she was so obviously distressed, he smothered the laugh and didn't tell her he couldn't imagine her getting so much as a parking ticket. "I didn't think that, but people generally have a reason for running away from home. Does your family know where you are?"

"I don't have any family. I lost my parents about a year ago."

"I'm sorry."

"It was an accident. A house fire. At night." She lifted her hands, dropped them into her lap again. "They didn't wake up."

"That's a lot to deal with."

"There was nothing anyone could do. They were gone, the house was gone. Everything. I wasn't home. I'd just moved into my own apartment a few weeks before. Just a few weeks. I…" She pushed absently at her fringe of bangs. "Well."

"So you decided to get away?"

She started to agree, to make it simple. But it wasn't the truth, and she was such a poor and guilty liar. "No. Not exactly. I suppose that's part of it. I lost my job a few weeks ago." It still stung, the humiliation of it. "I was going to lose my apartment. Money was a problem. My parents didn't have much insurance, and the house had a mortgage. And the bills." She moved her shoulders. "In any case, without a paycheck, I wasn't going to be able to pay the rent. I didn't have that much saved myself, after college. And sometimes I… I'm not very good with budgets, I suppose."

"Money's not going to be a problem now," he reminded her, wanting to make her smile again.

"I don't see how you can just give me almost two million dollars."

"You *won* almost two million dollars. Look." He

took her hand, nudging her around until she could see the screens. "People step up to the tables, every hour, every day. Some win, some lose. Some of them play for entertainment, for fun. Others play hoping to make the big score. Just once. Some play the odds, some play a hunch."

She watched, fascinated. Everything moved in silence. Cards were dealt, chips were stacked, raked in or slipped away. "What do you do?"

"Oh, I play the odds. And the occasional hunch."

"It looks like theater," she murmured.

"That's what it is. With no intermission. Do you have a lawyer?"

"A lawyer?" The amused interest that had come into her eyes vanished. "Do I need a lawyer?"

"I'd recommend it. You're about to come into a large amount of money. The government's going to want their share. And after that, you're going to discover you have friends you've never heard of, and people who want to offer you a terrific opportunity to invest. The minute your story hits the press, they'll crawl out of the woodwork."

"Press? Newspapers, television? No, I can't have that. I can't have that," she repeated, springing up. "I'm not going to talk to reporters."

He bit back a sigh. Yes indeed, he thought, this one would need a hand to hold on the walk through the forest. "Young, orphaned, financially strapped librarian from Kansas walks into Comanche Vegas and drops her last dollar—"

"It wasn't my last," she insisted.

"Close enough. Her last dollar in the slot and wins

a million-eight. Darling, the press is going to do hand-springs with a lead like that."

He was right, of course. She could see it herself. It was a wonderful story, just the kind she wanted to write herself. "I don't want it to get out. They have televisions and newspapers in Trader's Corners."

"Hometown girl makes good," he agreed, watching her. Suddenly he realized something else was putting panic into her eyes. "They'll probably name a street after you," he said casually.

"I don't want this to get back there. I didn't tell you everything." Because she had no choice but to hope he could help, she sat again. "I didn't tell you the main reason I left the way I did. There's a man. Gerald Peterson. His family's very prominent in Kansas. They own quite a bit of land and many businesses. Gerald, for some reason, he wanted me to marry him. He insisted."

"Women are still free to say 'no, thank you' in Kansas, aren't they?"

"Yes, of course." It seemed so simple when he said it, she mused. He would think she was an idiot. "But Gerald's very determined. He always finds a way to get what he wants."

"And he wants you," Mac prompted.

"Well, yes. At least he seems to think he does. My parents were very pleased that he was interested in me. I mean, who would think I'd catch the eye of a man like him?"

"Are you joking?"

She blinked. "What?"

"Never mind." He waved it away. "So Gerald wanted to marry you, and I take it you didn't want to marry him. What then?"

"A few months ago, I said I would. It seemed like the only reasonable thing to do. And he just assumed I would, anyway." Ashamed, she stared down at her linked fingers. "Gerald assumes very firmly. He doesn't hear the word no. It's like a genetic thing." She sighed. "Agreeing to marry him was weak, and stupid, and I regretted it immediately. I knew I couldn't go through with it, but he wouldn't listen when I tried to tell him. There was the whole ring thing, too," she added with a frown.

Fascinated and entertained, Mac cocked his head. "Ring thing."

"Well, it was silly, really. I didn't want a diamond engagement ring. I wanted something different, just… different. But he didn't hear that, either. I got a two-carat diamond, which was properly appraised and insured. He explained all about the investment value." She shut her eyes. "I didn't want to hear about the investment value."

"No," Mac murmured. "I don't imagine you did."

"I wasn't expecting romance. Well, no, yes, I was, but I knew it wasn't going to happen. I thought I could settle." She looked past him, past the screens. "I should have been able to settle."

"Why?"

"Because everyone said how lucky I was. But I didn't feel lucky. I felt smothered, trapped. He was very angry when I gave him back the ring. He barely said a word, but he was furious. Then he wasn't. He was very calm and told me he had no doubt I'd come to my senses shortly. Once I did, we'd forget it had ever happened. Two weeks later, I lost my job."

She made herself look back at Mac. He was listening, she realized with some surprise. Really listening.

Hardly anyone really listened. "They talked about budget cutbacks, my performance evaluation," she continued. "I was so shocked that it took me a little while to realize he'd arranged it. The Petersons endow the library. And they own my apartment building. He had to have known I'd come crawling back."

"Sounds to me like you gave him a good kick in the ass. Not as much as he deserved, but a solid shot."

"He'll be humiliated, and very, very angry. I don't want him to know where I am. I'm afraid of him."

Something new and icy flickered into Mac's eyes. "Did he hurt you?"

"No. Gerald doesn't have to use physical force when intimidation works so well. I just want to disappear for a while. He only wants me now because he can't tolerate being refused. He doesn't love me. I simply suit his needs in a wife. Neat, quiet, well educated and behaved."

"You'd feel better if you stood up to him."

"Yes." She lowered her gaze. "But I'm afraid I won't."

Mac considered a moment. "We'll do what we can to keep your name out of it. The press should run with the mystery woman angle happily enough for a while. But it won't last, Darcy."

"The longer the better."

"Okay, let's deal with the basics. I can't distribute the money yet. You don't have any identification for one thing, and that makes it sticky. You'll need to get some. Your birth certificate, driver's license, that sort of thing. So we're back to a lawyer."

"I don't know any. Just the firm back home who handled things for my parents, and I wouldn't want to use them."

"No, they wouldn't do, not for a woman who wants to start a new life from scratch."

Her smile bloomed slowly, drawing his attention to the shape of her mouth, the full bottom lip, the deep dip centered in the top one. "I guess that's what I'm doing. I want to write books," she confessed.

"Really? What sort?"

"Love stories, adventures." She laughed and leaned back in the cushions of the chair. "Wonderful stories about people who do amazing things for love. I suppose that sounds crazy."

"It sounds rational to me. You were a librarian, so you must love books. Why not write them?"

She goggled first, then her eyes went bright and beautiful. "You're the first person I've ever told who's said that. Gerald was appalled at the very notion that I'd consider writing at all, much less romance novels."

"Gerald's an idiot," Mac said dismissively. "We've already established that. I guess you'd better buy yourself a laptop and get to work."

Staring again, she pressed a hand to her throat. "I could, couldn't I?" When her eyes began to fill, she shook her head quickly. "No, I'm not going to start that again. It's just that a life can change so completely and so quickly. The best and the worst. In a blink."

"You're handling this very well. You'll handle the rest." He rose and missed the startled look she shot him. No one had ever expressed such casual confidence in her before. "I'm not sure it's ethical, but I can contact my uncle. He's a lawyer. You can trust him."

"I'd appreciate it. Mr. Blade, I'm so grateful for—"

"Mac," he interrupted. "Whenever I give a woman

almost two million dollars, I insist on a first-name basis."

Her laugh burst out, then was quickly muffled by her hand. "Sorry. It's just strange hearing that out loud. Two million dollars."

"A fairly amusing number," he said dryly, and her laughter stopped instantly.

"I never thought—I mean about your part. What it means to you, this place. You don't have to pay me all at once," she said in a rush. "It can be in installments or something."

On impulse he reached down, cupped her chin in his hand and studied her face. "You're incredibly sweet, aren't you, Darcy from Kansas?"

Her mind washed clean. His voice was so warm, his eyes so blue, his hand so firm. Her heart did one long, slow twist in her chest and seemed to sigh. "What did you say? I'm sorry?"

He skimmed his thumb over her jawline. Fairy bones, he thought absently, and catching himself wondering about her, he dropped his hand. *Don't go there, Mac,* he warned himself, and stepped back.

"The Comanche never makes a bet it can't afford to lose. And my grandfather doesn't really need that operation."

"Oh, God."

"I'm joking." More delighted with her than ever, he roared with laughter. "You're easy. Much too easy." They'll eat her alive, he thought. "Do yourself a favor, keep a low profile until my uncle starts the ball rolling. I'll advance you some cash."

He moved behind the desk and unlocked a drawer where he kept the petty cash. "A couple thousand should hold you. We've arranged for credit at the shops here for you. I imagine you'll want to make arrangements to have your car towed in." Expertly he counted out hundreds, then fifties.

"I'm having a little trouble breathing," Darcy said weakly. "Excuse me."

Mac glanced up, watched in some alarm as she lowered her head between her knees.

"I'll be all right in a minute," she told him when she felt his hand on the back of her head. "I'm sorry. I'm being an awful lot of trouble."

"No, but I'd definitely prefer it if you didn't faint again."

"I won't. I was just a little light-headed for a second." When the phone rang, she jolted, then sat straight up. "I'm taking too much of your time."

"Sit." He pointed, then snatched up the phone. "Deb, tell whoever it is I'll get back to them." He hung up again, narrowed his eyes and felt a genuine wave of relief that her color was back. "Better?"

"Much. I'm sorry."

"Stop apologizing. It's a very annoying habit."

"I'm—" She pressed her lips together, cleared her throat.

"Good." He picked up the stack of bills and handed it to her. "Go shopping," he suggested. "Go play. Get a massage or a facial, sit by the pool. Enjoy yourself. Have dinner with me tonight." He hadn't meant to say that, hadn't a clue where it had come from.

"Oh." He was frowning at her now, which was only more confusing. "Yes, I'd like that." Feeling awkward, she rose and pushed the bills into her pocket. She hadn't brought the lovely little shoulder bag the boutique had sent her, because she'd had nothing to put in it. "I don't know what to do first."

"It doesn't matter. Just do it all."

"That's a wonderful way of thinking." Unable to help herself, she beamed at him. "Just do it all. I'll try that. I'll let you get back to work." She started for the door, but he went to it with her and opened it. She looked up again, groping for the right words. "You saved my life. I know that sounds dramatic, but it's the way I feel."

"You saved it yourself. Now take care of it."

"I'm going to." She offered her hand, and because it was irresistible, he lifted it to his lips.

"See you later."

"Yes. Later." She turned and walked away without her feet touching the ground.

Mac shut the door, then dipping his hands into his pockets, stood staring at it. Darcy the Kansas librarian, he mused. Not his type. As far from his type as they came. The little pull he felt, he assured himself, was just concerned interest. Almost brotherly.

Almost.

It was the eyes that were doing it, he supposed. How was a man supposed to resist those big, wounded fawn eyes? Then there was the shy little hesitation in her voice followed by those quick bursts of enthusiasm. And the genuine sweetness of her. Nothing saccharine or cloying, just innocence, he supposed.

Which circled right back to the point. Not his type. Women were safer when they knew how to play the game. Darcy Wallace didn't have a clue.

Well, he couldn't very well hand her the money then toss her into the fray without a shield, could he?

Just steer her in the right direction, he promised himself, then wave goodbye.

With this in mind, he went back to his desk and picked up the phone. "Deb, get me Caine MacGregor's office in Boston."

Chapter 3

It was a different world. Perhaps even a different planet. And she, Darcy thought as she stepped cautiously into the sparkling boutique, was now a different woman.

The Darcy Wallace who so often had her nose pressed against the window of such pretty places was now inside. And she could have whatever she wanted. That gorgeous beaded jacket there, she thought—not daring to touch it—or that fluid column of ivory silk.

She could have them, both of them, all of them. Because the world had turned upside down and somehow had shaken her out and dumped her right on top.

She stepped in a little farther, peeked into a long glass display cabinet. Beautiful, sparkly things. Foolishly wonderful decoration for ears and wrists and fingers. She'd always wanted to wear something that sparkled.

Odd, she'd never felt that special thrill she'd expected when she'd worn Gerald's ring on her finger. His ring, she realized now. Of course, that was it. It hadn't really been hers at all.

"May I help you?"

Startled, she looked up and nearly backed guiltily away from the display. "I don't know."

The woman behind the counter smiled indulgently. "Are you looking for anything special?"

"Everything seems special."

The indulgent smile warmed. "I'm glad you think so. We're very proud of our selection. I'd be happy to help you if I can, or you can feel free to browse."

"Actually I have a dinner tonight, and nothing to wear."

"That's always the way, isn't it?"

"Literally nothing." When the clerk didn't appear especially shocked by this confession, Darcy drummed up the courage to go on. "I suppose I need a dress."

"Formal or casual?"

"I have no idea." Realizing the quandary, Darcy scanned the gowns and cocktail suits on display. "He didn't say."

"Dinner for two?"

"Yes. Oh." She turned back. "It's not a date. Exactly."

Willing to play, the clerk angled her head. "Business?"

"In a way. I suppose." She pushed at the hair that was tickling her ear. "Yes, that must be it."

"Is he attractive?"

Darcy rolled her eyes. "That doesn't begin to describe him."

"Interested?"

"You'd have to be dead ten years not to be. But it's not that sort of…thing."

"Maybe it could be. Let's see." Lips pursed, the clerk studied Darcy through narrowed eyes. "Feminine but not fussy, sexy but not obvious. I think I have a few things you might like."

The clerk's name was Myra Proctor. She'd worked at the Dusk to Dawn Boutique for five years since she and her husband had moved to Vegas from Los Angeles. He was in banking, and she had worked in retail most of her adult life. She had two children, a boy and a girl. The girl had just turned thirteen and would surely make her mother's hair gray. Though, at the moment, Myra's hair was a sleek auburn.

Darcy learned all this because she asked. And asking helped put her at ease while Myra approved or rejected outfits.

One cocktail dress, beaded jacket, evening purse and sparkly earrings later, Myra gave her a gentle nudge toward the salon.

"You ask for Charles," Myra advised. "Tell him I sent you. He's an absolute genius."

"What," Charles demanded when Darcy sat in the cushioned silver salon chair, "happened to your hair? An industrial accident? A near-terminal illness perhaps? Mice?"

Wincing, Darcy cowered under the stark white cape that had been draped around her. "I'm afraid I cut it myself."

"Would you remove your own appendix?"

She could only hunch her shoulders as he glowered

down at her with searing green eyes under dark, beetled brows. "No. No, I wouldn't."

"Your hair is a part of your body and requires a professional."

"I know. You're right. Absolutely." The back of her throat began to tickle and she swallowed gamely. It wasn't the time to laugh, however nervously, she reminded herself. Instead she tried an apologetic smile. "It was an impulse, a rebellion actually."

"Against what?" His fingers dove into her hair and began to knead and tug. "Being well-groomed?"

"No. Well…there was this man, and he kept telling me how I should wear it, and how it should be, and it made me mad, so I whacked it off."

"Was this man your hairdresser?"

"Oh, no. He's a businessman."

"Ha. Then he has no business telling you how you should wear your hair. Cutting it off was brave. Foolish, but brave. The next time you want to rebel, go to a professional."

"I will." She took a deep breath. "Can you do anything with it?"

"My dear child, I've worked miracles with much worse." He snapped his fingers. "Shampoo," he ordered.

She'd never felt more pampered in her life. It was so beautifully indulgent to lie back, to have her hair washed, her scalp massaged, to listen to the birdlike murmurs of the shampoo girl. Even when she was back in Charles's chair, she felt none of the stomach-quivering anxiety that often rode hand in glove with a haircut.

"You need a manicure," Charles ordered, snipping

away. "Sheila, squeeze in a manicure and pedicure for—what was your name, dear?"

"Darcy. A pedicure?" The thought of having her toes painted was so…exotic.

"Hmm. And you'll stop biting your nails immediately."

Chastised, Darcy tucked her hands under the cape. "It's a terrible habit."

"Very unattractive. You're fortunate, though. You have thick, healthy hair. A nice color. We'll leave that alone." He brought a section of hair up between two fingers, snipped. "What do you use on your face?"

"I have some moisturizer, but I lost it." Self-consciously she rubbed at her nose.

"The freckles are charming. You'll leave them alone, too."

"But I'd rather—"

"Are you picking up the scalpel?" he asked, arching one of his thick, black brows, then nodding, satisfied, when she shook her head. "I'm going to do your face myself. If you don't like the look, you don't pay. If you do like it, you not only pay, you buy the products."

Another gamble, Darcy thought. Maybe she was on a roll. "Deal."

"That's the spirit. Now…" He angled her head, snipped again. "Tell me about your love life."

"I don't have one."

"You will." He wiggled those eyebrows. "My work never fails."

By three, Darcy walked back into her suite. She was loaded down with purchases, and still floating. On impulse, she dumped everything on the sofa and dashed to the mirror. Myra had been right. Charles was a genius. Her hair looked pert, she decided with a chuckle. Almost sophisticated. Though it was even shorter than she had dared cut it, it was sleek and just a little sassy.

Her bangs didn't flop now, but spiked down over her forehead. And her face... Wasn't it amazing what could be done with those tubes and brushes and powders? They couldn't make her a raving beauty, but she thought—she hoped—she'd stepped up to the threshold of pretty.

"I'm almost pretty," she said to her reflection, and smiled. "I really am. Oh, the earrings!" She whirled and dashed toward the bags, thinking the glitter against her face might just take her that final step.

Then she saw the red message light blinking on her phone.

No one knew where she was. How could anyone call her when no one knew? The press? Had the news gotten out already? No, no, she thought, clutching her hands together. Mac had promised not to give out her name. He'd promised.

Still her pulse hammered in her throat as she picked up the phone and pushed the message button. She was informed she had two new voice mail messages. The first was from Mac's assistant and had her releasing the breath she'd been holding. Mr. Blade would pick her up for dinner at seven-thirty. If that wasn't suitable, she had only to call back and reschedule.

"Seven-thirty is fine," she whispered. "Seven-thirty is wonderful."

The last message was from Caine MacGregor, who identified himself as Mac's uncle and invited her to call him back at her convenience.

She hesitated over that. She found she didn't want to face the practical business of it all. Somehow it seemed much more romantic when it all remained dreamlike and impossible. But she'd been raised to return phone calls promptly, so she pulled out the chair at the desk, sat, and dutifully made the long-distance call to Boston.

When Darcy opened her door and found Mac holding a single white rose, she considered it another miracle. He was something out of one of the stories she'd secretly scribbled in notebooks for years. Tall, dark, elegantly masculine, heart-stoppingly handsome with just an edge of danger to keep it all from being too smooth.

The miracle was that he was there, holding out a long-stemmed rosebud the color of a summer cloud, and smiling at her.

But what popped out of her mouth was the single thought that had revolved in her muddled brain since her call to Boston.

"Caine MacGregor is your uncle."

"Yes, he is."

"He was attorney general of the United States."

"Yes." Gently Mac lifted Darcy's hand and placed the rose stem in it. "He was."

"Alan MacGregor was president."

"You know, I heard that somewhere. Are you going to let me in?"

"Oh. Yes. But your uncle, he was *president*," she said again, slowly, as if she'd been misunderstood. "For eight years."

"You pass the history quiz." Mac closed the door behind him and took a good long study of her. A warm hum of approval moved through his blood. "You look fabulous."

"I—really?" Distracted not only by the compliment, but the delivery, she glanced down. "I would never have chosen this," she began, running a hand over the copper-hued skirt of a dress that was shorter, snugger and certainly more daring than anything in her previous wardrobe. "Myra at the boutique, the evening wear boutique downstairs, picked it out. She said I belonged in jewel colors."

"Myra has an excellent eye." And likely deserved a raise, he thought, making a circling motion with his finger. "Turn around."

"Turn—" Her laugh was both pleased and self-conscious as she executed a slow twirl.

A big raise, Mac decided as the flippy little skirt danced around surprisingly delightful legs. "They're not there."

"What?" Her hand fluttered to the dipping bodice, checking. "What isn't there?"

"Wings. I expected to see little fairy wings."

Flustered, she laughed again. "The way this day has gone, I wouldn't be surprised to see them myself."

"Why don't we have a drink before we go to dinner, and you can tell me how the day's gone?"

He walked to the bar to take a bottle of champagne out of the minifridge. She loved to watch him move. It was the animal grace she'd only read about, sleek and confident. And again, slightly dangerous. But to see it…she let out a little sigh. It was so much better than just imagining.

"Charles cut my hair," she began, thrilling to the celebratory sound of the cork popping.

"Charles?"

"In your salon?"

"Ah, that Charles." Mac selected two flutes from the glass shelves and poured. "The customers tremble, but always go back to Charles."

"I thought he was going to boot me out when he saw what I'd done." She gave her short locks a tug. "But he took pity on me. Charles has definite opinions."

Mac skimmed his gaze over her hair, then down until his eyes met hers. "I'd say in your case he saw the wings."

"I'm only to pick up scissors to cut paper from now on." Her eyes danced as she accepted the glass Mac offered. "Or pay the consequences. And, if I bite my nails, I'll be punished. I was afraid to ask him how. Oh, this is wonderful," she murmured after a sip. Closing her eyes, she sipped again. "Why would anyone drink anything else?"

The pure sensual pleasure on her face had the hum in his blood quickening. A babe in the woods, he reminded himself. It seemed wiser all around to keep the bar between them. "What else did you do?"

"Oh, the salon took forever. Charles kept finding other things he said were absolutely essential. I had a pedicure." Humor danced into her eyes again. "I had no idea how wonderful it is to have your feet rubbed. Sheila put paraffin on my feet. Can you imagine? My hands, too. Feel."

He took the hand she held out, in all innocence. It was small and narrow, the skin as smooth as a child's. He had to check the urge to nibble. "Very nice."

"Isn't it?" Delighted with herself, Darcy smiled and stroked a finger over the back of her hand. "Charles said I have to have a full body loofah and some sort of mud bath, and… I can't even remember. He wrote it all down and sent me to Alice at the spa. She makes the appointments. I have to be there at ten—after I work out in the health club, because he believes I've been neglecting my inner body, too. Charles is very strict. May I have some more?"

"Sure." A little war between amusement and baffled desire waged inside him as he poured more champagne.

"This is a wonderful place. It has everything. Wonderful surprises around every corner. It's like living in a castle." Her eyes closed with pleasure as she drank. "I always wanted to. I'd be the princess under a spell. And the prince would scale the walls, tame the dragon— I always hated when they killed the dragon. They're so magical and magnificent. Anyway, once the prince came, the spell would be broken, and everything in the castle would come to life. The colors and the sounds. There'd be music and dancing. And everyone would be so happy. Ever after."

She stopped, laughed at herself. "The champagne's going to my head. This isn't at all what I wanted to talk to you about. Your uncle—"

"We'll talk about it over dinner." He slipped the flute from her hand and set it aside. He spotted the glittery little evening bag on a table and handed it to her.

She slanted him a look as he led her to the elevator. "Can I have more champagne at dinner?"

Now he had to laugh. "Darling, you can have whatever you want."

"Imagine that." With a blissful sigh, she leaned against the smoked glass wall.

He pushed the button for the circular restaurant on

the top floor. She'd bought perfume, he thought, something woodsy and perfect for her. He decided the best place for his hands was in his pockets. "Did you try out the casino?"

"No. There was so much else to do. I looked around a little, but I didn't know where to begin."

"I think you began pretty well already."

She beamed up at him as the doors opened. "I did, didn't I?"

He led her through a small palm-decked foyer and into a candlelit dining room ringed by windows where silver gleamed against white linen.

"Good evening, Mr. Blade. Madam." The maître d' made a slight bow and, with his shoe-black hair and round body, reminded Darcy of Tweedledee of Alice fame.

Another rabbit hole, she thought as they were led to a curved banquette by the window. She never wanted to find her way out.

"The lady enjoys champagne, Steven."

"Of course. Right away."

"It must be so exciting living here. It's like a world to itself. You like it, don't you?"

"Very much. I was born with a pair of dice in one hand, and a deck of cards in the other. My mother and father met over a blackjack table. She was working as a dealer on a cruise ship, and he wanted her the minute he saw her."

"A shipboard romance." It made her sigh. "She was beautiful."

"Yes, she is beautiful."

"And he would have been dark and handsome, and maybe a little dangerous."

"More than a little. My mother likes to gamble."

"And they both won." Her lips tipped up, deepening the dip in the center. "You have a big family."

"Unwieldy."

"Only children are always jealous of big, unwieldy families. You're never lonely, I bet."

"No." She had been, he thought. There was no doubt of it. "Loneliness isn't an option." He nodded approval to the label as the sommelier offered the bottle of champagne.

Thrilled by the ritual, Darcy studied every step, the elegant spin of the white cloth, the subtle movement of the sommelier's hands, the muffled pop of cork. At Mac's signal, a small amount was poured into Darcy's glass for tasting.

"It's wonderful. Like drinking gold."

That earned her a pleased smile from the sommelier, who finished pouring with a flourish before nestling the bottle in a silver bucket of ice.

"Now." Mac tapped his glass lightly against hers. "You talked with my uncle."

"Yes. I didn't realize, not until I'd made the call. Then I did—Caine MacGregor, Boston. I know I started to stutter." She winced. "He was very patient with me." A laugh bubbled up and was partially swallowed. "The former attorney general of the United States is my lawyer. It's so odd. He said he would take care of things—my birth certificate, the red tape. He didn't seem to think it would take very long."

"MacGregors have a way of moving things along."

"I've read so much about your family." Darcy accepted the leather-bound menu absently. "Your grandfather's a legend."

"He loves hearing that. What he is, is a character. You'd like him."

"Really? What kind of a character?"

How did one describe Daniel MacGregor? Mac wondered. "An outrageous one. Big, loud, bold. A Scotsman who built an empire on grit and sweat and shrewdness. He sneaks cigars—or my grandmother lets him believe he's sneaking them. He'll skin you at poker. Nobody bluffs better. He has an amazing heart, strong and soft. For him, family comes first and last and always."

"You love him."

"Very much." Because he thought she'd enjoy it, he told her of how a young, brash Daniel had come to Boston looking for a wife, had set his eyes on Anna Whitfield and, tumbling into love, had wooed and won her.

"She must have been terribly brave, becoming a doctor. There were so many obstacles for a woman."

"She's amazing."

"And you have brothers? Sisters?"

"One brother, two sisters, assorted cousins, nephews, nieces. When we get together it's...an asylum," he decided, making her laugh.

"And you wouldn't change it for the world."

"No, I wouldn't."

She opened her menu. "I always wondered what it would be like to—oh, my. Look at all this. How does anyone decide what to order?"

"What do you like?"

She looked up, gold eyes sparkling. "Everything."

She sampled all she could manage. Tureen of duck, wild greens, little salmon puffs topped with caviar. Unable to resist, Mac scooped up some of his own stuffed lobster and held the fork to her lips. Her eyes closed, a quiet moan rippled in her throat, her lips rubbed gently together. And his blood flashed hot.

He'd never known a woman so open to sensual pleasure, or so obviously new to it. She'd be a treasure in bed, absorbing, lingering over every touch, every taste, every movement.

He could imagine it clearly—much too clearly—the little sighs and murmurs, the awakenings.

She gave one of those little sighs now as her long lids opened slowly over dreamy eyes. "It's wonderful. Everything's wonderful."

It was all flowing through her, mind and body, soft lights, strong flavors, the froth of wine and the look of him. She found herself leaning forward. "You're so attractive. You have such a strong face. I love looking at it."

From another woman it would have been an invitation. From her, Mac reminded himself, it was a combination of wine and naiveté. "Where do you come from?"

"Kansas." She smiled. "That's not what you meant, is it? I have no finesse," she confessed. "And when I relax, I tend to say things that pop into my head. I'm usually nervous around men. I never know what to say."

He arched a brow. "Obviously I don't make you nervous. That's my ego you hear thudding at your feet."

She chuckled, shaking her head. "Women are always going to fantasize about men like you. But you don't make me nervous, because I know you don't think of me that way."

"Don't I?"

"Men don't." She gestured with her glass before sipping. "Men aren't quickly attracted to women who aren't particularly physically appealing. Willowy blondes," she continued, eyeing his plate and wondering how to ask for another bite. "Sultry brunettes, glamorous redheads. Attention focuses on them, it's only natural. And strongly attractive men are drawn to strongly attractive women. At least initially."

"You've given this a lot of thought."

"I like to watch people, and how they circle toward each other."

"Maybe you haven't looked closely enough. I find you very appealing, physically." He watched her blink in surprise as he slid a little closer. "Fresh," he murmured, giving in to the urge to cup a hand at the back of her slender neck. "And lovely."

He saw her gaze flit down to his mouth and return, startled, to his eyes. He heard the little rush of breath shudder through her lips. It was tempting, very tempting to close the slight distance, to complete the circle she'd spoken of. But she trembled under his hand, a trapped bird not entirely sure of her wings.

"There," he said quietly. "That shut you up. Nervous now?"

She could only move her head in short, rapid nods. She could all but feel his mouth on hers. It would be firm, and hot and so clever. The fingers at the back of her neck had stroked some wild nerve to life. She could feel it career through her, bumping her pulse to light speed.

The dawning awareness in her eyes, the flicker of panic behind it had his fingers tightening briefly on her nape. "You shouldn't dare a gambler, Darcy." He gave her neck what he hoped was a friendly squeeze before easing back. "Dessert?"

"Dessert?"

"Would you like some?"

"I don't think I could." Not with her stomach muscles in knots and her fingers too unsteady to hold a fork.

He smiled slowly. "Want to try your luck?" When she swallowed, he added, "At the tables."

"Oh. Yes. I think I would."

"What should I play?" she asked him when they walked into the noise and lights of the casino.

"Lady's choice."

"Well." She bit her lip, tried to keep her mind off the fact that he had his hand at the small of her back. It did no good to tell herself she had no business thinking of him that way. "Maybe blackjack. It's just adding up numbers, really."

He ran his tongue around his teeth. "That's part of it. Five-dollar table," he decided. "Until you get your rhythm." He led her toward a vacant chair in front of a dealer he knew to be both patient and personable with novices. "How much do you want to start with."

"Twenty?"

"Twenty thousand's a little steep for a beginner."

Her mouth dropped open, then curved on a laugh. "I meant dollars. Twenty dollars."

"Dollars," Mac said weakly. "Fine—if you think you can stand the excitement."

When he reached for his wallet, she shook her head. "No, I have it." She pulled a twenty out of her bag. "It feels more like mine this way."

"It is yours," he reminded her. "And at twenty, not a hell of a lot's going to be mine again."

"I might win." She slid onto a stool beside a portly

man in a checked jacket. "Are you winning?" she asked him.

He tipped a beer to his lips and winked at her. "I'm up about fifty, but this guy." He gestured toward the dealer. "He's tough."

"You keep coming back to my table, Mr. Renoke," the dealer said cheerfully. "Must be my good looks."

Renoke snorted, then tapped his cards. "Give me a little one, pal."

The dealer turned up a four. "Your wish, my command."

"There you go." Renoke waved a finger over the cards to indicate he'd hold with nineteen. When the dealer held on eighteen, Renoke patted Darcy's shoulder. "Looks like you brought me some fresh luck."

"I hope so. I'd like to play," she added.

"Changing twenty," the dealer announced and shoved the bill into a slot with a clear plastic box. Darcy neatly stacked her four five-dollar chips. "Bets?"

"Put a chip on the outline there," Mac instructed.

The cards moved quickly, slipping out of the shoe and snapping lightly on felt. She was dealt a six and an eight, with the dealer showing ten.

"What do I do now?"

"Take a hit."

She tilted her head, looked up at Mac. "But I'm beating him, and a ten would put me over, wouldn't it?"

"Odds are his down card is over two. Play the odds."

"Oh. I'll take a hit." She pulled a ten, then frowned. "I lost."

"But you lost correctly," the dealer told her with a grin.

She lost correctly twice more and, with brows knit

in concentration, slid her last chip into place. And hit blackjack. "I didn't even have to do anything." She wiggled more comfortably on the stool and sent Mac an apologetic look. "I think I'll play incorrectly for a while, just to see what happens."

"It's your game."

With some surprise, he watched her play against all logic and build her little stack of chips up to ten, dwindle them down to three, then build them back up again. She chatted with Renoke, learned about his two sons in college and neatly stacked her chips.

A twenty-dollar stake, he mused, and she was up to two hundred. The woman was a marvel.

He caught the eye of a dealer at another table, a subtle signal of trouble on the brew. "I'll be right back," he murmured to Darcy, giving her shoulder a light squeeze.

It wasn't hard to spot where the trouble was centered. The man in the first chair was down to three hundred-dollar chips. Mac judged him to be roughly forty, a little worse for liquor and a poor loser.

"Look, you can't deal cleaner than that, you ought to be fired." The man jabbed a finger at the dealer while other players eased out of their chairs and looked for calmer water. "I can't win more than one hand out of ten. And that little bitch who was dealer before you's no better. I want some damn action here." He thumped his fist on the table.

"Problem?" Mac stepped up to the table.

"Back off. This is none of your damn business."

"It's my business." A subtle signal had his floor man, already moving toward the table, stopping. "I'm Blade, and this is my place."

"Yeah?" The man lifted his glass, gulped. "Well,

your place is lousy. Your dealers think they're slick, but I can spot them." He slammed his glass down. "Bled me for three grand already. I know when I'm being taken."

Mac's voice remained low, his eyes cool. "If you want to lodge a complaint, you're welcome to do so. In my office."

"I don't have to go to your stinking office." In one violent gesture, he knocked his glass from the table. "I want some satisfaction here."

Mac held up a hand to hold off the two security guards who were moving rapidly in his direction. "You're not going to get it. I suggest you cash in and take your business elsewhere."

"You're kicking me out?" The man shoved away from the table. On his feet he wasn't steady, but he was big, burly and his fists were clenched. "You can't kick me out."

Ready violence flashed into Mac's eyes in a quick, icy flare. "Want to bet?"

Rage had the man trembling, visibly. But drunk or not, he recognized the cold fury staring him down. "The hell with it." He snatched up his chips, sneered. "I should've known better than to trust some Indian dive."

Mac's hand shot out like a lightning bolt, grabbed the man by the shirtfront and hauled his bulk onto his toes. "Stay out of my place." His voice was dangerously quiet, his eyes flat as ice. "I see you in here again, and you won't leave standing. Escort this…gentleman to the cashier," Mac instructed his security team. "Then show him the door."

"Yes, sir."

"Half-breed son of a bitch," the man shouted as he was led away.

Mac's head jerked around when a hand touched his arm. Instinctively Darcy backed away from the frigid fury on his face. The muscles beneath her fingers were like iron and she quickly dropped her hand. "I'm sorry. I'm so sorry. He was dreadful."

"Plenty more where he came from."

All she could think was if anyone ever looked at her with eyes that icy, that powerfully cold, she would shatter into tiny shards. "There shouldn't be." She bent down, started to pick up the glass the man had knocked to the floor, but Mac snagged her hand and tugged her up again.

"What are you doing?"

"I was going to clean up the—"

"Stop." His temper was still on the end of a straining leash, and the order snapped out. "You don't belong here," he muttered, and began to pull her away from the tables and the still-gawking crowd. "It isn't all fun and games. It isn't a damn castle. There are people like that in every corner."

"Yes, but—" He was striding so quickly through the breezeway to the hotel area that she had to trot to keep up.

"You ought to be back in Kansas, tucked away in your library."

"I don't want to go back to Kansas."

He pulled her into the elevator and jammed in his master card for her suite. "They'll gobble you up in one tasty bite. I damn near did it myself."

"I don't know what you're talking about."

"Exactly." He rounded on her, frustration, fury, self-disgust punching inside his gut. Her eyes were as big as saucers, that delectably curved top lip just beginning to tremble. "Exactly," he said again, struggling for calm. "I have to go down and take care of this. Stay up here."

"But—"

"Stay up here," he repeated, pausing between each word, then giving her a nudge out of the elevator and into her suite before he did something insane. Like clamping his mouth on hers. "You worry me," he muttered as she stared at him. "You're really starting to worry me."

They continued to stare at each other until the doors shut.

Chapter 4

Darcy kept her spa appointments the next morning because she thought it would be rude not to. But her heart wasn't in it. Even being scrubbed with exotic sea salts, massaged with oils that made her think of some Egyptian handmaiden and having her face packed with thick cool goo the color of ripe pomegranates didn't lift her mood.

He wanted her to leave, and she really had nowhere to go.

It didn't seem to matter that as soon as the documents came through she'd be able to travel to all the dazzling places she'd read and dreamed about. She wanted to stay here, in this wonderful, exciting place, with all the lights and the sounds and the crowds and the seamy edges.

She wanted to gamble again, to drink champagne, to buy more sparkling earrings. She wanted just a little more time in a world where men with faces that should be sculpted in copper paid attention to her as if she were worthy of their interest.

She wanted, more than anything, a few more magical days with Mac before her coach turned into a pumpkin and the glass slipper no longer fit.

She wanted him to smile at her again in the way that transformed his face into one glorious piece of art.

He was so lovely, not just to look at, she thought, but to be with. He had a way of turning those wonderful blue eyes on her and making her think he really cared about what she thought, how she felt, what she had to say.

She'd never been able to talk to another man the way she could talk to him. Without feeling inadequate and foolish. Or simple, she supposed.

But she'd taken up too much of his time, gotten in the way. She'd always been better off fading into a corner and watching other people live. Once you stepped out too far, into those lights, you ended up doing something silly or foolish that made those who knew...*things* wish you'd slip away again.

The money wasn't going to change who she was. A pretty dress, a new haircut—it was only gloss. Under it, she was still awkward and average.

"You're going to love this."

Shaking off the blue mood, Darcy looked over at the technician. She'd already forgotten the woman's name, which was, in Darcy's opinion, as rude as not keeping the appointment in the first place. Flat on her back on the padded table, she focused on the nameplate pinned to the breast of the soft pink uniform.

"Am I, Angie?"

"Absolutely."

To Darcy's shock, Angie tugged down the thin blanket and began to paint warm brown mud on her breasts. "Oh!"

"Too warm?"

"No, no." She would not blush, she would not blush, she would *not* blush. "What's this for?"

"To make your skin irresistible."

"Nobody's going to see it where you're putting it on," Darcy said dryly, and Angie laughed.

"Hey, this is Vegas. Your luck could change any time."

"Maybe you're right." Giving up, Darcy closed her eyes.

She and her new, irresistible skin had barely stepped back into her suite when the buzzer sounded. Her tongue tied itself into knots the minute she opened the door and saw Mac.

"Got a minute?" he asked, then stepped inside when she only nodded. "I don't have much time, but I wanted to let you know the press has the bit between their teeth. The mystery woman angle has them fired up. They'll play that for a few more days, but it won't stop there. There's bound to be a leak sooner rather than later. You'll need to be prepared for that."

"I'm not going back to Kansas." It came out in a burst, fueled by an anger that surprised them both.

Mac raised his eyebrows. "So you said."

"I'm not going back," she repeated. "I have enough of the cash you advanced me to get a hotel room."

"And you'd do that because…"

"You said I shouldn't be here."

"I don't believe I did." But he remembered his temper of the night before, and thought he might have said something along those lines. "It's certainly not what I meant." Annoyed with himself, he dragged a hand through his hair. "Darcy—"

"I know I've been taking up a lot of your time. You feel responsible for me, but you don't have to. I'm perfectly content to keep out of the way. I can just stay up here and write. That's what I did last night after… well, after."

He held up a hand, guessing correctly it would stop the flood of words. "I'm sorry. I was out of line. I let that idiot last night get to me, and I took it out on you." He dipped his hands into his pockets. "But it did make me realize that you shouldn't have been there, and that you certainly shouldn't be wandering around a casino alone."

She'd been on the point of yielding when his final statement put her back up again. "You think I'm stupid and naive."

"I don't think you're stupid."

Her eyes flashed, fascinating him with the sudden and unexpected fire of gold. "Just naive, then. Probably a bit incompetent and certainly too…" Her mind went on a fumbling search for the word. "Too midwestern to take care of myself in the big, bad city."

His eyebrow arched in a way she found both charming and infuriating. "You are the one who walked into town with less than ten dollars, no purse and nothing but the clothes on her back, aren't you?"

"So what! It got me here, didn't it?"

"Point taken," he murmured.

"And last night wasn't the first time I've seen an evil-minded drunk, either. I'm from Kansas, not Dogpatch. We've got plenty of drunks in Kansas."

"I stand corrected." And struggling mightily not to grin.

"And you needn't feel obligated to look after me as if I were some stray puppy who might run out into traffic. There's absolutely no reason for you to worry about me."

"I didn't say I was worried about you. I said you worried me."

"It's the same thing."

"It's entirely different."

"How?"

He studied her. Color was warm in her face, her eyes were dark and shining. It wasn't just anger she was feeling, he realized, but bruised pride as well. And that was undeniably his fault. He sighed. "You're really leaving me no choice. You worry me," he repeated, and laid his hands on her shoulders. "Because…" Slid them down her arms, around her waist. Watched her lips part in surprise just before he covered them with his.

The world tilted. Every coherent thought in her mind tumbled out and scattered. Hopelessly lost. His mouth was just as she'd imagined it would be. Hot and firm and clever. But now it was on hers, luring her into some exciting airless space where everything shimmered and shook. Colors brightened, blurring around the edges before they melted together and turned as liquid as her bones.

His tongue swept over hers, teasing, inviting, mixing his dark, intimate taste with her own. Smooth, so smooth, that glide of tongue, that slide of lips, that she seemed to coast bonelessly down the long chute of sensation toward a spreading pool of liquid heat.

Her hands had come up to clutch at his arms for balance. He could feel the pressure of her short nails through his jacket, a contrasting signal of anxiety even as her lips opened and gave. Nerves and surrender, a dangerous mix, punctuated by the helpless little whimpers of pleasure that sounded in her throat, combined to take him deeper than he'd intended, to make him want more, much more than he'd expected.

What he'd begun churned through him and demanded he finish—his way. Then and there, and thoroughly. She was aroused. So was he. However innocent, she wasn't a child. And he wanted her. God, he wanted her.

Her eyes remained closed as he drew her away. He watched the tip of her tongue trace her curvy, unpainted lips before she pressed those lips together, like a woman lingering over a particularly lush taste. Even as her lashes fluttered, a hot fist of need balled in his gut.

Her eyes were dark and clouded, fixed now on his. A flush glowed on her cheeks. A swallow rippled her throat.

Damn, he wanted, desperately wanted to take her in one greedy gulp until nothing was left but the sighs.

"Why…" Her breath was coming too fast for the words to be steady. "Why did you do that?"

Be careful with her, he reminded himself. *Very careful.* "Because I wanted to. Is that a problem?"

She stared at him for a long moment. "No," she answered with such weighty seriousness he nearly smiled. "I don't think so."

"Good. Because I'm not finished yet."

"Oh." His arms were tightening, easing her close again. Bodies met again. "Well..." Her eyes drifted shut. "Take your time."

Her innocence was as bright as a beacon, and outrageously arousing. No, not a child, he thought again, but the odds were weighted heavily against her. And he had no right to use that as leverage. Grappling for control, he rested his forehead on hers. *Slow down,* he ordered himself. *Better yet, stop.*

"Darcy, you're a dangerous woman."

Her eyes flew open. "Me?"

The shock in her voice did nothing to relieve the tension centered in his gut. The tension was a bad sign, he decided, a signal not just of desire, but of desire for her. Very specific, very exact and completely inappropriate. "Lethal," he murmured, then stepped back.

But he kept his hands on her shoulders, not quite able to break all contact. She was searching his face now, her big gold eyes still blurred from the first kiss, her mouth pursed in anticipation of the next. He could have lapped her up like cream.

"Have you ever had a lover?"

She blinked, then her gaze lowered to stare at the buttons of his shirt. The shirt was black and silky. It had felt warm and smooth under her hands. She wanted to touch it again. To touch him. "Not exactly."

His brow lifted again. "Despite its infinite and entertaining varieties, sex remains a fairly exact pastime."

She had the distinct impression he didn't intend to kiss her again, after all. Sexual frustration was a new, and not entirely pleasant, sensation. Vaguely insulted, she frowned up at him. "I know what sex is."

No, he thought, she didn't. She didn't have a clue

what he wanted to do with her, to her. If she did, he imagined she'd run as far and as fast as her pretty fairy legs would carry her. "You don't know me, Darcy. You don't know the rules around here, or the pitfalls."

"I know how to learn," she said testily. "I'm not a moron."

"Some things you're better off not learning." He gave her shoulders a light squeeze when the phone began to ring. "Answer the phone."

She turned on her heel, stalked over to the desk and snatched up the receiver. "Yes? Hello?"

"And who might this be?"

The abrupt demand in a thick burr was so commanding she answered immediately. "This is Darcy Wallace."

"Wallace? Wallace, is it? And would you spring from William Wallace, the great hero of Scotland?"

"Actually..." Confusion had her pushing a hand through her hair. "He's an ancestor on my father's side."

"Good blood. Strong stock. You can be proud of your heritage, lass. Darcy, is it? And are you a married woman, Darcy Wallace?"

"No, I'm not. I—" She snapped back and her brows drew together. "Excuse me, who is this?"

"This is Daniel MacGregor, and I'm pleased to make your acquaintance."

She managed to close her mouth, take a breath. "How do you do, Mr. MacGregor?"

"I do fine, fine and dandy, Darcy Wallace. I'm told my grandson is paying a call on you."

"Yes, he's here." Weren't her lips still tingling from his? "Um. Would you like to speak to him?"

"That I would. You have a fine, clear voice. How old might you be?"

"I'm twenty-three."

"I wager you're a healthy girl, too."

Totally at sea, she nodded her head. "Yes, I'm healthy." She only blinked at Mac when he cursed under his breath and grabbed the phone away from her.

"Shall I check her teeth for you, Grandpa?"

"There you are." Pleasure, and no remorse, rang in Daniel's voice. "Your secretary transferred me. Of course, I wouldn't have to be transferred all over hell and back to have a word with my oldest grandchild if you ever bothered to call your grandmother. She's feeling neglected."

It was an old ploy, and made Mac sigh. "I called you and Grandma less than a week ago."

"At our age, boy, a week's a lifetime."

"Bull." He couldn't stop the smile. "You'll both live forever."

"That's the plan. So, I hear from your mother—who bothers to call home from time to time—that you lost yourself a million-eight and change."

Mac ran his tongue around his teeth, glancing over as Darcy wandered to the window. "You win some, you lose some."

"True enough. And was the lass I was just speaking to the one who robbed you?"

"Yes."

"A Wallace. Good, clear voice, good manners. Is she pretty?"

Mac eased a hip on the desk. He knew his grandfather well. "Not bad, if you overlook the hunchback and the crossed eyes." Idly he flipped open the notebook on the desk as Daniel's hearty laughter rang in his ear.

"She's pretty then. Got your eye on her, do you?"

Mac lifted his gaze from the pages crowded with margin-to-margin writing, and studied the way Darcy stood facing the window. The sun was a halo over her hair. Her hands were linked together in front of her. She looked as delicate as a wildflower in the unforgiving heat of the desert.

"No." He said it definitely, finally, wanting to mean it. "I don't."

"And why not? Are you going to stay single all your life? A man your age needs a wife. You should be starting a family."

As Daniel blustered on about responsibility, duty, the family name, Mac cocked his head and read a page. It was about a woman sitting alone in the dark, watching the lights of the city outside her window. The sense of solitude, of separation, was wrenching.

Thoughtfully he closed the book again, laying a hand over it as he watched Darcy watch the city. "But I'm having such fun, Grandpa," he said, when Daniel finally paused for breath, "working my way through all the showgirls."

There was a moment's pause, then a roar of laughter. "You always had a mouth on you. I miss you, Robbie."

Daniel was the only one who ever called Mac by his childhood name—and then he used it rarely. Love, Mac thought, was inescapable. "I miss you, too. All of you."

"Well, if you'd tear yourself away from those showgirls, you could come visit your poor old granny."

Obviously Anna MacGregor wasn't within hearing distance. Mac could imagine the punishment she would mete out if she heard her husband call her "poor," "old" or "granny." "Give her my love."

"I will, though she'd prefer you give it to her yourself. Put the lass back on the phone."

"No."

"No respect," Daniel muttered. "I should have taken a strap to you when you were a boy."

"Too late now." Mac grinned. "Behave yourself, Grandpa. I'll talk to you soon."

"See that you do."

Mac stayed where he was after he replaced the receiver. "I'll apologize for The MacGregor's interrogation."

"It's all right." She kept her back to him, stared out at the sun shining on towering buildings. "He sounds formidable."

"Hard shell, soft center."

"Mmm." She hadn't meant to eavesdrop, but how could she have helped hearing Mac's part of the conversation? The love and exasperation in his voice had touched her. And his words had cleared up her confusion.

Showgirls. Of course he would be attracted to the long legs, the beautiful bodies, the exotic faces. He'd only been curious, she supposed. That's why he'd kissed her. But damn him, damn him for stirring up all this need that she'd managed to live very contentedly without until now.

"I seem to have gotten distracted from the point of coming to see you." He waited for her to turn and face him. At a casual glance she appeared perfectly composed. But he couldn't seem to glance at her casually. He was compelled to search, and a search of those eyes revealed bruises and storms. "Now you're angry."

"No, I'm irritated, but I'm not angry. What was the

point," she began, then paused significantly, "of your coming to see me?"

That flair for sarcasm surprised him. The edge of it pricked at him enough to have him pushing off the desk and shoving his hands into his pockets. "The point was the press. I know you're concerned about your name getting out. We're being deluged with calls for the full story. I can hold them off, but it's bound to leak, Darcy. The hotel employs hundreds, and several people already know your name. Sooner rather than later, one of them is going to talk to a reporter."

"I'm sure you're right." She supposed she should be grateful he'd given her something else to worry about. "I'm sure you think I'm a coward, not wanting Gerald to know where I am."

"I think that's your business."

"I am a coward." She said it defiantly, tossing up her chin in a challenging gesture that contrasted with her words. "I'd rather agree than quarrel, rather run that fight. But that's why I'm here, isn't it? Here with you, about to become wealthy. Cowardice works for me."

"He can't hurt you, Darcy."

"Of course he can." Lifting her hands, she gave a weary sigh. "Words hurt. They bruise the heart and scar the soul. I'd rather be slapped than battered with words." Then she shook her head. "Well, whatever happens, happens. How much time do you think I have before my name gets out?"

"A day or two."

"Then I should make the most of it. I appreciate you letting me know. You must be busy. I don't want to keep you."

"Kicking me out?"

She managed a small smile. "We both know you have other things to do. I don't need you to baby-sit."

"All right." He started for the door, then stopped and turned with his hand on the knob. "I wanted to kiss you again." He watched her gaze flick warily to his face. "A little too much for your own good, and maybe for my own."

Her heart stuttered. "Maybe I'm tired of my own good, and willing to gamble."

Something flashed into his eyes that made her shudder. "High stakes, bad odds. Too risky for a novice, Darcy from Kansas. First rule is never bet what you can't afford to lose."

When he closed the door quietly behind him, she let out the breath she'd been holding. "Why do I have to lose?"

She kept to herself the rest of the day, writing furiously in her notebook. The garage that had towed in her car called to tell her it was repaired. On impulse she asked the mechanic if he knew anyone who would buy it. She was finished with it, after all, and with everything else—save her notebooks—that she'd brought with her from Trader's Corners.

When the mechanic offered her a thousand dollars, she snapped it up without bargaining, and hurried out to sign over the paperwork.

There was a slick little laptop computer sitting on her desk when she returned, with a note telling her that it was hers to use during her stay, courtesy of The Comanche. Thrilled, Darcy stroked it, examined it, experimented with it, then settled down to transcribe her notes onto the screen.

She worked straight through dinner and into the evening until her eyes blurred and her fingers went numb. Hunger rumbled in her stomach. It was tempting to reach for the phone, to order something to be brought to the room. To stay hidden.

Instead she picked up her purse, squared her shoulders. She was going out, she decided. She'd have a meal, some wine if she wanted. Then, by God, she was going to gamble.

The tables were crowded and the air stung with smoke and perfume when she entered the casino. She wanted to watch, to study. Figure the odds, Mac had said. Learn the rules. She intended to do just that. She liked the world here, the hard-edged brightness of it, the thrill of risk.

She wandered through, loitering by a blackjack table long enough to see a man in shirtsleeves with a thin black cigar clamped between his teeth lose five thousand dollars without flinching.

Amazing.

She studied the spin of the wheel, the teasing bounce of the little silver ball at roulette. Saw stacks of chips come and go. Odd or even. Black or red.

Fascinating.

Behind it all was the never-ending beeps and whistles and clinks of the slots. Lights beckoned. Jackpot. She studied the technique of an elderly woman who leaned on a walker and mumbled to the spinning face of a machine. And gave a cheerleader's shout when quarters cascaded into the metal dish.

"Fifty bucks," the woman said, shooting Darcy a steely smile. "About time this sucker paid off."

"Congratulations. It's poker, isn't it?"

"That's right. Been nickel-and-diming me for two hours. But it's heating up now." She gave the machine a friendly thump with her walker, then stabbed the red button again. "Let's go, sweetheart."

It looked like fun, Darcy decided. Simple, uncomplicated, and an excellent place to start. She walked down the line until she came to an unoccupied machine, then slid onto the stool. After reading the instructions, she put a twenty in the slot and watched her credits light. She pushed the button, grinning as her hand was dealt.

In his office, Mac watched her on-screen. He could only shake his head. In the first place, she was playing like a chump, one credit at a time. If she wanted to hit, she needed to play four, a buck a hand. Now she was holding two kings instead of going for the straight flush.

It was pitifully obvious she'd never played poker before in her life.

Well, he'd keep an eye on her, make certain she didn't lose more than a few hundred.

He glanced over at the door when a knock sounded, then his smile spread with delight when his mother poked her head in. "Hello, handsome."

"Hello, gorgeous." He caught her around the waist in a fierce hug and pressed his lips to her soft, burnished gold hair. "I didn't expect you for another day or two."

"We finished up early." She cupped his face in her hands and smiled at him. "And I wanted to see my boy."

"Where's Dad?"

"He'll be right along. He got waylaid in the lobby so I deserted him."

Mac laughed and kissed her again. She was so beautiful, with soft skin, exotic eyes a unique shade of lavender, and strong facial bones that guaranteed grace and beauty for a lifetime. "Serves him right. Come sit down. Let me get you a drink."

"I would love a glass of wine. It's been a long day." With a sigh Serena sat in one of the leather chairs, stretched out long legs that rustled with silk. "I talked to Caine this morning. He tells me he's getting the paperwork finished up for this woman who hit the big machine here. The press is full of Madam X," she added.

With a short laugh, Mac poured a glass of his mother's favorite white wine. "I can't think of a title that suits her less."

"Really. What's she like?"

"See for yourself." He gestured to the screen. "The little blonde in the blue blouse at the poker slot."

Serena shifted, sipping her wine as she studied the monitor. She lifted a brow as Darcy held a pair of eights and tossed away the best part of a flush. "Not much of a player, is she?"

"Green as they come."

Serena's gambler's heart warmed when Darcy pulled another two eights. "Lucky little thing, though. And pretty. Is it true she was dead broke when she walked in here?"

"Just about down to her last dollar."

"Well, good for her." Serena lifted her glass to toast the screen. "I'm looking forward to meeting her. Oh, good, someone's going to give her a little help."

"What?" Alerted, Mac looked back at the screen and saw a man slip onto the stool beside her. He saw the quick, flirtatious grin, the easy brush of a hand on Darcy's shoulder. And Darcy's wide-eyed, attentive smile. "Son of a bitch."

Mac was halfway out the door before Serena could leap to her feet. "Mac?"

"I've got to get down there."

"But why—"

As her son dashed off, Serena decided there was only one way to find out why. She set her wine aside and hurried after him.

Chapter 5

People were so nice, so friendly, Darcy thought. And so helpful, she decided as she smiled at the attractive man in the Stetson who'd settled down beside her at the slots.

His name was Jake, and he was from Dallas, which, as he said, practically made them neighbors.

"I'm really new at this," she told him confidentially, and his sunshine blue eyes laughed into hers.

"Why, I could spot that right off, sugar. Now like I said first off, you want to plug in the maximum credits for each hand, otherwise you don't get yourself a full payoff when you hit."

"Right." Dutifully Darcy pressed the credit button, then punched for the deal. She studied her hand thoughtfully. "I've got two threes, so I hold them."

"Well now, you could." Jake laid a hand over hers before she could press to hold the cards. "But you see, you're after that royal straight flush, right? That's the jackpot. You got yourself the ace, queen and the jack of hearts there. Couple treys aren't going to get you anything. Even a triple's just keeping you in the game."

She nibbled her lip. "I should throw away the threes?"

"If you're going to gamble—" he winked at her "—you should gamble."

"Right." She furrowed her brow and let the threes go. She plucked an ace and a five. "Oh, well, that's no good." Still she remembered what the blackjack dealer had said, and turned to Jake with a smile. "But I lost correctly."

"There you go." She was cute as a brass button, he thought, sweet as a daisy and looked to be just as easy to pick. Charmed, he leaned in a little closer. "Why don't I buy you a drink, and we'll talk poker strategy."

"The lady's unavailable." Mac dropped a proprietary, and none too gentle hand on Darcy's shoulder.

Her head whipped up, her shoulders tensed. "Mac." He had that frigid look in his eyes again, she noted. Not that he spared her a glance. The ice was all for her new friend from Dallas. "Ah, this is Jake. He was showing me how to play the poker machine."

"So I see. The lady's with me."

Jake ran his tongue around his teeth and, after a brief internal debate, decided he wanted to keep those teeth just where they were. "Sorry, pal. Didn't know I was poaching." He rose, tipped his hat to Darcy. "You hold out for that royal straight flush now."

"Thank you." She held out her hand, confused when Jake's eyes shifted to Mac's before he accepted.

"My pleasure." After a short and silent male exchange, Jake swaggered off.

"I'd been doing it wrong," Darcy began. And that was as far as she got.

"Didn't I tell you not to come down here at night alone?" The fact that he was speaking softly didn't lessen the power and fury behind the words. It only added to them.

"That's ridiculous." She wanted badly to cringe, and had to force herself not to. "You can't expect me to sit in my room all night. I was only—"

"This is exactly why. Ten minutes at a machine and you're getting hit on."

"He wasn't hitting on me. He was helping me."

Mac's opinion of that was short and pithy and put some steel back in Darcy's spine.

"Don't swear at me."

"I was swearing in general." He put a hand under her elbow and hauled her to her feet. "The cowboy wasn't going to buy you a drink to be helpful. He was just priming the pump, and believe me, yours is easily primed."

She started to shake, and realized it was just as much from anger as fear. "Well, if he was, and it is, it's my business."

"My place. My business."

She hissed in a breath, tried to jerk free and failed. "Let go of me. I don't have to stay here. If I'd wanted some overbearing male ordering me around, I'd still be in Kansas."

His smile was as thin and sharp as his name. "You're not in Kansas anymore."

"That's both obvious and unoriginal. Now let go of me. I'm leaving. There are plenty of other places where

I can gamble and socialize without being harassed by the management."

"You want to gamble?" To her shock and—God help her—excitement, he backed her up against the machine with something close to murder in his eyes. "You want to socialize?"

"Mac?" Deciding she'd seen quite enough, Serena stepped up, a bright, friendly smile in place. "Aren't you going to introduce me?"

He turned his head and stared. He'd completely, totally forgotten about his mother. He saw easily beyond the smile to the command in her eyes. And felt twelve years old again.

"Of course." With a smoothness that blanketed both his straining temper and embarrassment, he shifted his grip on Darcy's arm. "Serena MacGregor Blade, Darcy Wallace. Darcy, my mother."

"Oh." Not nearly as skilled as Mac, Darcy didn't come close to hiding both her distress and mortification. "Mrs. Blade. How do you do?"

"I'm so happy to meet you. I just got into town and was about to ask Mac about you." Still smiling, she slid an arm around Darcy's shoulders. "Now I can ask you in person. Let's go get a drink. Mac," she added, casting a smug look over her shoulder as she led Darcy away, "we'll be in the Silver Lounge. Tell your father where I am, will you?"

"Oh sure," Mac muttered. "Fine." He resisted, barely, giving the slot a swift kick, and instead dutifully cashed Darcy out.

In a relatively quiet corner of a cocktail lounge gleaming with silver tables and rich black cushions,

Darcy ran her fingers up and down the stem of a glass of white wine. She'd taken one sip, to clear her dry throat, but was afraid to take more.

Mac was probably right about one thing, she'd decided. She didn't hold her liquor very well.

"Mrs. Blade, I'm so terribly sorry."

"Really?" Serena relaxed against the cushions and took stock of the young woman facing her. Prettier still up close, she mused, in a delicate, almost ethereal, way. Big innocent eyes, a doll's mouth, nervous hands.

Not the type her son usually looked at twice, she reflected. She knew very well his taste generally ran to the long, lean and, in her opinion, somewhat brittle sort of woman. She also knew him well enough to be sure he rarely, very rarely lost his temper over one.

"Mac did ask me not to come down to the casino alone at night."

Serena arched a brow. "I can't see that he'd have any right to do that."

"No, but…he's been so kind to me."

"I'm glad to hear that."

"What I mean is, he really only asked me that one thing. It's understandable he'd be angry I didn't listen."

"It's understandable he'd be angry because he's used to getting his way." Serena studied Darcy over the rim of her glass. "That's not your problem."

"He feels responsible for me."

It was said in such a miserably depressed tone that Serena had to swallow a chuckle. She had an inkling her son felt a bit more than responsibility. "He's always taken his responsibilities seriously. Again, not your problem. Now, tell me everything." She leaned forward, inviting confidences. "I've gotten it all second hand—either from what Mac told my husband or the papers. I want the whole story, straight from the source."

"I don't know where to start."

"Oh, at the beginning."

"Well." Darcy contemplated her wine, then risked another sip. "It was all because I didn't want to marry Gerald."

"Really?" Delighted, Serena inched closer. "And who is Gerald?"

An hour later, Serena was fascinated, charmed and feeling sentimentally maternal toward Darcy. She'd already decided to extend her quick trip to several days when she covered Darcy's hand with hers. "I think you've been incredibly brave."

"I don't feel brave. No one's ever been as kind to me as Mac has, and I've made him so angry. Mrs. Blade—"

"I hope you'll call me Serena," she interrupted. "Especially since I'm going to offer you some unsolicited advice."

"I'd appreciate some advice."

"Don't change anything." Now Serena squeezed Darcy's hand. "Mac will deal with it, I promise you. You be exactly what you are, and you enjoy it."

"I'm attracted to him." Darcy winced then scowled down at her empty glass. "I shouldn't have had the wine. I shouldn't have said that. You're his mother."

"Yes, I am, and as such I'd be insulted if you weren't attracted to him. I happen to think he's a very attractive young man."

"Of course. I mean…" She trailed off, her eyes shifting up, then going wide. "Oh." She barely breathed as she stared at the man who stepped up to the table. "You *are* the chief."

Justin Blade flashed a grin at her, then slid into the booth beside his wife. "You must be Darcy."

"He looks so much like you. I'm sorry. I don't mean to stare."

"The day I mind being stared at by a pretty young woman is the day life stops being worth living."

Justin draped an arm around his wife's shoulders. He was a tall, lean man with black hair streaked with silver as bright as the table and his eyes were green, sharp and deep in a tanned and weathered face. They skimmed over Darcy with both approval and interest.

"Now I know what Mac meant about the fairy wings. Congratulations on your luck, Darcy."

"Thank you. It doesn't seem real yet." She glanced around the glittery lounge. "None of it does."

"Any plans for your new fortune? Other than giving us the chance to win some of it back."

She smiled now, fully. "Oh, he is like you. Actually, I seem to win a little every time I play." She tried to make it sound apologetic, but spoiled it with a chuckle. "But I have put some back—into the shops and salons."

"A woman after my own heart," Serena declared. "We do have wonderful shops here."

"And they genuflect when they see you coming." Justin's fingers drifted up into his wife's hair and began toying with the strands.

It made Darcy realize she'd never seen her parents touch like that, so casually, so intimately. Not in public or private. And realizing it made her unbearably sad.

"Another round, ladies?" Even as he asked, Justin was signaling for a waitress.

"Not for me. Thank you. I should go up. I thought I'd look for a new car tomorrow."

"Want company?"

Darcy fumbled with her purse as she rose, and smiled hesitantly at Serena. "Yes, if you'd like."

"I'd love it. Just call my room when you decide what time you want to go. Someone will find me."

"All right. It was nice meeting both of you. Good night."

Justin waited until Darcy was out of earshot before lifting an eyebrow at his wife. "What's going on in your head, Serena?"

"All sorts of interesting thoughts." She turned her head so that her lips brushed his.

"Such as?"

"Our firstborn nearly punched a cowboy for having a mild flirtation with our Kansas pixie."

"Another wine for my wife, Carol, and a draft for me," he said to the waitress before shifting to face Serena. "You must be exaggerating. Duncan's the one who likes to trade punches over pretty women, not Mac."

"I'm not exaggerating in the least. Fangs were bared, Blade," she murmured. "And murder was in the air. I believe he's seriously smitten."

"Smitten?" The word made him laugh, then his laughter faded into unexpected anxiety. "Define 'seriously.'"

"Justin." She patted his cheek. "He's nearly thirty. It has to happen sometime."

"She's not his type."

"Exactly." She felt her eyes sting and sniffled. "She's nothing like his type. She's perfect for him." Resolutely she blinked back the tears. "Or I'll find out if she's perfect before long."

"Serena, you sound uncomfortably like your father."

"Don't be absurd." Sentimental tears dried up with the insult. "I have no intention of manipulating or scheming or plotting." She tossed her head. "I'm simply going to…"

"Meddle."

"Discreetly," she finished, and beamed at him. "You are very attractive." She skimmed her fingers through the silver wings of his hair, lingered there. "Why don't we take these drinks upstairs, up to bed."

"You're trying to distract me."

"Of course I am." Her smile was slow, seductive and sure. "Is it working?"

He took her hand to pull her to her feet. "It always has." He kissed her fingers. "Always will."

Habitually, Mac slept from about three in the morning to nine, straddling shifts and ending his day after peak hours. Barring trouble, he could safely leave the full responsibility of the casino for that stretch of time to his shift and pit bosses and floor men. Morning hours routinely were dedicated to the massive paperwork the casino demanded—the banking, accounting, staff meetings, the hirings and firings.

He'd taken over as casino manager of Comanche Vegas when he'd been twenty-four, and had set the tone. The surface was friendly, noisy, full of movement and action. But underneath, it was ruthlessly organized and the bottom line was profit.

As he was one himself, he could spot a card counter across the blackjack pit after a five-minute study.

He knew when to let them ride, or when to move them along. Employees were expected to be personable and honest. Those who met his standards were rewarded. Those who didn't were fired.

There were no second chances.

His father had built The Comanche out of guts and grit, and had turned it into a polished, sharp-edged jewel in the desert. Mac's responsibility was to keep the sheen high and he took his responsibilities seriously.

"The first half of the year looks good." Justin leaned back in his chair, removed the reading glasses he privately despised, then handed Mac back the computer-generated spreadsheet. "Up about five percent from last year."

"Six," Mac said with a flash of grin. "And a quarter."

"You've got your mother's head for math."

"I live for numbers. Where is Mom? I thought she'd want to sit in on this meeting."

"She's off with Darcy."

Mac set down the personnel file he'd just picked up. "With Darcy."

"Shopping. Refreshing young woman." Justin's face was as bland as it would have been if he'd held three aces. "Makes it hard to regret handing her seven figures."

"Yeah." Mac caught himself drumming his fingers on the file and stopped. "The press is pushing for a name. I've got half a dozen assistants fielding calls."

"Even without her name, the publicity's humming. It can't hurt business."

"The hotel manager reports an upswing in reservations in the last two days. Play on the machine she hit on is up thirty percent."

"When her story gets out—and that pretty face is splashed over the national news—they'll flood in here."

"I'm putting on three extra floor men, and I'd like to promote Janice Hawber to pit boss."

"You know your staff." Justin took out a slim cigar. "We'll likely get the ripple effect at other locations." When Mac opened the file, Justin waved the cigar, spiraling smoke. "Let's take a break here. Whatever happened to that long-legged brunette who liked baccarat and Brandy Alexanders?"

"Pamela." His father didn't miss a trick, Mac thought. "I believe she's playing baccarat and drinking Brandy Alexanders over at the Mirage these days."

"Too bad. She added a nice…shine to the tables."

"She was looking for a rich husband. I decided to fold before things got sticky."

"Hmm. Seeing anyone else?" At Mac's lifted brow, Justin grinned. "Just trying to keep up with the tour, pal. Duncan changes dancing partners so often I just give them numbers."

"Duncan juggles women like apples," Mac said, thinking of his brother. "I find one at a time's less complicated. And no, I'm not dancing at the moment. You can report back to Grandpa that his oldest grandchild continues to be lax in his duty to continue the line."

Justin chuckled and puffed on his cigar. "You'd think four great-grandchildren would satisfy him for a while."

"Nothing will satisfy The MacGregor until every last one of us is married and clucking around a brood of kids." Mac moved his shoulders restlessly. "At least he could nag one of the others for a bit. Pick on D.C."

"He does pick on D.C." Justin grinned. "Alan tells me he picks at the boy until D.C. holes up in his garret, paints and swears he'll die a bachelor just to spite Daniel. So then Daniel goes to work on Ian, who just smiles charmingly, agrees with everything Daniel says, and cheerfully ignores him."

"Maybe I'll slip one of their names into our next conversation—strictly in the spirit of self-preservation—and shift his focus for a while."

The door burst open. "Speak of the devil," Mac murmured as he got to his feet.

The MacGregor stood in the doorway, grinning widely. His white hair flowed back from a broad and deeply seamed face offset by eyes that twinkled bright blue and a wild, snowy beard. His shoulders were as broad as the grill of a truck. And the hand that slapped Justin enthusiastically on the back was as big as a ham.

"Give me one of those pitiful excuses for a cigar," Daniel boomed, then caught Mac in a bear hug that could have toppled a rabid grizzly. "Pour me a Scotch, boy. Flying cross-country puts a thirst in a man."

"You had a Scotch on the plane." Caine MacGregor strode into the room. "Charmed the flight attendant out of one when I wasn't looking. If Mom finds out, she'll kill me."

"What she doesn't know won't hurt you." Daniel plopped his bulk into a chair, sighed lustily and looked around with great pleasure. "Well now, how about that cigar?"

Knowing the rules—and Anna MacGregor's wrath—Justin turned to his brother-in-law. "Anna dump him on you?"

"Ha!" Daniel thumped the cane he used as much for looks as for convenience.

"He wouldn't stay home. She sends her love and her

sympathy. Good to see you." Caine gave both Justin and Mac a hard hug. "Where's Rena?"

"Shopping," Justin told him. "She should be back shortly."

"Give me a damn cigar." Daniel glowered and thumped his cane again. "And where's the lassie who skinned you for over a million? I want to meet her."

Mac turned to study his grandfather. Formidable, Darcy had said. It appeared she was going to find out firsthand just how formidable.

Dazed and flushed, Darcy carted bags and boxes into her suite. Similarly burdened, Serena was right behind her.

"Oh, that was fun." With a sigh, Serena dumped everything on the floor and dropped into a chair. "My feet are killing me. Always a good sign of shopping success."

"I don't even remember what I bought. I don't know what came over me."

"I'm a terrible influence."

"You were wonderful." It had been one of the most monumental days in Darcy's life. Being propelled from store to store, having blouses and dresses tossed at her, modeling them in front of Serena's assessing eyes. "You know everything about clothes."

"A lifetime love affair. Darcy, run up and put on that yellow sundress. I'm dying to see it on you again. Try it with the white sandals and the little gold hoop earrings." She rose to nudge Darcy toward the stairs. "Indulge me, won't you, honey? I'll order us up a well-deserved cold drink."

"All right." Halfway up, she turned and looked back.

"I had the best time. I don't think I'll be able to bring myself to buy that sports car, though. It's so impractical."

"We'll worry about that later." Humming to herself, Serena walked away to order some lemonade.

The child was starved for attention, she thought. It was so easy to see, and so easy to read between the lines when Darcy spoke of her childhood. She doubted anyone had ever taken her on a whirlwind shopping spree, or giggled with her over foolish lingerie, or told her how pretty she looked in a yellow dress.

It made Serena's heart ache to remember how stunned Darcy had looked when she'd laughed and hugged her as they'd debated over earrings. And the wistful glance she'd sent the bright blue sports car before she'd given her attention to the sober and practical sedan she said was more suitable.

As far as Serena could tell there had been far too much suitable in Darcy's young life, and not nearly enough fun.

That, she determined, was going to change.

When the phone rang, Darcy called from upstairs. "Oh, can you—I'm not—"

"I'll get it." Serena picked up the phone. "Ms. Wallace's suite." Her eyes gleamed, her smile spread as she listened to the voice. "Yes, indeed, we're back."

Her mind calculated at a speed and in a direction that would have made Daniel puff out with pride. "Why don't we do that here? I'm sure she'd be more comfortable. Yes, now's fine. See you in a minute."

Humming again, Serena strolled to the base of the stairs. "Need any help?"

"No. There are so many boxes. I just found the dress."

"Take your time. That was Justin on the phone. You don't mind if we do a little business, do you?"

"No."

"Good. I'll order up more drinks." Champagne, she decided, considering.

Ten minutes later, Darcy took the first turn on the steps just as the elevator opened. She froze where she was, staggered by the rich mix of male voices, the sudden rush of energy that poured out of the elevator along with them.

Then she could only see Mac.

Serena watched the way her son's eyes locked on Darcy's, the way they darkened, held. And she was sure.

"There's my girl." Daniel grabbed his daughter in a fierce hug. "You don't call your mother enough," he scolded her. "She pines."

"I've been spending a lot of time nagging my children." She kissed him lavishly on both cheeks, then turned to embrace her brother. "How are you? How's Diana? How're the kids?"

"Everyone's fine. Diana's tying up a case and couldn't get away. She'll be sorry she missed you."

"Well now." Daniel leaned on his cane and studied the woman who'd frozen like a statue on the stairs. "You're just a wee lass, aren't you? Come on down, and let's have a better look at you."

"He rarely bites." Mac crossed to the base of the steps, held out a hand.

Her legs were wobbly, and she knew her fingers weren't steady so she pretended not to see his hand. But he took hers anyway, giving it a reassuring squeeze that clutched at her heart.

"Darcy Wallace, The MacGregor."

She was afraid she wouldn't find her voice. He looked so big, and so fierce with white brows knitted together over sharp blue eyes. "I'm happy to meet you, Mr. MacGregor."

The scowl stayed in place another moment, then transformed into a smile so wide and so bright she blinked. "Pretty as a sunbeam." He gave her cheek a gentle pat with his huge hand. "Tiny as an elf."

Her lips curved up in response. "It's only that you're so big. If William of Scotland had had more like you, he would have won."

Daniel let out his bark of a laugh, and winked at her. "Now, there's a lass. Come sit and talk to me."

"You can interrogate her later. I'm Caine MacGregor."

She shifted her gaze to the tall man with silver and gold hair and strong blue eyes. "Yes, I know. I'm so nervous." She clutched her hands together. How many legends could one person meet in one day? "I studied about you in school. Everyone thought you'd run for president."

"I leave the politics to Alan. I'm just a lawyer. Your lawyer," he added, taking her arm and leading her to a chair at the glossy conference table. "Want me to clear this rabble out while we consult?"

"Oh, no, please." She scanned the faces around her, lingered on Mac's. "Everyone here has a part in this."

"All right. It's straightforward enough." He sat and opened his briefcase. "I've got your birth certificate, your social security card, a copy of the police report from the purse snatching last week. You're unlikely to recover anything from that."

She stared down at the papers he handed her. "It doesn't matter. You got all of this so quickly."

"Connections," he said with a wolfish grin. "I have copies of your last two years' tax returns. There are some forms for you to fill out and sign. A number of them."

"All right." She tried not to gape at the stack he began to produce. "Where do I start?"

"I'll explain them as we go along." He glanced up, wiggling his brows at his family. "Haven't you all got something better to do?"

"No." Daniel took a chair for himself. "Can't a man get a drink around here while all this legal mumbo jumbo's going on?"

"I ordered drinks." To distract him, Serena sat on the arm of his chair and began to tell him about her grandchild's latest accomplishments.

Listening carefully, Darcy filled out each form. She hesitated over the address, then wrote in the name of the hotel. When Caine didn't correct her, she relaxed a little and continued to note down the required information.

"Your identification's in order," Caine told her. "You'll be able to reapply for a driver's license, credit cards, that sort of thing. You didn't indicate a bank."

"A bank?"

"The transfer of funds will be done electronically, from account to account. The oversize check Mac will present you with is just for publicity. Photo op, and positive publicity for The Comanche. The actual business is accomplished quickly and efficiently by transferring the amount of your winnings from The Comanche's account to yours. Do you want the money sent to your bank in Kansas?"

"No." She refused swiftly, then fell into silence.

"Where do you want it sent, Darcy?" Caine asked gently.

"I don't know. Maybe it could just stay in the same bank. Here?"

"That's not a problem. You're aware that the IRS gets the first bite."

She nodded, signing her name to the last form. Under her lashes, she watched Mac go to the door to let in the room-service waiter.

Mac wore black trousers and a white shirt. Both looked soft, almost fluid, and she wondered about the texture, wished she could run her fingertips over them. Over him.

"You're going to need financial advice."

"What?" Flushing, berating herself for not paying attention, she looked over at Caine. "I'm sorry."

"Tomorrow morning, you're going to have a great deal of money. You'll need a financial advisor."

"You can't do that?"

"I can give you some basic and initial guidance. After that, you're going to want someone who specializes. I can give you some names."

"I'd appreciate it."

"That's pretty much it." He leaned back. "We'll open you an account, the money will be transferred. And you're set."

"Just like that?"

"Just like that."

"Oh." She pressed a hand to her suddenly jittery stomach. "God." Once again she searched out Mac's face, hoping he'd tell her what to do, what to say. But he only watched her, his eyes steady and unreadable.

With an impatient huff for her son, Serena rose. "I'd say this calls for a celebration. Mac, darling, open the champagne. Darcy, you get the first glass."

"It's so nice of you, all of you, but—" She jolted when the cork popped.

"I've never lost a million to anyone more appealing." Justin took the glass from his son and carried it to Darcy. "Enjoy it." He leaned down to kiss her cheek.

Warmth spread in her stomach, pressure weighed on her chest. "Thank you."

"Congratulations." Caine took her hand, covered it with both of his.

Then everyone was lifting glasses, and talking. She was hugged, kissed by everyone, with the notable exception of Mac. He only lifted a hand to her cheek, skimmed a finger down it.

There was laughing, and arguments over the time and place for a family dinner, which, she realized with shock, included her. Serena draped an arm casually around her shoulder while telling Caine he was an idiot if he thought she'd settle for pizza for such an occasion.

Emotions were clawing at her, rising up to squeeze her heart, to close her throat and burn her eyes. She heard her own breath begin to hitch and clamped down hard.

"Excuse me." She managed to mumble it before turning quickly for the stairs. Horribly aware the laughter had stopped, she rushed up, closed herself in the bathroom. She held on, carefully turning the water on full in the sink so the sound would cover her sobs.

She sat on the floor, curled up into herself and wept like a baby.

Chapter 6

The suite was quiet when Darcy came out again. She didn't know whether to be relieved or mortified to realize they'd left her alone. She would have to fumble her way through apologies and explanations, she told herself. But for now she could settle her nerves and emotions.

She glanced around the bedroom, scanning the shopping bags, the boxes. The right thing to do, she told herself, was to put everything away, to tidy up, to put at least this part of her life in order.

She was just unwrapping a new blouse when she heard footsteps on the stairs. Clutching the blouse, she stared at Mac as he stopped at the top of the suite.

"Are you all right?"

"Yes. I thought everyone had gone."

"I stayed," he said simply, then crossed to her. He

glanced down at the blouse she continued to hold in white-knuckled fingers. "Nice color."

"Oh. Yes. Your mother picked it out." Feeling foolish, Darcy relaxed her fingers and turned away to hang the blouse in the closet. "I was so rude, leaving that way. I'll apologize to everyone."

"There's no need for that."

"Of course there is." She spent several seconds adjusting the shoulders of the blouse on the padded hanger as if their evenness was of monumental importance. "It's just that everything seemed to hit me all at once." She went back to unfold slacks, then repeated the procedure, lining up the edges of the hem perfectly.

"That's understandable, Darcy. It's a lot of money. It'll change your life."

"The money?" Distracted, she glanced back, then fluttered her hands. "Well, yes, I suppose the money's part of it."

He angled his head. "What else?"

She started to pick up a box, then set it back on the bed and wandered to the window. It still felt odd to stand there against the glass, with a world she'd only begun to touch spread like a banquet at her feet.

"Your family's so…beautiful. You have no idea what you have. You couldn't. They've always been yours, you see, so how could you know."

She watched the signs of the casino across the street, beckoning, daring, inviting. *Win, Win, Win.*

It wasn't so terribly hard to win, she thought. But it was much, much trickier to keep the prize.

"I'm a watcher," she told him. "I'm good at it. That's why I want to write. I want to write about things I see, or want to see. Things I'd like to feel or experience."

She lifted her hands to rub her arms, then made herself turn back to him. "I watched your family."

She looked so lovely, he thought. And so lost. "And what did you see?"

"Your father playing with your mother's hair when they sat together in the lounge last night." She saw the confusion in his eyes and smiled. "You're used to seeing them touch each other—casually, affectionately, so you don't notice when it happens. Why would you?" she murmured, swamped with envy. "He put his arm around her, and she leaned into him, sort of..." Eyes half-closed, she moved her body as if yearning for another. "Settled into the curve because she knew exactly how she'd fit there."

Darcy closed her eyes, laid a hand over her own heart as she brought the scene back into focus. "And while he talked to me, he toyed with the ends of her hair. Tangled them, combed them through, wound the strands around his finger. It was lovely. She knew he was doing it, because there was a little light in her eyes. I wonder if it takes another woman to recognize that."

She opened her eyes again and smiled. "I never saw my parents touch that way. I think they loved each other, but they never touched that way, that easy and wonderful way. Some people don't. Or they can't."

She sighed and shook her head. "I'm not making sense."

He could see it himself, now that she'd painted it for him. And she was right, he realized. It was so much a part of his life, a part of his family, he didn't notice it.

"Yes, you are."

"It's more—it's all of it. Everyone piling in here a little while ago. You were part of it again, so you couldn't have really seen it. The way your grandfather hugged your mother. So strong and tight. For that instant she was the center of his world, and he of hers. And more, when she sat on the arm of his chair. He laid his hand on her knee. Just put it there, to touch. It was so lovely," she said quietly. "The way she and your uncle argued about where to have dinner, and laughed at each other. All the little looks and pats and the shorthand of people who know each other, and like each other."

"They do like each other." He could see that her eyes were overbright again, and reached out to touch her hair. "What is it, Darcy?"

"They were so kind to me. I'm taking money from them, a lot of money, but everyone's drinking champagne and laughing and congratulating me. Your mother put her arm around my shoulders." It made her voice break, forced her to fight to steady it. "It sounds ridiculous, I know it, but if I hadn't gone up right then, I would have grabbed on to her. Just grabbed on and held. She would have thought I was crazy."

Lonely? Had he thought she was lonely? He understood now the word didn't come close. "She would have thought you wanted a hug." He slipped his arms around her, felt her tremble lightly. "Go ahead, grab on to me. It's all right."

He eased her closer, pressed his cheek to her hair. He could feel her hesitation, the battle of emotions that had her standing very still. Then her arms came around him, wrapped tight. Her breath came out on a long, broken sigh.

"We're big on grabbing in my family," he told her. "You won't shock any of us if you take hold."

It felt so good to press up against the strong wall of

his chest, to hear the steady beat of his heart, to smell
the warmth of his skin. Closing her eyes, she let herself absorb the comfort of his hand stroking gently over
her back.

"It's just so foreign to me. All of this. All of them.
You. Especially you."

Her voice was husky and low. Her hair was soft under
his cheek and fragrant as a meadow. Affection, he reminded himself as her slender little body molded to his,
not lust. Friendship, not passion.

Then she turned her head as if to sniff his neck and
needs stirred restlessly.

"Better now?" He started to ease away, but she clung.
His lips brushed her temple, lingered. He held her, let
her hold him and told himself it was only because she
needed it.

"Mmm."

The dress had thin straps crossing over the smooth
flesh of her back. His fingers began to trace along them,
under them. She moved in a long, catlike stretch under
the caress, jangling his brain.

It was the only excuse he had for the fact that his
lips trailed down her face, found hers and plundered.

He forgot to be gentle. She was pressed against him
in the stream of sunlight, all gold and soft and willing.
The kiss demanded surrender, and she gave it, flowing into his arms like heated wine, her mouth yielding
under the assault of his as if it had only been waiting.
Had always been waiting.

Her mind was spinning in slow, expanding circles
that spiraled up toward something desperately wanted.
The strength of him, the power of those arms that
wrapped possessively around her was desperately ex-

citing. Knowing she was helpless against him made her quiver, yet she gloried in the power of him.

This was need, she thought wildly. This, finally this. A wild burst of light and energy and raw nerves. The thumping heart, the racing pulse, the explosion of heat.

Thrilled, she gave herself to it, to him.

In one strong stroke, his hands slid down her back, over the curve of her bottom, lifting her, pressing heat desperately to heat. His mouth swallowed her gasps, greedily, ravenously. He could imagine himself filling her, buried in her, taking her where they stood and driving into her until the hot ball of frustration broke free and gave him peace.

He caught himself as his hands gripped those delicate straps over her back, at the point of rending. He looked down into her eyes, wide, unseeing and still swollen from tears.

He set her aside so abruptly she staggered, scalded her with a look when she crossed her hands over her heart as if to hold it in place.

"You're too damn trusting." The words whipped out at her, but the lash was for himself. "It's a miracle you survived a day on your own."

God, my God, was all she could think. Was the blood supposed to burn like this? It was a wonder her skin didn't burst into flame. She lifted her fingers to her mouth where her lips continued to tingle and ache. "I know you won't hurt me."

He'd come close, dangerously close, to ripping off her clothes, shoving her against the wall and taking her without thought or care. Now, he thought, she was standing there, staring at him out of eyes filled with arousal and—worse, much worse—trust.

"The hell I won't." He said it roughly, hoping to save them both. "You don't know me, and you don't know the game, so I'll tell you, don't bet against the house. The house always wins in the end. Always."

She couldn't catch her breath. "I won."

His eyes flashed. "Stick around," he challenged. "I'll get it back. And more. More than you'll want to lose. So be smart."

His hand whipped out, cupped the back of her neck firmly. He wanted her to cringe. If she did he'd be able to resist all the things he wanted to do. "Run away. Take the money and run far and fast. Buy yourself a house with a picket fence and a hatchback in the driveway and shade trees in the yard. Because my world isn't yours."

She almost shuddered at his words. But if she did, she'd prove everything he said was true. "I like it here."

His lips curved into something between a smile and a sneer. "Honey, you don't even know where you are."

"I'm with you." And that, she realized with a fresh and towering thrill, was all she really wanted.

"You think you want to play with me?" He angled his hand at the back of her neck to bring her to her toes. "Little Darcy from Kansas? First raise and you'll fold your cards and scramble."

"You don't scare me."

"Don't I?" He damn well should, he thought. And he damn well would, for her own good. "You haven't even got the guts to risk having some jerk back home find out where you are. You'd rather sneak out of your own town like a thief instead of taking a stand. Now you think you can play with the high rollers?" With another short laugh, he released her and turned to leave. "Not bloody likely."

His words were a sharp slap of shame to an exposed cheek. She winced from the blow but steadied herself. "You're right."

He stopped at the top of the stairs and turned back. She was still standing by the window with her arms wrapped tight around her body, her eyes lit with a passion that contrasted sharply with the defensive stance.

He wanted, quite desperately, to go back, gather her close again and just hold her. Not simply because she needed it, he realized with something akin to panic. Because he did. Outrageously.

Her breath came out in one explosive puff. "You're absolutely right. How do we do it?"

The images that careered through his mind had him taking careful hold of the banister. "Excuse me?"

"How do we inform the press? Do you just give out my name, or do we have to do something like a release or a press conference?"

The combination of shame and irritation he felt was lethal. He took a moment, rubbing a hand over his face as he searched for control. "Darcy, there's no point in rushing into that."

"Why wait?" She stiffened her spine. "You said that it was going to leak shortly anyway. I'd prefer to have some control. And I can hardly expect you to have any respect for me if I continue to hide this way."

"This isn't about me. It's long past time you started thinking not just *for* yourself, but thinking *of* yourself."

"I am. And it is about me." Odd, she thought, how saying that, realizing that, felt so calming. "It's about taking a stand, not being pushed around, pressured or maneuvered. I might not be a high roller, Mac, but I'm ready to play my hand."

She turned, moving quickly before she could change her mind, and picked up the bedside phone. "Do you call the press, or do I?"

He studied her another moment, waiting for her to fold. But her eyes stayed level, her jaw remained set. Saying nothing, he walked to her, took the phone out of her hand, then punched in an extension.

"This is Blade. I need you to set up a press conference. We'll use the Nevada Suite. One hour."

"I pushed her into this." Behind the service entrance of the Nevada Suite, Mac shoved his hands into his pockets and watched as Caine briefed Darcy on the press conference.

"You gave her breathing room," Serena corrected. "If you hadn't run interference, she'd have been dropped straight into the media days ago. Without time to settle and prepare." She gave her son a quick, supportive pat on the arm. "And without one of the top lawyers in the country beside her."

"She's not ready for this."

"I think you underestimate her."

"You didn't see her an hour ago."

"No." And though she wondered what had passed between Darcy and her son, she resisted prying. "But I'm seeing her now. And I say she's ready."

Serena linked an arm through her son's and studied the woman listening attentively to Caine. Darcy had topped the yellow sundress with a short white jacket. It was a smart look, Serena decided. Simple and sunny.

The girl was a little pale, she mused, but she was holding her own.

"She's going to surprise herself," Serena murmured.

And you, she added silently. "Caine's going to be right there with her—and all of us are here, backing her up."

Justin slipped through the heavy door, nodded to his son, laid a hand lightly on his wife's shoulder. "We're set. The audience is a bit restless. Do you want me to make the announcement?"

"I'll do it." He watched the way his mother's hand lifted to lie over his father's, the way their bodies brushed. The unit they made. It was something so natural to both of them, he realized he wouldn't have noticed, or would have taken it for granted. Until Darcy.

"I haven't appreciated you enough." He covered their joined hands with his. "Not nearly enough."

Justin frowned thoughtfully as Mac walked to Darcy. "Now, what was that about?"

"I'm not sure." Serena smiled, a bit mistily. "But I like it. Let's go keep The MacGregor distracted so Darcy can get through this smoothly."

Darcy was terrified. Everything Caine had told her was already jumbled into mush in her head. Pride kept her rooted to the spot even when her imagination conjured a picture of herself running like a rabbit.

Her heart drummed hard staccato beats in her head as Mac came toward her.

"Ready?"

Time to stop running, she told herself. "Yes."

"I'm going to go in, give them a brief rundown, then you'll come in and field some questions. That's all there is to it."

He might as well have told her she was to perform a tap dance while juggling swords. But she nodded. "Your uncle's explained how it works."

"The girl's not a moron," Daniel barked. "She knows how to speak for herself. Don't you, lass?"

The bright blue eyes demanded confidence. "We're about to find out." She squared her shoulders and walked to the side door to peek out. "So many." Her stomach did a painful lurch as she scanned the dozens of faces in the ballroom. "Well." She stepped back. "One or a hundred it's the same thing."

"Don't answer anything you're not comfortable with," Mac said briefly, then stepped out.

The noise level rose with rustling movements and speculative murmurs as he climbed the short stairs to a long platform.

Confidence, Darcy reflected, watching the way he moved, the easy way he stood behind the dais and spoke into the microphone. His voice was clear, his smile easy. When laughter broke out among the gathered reporters, she blinked.

She hadn't heard the words, just the tone. She understood he was setting a casual and friendly one.

It was so easy for him, she thought. Facing strangers, thinking on his feet, being in control. The sea of faces didn't have his nerves jangling, the shouted questions didn't shake his poise in the least.

"Okay?" Caine put a hand to the small of her back.

She drew in a breath, held it, let it out. "Okay."

Attention shifted in a wave when she stepped out. Cameras whirled as photographers jockeyed for a better angle. Television crews zoomed in. A barrage of questions was hurled at her the minute she stepped up to the mike. She jolted a little when Mac reached down to adjust it for her.

"I—" Her voice boomed back at her, making her

want to giggle nervously. "I'm Darcy Wallace. I, ah…" She cleared her throat and struggled to dredge something coherent out of the jumble of thoughts in her mind. "I hit the jackpot."

There was laughter, some appreciative applause. And the questions shot out too fast to separate one from the other.

"Where are you from?"

"How do you feel?"

"What are you doing in Vegas?"

"What happened when…"

Why? How? Where?

"I'm sorry." Her voice frayed around the edges, but when Mac moved closer, she shook her head fiercely. She would do this, she promised herself. And she would do it without making a fool of herself. "I'm sorry," she repeated. "I've never talked to reporters before, so I don't really know how. Maybe it would be better if I just told you what happened."

It was easier that way, like telling a story. As she spoke, her voice steadied, and the fingers that had gripped the edges of the dais like a lifeline relaxed.

"What was the first thing you did when you realized you'd won?"

"After I fainted?" There was such quick laughter at her answer that her lips curved up in a smile. "Mr. Blade gave me a room—a suite. They have beautiful rooms here, like something out of a book. There's a fireplace, and a piano and gorgeous flowers. I don't think it all even started to sink in until the next day. Then the first thing I did was buy a new dress."

"Lass has a way with her," Daniel announced.

"She's caught them." Serena beamed approval. "She has no idea how charming she is."

"Our boy's taken with her." Daniel wiggled his eyebrows when his daughter sent him an arched look. "See how he hovers over her, like he's ready to scoop her up and cart her off if anyone gets too close. He's smitten."

She wasn't quite ready to give him the satisfaction of agreeing. "They've only known each other a few days."

Daniel merely snorted, then leaned in close to whisper in her ear. "And how long did it take you to catch this one's eye?" He jerked a shoulder toward Justin.

"Slightly less time than it took me to realize you'd maneuvered us together in the first place."

"Married thirty years now, aren't you?" Unrepentant, Daniel grinned. "No, don't thank me," he continued, patting her cheek. "A man's got to look after his family, after all. They'll make pretty babies together, don't you think, Rena?"

She only sighed. "At least try to be subtle about it."

"Subtle's my middle name," Daniel said with a wink.

"Good job." Caine gave Darcy a congratulatory embrace the minute the door closed behind them.

"It wasn't as hard as I thought it would be." Relief flooded through her. "And now it's over."

"It's just beginning," Caine corrected, sorry to put that doe-on-alert look back in her eyes. "Mac will keep them busy for now," he said, nodding as his nephew went out to bat cleanup for the press.

"But I told them everything."

"They're always going to want more. And you can expect dozens of calls requesting personal interviews, photos. Offers for your life story."

"My life story." That, at least, made her laugh. "I barely had a life before a few days ago."

"The contrast is only going to add fuel. The tabloids are going to play with this, so be prepared for speculation that you were directed to Vegas by psychic aliens."

When she laughed, he guided her at a quick pace toward the service elevator. He didn't want to frighten her, or dull that bloom of success, but knew she needed to be prepared.

"The calls to offer you tremendous investment opportunities are going to start, too. Financial advisors, legitimate and not, are going to camp on your doorstep. The stepsister of the cousin of the kid who sat behind you in first grade is going to try to hit you up for a loan."

"That would be Patty Anderson," Darcy improvised with a weak smile. "I never liked her anyway."

"Good girl. Do yourself a favor. Don't answer the phone for a couple of days. Better yet, we can arrange for Mac to have the desk take your calls until things cool off a bit."

"That's like running again, isn't it?"

"No. It's protecting yourself, and it's staying in control. If you want to do interviews, you can set them up. When you've figured out what it is you want to do, you contact a financial advisor. Whatever you do, you do at your pace."

"I'm in charge," Darcy said when they stopped at the door of her suite.

"Exactly. If you have any questions or concerns, you can call me. I'll be around through tomorrow. After that, you can reach me in Boston."

"I don't know how to begin to thank you."

"Enjoy yourself." He gave the hand she offered a

squeeze. "And don't forget how much fun it was to buy a new dress."

"Keep it simple," she murmured, understanding.

"Atta girl." He bent to kiss her cheek. "I'll see you later."

Alone, Darcy stepped into the suite. Keeping it simple wasn't as easy as it sounded. She was a rich woman with her fifteen minutes of fame in its initial seconds. The message light on her phone was blinking, and the phone itself began to ring. Taking Caine's advice, she ignored it, waiting until it stopped, then taking the receiver off the hook.

Problem solved, she thought, for now.

But she had much deeper, much more complex problems that sudden wealth had nothing to do with.

She was in love and knew there was no point in questioning it, debating it or denying it. Her heart was the one thing she'd always been sure of.

Often she'd imagined what it would be like to lose it, the thrill and the anxiety of the fall. She'd always wondered who it would be who would make everything inside her yearn. How they would be together—for in her dreams he'd loved her as well.

But this wasn't a dream or imagination. Loving Mac was simply and brutally real, with the physical needs so much sharper and more vital than she'd believed herself capable of.

She wanted him, to touch him, to taste, to fulfill the promise of that frantic kiss. She wanted to tremble with the knowledge she was desirable, and oh, she wanted to know what it was to lose herself in sensations.

Just as much, she wanted to curl up against him and know she was welcome there. Even expected there. She wanted to exchange those quiet looks that people who were truly intimate could use as effectively as words.

To be loved in return.

That wasn't a simple matter.

But something about her stirred him, and that in itself was a miracle. If he could want her, perhaps there was a chance for more. It wasn't any more impossible, she supposed, than winning more than a million dollars on the single pull of a lever.

Comforted by that, she snuggled into the corner of the sofa, rested her head on the big, soft pillow tucked there and let herself imagine.

She dreamed of showgirls, dozens of them with endless legs and bountiful breasts showcased in brief, glittering costumes and colorful, floating feathers.

She stood among them, miles too short, wearing layers too plain to be noticed. A wren among exotic birds.

Their long legs flashed, their lush bodies turned and twirled while she stumbled through the complex routine. She couldn't keep up, couldn't compete. No matter how hard she tried, she was always a step behind.

Mac stood watching, a small, amused smile on his face. Beautiful women with long, curvy bodies spun gracefully, seductively around him. Take your pick, they seemed to say.

His gaze flicked down to her face when she stopped in front of him. *Where did you come from? You don't belong here.*

But I want to stay.

He only patted her cheek, then gently nudged her along. *This isn't the place for you, Darcy from Kansas. You don't even know where you are.*

I do know. I do. And it could be the place for me. I want it to be.

And there was Gerald, taking her hand, tugging her away. He had that impatient frown on his face, that irritated scowl in his eyes.

It's time to stop this foolishness. If you insist on pretending to be what you're not, you're only going to embarrass yourself. I'm tired of waiting for you to come to your senses. We're going home.

"I'm not going back." She murmured it as she broke through the surface of the dream. "I'm not going back," she said more definitely, opening her eyes to find the room had become dark while she'd slept.

She lay there another moment, ordering both the dream and the depression that accompanied it to fade.

"I'm staying here." She wrapped her arms around the pillow. "No matter what."

Chapter 7

Darcy had been at The Comanche nearly a week and was amazed at how much of the hotel she'd yet to explore.

She'd managed to catch the stunning display of horsemanship presented in the auditorium twice a day, where beautiful fast horses and daring riders in authentic Comanche costumes teamed up for a spectacular performance.

She'd wandered around the lavish outdoor pool with its sparkling water contained in bright tile cannily shaped in a wide *C,* and dipped her fingers into the smaller lagoon, secluded by palms and fed by a musical waterfall.

She'd indulged herself in the spa and treatment center, had roamed nearly half the wide array of shops, but had yet to slip inside any of the three theaters or walk through the many ballrooms and conference rooms, or find an excuse to visit the business center.

The longer she was a guest of The Comanche, she thought, the more it seemed to grow.

When the elevator let her out on the roof, she stepped into a lush oasis of palms and tangling flowered vines. The morning sun showered onto the rich blue waters of the pool, shooting diamonds of light onto the surface.

Chaises and chairs in the hotel's colors of sapphire and emerald were arranged to offer ease to sun worshipers or those who preferred the shade.

Seated at one of the glass tables under the jewel tone stripes of a slanted umbrella was Daniel MacGregor.

He got to his feet when he saw her, and Darcy was again struck by the raw power of the man who had lived nearly a century, had built empires, raised a president, stood at the head of a fascinating family.

"Thanks so much for agreeing to see me like this, Mr. MacGregor."

He winked and gallantly pulled out a chair for her. "A pretty woman calls and asks to see me alone, I'd be a fool to say no." He took his seat across from her. Instantly a waiter appeared with a pot of coffee. "Do you want breakfast, lass?"

"No." She smiled weakly. "I'm too nervous to eat."

"Food's just what you need then. Bring the girl some bacon and eggs—you need some meat on you," he said to Darcy. "Scramble the eggs, and don't be stingy with the hash browns. And bring me the same."

"Right away, Mr. MacGregor."

And that, Darcy mused as the waiter scurried away, was likely the typical response of those who came into

Daniel MacGregor's orbit. Right away, Mr. MacGregor, and off they rushed to follow orders.

"Now." He picked up his cup. "You'll eat and see if you don't feel steadier. A lot's happened to you in a short time. Anybody'd be a bit rocky. My grandson's taking good care of you?"

"Yes. He's been wonderful. All of you have been wonderful."

"But the ground seems a bit boggy under your feet."

"Yes." Her breath came out in a whoosh of relief that he understood. "It's all so…foreign. Exciting," she added, scanning the lush rooftop garden. "I feel as if I've dropped down into the middle of a book, and I'm vague on the first chapters and don't have any idea how it's going to end."

"Nothing wrong with enjoying the page you're on."

"No, and I have been." Self-consciously she lifted a hand to finger the silver-and-gold twists that dangled from her ear. "But I have to think about what's going to happen when I turn that page. I can't keep buying new clothes and earrings, and living in the moment. Money's a responsibility, isn't it?"

He leaned back, lips pursed as he studied her. Delicate she might look, he mused, but there was nothing delicate about her brain. He had a feeling it was both strong and flexible. All the better, he decided. The wife of his grandson should possess a nimble mind and not a shallow one.

"That it is," he said, and smiled at her.

The smile confused her. It was so…canny. And there were secrets dancing in those bright blue eyes. A little flustered, she picked up her coffee, forgetting to add her customary cream. "There were dozens of calls on my voice mail when I checked it this morning."

"That's to be expected."

"Yes, I know. Mac told me it would happen, but I didn't imagine there would be so many. Reporters..." She laughed a little. "People from magazines I've read, television shows I've watched suddenly want to talk to me. I haven't done anything. I haven't saved a life or found the cure for the common cold or given birth to quintuplets."

His brows shot up. "Do multiple births run in your family?"

"No."

"Pity," he murmured. He'd have enjoyed twin babies. Still, he brushed that aside as Darcy stared at him in confusion. "You've lived a common fantasy. Instant wealth. And you're young, pretty, you come from a small town in the Midwest and you were down to your last dollar. It's a good story. People who read it or hear it can root for you, and imagine it could happen to them."

"Yes, I suppose that's true. It's only fair I talk to some of them." She paused as the waiter returned with two heaping plates. Daunted, Darcy stared down at hers while Daniel dug into his with gusto.

"Eat up, girl. You need some fuel."

She picked up her fork. "I didn't know they served meals up here."

Daniel grinned. "They don't. Just drinks and such as a rule. But it's a fine thing to break the rules now and then. You wanted to be private," he reminded her. "And not many come up here so early in the day. The restaurants inside will likely be packed with people wanting the special buffet and the like."

"There are six restaurants," she told him. "I read about them in the hotel guide. Six. And four swimming pools."

"People have to eat, and some like to be seen around the pool when they're not gambling."

"I can't get over how…huge this place is. Theaters and lounges, the open-air auditorium. It's a maze."

"And all roads lead back to the casino. It's not a casual design," he added with a wink. "Whatever else there is to do in a hotel of this nature, gambling's the hub."

"It's beautiful and exciting. Then you come up here, and you can look beyond it all and see the desert. I love looking at the desert."

"One of the reasons there aren't any windows in the casino. Wouldn't want any distraction." He shot her a warrior's grin. "You should eat a good breakfast, then when it's settled, take yourself a nice swim. I swim most every day. Keeps me young."

It was more than that, Darcy thought. It was the energy, the avid interest in life, the delight in the challenge of it that kept him vital. She was counting on that interest and that delight. "Um… Mr. MacGregor, Caine— gave me a list of names. Financial advisors, brokers, that sort of thing."

Daniel grunted and, since no one was around to stop him, dashed salt on his potatoes. "You need to protect your capital."

"I understand that, particularly since a large percentage of the calls on my voice mail were from people wanting to discuss my finances. One offered to fly me into Los Angeles, put me up at the Beverly Wilshire so that I could take a meeting."

Frowning, she buttered a piece of toast. "Most of them sounded very interested in discussing portfolios and investments, but none of them were on the list your son gave me."

"That doesn't surprise me."

"I wrote them down. I have both lists. I wondered if you would mind looking at them? I know your son prefers giving me a range of choices, but I think I'd do better if I was pointed in a specific direction."

"Let's have a look." Daniel pulled his glasses out of his pocket, perched them on his nose as Darcy took her lists from her purse. "Ha! Vultures, fly-by-nights. Grifters." With barely a glance he slapped the first list facedown. "You'll want to stay away from these, lass."

She nodded. "That's what I thought. That's the list of the ones who called. This is the one your son gave me."

He tapped his fingers on the table as he read the second list. "The boy learned, didn't he?" Pleased with the names Caine had offered, Daniel scratched his chin through his beard. "Any one of these would do well for you. The best thing is for you to interview the top man at each firm, get a feel for it. Let them woo you, then trust your gut."

She was already trusting her gut but wasn't quite ready to tell him what she wanted. "I've never had any money, never had more to worry about—and over—than what I could juggle in my checking account month to month. Last night, I tried to imagine what a million dollars would look like. I couldn't. And now, even after taxes, I have a bit more than what I can't even imagine."

Daniel poured himself a second cup of coffee. Anna would hate it, he thought with delight, if she knew he was slurping up that much caffeine. "Tell me what you want from your money."

From it, she thought. Not what she wanted to do with it, but what she wanted from it. "Time," she said immediately. "Time enough so that I can do what I've always wanted to do. I've always wanted to write, and always had to steal the time to do it. I want that first, the time to finish my new book, then time to start the next," she said with a smile. "Because I want to be a writer, and the only way to be one is to write."

"Are you any good at it?"

"Yes, I am. It's the only thing I've ever really been good at, really felt confident about. I just need another few weeks to finish the one I'm working on."

"The money'll buy you more than a few weeks."

"I know. I intend to have fun with it, too." Her eyes glinted as she leaned forward. "I'm starting to realize that fun wasn't a big part of my life. I'm going to correct that. Whoever said money couldn't buy happiness must have been happy to begin with. Because if it can't, at least it can buy the opportunity to explore being happy." She laughed and settled back. "I'm going to explore being happy, Mr. MacGregor."

"That's a sensible thing."

"Yes, I think it is. Being happy isn't something I'm going to take for granted," she said quietly, "or something I intend to waste."

He laid his big hand over hers. "Have you been so unhappy?"

"I suppose in some ways I have been." She moved her shoulders restlessly. "But I have a chance now to make choices, for myself. It makes all the difference in the world. So I want to make good choices."

"I think you will." He gave her hand a squeeze and a pat. "You've already started to."

"I want to use the money well. And I want to give some back."

"To my grandson?"

"Oh." She laughed again and propped her elbows on the table. "In the casino. Yes, indeed. That's part of the fun, isn't it? But I meant to give some of that money, that time and that opportunity to explore happiness back. I want to make a donation, to literacy, I think. It fits, doesn't it?"

"Aye." He reached out to pat her cheek. "It fits, and you wear it well."

"I don't know how it's done, though. I thought you would."

"I'd be happy to help you with it." When the waiter came to remove their plates, Daniel waved a hand. "Leave hers," he ordered. "She hasn't eaten enough. Now," he continued as Darcy and the waiter exchanged resigned glances, "you'll have your time, your opportunity, and you'll have given something back. Unless you intend to toss around money like confetti, and you don't strike me as an idiot, you'll have quite a bit left over. What do you want from that?"

She bit her lip, easing forward. "More," she said, then blinked when he threw back his head and roared with laughter.

"Now there's a lass with a head on her shoulders. I knew it."

"It sounds greedy, but—"

"It sounds sane," he corrected. "Why should you want less? More is better, after all. You want your money to work for you. I'd call you a fool if you wanted otherwise."

"Mr. MacGregor." She took a deep breath and rolled the dice. "I want you to take my money and make it work for me."

The blue eyes narrowed. "Do you now? And why is that?"

"Because it seems to me I'd be a fool to settle for less than the best."

His eyes remained narrowed, fixed on her face so intensely she felt heat rising to her cheeks. Certain she'd gone too far, she started to babble an apology.

Then the mouth surrounded by that white beard began to curve. "Neither of us are fools, are we, lass?"

"No, sir."

"Well then." Grinning, his eyes sparkling with challenge, he twisted the gold knob on his cane. When it hinged back, he slipped out a thick cigar. With the lighter he took out of his pocket, he touched tip of flame reverently to tip of cigar, his bright eyes closing in pleasure as he took the first puffs.

"I know it's a lot to ask, Mr. MacGregor, but—"

"Daniel," he said, and grinned fiercely. "We're partners, aren't we? Eat," he ordered when Darcy only stared at him. "I've a couple ideas for how to get you that 'more' you'd like. Are you a gambler, little girl?"

With her head light and her heart soaring, Darcy bit into a piece of bacon. "It looks like I am."

Mac had a lot on his mind. The media was executing a full-court press, scrambling for access to Darcy. Reporters were wild for interviews and personal data. The morning editions, both local and national, had played variations on the theme.

Little Darcy From Kansas Hits Yellow Brick Road
From Kansas To Oz On Three-Dollar Bet
Over The Rainbow With A Million For Kansas Librarian

Normally he would have been amused, and certainly pleased at the positive publicity the story generated for Comanche Vegas. Reservations in the hotel were soaring, and he had no doubt that the casino would be three deep at the slots and tables as long as the story was hot.

He could handle the demands on his time, the incessant requests for interviews and photos. He could add staff to each shift, and intended to work the floor himself during peak periods. In fact, his parents had already agreed to extend their stay a few days and pitch in. And he preferred, just now, to have his plate overfull.

God knows he needed the distraction to keep his mind off his libido. It was suddenly and insistently on edge due to one small, big-eyed woman with a shy smile.

He wasn't inclined toward a serious relationship and certainly didn't intend to become involved with an innocent, naive woman who didn't know the difference between a straight and a flush.

He considered himself a disciplined man who knew how to control his baser instincts and resist temptations. He didn't play at love like his brother, Duncan. Nor did he consider it a pesky fly to be swatted aside like his sister Amelia. And he certainly had no intention of settling down and raising a family at this stage of his life as his sister Gwen was doing.

For Mac love was something to be dealt with eventually, when there was time, when the odds were favorable and when there was a good chance of raking in all the chips.

He wanted what his parents had. Perhaps he hadn't realized that quite so clearly until Darcy had pointed out just what they did have together. But he could admit he had always used them as his yardstick where relationships were concerned.

It was undoubtedly the reason he'd avoided any long-term or serious ones up to this point.

He enjoyed women, but involvement beyond a certain level led to complications, and complications invariably led to hurt on one side or the other. He'd been very careful not to hurt any of the women who had brushed in and out of his life.

He had no intention of breaking that particular rule now.

As far as Darcy Wallace was concerned, he'd decided it was a bad bet all around. She was too inexperienced, too vulnerable.

He was setting her firmly off-limits. Friendship, he ordered himself. A steadying hand until she had her feet firmly under her, and nothing more.

Then he stepped onto the rooftop garden and saw her. She was sitting at one of the tables, her big, elfin eyes wide and intent on his grandfather's face. Their heads were close together, like conspirators, he thought, and wondered what the hell was going on between them.

She looked so…fragile, he decided, so slimly built with those pretty, ringless hands clasped together like a schoolgirl's. She'd worked a foot out of one strappy sandal, and was waving the shoe by a single strap hooked around toes painted a soft shell pink.

The image that flashed through his mind of nibbling on those pretty toes and working his way up those slender legs had him muttering a curse.

Lust, something he normally accepted and enjoyed, was currently driving him mad.

Irritation still simmered in his eyes as he stepped through the palms and up to the table. Daniel leaned back, beamed and wiggled his eyebrows. "Well, there's a likely lad. Want some coffee, boy?"

"I could do with a cup." Because he knew Daniel well, Mac didn't trust him a whit. He scraped back a chair, straddled it and met his grandfather's cheerful gaze. "What's going on here?"

"Why, I'm having breakfast with this pretty young thing, which you'd be doing yourself if you weren't slow-witted."

"I've got a casino to run," Mac said shortly, and turned his sharp eyes to Darcy. "Did you get some rest?"

"Yes, plenty, thank you." She jolted when Daniel thumped his fist on the table.

"God Almighty, boy, is that any way to greet a woman in the morning? Why aren't you telling her how pretty she looks, or asking her if she'll take a drive with you this evening?"

"I'm working this evening," Mac said mildly.

"The day a MacGregor can't find time for a sweet-eyed woman is a sorry day. A sorry day, indeed. You'd like a drive, wouldn't you, lass, up into the hills in the moonlight?"

"I—yes, but—"

"There." Daniel thumped his fist again. "Are you going to do something about this, boy, or do I have to hang my head in shame?"

Considering, Mac picked up the cigar smoldering in the ashtray. He studied it thoughtfully, turned it in his hand. "And what's this?" Lifting his brow, Mac smiled thinly at his grandfather. "This wouldn't be yours, would it, Grandpa?"

Daniel's gaze slid away. He studied his own fingernails intently. "I don't know what you're talking about. Now—"

"Grandma would be very displeased if she thought you were sneaking cigars behind her back again." Idly Mac tapped the ash. "Very displeased."

"It's mine," Darcy blurted out, and both men turned to stare at her.

"Yours?" Mac said in a voice that dripped like honey.

"Yes." She jerked her shoulder in what she hoped was an arrogant shrug. "So what?"

"So…" Mac's teeth flashed in a grin. "Enjoy," he suggested, and handed her the cigar.

The challenge in his eyes left her little choice. Defiantly she took a puff. Her head spun, her throat closed, but she managed to muffle most of the cough. "It's very smooth." She wheezed as she choked on smoke.

Her eyes teared as she gamefully puffed again. Mac had to resist an urge to tug her into his lap and nuzzle her. "I can see that. Want a brandy to go with it?"

"Not before lunch." She coughed again, felt her stomach pitch. "Your grandfather—" She coughed, blinked away tears. "Your grandfather and I were discussing business."

"Don't let me stop you. Done with this?" He picked up a slice of her bacon. He bit in neatly then grinned. She was turning a very interesting shade of green. "Put that down, darling, before you pass out."

"I'm perfectly fine."

"You're a rare one, Darcy." Adoring her, Daniel rose. He tipped up her chin, kissed her full on the mouth. "I'll get started on that business we were speaking of." He sent his grandson a glowering look. "Don't shame me, Robbie."

"Who's Robbie?" Darcy asked dizzily when Daniel strode off.

"I am, to him, occasionally."

"Oh." She smiled. "That's sweet."

"You're going to make yourself sick," Mac muttered, and took the cigar from her fingers. "I didn't think you'd do it."

She let her reeling head fall back. "I don't know what you're talking about."

With a sigh, Mac picked up her water glass and held it to her lips. "Did you really think I'd rat on him? Come on, sip a little. The smoke's made you punchy."

"It's not so bad. I kind of like it." She turned her head to smile at him. "You wouldn't have told? About the cigar?"

"It wouldn't have mattered. My grandmother knows he sneaks them every chance he gets."

"I wish he were my grandfather. I think he's the most wonderful man in the world."

"He likes you, too. Steady now?"

"I'm fine." She studied what was left of the cigar as it smoked in the ashtray. "I may just take it up." But she drank the water again to cool her throat. "He shouldn't have teased you that way, about taking me for a drive."

With a few deliberate taps, Mac put out the cigar. "He's decided you suit me."

"Oh." The idea wound through her mind, then warmed her heart. "Really?"

"The MacGregor's fondest wish is to see all of his grandchildren married and producing babies. And the more he has to do with it, the better. He actually arranged for my sister, and two of my cousins, to meet men he'd specifically picked out for them."

"What happened?"

"In those cases, it worked, which only makes him more difficult to control. He's on a streak. And just now…" He angled his head, skimmed his gaze over her face. "He's decided you'll do for me."

"I see." She supposed the quick thrill and sense of glee was inappropriate. But it was very hard to control the curve of her lips. "I'm flattered."

"So you should be. I am, after all, the oldest grandchild—and he's a fussy man when it comes to family."

"But it irritates you."

"Mildly," he admitted. "As much as I love him, I've no intention of going along with his grand schemes. I apologize if he got you out here this morning to put ideas in your head, but I'm not looking for marriage."

Her eyes went wide and dark. "Excuse me?"

"I suspected, when I was told the two of you were together up here, that he'd been planting seeds."

The warmth that had settled inside her iced over and went rock hard. "And, of course, someone like me would be fertile ground for such seeds."

Her tone was so quiet, so pleasant, he missed the flash. "He can't help it. And your name being Wallace put a cap on it. Strong Scot blood," he said with a grin and a burr. "He'd consider you tailor-made to bear my children."

"And since you're not in the market for a wife or children, you thought it only fair to nip in the bud any ideas he might have planted in my vulnerable mind in that area."

He caught the underlying frost in the tone now. "More or less," he agreed, cautiously. "Darcy—"

"You arrogant, self-important, *insulting* son of a bitch." She sprang to her feet so abruptly the table jerked. The water glass toppled over and crashed on the tiles as she stood vibrating with temper, her fists clenched and eyes blazing. "I'm not the empty-headed, dim-witted, *needy* fool you seem to think I am."

"That's not what I meant." More than a little wary, he got to his feet. "That's not at all what I meant."

"Don't stand there and tell me what you didn't mean. I know perfectly well when I'm being considered a corn-for-brains moron. You're not the first who's made that mistake, but I swear to God, you're going to be the last. I'm perfectly aware that you don't want me."

"I never said—"

"Do you think I don't know I'm not your type?" Furious, she shoved the chair into the table, and sent another glass crashing. "You prefer big-busted showgirls with eight feet of leg and yards of hair."

"What? Where the hell did that come from?"

Straight out of her dream the night before, but she'd be damned if she'd tell him. "I don't have any delusions about you. Just because I would have slept with you doesn't mean I expected you to sweep me off to the altar. If all I wanted was marriage, I could have stayed exactly where I was."

She still looked like a fairy, he noted, one who could—and would—spitefully turn an incautious man into a braying jackass. "Before you break any more glassware, let me apologize." He put a restraining hand on the back of the chair before she could jam it into the table again. "I didn't want my grandfather to put you in an uncomfortable position."

"You've accomplished that all on your own." Mortification mixed with temper to send her color high. "It may surprise you to know that I asked Daniel to meet me here this morning, and—though it may crush your outrageous ego—it had nothing whatsoever to do with you. It was a business meeting," she said rather grandly.

"Business?" He squinted against the sun. "What sort of business?"

"I don't believe that's any of your concern," she told him coldly. "But since you'll undoubtedly harass Daniel over it, I'll tell you. Daniel has agreed to be my financial advisor."

Intrigued, Mac slipped his hands into his pockets and rocked on his heels. "You asked him to handle your money?"

"Is there any reason I shouldn't?"

"No." Hoping to cool her off a bit, he smiled and inclined his head. "You couldn't do better."

"Precisely."

And he, Mac thought, couldn't have done any worse. "Darcy—"

"I don't want your apology." Her voice glittered with ice. "I don't want your excuses or your pitiful reasons. I believe we both understand perfectly well the status of our relationship." She snatched up her purse. "You can bill me for the cost of the glasses."

He couldn't stop the wince as she stormed off, slapping her way though the palms. He had both feet up to the knees in his mouth, he decided, grimacing at the sparkle of shattered glass on the tiles.

Getting them out would be the first problem, he thought.

The second problem would be a great deal more complex.

Just how was he going to deal with the fact that the woman who had just ripped the skin off his hide utterly fascinated him?

Chapter 8

For the next two days Darcy concentrated on her writing. For the first time in her life, she decided, she was going to do what she wanted, when she wanted. If she wanted to work until three in the morning and sleep until noon, there was no one to criticize her habits. Dinner at midnight? Why not?

It was her life now, and sometime during those first furious hours, she realized she was finally living it.

She was going to miss Daniel, she thought. He'd returned East the day before, with a promise to keep in close contact on the investments he was making for her. He'd issued an open invitation for her to visit his home in Hyannis Port.

Darcy intended to take him up on it. She'd grown very fond of the MacGregors. They were warm, generous and delightful people—even if one particular member of the clan was arrogant, insulting and infuriating.

He actually thought sending her flowers was going to make up for it. She sniffed as she glanced over at the lush arrangement of three dozen silvery white roses she'd instructed the bellman to place on the conference table. They were the most beautiful flowers she'd ever seen—which he undoubtedly knew, she thought, hardening her heart as she sat at the desk.

She hadn't acknowledged them, or the sweet basket of button-eyed daisies that stood perkily on her bathroom counter, or the vase of stunning tropical blooms that graced the bureau in the bedroom.

The roses had come first, she remembered, tapping her fingers on the desk. Barely an hour after she'd stormed back into her room after the conversation with Mac, the bellman had knocked on her door. The note with them had been a smooth apology she'd easily ignored.

It was no one's business but hers that she'd tucked the card away in her lingerie drawer.

The daisies had come the next day, with a request that she call him when she had a moment. She'd tucked that card away, too, and had ignored the request—just as she'd ignored his insistent knocking at her door the previous evening.

This morning it was birds-of-paradise and hibiscus with a much pithier request.

Damn it, Darcy. Open the door.

With a short, humorless laugh, she turned on her laptop. She would *not* open the door, not to him. Not the literal door of her room, or the metaphorical door to her heart. It wasn't simply mortifying that she'd allowed herself to fall in love with him, it was…typical, she thought and clenched her teeth.

Pitiful, lonely woman meets sophisticated, handsome man and tumbles face-first at his feet.

Well, she'd picked herself up now, hadn't she? He could send her an acre of flowers, a ream of notes, but it wasn't going to change a thing.

She had her direction now. As soon as she completed the draft of her book, she was going to a Realtor. She intended to buy a house—something big and sand colored that faced the open mystery of the desert and the majestic ring of mountains.

Something with a pool, she decided, and skylights. She'd always wanted skylights.

Settling here had nothing to do with Mac, she told herself. She liked it here. She liked the hot winds, the sprawling desert, the pulse of life and promise that beat in the air. Las Vegas was the fastest growing city in the U.S., wasn't it, and reported to be one of the most livable?

It said so in the glossy hotel guide on her coffee table.

Why shouldn't she live here?

When the phone rang she merely scowled at it. If it was Mac thinking she was the least bit interested in speaking to him, he could think again. She ignored the call, rolled her shoulders once, then dove back into the story.

Mac prowled his office restlessly while his mother scanned the printout of bookings for the next six months. "You've got a wonderful lineup here."

"Mmm." He couldn't concentrate, and it infuriated him.

He'd only wanted to warn her about his grandfather's tendency for plots and schemes. For her own good, he thought, moving from window to window as if to improve his view. And he'd apologized repeatedly. She didn't even have the courtesy to acknowledge it.

He'd come close, far too close, to using his passkey and circumventing the control on her private elevator. And that, he reminded himself would have been an unforgivable invasion of her privacy and a breach of his responsibilities to The Comanche.

But what the hell was she doing in that suite? She hadn't had a meal outside of it since that breakfast on the roof. She hadn't stepped foot in the casino, or any of the lounges.

Sulking. It was so unattractive, he decided, and sulked a bit himself.

"It serves me right for trying to look after her," he muttered.

"What?" Serena glanced over, then shook her head. She knew very well she'd had only the stingiest slice of her son's attention for the past hour. "Mac, what's wrong?"

"Nothing's wrong. Do you want to see the entertainment schedule?"

She lifted her eyebrows and waved the printout. "I'm looking at it."

"Oh. Right." He turned to scowl out the window again.

With a sigh, Serena set the papers aside. "You might as well tell me what's bothering you. I'll just nag you until you do anyway."

"Who'd have thought she could be so stubborn?" The words exploded out of his mouth as he whirled back. "If she can be this damn perverse, how the hell did she get pushed around so much?"

Serena hummed in her throat then, crossing her legs, settled back. Women rarely ruffled Mac, she mused, and took it as a very good sign. "I assume you're talking about Darcy."

"Of course, I'm talking about Darcy." Frustration simmered in his eyes. "I don't know what the hell she's doing, locked in that suite day and night."

"Writing."

"What do you mean writing?"

"Her book," Serena said patiently. "She's trying to finish the first draft of her book. She wants to have that done before she starts querying agents."

"How do you know?"

"Because she told me. We had tea in her suite yesterday."

It took monumental control to keep his mouth from falling open. "She let you in?"

"Of course, she let me in. I talked her into taking a short break from it. She's a very disciplined young woman, and very determined on this. And talented."

"Talented?"

"I persuaded her to let me read a few pages of the book she'd finished last year." Serena's lips curved up into a pleased smile. "I was impressed. And entertained. Does that surprise you?"

"No." He realized it didn't, not in the least. "So she's working."

"That's right."

"That's no excuse for being rude."

"Rude? Darcy?"

"I'm tired of the silent treatment," he muttered.

"She's not speaking to you? What did you do?"

Mac set his teeth and shot a withering look at Serena. "Why do you assume I did anything?"

"Darling." She rose, crossing over to lay a hand on

his cheek. "As much as I love you, you're a man. Now, what did you do to upset her?"

"I was simply trying to explain The MacGregor to her. I came across them with their heads together, and Grandpa started in on why didn't I take this pretty young girl for a drive in the moonlight. You know the routine."

"Yes, I do." Daniel "Subtle" MacGregor, she thought with a windy sigh. "Exactly how were you trying to explain him to her?"

"I told her he wanted his grandchildren married, settled and producing more little MacGregors, that it appeared he'd picked her out for me. I apologized for him, and explained that I wasn't looking for marriage, and she shouldn't take him too seriously."

Serena stepped back, the better to stare at her firstborn. "And you used to be such a bright child."

"I was only thinking of her," he retorted. "I thought he was setting her up. How was I supposed to know she'd asked him to meet her on business? I admit I put my foot in it." He jammed his hands into his pockets. "I apologized, several times. I sent her flowers, I've called—not that she'll answer the damn phone. What the devil am I supposed to do? Grovel?"

"It might be good for you," Serena murmured, then laughed as he hissed at her. "Mac." Gently she cupped her hands on his face. "Why are you so worried about it? Do you have feelings for her?"

"I care what happens to her. She stumbled in here like a refugee, for God's sake. She needs someone to look out for her."

She kept her eyes level on his. "So your feelings for her are...brotherly."

He hesitated just a moment too long. "They should be."

"Are they?"

"I don't know."

Loving him, she skimmed her fingers back into his hair. "Maybe you should find out."

"How? She won't talk to me."

"A man who has both MacGregor and Blade blood in his veins wouldn't let something like a locked door stop him for long." She smiled, kissed him firmly. "My money's on you."

Darcy's eyes were closed as she tried to visualize the scene before letting the words come. Now, finally, though danger shadowed every corner, her two main characters would come together. No longer would they resist this vital and primitive pull, no longer would needs that swam in the blood and slammed in the heart be denied. It was now. Had to be now.

The room was cold and smelled of damp the blazing fire had yet to conquer. The blue haze of a winter moon slipped through the windows.

He would touch her. How would he touch her? A brush of knuckles on her cheek? Her breath would catch, strangle in her throat, shudder through her lips. Would she feel the heat of his body as he drew her close? What would be the last thing running through her mind in those seconds just before his mouth lowered, took possession of hers?

Insanity, Darcy thought. And she would welcome it.

Keeping her eyes closed, Darcy let the words run through her mind and onto the page. The sudden shrill of the phone was so abrupt and out of place in her chilly cabin in the mountains, she snatched it up without thinking.

"Yes, yes, hello?"

"Darcy." The voice was grave, undeniably irritated, and all too familiar.

"Gerald." The passion and promise of the scene vanished, replaced by nerves. "Ah, how are you?"

"How would you expect me to be? You've caused me a great deal of trouble."

"I'm sorry." The apology was automatic, making her wince the moment it was out of her mouth.

"I can't imagine what you were thinking of. We'll discuss it. Give me your room number."

"My room number?" Nerves shot directly to panic. "Where are you?"

"I'm in the lobby of this ridiculous place you chose to land in. It's beyond inappropriate—which I should have expected given your recent behavior. But we'll straighten it out shortly. Your room number, Darcy?"

Her room? Her haven. No, no, she couldn't let him invade her sanctuary. "I—I'll come down," she said quickly. "There's a seating area near the waterfall. It's on the left of the reception desk in the main lobby. Do you see it?"

"I could hardly miss it, could I? Don't dawdle."

"No, I'll be right down."

She hung up, pushed away from the desk. Despair closed in and was resolutely fought back. He couldn't make her do anything she didn't want to do, she reminded herself. He had no power here, no control. He had nothing that she didn't give him.

But the hand that picked up her purse wasn't completely steady. Her legs wanted badly to shake as she walked to the elevator. She concentrated on keeping her knees from knocking together all the way down.

The lobby was crowded with people, families of tourists who wandered through to toss coins into the pool at the base of the waterfall or to see the live-action show in the open-air amphitheater. Guests checked in, checked out. Others were lured by the ching of slots and headed for the casino.

Gerald sat in one of the curved-back chairs near the bubbling pool. His dark suit was without a wrinkle, his hard, handsome face without a smile as he scanned the activity around him with a glint of derision in his dark eyes.

He looked successful, Darcy thought. Removed from the chaotic whirl around him. Cold, she decided. It was his cold nature that had always frightened her.

His head turned as she approached. Even as his eyes skimmed over her, registering both surprise and disapproval of her choice of pale green shorts and a peach blouse, he got to his feet.

Manners, she thought. He'd always had excellent manners.

"I assume you have an explanation for all of this." He gestured to a chair.

The gesture, she mused, was just one of the ways he took control. *Sit, Darcy.* And she'd always quietly obeyed.

This time she stood.

"I decided to relocate."

"Don't be absurd." He dismissed this with a wave of his hand before taking her arm and pulling her firmly into a chair. "Do you have any idea what embarrassment you've caused me? Sneaking out of town in the middle of the night—"

"I didn't sneak." Of course she had, she thought.

He merely arched a brow, adult to child. "You left without a word to anyone. You've been irresponsible, which again, I should have expected. Taking a trip like this without any planning. What did you expect to accomplish?"

Escape, she thought. Adventure. Life. She linked her fingers together, laid them in her lap and tried to speak calmly. "I wasn't taking a trip. I was leaving. There's nothing for me in Trader's Corners."

"It's your home."

"Not anymore."

"Don't be more foolish than necessary. Do you have any idea what sort of position you've put me in? I find my fiancée gone—"

"I'm not your fiancée, Gerald. I broke our engagement some time ago."

His gaze never wavered. "And I've been more than patient, giving you time to come to your senses and calm your nerves. This is how you behave. Las Vegas, for pity's sake."

He placed his hands neatly on his knees and leaned forward. "People are gossiping about you now. And that reflects poorly on me. You've been splashed all over the national news—some sort of three-day wonder."

"I won nearly two million dollars. That's news."

"Gambling." He sneered on the word, then leaned back again. "I'll handle the press, of course. The interest will die down soon enough, and it's a simple matter to put a positive spin on the incident, to play down the sordid."

"Sordid? I put money into a slot machine. I hit the jackpot. What's sordid about it?"

He spared her a weary glance. "I wouldn't expect

you to understand the underlying thrust of this, Darcy. Your innocence, at least, does you credit. We'll arrange for the money to be transferred—"

"No." Her heart was beginning to pound in her throat.

"You can hardly leave it in Nevada. My broker will invest it properly. We'll see that you get a nice allowance from the interest."

An allowance, she thought, through the dull buzzing in her head. As if she were a child who could be indulged with carefully controlled spending money. "It's already being invested. Mr. MacGregor, Daniel MacGregor is handling it."

Shock reflected in his eyes as his hand shot out to grip hers. "My God, Darcy, you're not telling me you've given over a million dollars to a stranger?"

"He's not a stranger. And actually, he has slightly under a million for now. There are taxes and living expenses to consider."

"How could you be so stupid?" His voice rose, making her cringe back from it, and the disgusted fury in his eyes. "Put it together—a simpleton could see it. MacGregor has a financial interest in this hotel. And now he has the money you took from this hotel."

"I'm not stupid," Darcy said in a quiet voice. "And Daniel MacGregor isn't a thief."

"My lawyer will draw up the necessary papers to transfer the funds—what there are left of them. We'll have to work quickly." He glanced at his watch. "I'll have to call him at home. Inconvenient, but it can't be helped. Go up and pack while I deal with this latest mess you've made. The sooner I get home, the sooner this can be mended."

"Did you come for the money or for me, Gerald?"

She flexed her hand in his, then let it lie passively. She would never win in a physical altercation so she concentrated her efforts, and her anger, into the verbal. "It occurs to me that your pattern would have been to call and order me home once you knew where I was. You wouldn't have bothered to rearrange your busy schedule and come in person. You wouldn't have felt the need. You'd have been so sure I'd have tucked my tail between my legs and come back when you snapped your fingers."

"I don't have time for this now, Darcy. Go pack, and change into something suitable for travel."

"I'm not going anywhere."

Fury had his fingers biting into hers as he jerked her to her feet. "Do what you're told. Now. I will not tolerate a public scene."

"Then leave, because you're about to get one."

A hand dropped lightly onto her shoulder. She knew before he spoke that it was Mac. "Is there a problem here?"

"No." She didn't look at him, couldn't. "Gerald, this is Mac Blade. He runs The Comanche. Mac, Gerald was just leaving."

"Goodbye, Gerald," Mac said in a mild tone that flashed just around the edges. "I believe the lady would like her hand back."

"Neither Darcy nor I require your interference."

Mac stepped forward until they were eye-to-eye. "I haven't begun to interfere, but I'd be happy to." His smile was lethal. "In fact, I've been looking forward to the opportunity."

"Don't." More angry than frightened now, Darcy

pushed her way between them. "I'm perfectly capable of handling my own problems."

"Is this what you've been up to, Darcy?" Disgust laced Gerald's voice as he stared down at her. "Letting yourself be seduced by this…person? Deluding yourself that he would want anything more from you than to cheat you out of the money you took from him, and some cheap sex on the side?"

She felt the ripple behind her, sensed that Mac was braced to attack, and quickly swung her hands back to grip his arms. "Please, don't. Please." The muscles seemed to vibrate against her restraining fingers. "It won't help. Please."

She ignored the interested onlookers who were busy pretending not to watch. Perhaps it helped, just a little, that her back was firmly pressed against the solid wall of Mac's chest. But she knew she had to stand on her own now, or she'd never manage to do so.

"Gerald, what I do, where I do it and with whom has nothing whatever to do with you. I apologize for ever agreeing to marry you. It was a mistake I tried to rectify, but you never wanted to hear me. Other than that, I have nothing to be sorry for."

She drew a fresh, steadying breath while she watched his jaw clench. He wanted to hit her, she realized, and found she wasn't surprised. If she hadn't found the courage to run, he would have ended up using fists, as well as words. Sooner or later, intimidation wouldn't have been enough.

The certainty of that gave her the will to finish it. "You maneuvered and manipulated me, because you could. And that's why you wanted to marry me—at first anyway. After that, you insisted on it because you couldn't and wouldn't accept some little no one refusing you—and having to explain a broken engagement to the neighbors."

His face had gone stone cold. "I'm not going to stand here while you air our personal business in public."

"You're free to leave anytime. You came here because I'm suddenly some little no one with a great deal of money. That ups the stakes—and so does the press. I'm sure a few enterprising reporters have made their way to Trader's Corners, and it wouldn't take much for any of them to dig up that we'd once been engaged. Embarrassing for you, but it can't be helped.

"I'm telling you now, as clearly as I know how, that you'll never get your hands on me or my money. That I'm never coming back. I live here now, and I like it. I don't like you, and I realize I never have."

He stepped back from her abruptly. "I can see now that you're not the person I believed you to be."

"I can't tell you how happy that makes me. Cut your losses, Gerald," she said quietly. "And go home."

He angled his head, studying both her and Mac with equal disdain. "As far as I can see, the two of you are well suited to each other, and this place. If you mention my name in the media, I'll be forced to take legal action."

"Don't worry," Darcy murmured as he strode away. "I seem to have forgotten your name already."

"Well done." Unable to resist, Mac lowered his head and pressed a kiss to the top of hers.

She only closed her eyes. "However it was done, it's over. Thanks for offering to help."

"You didn't appear to need it." But she was starting to tremble now. "Let me take you upstairs."

"I know the way."

"Darcy." He turned her around, leaving his hands on her shoulders. "You wouldn't give me the satisfaction of breaking his face. You owe me."

She drummed up something that passed for a smile. "All right. I always pay my debts."

He kept an arm around her shoulders as he walked her to the elevator. Instinctively he rubbed a hand up and down her arm to ease the trembling. "Did you get my flowers?"

"Yes, they're very nice." Her voice went prim, pleasing him. "Thank you."

He used his passkey to access her floor. "My mother tells me you've been working."

"That's right."

"So…the reason you haven't answered my calls— or let me into your room is because you've been busy writing. Not because you hold a grudge."

She shifted uncomfortably. "I don't hold grudges. Usually."

"But you're making an exception for me."

"I suppose."

"Okay. You've got two choices. You can forgive me for being… I believe 'arrogant' and 'insulting' was the way you put it, or I'm going to be forced to go after Gerald and pound my frustrations out on him."

"You wouldn't do that."

"Oh, yes." He smiled darkly. "I would."

She stared at him even after the elevator doors slid open. "You would," she realized with something between shock and horrified delight. "It wouldn't solve anything."

"But I'd enjoy it so much. So are you going to invite me inside, or do I go find him?"

She jerked a shoulder and tried not to be pleased. "Come in. I'm probably too distracted to work anyway."

"Thanks." He glanced toward her desk. "How's it going?"

"Very well."

"My mother said you let her read a couple pages."

"She made it hard to say no. Would you like a drink? Some coffee?"

"Nothing right now. Are you going to let me read some of your book?"

"When it's published you can read the whole thing."

He shifted his gaze from the desk to her face. Her color was back, which relieved him. She'd looked much too pale, and much too fragile, downstairs. "I can make it hard to say no, too. It runs in the family. But you're a little shaky at the moment, so I'll wait."

"It's just a reaction." She cupped her elbows in her palms. "I was afraid when he called."

"But you went down and met him."

"It had to be done."

"You could have called me. You didn't have to do it alone."

"Yes, I did. I had to know I could. It seems foolish now to realize I'd ever been intimidated by him. He's so pathetic, really." She hadn't understood that before, she thought now. Hadn't seen the sorry man under the bully. "Still, if I hadn't been, I might not be here. I might not have met you. I have to be grateful for that."

She clasped her hands together. "I appreciate you not hitting him after he insulted you that way."

His eyes stayed on her face. "I wouldn't have hit him for me."

New emotions swam into her eyes. "I knew, when you came, it would be all right. That I would be all right. And I wasn't afraid anymore. He thought that we've been... I was glad he did, because I'd never let him touch me. And he thinks you have."

He knew it was a mistake to cross to her. The odds were weighted wrong for both of them. "He'll stew about that for a long time. It's almost as good as beating him senseless."

The warmth spreading in her chest was nearly painful. "I'm glad you were there."

"So am I. Are we friends again?"

His knuckles brushed her cheek, made her breath catch, strangle in her throat and shudder through her lips. "Is that what you want to be?"

Her eyes were wide and dark. Her lips parted, full of anticipation, invitation. And irresistible. "Not entirely," he murmured and lowered his mouth to hers.

She knew now what thoughts scrambled through the brain in those last seconds before the mating of lips. Wild and desperate images so bold and tangled they had no name. She stretched up to her toes, her body pressing into his, her hands streaking up his chest to grip his shoulders as she let herself tumble into those shockingly bright colors and shapes.

Her mouth was so eager, so soft and warm and giving. He wanted more of it. Her body was so slight, so pliant, so ready. He wanted all of it. The need was huge, raw as a groan, and forced him to fight for control.

"Darcy—" He started to ease her away, swore that he would, but her arms wound around his neck.

"Please." Her voice was husky, a tremble of urgency. "Oh, please. Touch me."

The whispered request was as seductive as a rustle of black silk. Desire swarmed through him, roaring in his head, throbbing in his loins. "Touching won't be enough."

"You can have enough." She could drown in need, she thought frantically. Already she was going under. "Make love with me." Her voice sounded desperate and very faraway as her lips raced over his face, melted onto his. "Take me to bed."

It was as much demand as offer. Everything inside him responded to both. "I want you." He tore his mouth from hers to press it to her throat. "It's insane how much I want you."

"I don't want to be sane. I don't want you to be. Just once—be with me."

He let the wheel spin. He swept her up in his arms and watched her eyes turn gold with awareness. The fact that she weighed little more than a child terrified him. "I won't hurt you."

"I don't care."

But he did. He nuzzled a sigh from her as he carried her to the stairs and started up. "The first time I brought you up here, I wondered about you. Who is she? Where does she come from?" He laid her on the bed, stroked his fingers down the column of her throat. "What am I going to do with her? I still haven't figured it out."

"When I woke up and saw you, I thought I was dreaming." She lifted a hand to his cheek. "Part of me still does."

He turned his head to press his lips into the cup of her palm. "I'll stop if you ask me." He took her mouth again, going deep, sinking in. "For God's sake, don't ask me."

How could she? Why would she, when nerves and pleasure and needs were dancing just under her skin? The spread was slick under her back, and his hands were already stroking small, separate fires into life over her body. His mouth drew and drew and drew from hers as if she contained some life force he craved.

Craved.

No one had ever made her feel wanted like this.

His fingers trailed over her as though he found her delicate, special. And when his hand closed over her breast, molded it, her mind emptied.

She was unbearably responsive, her body arching, giving, inviting him to do as he wished. Gently, he ordered himself, go gently here. He blurred her mind, and his, with kisses as he opened her blouse and began to explore warm, smooth flesh.

Her trembles aroused him, almost brutally. Every quiver of her muscles was a miracle to be exploited, then savored. For he found he could savor, the texture of that skin curving subtly above the cup of her bra, the flavor of her throat where the pulse beat so hard and fast.

He drew her up, nibbling tortuously at her mouth as he slipped her blouse aside.

Hesitantly she reached for the buttons of his shirt. She wanted to touch him, to see. To know. A sound of dizzy delight escaped her when she saw her white hands against the dusky gold of his chest.

So strong, she thought, fascinated by the ridge of muscles under her fingertips. So hard and strong and male. Thrilled, she leaned forward to press her lips to his shoulder, to absorb the taste.

He felt something like a growl working through him and pushed down a sudden, violent need to devour. Instead he took her face in his hands, watching her, drinking her in even as his mouth took hers again. Watching still, for those flickers of surprise and pleasure in her eyes, as he slipped her bra aside, as he cupped her breasts in his hands, skimmed his thumbs over nipples that went hot and stiff.

Then he laid her back to capture one sensitized point with his mouth.

Her hand fisted in the spread, dragging at it as hot, liquid sensation flooded her system. A pulse was pounding between her legs, all but burning there. She heard her own moan, a wanton, throaty sound of pleasure as she wrapped around him, racked by edgy, questing needs.

"Easy." He wasn't certain if he were calming her or himself. But her restless movements beneath him had control nearly slipping out of his hands.

He rolled with her, tugging away the spread she'd tangled around them, sinking with her into the pool of pillows. He dragged at her shorts, drawing them down, away, then toyed with the last barrier, the little swatch of blush-colored lace.

"Oh, my." Her hips jerked and her vision blurred. "I can't—"

"You should be dancing through the woods under a full moon." He murmured it, delighting in her body, the shape of it, the glorious response of it to every touch. He traced a scatter of freckles on her quivering belly and smiled as he shaped a star. "Should've figured it."

Then he slid a finger under the lace.

Pressure slammed into her, a smothering weight of

velvet that had her fighting for one gulp of air. Heat flashed with the shock of a fireball. Her eyes went blind, the stunned cry ripped from her throat, and the pressure burst into a flare of pleasure dark as moonless midnight.

She went limp with it, the hand that had gripped his shoulder sliding bonelessly to the tangled sheets.

So hot, he thought, and his hands weren't completely steady as he drew the lace down her legs. So wet. So beautifully ready. He felt his heart slamming in his chest as her heavy eyes flickered open and that clouded gold fixed on him.

"I've never…"

"I know." He was the first, and it made him mad to have her. "Again," he murmured, and brought her close, so desperately close that her hips arched up to meet him when he came into her.

His muscles screamed, his blood seemed to snarl as he met both heat and resistance. "Hold on." He panted it, linked his hands with hers.

She felt herself reaching again, flying toward that astonishing peak. The pain was a shock, so mixed with pleasure she couldn't separate the two. Then she was opening for him, taking him into her. Mating. And there was only pleasure.

Movement and magic combined to sweep her off on some high, curving wave that crested so slowly, so gracefully that she seemed to tremble on its peak endlessly before sliding down, and down into a quiet and shimmering pool.

Resting there, with him on her, in her, she wrapped herself around him and sighed his name.

Chapter 9

She could smell the heady and exotic fragrances of the tropical bouquet on her dresser. The sun poured through the windows and beat warmly against her face.

If she kept her eyes closed she could picture herself in some lush and deserted jungle, gloriously naked and tangled around her lover.

Her lover. What a marvelous phrase that was.

She let it repeat in her mind, over and over, as she turned her head to press her lips to his throat. But when he started to shift, she tightened her grip.

"Do you have to move?"

His mind didn't seem to want to clear. She was still inside it as completely as he was still inside her. "You're so little."

"I've been working out." She wanted to keep tasting it, the hot, dusky flavor of his throat. "I'm starting to get biceps."

He had to smile. He eased back just enough to pinch her upper arm where the tiny muscle melted like wax under his fingers. "Wow."

She laughed. "Okay. I'm *almost* getting biceps. In a few more weeks, nobody's going to call me Pencil-Arm."

"You don't have pencil arms," he murmured, distracted by the texture of her skin along her elbow. "They're slender. Smooth."

She studied his face, marveling at the concentration in his eyes as he traced his finger from her shoulder to her wrist. Did he have any idea just what that absent brush of fingers did inside her body? She didn't see how he could, or how he could possibly understand what it was like for her to look at that beautifully sculpted profile and know that for a little while he belonged to her.

Was it because she was in love with him that their lovemaking had taken on such a brilliant sheen? Was it because he was her first, her only, that she couldn't imagine being so close, so intimate with anyone else?

Whatever the reason, she would treasure what he'd given her. And she would hope she'd given him something he would remember in return.

"I have to ask." Her smile was a little apologetic. "I know it's probably pitifully typical, but…well, I need to know."

His gaze had come back to her face, and it was wary. He was afraid she would ask him how he felt, what he wanted, where this was leading. Since he was still struggling with the first part of that, he had no idea what followed.

"Was I—was it…" How did one phrase it? "Was it all right?" she asked him.

Then tension in his stomach dissolved. "Darcy." Struck by a wave of tenderness, he lowered his mouth and kissed her, long and deep. "What do you think?"

"I stopped being able to think." Her eyes opened slowly, glowed into his. "Everything got jumbled. I always imagined that I'd remember all the details, sort of step-by-step. But I couldn't pay attention. There was so much to feel."

"Sometimes…" He wanted her mouth again, and took it. "Thinking's overrated."

"Thoughts just slide out of my head when you do that." Her hands stroked down his back as she floated on the kiss. "And when you started to touch me, everything got so…hot."

He groaned against her mouth, then swallowed her gasp as he hardened inside her. "You don't have to pay attention," he told her. "Just let me have you."

Her breath came fast and thick, shattered on each long, slow stroke. She came on a moan and a shudder that ripped through him like claws. He gripped her hips, lifted them. "More. Give me more this time," he demanded, and drove deep, dragging her over the edge with him.

Later, when she was alone, she caught her reflection in the mirror over the bed. Her eyes went wide with shock at the image of herself, hair tousled, face glowing, her naked body sprawled over a tangle of sheets.

Could this be Darcy Wallace? The dutiful daughter, the conscientious librarian, the shy and pitiful doormat from Kansas?

She looked…ripe, she decided. Aware. And oh, so satisfied. Then she bit her curving lip as she wondered if she'd have the nerve to look up into the mirror the next time Mac made love with her.

The next time.

Overcome with joy, she hugged a pillow and rolled. He wanted her. She didn't care what the reasons were, it was enough that he did. There had been simmering promise in the kiss they'd shared before he'd left her. He'd asked her to have a late supper with him in his office.

He wanted her.

Was it so impossible to believe she could find a way to make him keep wanting her? And to find a way to turn that wanting into love?

Curling into the pillow, she rested her head. It would be a gamble. She would be risking what she had now in the hope for more. Because he'd been right, she admitted. What he'd said in the rooftop garden had been a bull's-eye. She did want marriage and family and permanence. She wanted children. She wanted, desperately, to be able to take this love that threatened to flood right out of her heart and give it.

And for once in her life, she wanted to feel loved in return. Not the lukewarm affection of duty, not the kindly indulgence of affection, but the hot-blooded and dangerous love that sprang from passion and lust and blind need.

The kind of love that could hurt, she thought, squeezing her eyes shut. The kind that lasted and grew and shot up and down the hills of the roller coaster and demanded screams of delight and terror.

She wanted it all. And she wanted it with Mac Blade.

How would she win his heart? She sighed a little, absently snuggling into the pillow as her limbs grew heavy. She would figure it out, she promised herself and sighed toward sleep.

After all, the only way to win was to play. And she was on a hot streak.

She wore the beaded jacket she'd fallen in love with on her first day at the hotel. Under it was a daring little excuse for a dress in lipstick red. The jacket gave her confidence, made her feel glamorous.

The dress made her feel just a bit sinful.

She wanted to try her hand at blackjack again, decided she might make it her signature game. If she was going to live in Vegas—and she was—and be involved with a man who ran a casino—which she hoped to be— she needed to be skilled in at least one form of gambling.

The slots, she decided, didn't take skill. She'd proved that herself. Roulette appeared to be a bit repetitive, and craps…well, it looked wonderfully exciting and rousing, but she just couldn't follow the action.

But the cards were self-explanatory, and they always came up in a different and intriguing order.

She wandered for a while, just enjoying the crush of people, the raucous sounds, the pulse of excitement. The tables were crowded tonight, and the cards moved, fast and sharp. She was toying with joining a game, and had talked herself into risking a hundred dollars for the night when Serena came up beside her.

"I'm glad to see you decided to get out for a while." Angling her head, Serena took in the glittery jacket. "Celebrating?"

"Um." Darcy felt color flood her face. She could hardly tell Mac's mother she was, in her way, celebrating making love to him. "I just wanted to dress up. I bought all these clothes and I've been living in slacks and shorts."

"I know just how you feel. Nothing perks up the soul like a great dress. And that's a great one."

"Thanks. You don't think it's too…red?"

"Absolutely not. So are you going to try your luck here?"

"I was thinking about it." She nibbled her lip. "I hate to join a table where everyone knows what they're doing. It must be irritating to have a novice plop down and slow the game."

"It's part of the game, and the luck of the draw. If you stick to the five-or ten-dollar tables, most people will be willing to help you out a bit."

"You were a dealer."

"Yes, I was. And a good one."

"Would you teach me?"

"To deal?"

"To play," Darcy stated. "And to win."

"Well…" Serena's smile spread slowly. "Go get us a table in the bar. I'll be along in a minute."

"Split your sevens."

Eyes sober, Darcy followed instructions, setting the two sevens she'd been dealt side by side on the silver table in the lounge. "And this is supposed to be good, right? Not stressful because now I have two hands to worry about."

Serena just grinned. "Cover your bet on the second hand." She dealt Darcy her next cards. "Three for ten on your first hand, six for thirteen on your second. Dealer has an eight showing, what do you do?"

"Okay." Darcy wiped her damp palms on her knees. "I double down on the first hand, then take a hit." Remembering the ritual she'd been taught, she counted out the bar nuts standing in the place of chips, then tapped a finger on her cards. "A three—thirteen. I have to take another one."

"Pulled a six for nineteen. Holding on nineteen?"

"Yeah. Now we do this one." She tapped her finger on the second hand and winced at the steely eyes of the king she drew. "Well, at least that was fast."

"Busted on twenty-three." Serena raked in the nuts, and cards, then turned over her down card. "Dealer has eleven, fourteen, and breaks on twenty-four."

"So I win on the first hand, but I doubled the bet so it's like winning twice. That's good."

"You're getting it. Now if you want to buck the house, you let that bet ride on the next hand."

Darcy stared down at her pile of nuts. "It's a lot—twenty nuts on one hand."

"Two thousand." Serena twinkled at her. "Didn't I mention the nuts are a hundred a pop?"

"Good God, I've eaten a dozen. Let's go for it."

"Is this game open, ladies?"

Serena tipped up her face for her husband's kiss. "You got a stake, pal, you got a chair."

He snagged a bowl of pretzels from a neighboring table. "I think I can afford a few hands."

"Thousand-dollar chips. We got us a high roller." Delighted with the game, Serena rubbed her hands together. "Place your bets."

When Mac found them a half hour later, Darcy was sitting hip to hip with his father and giggling as she piled a mix of nuts and pretzels into a sloppy mountain on the table. "You're not supposed to hit on seventeen when the dealer's showing a two," Darcy said, sniffing experimentally at the smoke from Justin's slim cigar. "Why did you?"

"He's a card counter." Mac pulled up a chair and sat between his parents, eyeing his father. "We don't like card counters around here. We ask them politely to take their money elsewhere."

"I taught you how to count cards before you could handle a two-wheeler."

"Yeah." Mac's grin flashed and spread. "That's why I can spot 'em."

"Your father's still as slick as he was when he bet me a walk on the deck of the ship on one hand of twenty-one. He hit on seventeen then, too."

"Oh." Darcy's heart sighed. "That's so romantic."

"Serena didn't think so at the time." Justin sent Serena a long, slow smile. "But I changed her mind."

"I thought you were arrogant, dangerous and cocky. I still do," Serena added, sipping at her wine. "I just learned to like it."

"Are you two going to flirt with each other or play cards?" Mac demanded.

"They can do both," Darcy told him. "I've been watching."

"Learned anything?"

It was the delivery, smooth as silk, that flustered her as much as the words. She looked at him, large eyes shuttered by dark lashes. "If you don't bet, you don't win."

"I've got a couple hours off." He spoke to the table at large, but his eyes were on Darcy's as he rose, held out a hand. "I'll see you tomorrow," he said to his parents, then drew Darcy to her feet. "Let's go out."

"Out?"

"There's more to Vegas than The Comanche."

"Good night," she called over her shoulder as Mac was already pulling her away.

Justin drew on his cigar, tapped it idly. "The boy's a goner," he decided.

The minute she stepped outside, Darcy realized she hadn't been out of the hotel after sunset since she arrived. For a moment she simply stood, between the tumbling sapphire water of a fountain and the grand gilded statue of the chief.

The lights were dazzling, the traffic edgy. Vegas was a woman, she thought, part honky-tonk, part siren, bold, brassy and seductive.

"It's so…much," she decided.

"And there's always more. The Strip's a few blocks long, a few blocks wide, but you can smell money in every foot of it. Gambling's the core, but it's not a one-factory town anymore. Headliners, circus acts, wedding bells and rides for the kids."

He glanced back at the wide and towering double arch that was The Comanche. "We added a thousand rooms five years ago. We could add a thousand more and still fill them."

"It's a huge responsibility. Running an enterprise of this size."

"I like it."

"The challenge?" she wondered. "Or the power, or the excitement?"

"All of it." He turned back, then taking her hand stepped back. He hadn't gotten beyond her face in the bar. Those eyes of hers always seemed to capture his mind first. Now he took in the glittering glamour of her jacket and the invitational red of her dress.

"I should have stolen more than a couple hours. You need to be taken out on the town."

"I'd love a couple of hours. Where should we go?"

"I can't manage a drive into the mountains in the moonlight, but I can take you for a walk through a tunnel full of fantasies."

He took her walking on Freemont, where the street was covered and full of lights. Colors circled and bled overhead, and the ever present clack of the slots added a musical, carnival feel. She could marvel at the light show, delight in the music and walked hand in hand with him on what was so suddenly and unexpectedly an innocent date.

He bought her ice cream, and made her laugh.

She rode the elevator to the top of The Stratosphere with him, thrilled at the idea that she was rising up inside of that towering needle that stood at the edge of the Strip. And though she stared then gulped at the sight of the rooftop roller coaster, the silent challenge in his eyes had her scooting into the car with him.

"I've never ridden a roller coaster in my life."

"You might as well start with a champ," he told her.

"I tried a Tilt-A-Whirl once at a carnival but…" She trailed off. "Are you sure this is safe?"

"Almost everyone who gets on gets off again. The odds are good." He laughed at the horrified look in her eyes, then took advantage—as he'd intended to—when the coaster started its climb and she gripped him in a death hold. "I want to kiss you."

"Okay, but you could have done that on the ground." She lifted her face, which she'd buried in his shoulder.

"Not yet," he murmured, but laid his hands on her cheeks. "Not quite yet."

Lulled, she smiled and her heart began to beat normally again. "It's not so bad. I didn't realize it would be so nice and slow."

Then they dipped, spinning fast into a free fall that shot her stomach hard against her ribs and burned white-hot fear into her throat.

"Now." And he took her mouth greedily as they swung over the edge of the world.

She couldn't breathe. There wasn't even breath to scream. They were flying, rocketing up, plunging down, shoved into the void then snatched back while his mouth assaulted hers with a single-minded intensity that left her stupefied.

Speed, light, screams. And that firestorm of stunning heat that refused to be stopped. Dizzy, breathless, helplessly caught in the crosshatch of arousal and fear, she clung to him.

And gave him what he'd wanted—crazed, half-terrified surrender.

Her head was still reeling after they'd jerked to a stop. Her fingers continued to grip his jacket, as if fused there. "God." The word exploded from her lips. "I've never felt anything like that before." She shuddered once. "Can we do it again?"

His grin flashed. "Oh, yeah."

She felt drunk and giddy by the time they stood on the street again. "Oh, that was wonderful. It made my head spin." She laughed as he slipped a supporting arm around her waist. "I won't be able to walk a straight line for hours."

"Then you'll have to lean on me—which was part of my plan."

Laughing again, she threw back her head to watch an explosion of fireworks. Jewel colors shot into the black sky, and fountained there. "Everything's so bright here, so bold. Nothing's too high or too big or too fast." She turned into him. "Nothing's impossible here."

Wrapping her arms around his neck, she kissed him with a passion that had waited a long time to wake. "I want to do everything. I want to do everything twice, then pick the best and do it again."

He slid his arms under her jacket and discovered to his delight that the dress left her back bare to his hands. "We've got a little time before I have to get back. What would you like to do?"

"Well…" Her eyes sparkled in the neon. "I've never seen an exotic dancer."

"And your second choice would be?"

"I just wonder what it would be like in one of those places where the women dance topless and slide around on those poles."

"No, I'm definitely not taking you to a strip joint."

"I've seen naked women before."

"No."

"All right." She moved a shoulder, began to walk casually beside him. "I'll just go by myself some other time."

He shot her a look, narrowed his eyes, but she only smiled up sunnily. He considered himself highly skilled at judging a bluff. And knew when he was up against a better hand.

"Ten minutes," he muttered. "And you don't say a word while we're inside."

"Ten minutes is fine." Delighted with the victory, she tucked her arm through his.

"The patriotic one was double-jointed, I'm sure of it." With another fascinating experience under her belt, Darcy breezed into Mac's office just ahead of him. "The one with the little flag over her—"

"I know the one you mean." Every time he thought he had her pegged, Mac thought, she flustered him. She hadn't been the least bit embarrassed or shocked. Instead she'd been fascinated.

"The way they slid around on that pole, they must practice for hours. And the muscle control, it's phenomenal."

"I can't believe I let you talk me into taking you into a place like that."

"I had no idea."

"Obviously."

"No, I mean about you." She sat on the arm of a chair. He was already behind his desk, scanning the screens.

"What about me?"

"That under that suave, sophisticated exterior, you're really a fuddy-duddy at heart."

He stared at her, unsure if he should be amused or insulted. "Anyone who uses the expression 'fuddy-duddy' in a sentence automatically assumes fuddy-duddy status."

"I never heard that."

"It's written down somewhere. Are you hungry?"

"Not really." She couldn't sit still and rose to circle the room. "I had such a wonderful time. It's been the most incredible day of my life—and I've had some incredible days lately. Everything's churning about inside me." She wrapped her arms around herself as if to hold it all in. "I don't think there's any room for food."

Her jacket caught the lights as she moved, glittering like jewel-toned stars that reminded him of the fireworks. But it was her face—it always seemed to be her face—that held his attention. "Champagne?"

She laughed, a warm delighted sound. "There's always room for champagne. Imagine me being able to say that. It's like every minute I'm here is another little miracle."

He took a bottle from the small refrigerator behind the wet bar, watching her as he opened it. She was glowing, he thought, eyes, cheeks, lips. Everything about her seemed to pulse with energy and fresh, unshadowed joy.

Seeing it, feeling it, aroused, contented and unnerved him. *Be with me,* she'd asked him. And being with her, on a walk down a crowded street, alone in a tumbled bed, over a candlelit table, was becoming uncomfortably vital.

But she was glowing. How could he take his eyes off her? "I like seeing you happy."

"Then you must be having a good night, too. I've never been so happy." She took the glass he offered, twirling around as she sipped. "Can I stay here with you awhile, watch the people?"

Did she really have no idea how she affected him? he wondered. "Stay as long as you want."

"Will you tell me what you're looking for when you watch the screens? I don't see anything but people."

"Trouble, scams, tells."

"What are tells?"

"Everybody has them. Gestures, repetitive habits that tell you what's going on in the head." He smiled at her. "You link your fingers together when you're nervous. It keeps you from biting your nails. You cock your head to the left when you're concentrating."

"Oh. Like the way you put your hands in your pockets when you're frustrated—so you don't punch someone."

He lifted a brow. "Good."

"It's easy when you're watching a handful of people, but there are so many," she added, gesturing to the screens. "How do you pick them out?"

"You get to know what to look for. This is only backup. The first line of defense against scam artists is the dealer." He walked up behind her, laid a hand on her shoulder so they could watch the screens together. "Then the floor man, the pit boss, the shift boss. And over it all is the eye in the sky."

"This?"

"No, this is a wink. We have a control room with hundreds of screens like this. The staff in there watches the casino from every angle, and they're linked to the floor men, the shift and pit bosses with radios. They'll spot a hand mucker—"

"A what?"

"Card palming. The scam artist is dealt say a six and an eight, he palms them, and switches them with a queen and ace for a blackjack. Cheating's a problem— more now than it used to be when you were dealing with loaded dice and fast hands. We're talking body computers these days."

Body computers, she thought, scam artist. Hand mucking. Wouldn't that be a fascinating backdrop for a book? "What do you do when you catch someone cheating?"

"Show them the door."

"That's it?"

"They don't walk out with our money."

The chill in his voice had Darcy glancing back at his face. "I bet they don't," she murmured.

"We run a clean room, the cameras there and in all the counting areas help keep it honest. But the house always has the edge. It's not hard to win money in The Comanche, but odds are, you won't keep it."

"Because you want to keep playing." She understood that. It was so hard to stop when there was a chance for more.

"And the longer you play, the more you'll put back."

"But it's worth it, isn't it? If you've enjoyed yourself. If it's made you happy."

"As long as you know what you're risking." He saw that she understood they were no longer talking about table games and slots.

"The danger's part of the allure." Her heart began to thud as he took the glass from her hand and set it aside. "That, and the whiff of sin. You get a taste for it."

"And why stop at a bite or two, when you can have all you want." His gaze roamed over her face, lingering on her mouth, then sliding down. "Take off your jacket."

"We're in your office."

His eyes came back to hers, and his smile was slow and dangerous. "I wanted you, here, the first day you came in. Now I'm going to have you, here. Take off your jacket."

Mesmerized, she slipped it off, let it fall in a colorful pool over the arm of the chair. When she realized she'd linked her fingers together, she pulled them apart. And made him smile again.

"I don't mind you being nervous. I like it. It's exciting to know you're a little afraid, but when I touch you, you'll give." He reached out to toy with the sassy red strap on her shoulder. The dress clung to every quiet curve. "What've you got on under there, Darcy?"

Her breath shuddered out. "Hardly anything."

His eyes flashed, a clash of swords in the sun. "I don't want to be gentle this time. Will you risk it?"

She nodded, would have spoken, but he was already dragging her against him. His mouth was bruising and hungry and tasted of such raw passion she could only marvel he felt it for her.

Then he was pulling her to the floor, and the shock of that alone had her gasping. His hands took her over, body and mind, racing over her, taking, possessing, inciting a fury of sensations.

All she could think was that it was like the roller coaster, a fast and reckless ride. Glorying in it, she yanked desperately at his jacket, tugged at his shirt while the pulse pounding in her seemed to scream hurry, hurry, hurry.

She moaned as he peeled the dress down, and the sound raged through his blood. Her breasts were small and firm and when he filled his mouth with the taste of them she fisted her hands in his hair, urging him to take more. Desperate for the taste of flesh, her flesh, he used tongue and teeth until she writhed under him, her sobbing breaths like a drumbeat to his greed.

But still it wasn't enough.

His mouth streaked down, laying a line of heat on skin that had gone hot and damp. Her muscles quivered beneath his tongue, her body shivered under his busy, relentless hands. His own breath was ragged when he gripped her restless hips and lifted them.

The fast plunge ripped a scream from her throat. The fire that shot through her was molten, shocking her system with sensations so acute she feared for a moment they would simply tear her apart. The climax rushed through her, a towering wave of hot, hard pleasure that tossed her high, sucked her deep. Helpless, she tossed an arm over her eyes and let it drag her where it would.

When she thought there could be no more, he pulled her mercilessly over the next edge.

She lay bonelessly as he yanked off the rest of his clothes. Her skin glowed under the lights, flushed and damp. Her mouth was swollen from his. When he drew her up, her head fell weakly back, leaving him no choice but to plunder her soft mouth.

"Stay with me." He murmured it as he assaulted her neck, her shoulders. He shifted, bringing her over him, brought her down until she took him into her, closed that glorious heat around him.

Her moan was long and deep and broken. He watched as flickers of fresh pleasure moved over her face and into the clouded eyes that opened and fixed on his.

"Take what you want." His hands moved up her body and covered her breasts.

She was already moving. Her body was unable to rest. There was a shock of control, of power, a nervy kind of energy that demanded movement. Tantalizing. She arched back and drove herself mad.

Everything inside her was as bright, as brilliant, as reckless and bold as the world she now lived in. A world where nothing was too big or too fast, or too much.

He was quivering beneath her, and his hands were rough as they gripped her hips. A new thrill snaked through her, the knowing that she was taking him with her.

Stay with me, he'd demanded. And she wanted nothing more than to obey.

When the climax bowed her back, when it had her melting down on him, he rolled her over, his body plunging, his heart pounding, until both body and heart emptied themselves into her.

Chapter 10

The phone woke Darcy at five past nine. She thought blearily that her days of working an ordinary eight-hour day were over. It had been nearly four in the morning when she'd given in to exhaustion. And even then she'd been wrapped around Mac.

Since she was alone in the big bed, she had to assume he'd figured out a way to function on little to no sleep. If he could learn, so could she.

She yawned widely, reached for the phone with her eyes still hopefully shut. "Hello?" she mumbled, and buried both her head and receiver in the pillow.

Fifteen minutes later she was sitting straight up in bed, staring at nothing. Maybe she'd been dreaming, she thought, and stared at the phone. Had she actually just talked to an editor in New York? Had that editor actually asked to see her work?

She pressed a hand to her heart. It was beating, fast but steady. She could feel the light chill from the air-conditioning on her bare shoulders. She was wide-awake.

Not a dream, she told herself, bringing her knees up and wrapping her arms tightly around them. Not a dream at all.

Her story was all over the media—the editor had said as much. Darcy had told reporters that she was writing a book, and now the next miracle had happened. A publisher wanted to see it.

It was only because of the attention from the press, Darcy thought, resting her forehead on her knees. She was an oddity, a story in herself, and the publisher would consider her manuscript because of the public's interest in the writer, and not the work.

And that, she thought with a sigh, didn't make her a writer.

What difference did it make? She sat straight again, balling her fists. It was a foot in the door, wasn't it? A chance to see if—no, not to see, she corrected, to *prove* her work had merit.

She'd send the first book in, and the opening chapters of the second. She would let them stand or fall on their own.

Tossing the sheets aside, she scrambled out of bed, bundled into a robe and raced downstairs to turn those first two chapters into gems.

She said nothing to Mac, to anyone, afraid she would jinx herself. Superstition was another new character trait, or perhaps one she'd kept buried. She worked steadily through the day, ruthlessly cutting, lovingly polishing her words until she was forced to admit she could do no better.

While the pages printed out, she retrieved her list of agents. If she intended to be a professional, she told herself, then she would need professional representation. It was time to take the big risk. Finally take it.

They were just names to her, faceless power symbols. How would she know which one to pick, which one would see something inside her worthy of their time and attention?

The face of the slot had been only stars and moons, she remembered. She'd gambled everything once. It wasn't so hard to do it again. Following impulse, she shut her eyes, circled her finger in the air, then jabbed it onto the list.

"Let's see how lucky you are," Darcy murmured, and calculating she had fifteen minutes before offices closed on the East Coast, picked up the phone.

Twenty minutes later she had representation, or at least the promise to read the manuscript and sample of her work, and to negotiate if the publisher made an offer.

More than satisfied, Darcy typed up a cover letter, then called the desk to request an overnight bag and form before she could change her mind.

She nearly did so while the bellman waited for her to seal the envelope. She very nearly gave in to the dozens of excuses whirling in her head.

It wasn't ready. She wasn't ready. The book needed more work. She needed more time. She was sending work she'd slaved over to strangers. She should ask someone's advice before she mailed the pages. She should call the agent back and tell her she wanted to finish the second manuscript rather than submitting the first.

Coward, she berated herself and, setting her jaw, handed the bellman the envelope. "Will this go out today?"

"Yes, ma'am. It'll be in—" he glanced at the address on the form "—New York tomorrow morning."

"Tomorrow." She felt the blood drain out of her face. "Good. Thank you." She handed him some crumpled bills as a tip, then sat down the minute he was gone and dropped her head between her knees.

It was done. There was no going back now. In a matter of days she would know if she was good enough. Finally good enough. And if she wasn't...

She simply couldn't face failing at this. Not this. As long as she could remember, she'd wanted this one thing. Had set it aside time after time after time. Now there was no one to tell her to be practical, to accept her own limitations. There were no more excuses.

Steadier, she sat up, took two long breaths. She'd plugged in her stake, she told herself, and she'd pulled the lever. Now she would have to wait for the end of the spin.

When the phone rang, she stared at it, horrified. It was the editor calling back, she thought frantically, telling her there had been a mistake.

Holding her breath, she picked up the phone. "Hello," she said, with her eyes tightly shut.

"Hello yourself, little girl."

"Daniel." His name came out on something close to a sob.

"Aye. Is something wrong, lass?"

"No, no." She pressed a hand to her face and let out

a quick, nervous laugh. "Everything's fine. Wonderful. How are you?"

"Right as rain." The way his voice boomed through the receiver seemed to prove it. "I thought I should let you know, I lost every penny in a leveraged buyout."

"I—I—" She blinked so rapidly the room spun in front of her eyes. "All of it?"

His laughter roared out, forcing her to pull the receiver several inches away from her ear. "Just joking with you, lass."

"Oh." She pressed a hand to her speeding heart. "Ha-ha."

"Got your blood moving, didn't it? I'm just calling to let you know we made some money already."

"Made some? Already?"

"You know, Darcy girl, you're using the same tone for the good news as you did for the bad. That's a good sign of a steady nerve."

"I don't feel steady," she admitted. "But I feel lots of nerves."

"You'll do. We made a tidy little sum on a short-term deal, an in and out sort of thing. You should go buy yourself a bauble."

She moistened her lips. "How big a bauble?"

He laughed again. "That's my girl. We pulled in a quick fifty, just getting our feet wet."

"I can get some nice earrings for fifty dollars."

"Fifty thousand."

"Thousand," she repeated though her tongue seemed to tangle on the word. "Are you joking again?"

"Buy the bauble," he told her. "Making money's a fine way to pass the time, but enjoying it's better. Now tell me when you're coming to see me. My Anna wants to meet you."

"I may be coming East—on business—in the next few weeks."

"That's fine then. You plan to come here, spend some time, meet the rest of the family, or those I can gather up. Children scatter on you. It's a crime. My wife pines for them."

"I will come. I miss you."

"You've a sweet heart, Darcy."

"Daniel...do you..." It had to be delicately put, she thought, but it had to be put. "Mac mentioned, that is, he seemed to think you might have the idea that we'd suit each other. That you were, well, planting seeds along those lines."

"Planting seeds, is it! Planting seeds. Ha! The boy needs a cuff on the ear. Did I say a word? I ask you."

"Well, not exactly, but—"

"Where do they get this idea that I'm scheming behind their backs? I didn't drop you into his lap, did I?"

"No, but—"

"Not that it doesn't take a push to get these young people to do their duty—and to see what's best for them. Dawdle around is what they do. My wife deserves babies to bounce on her knees in her twilight years, doesn't she?"

"Yes, of course. It's just that—"

"Damn right I do—she does," he corrected quickly. "Boy's going to be thirty in another month or so, and is he settling down to make a family? He is not," Daniel rolled on before Darcy could speak. "And what's so wrong with giving him a bit of a nudge, I'd like to know, if you suit him?"

"Do I?" she murmured. "Do I suit him?"

"I'm saying so, and who'd know better?" He huffed, then his voice shifted, became sly and persuasive. "He's a good-looking young man, don't you think?"

"Yes, I do."

"Strong stock, a good brain. There's a kind heart in him, too, and a fine sense of responsibility. He's a steady one, stands for his friends and his family. A woman couldn't do better than my Robbie."

"No, I don't see how she could."

"We're not talking about she," Daniel said with some impatience. "We're talking about you. You've got a spark for him now, don't you, Darcy girl?"

She thought of the fireworks exploding over the city the night before. Her spark for Mac was every bit as huge and bright and volatile. "Daniel, I'm so desperately in love with him."

"Well now."

"Please." She winced at the booming pleasure in his voice. "I'm trusting you with that because I need to tell someone."

"Why aren't you telling him?"

"Because I don't want to scare him off." There, she'd said it, she thought, biting her lip. It was no more than a plot.

"So...you're giving him some time to woo you, and come around to thinking it was his idea."

Now she winced. "It's not really that devious. It's just—"

"What the devil's wrong with devious? Devious gets the job done, doesn't it?"

"I suppose." Her lips trembled into a smile. How could she help it? "He cares for me, I know he does,

but I think part of it comes from that fine sense of responsibility. I'm willing to wait until he doesn't feel
responsible."

"Don't wait too long."

"I'm hoping I won't have to." She smiled. "I have
some ideas."

She wasn't in the market for a bauble, but she rented
a car. Buying one was going to wait until she could decide if the sports car or the sedan suited her new and
developing lifestyle.

She secretly hoped it would be the sports car.

Armed with maps, she began the task of familiariz-
ing herself with the city, the one beyond the Strip. She
cruised downtown, noting the huge building cranes that
loomed like giant, hovering birds. Growth was everywhere, from the spectacular hotel resorts, to the devel-
opments that sprawled into the desert.

She parked and walked the malls, the grocery store
and drugstores, giving herself a chance to observe the
life that pulsed here beyond the casinos.

She saw children playing in yards, houses tucked
side by side in neighborhoods. She saw schools and
churches, quiet streets and crowded ones. She saw
sprawling homes that faced the eerie peace of the desert and the tumble of rocks that made the mountains
beyond.

She saw a life she could begin to build.

Circling back, she found a library and went inside to
gather more information on the place she would make
her home.

It was after seven when she got back to her suite,
pleasantly tired and more than eager to put her aching

feet up. She was certain she'd walked twenty miles. Though she hadn't bought a bauble, she had made an appointment to view a property the following day.

She thought she might become a home owner very soon.

"There you are." Mac stepped up to the elevator the moment the doors opened. "I was getting worried."

"I'm sorry. I was out exploring." She tossed her purse aside and started to smile, but her mouth was soon busy against his.

He knew the sense of relief was out of proportion, as was the irritation he'd felt when he hadn't been able to find her anywhere in the hotel. "You shouldn't have gone out alone. You don't know your way around."

Responsibility, she thought, and wanted to sigh. "I got a map. I thought it was time I saw a little more of the city."

She started to tell him about the house she planned to see the next day, then held her tongue. The news was hers for now, she thought, just as the call from New York was hers.

"You spent some time in the sun." He ran a fingertip down her nose and made her wrinkle it.

"I'll have to remember to get a hat before I turn into one big freckle. The air's so hot and dry. It must be murder on the skin, but I really love it."

"It's easy to get dehydrated."

"Mmm. You're right." She walked over to take a bottle of water from behind the bar. "I saw people with water bottles hooked on their belts. Like hikers or explorers, and so much building going on. Men in hard hats working a hundred, two hundred feet in the air. Slot machines in the grocery store."

"You went to a grocery store."

"I wanted to see what it was like," she said, evading. "All this boom in the downtown area, then suddenly, you're in a quiet suburban neighborhood, with kids and dogs in the yard, and it all seems so cozily settled."

"I'd have taken you around if I'd known you wanted to go."

"I knew you were busy."

"I'm not busy now. My parents booted me out, with orders to take the night off."

A smile curved her lips. "I really love your parents."

"So do I. Come for a drive with me." He held out a hand. "We'll find some moonlight."

In the distance, Vegas shimmered like a mirage. The floor of the desert stretched in every direction, barely marred by the slice of road. Overhead the sky was a clear, dark sea, studded by countless stars and graced by the floating ball of a white moon.

In the distant hills a coyote called, and the plaintive sound carried like a bell on the air that had cooled with moonrise.

He'd put the top down so that she could lay her head back and let starlight shower on her face. Wind danced lightly across the sand as they sat in silence.

"You forget this exists when you're in there." She looked toward the colors and shapes of the city. "The West, wild and dangerous and beautiful."

"A long way from Kansas." It was too easy to picture her there, away from the arid wind, the gaudy lights. "Do you miss the green? The fields?"

"No." She didn't have to think about it. "There's something so powerful in the siennas and soft reds, the baked-out greens and browns of this land. But you didn't grow up here, either." She turned her head to look at him. "You lived back East, didn't you?"

"The house is in New Jersey, just outside of Atlantic City. My parents didn't want to raise a family in hotel rooms over a casino. But we spent plenty of time there. Duncan and I used to hunker down in the security bay over the tables. Before everything was electronic, that's where they watched the room. My mother would have skinned me if she knew I'd taken him up there."

"Rightfully so. It must have been dangerous."

"Part of the appeal, right?" His grin flashed and to her secret joy he began to play absently with her hair. "There's a story about the night one of the men fell out and landed facedown on a craps table."

"Ow! Was he hurt? What happened?"

"Rumor persists that some guy bet five dollars on his ass. The game doesn't stop for much."

She chuckled and settled her head on his shoulder. "It was exciting for you, being a part of all of that. Why did you choose to work here and not back East?"

"There's only one Vegas. No point in settling for less than the best."

Her heart gave a little jerk at the sentiment, spoken with such casual confidence. But she ignored it. "Is the rest of your family involved with the casinos?"

"Duncan's managing the riverboat. It suits him down to the ground, cruising along the Mississippi and charming the ladies."

"You're close?"

"Yeah. We are, all of us. Geography doesn't change that. Gwen's a doctor, lives in Boston—as do several assorted cousins. She had a baby a few months ago."

"Boy or girl?"

"A girl. Anna, after my grandmother. I have two or three hundred pictures," he added with a smile, "if you'd like to see her."

"I'd love to. You have another sister, the youngest?"

"Mel. She's a live wire. The eyes of an angel and the right hook of a middleweight."

"I imagine she needed both," Darcy said dryly. "You probably teased her unmercifully."

"No more than was my right and duty. Besides, I'm the one who taught her how to punch. No girlie little slaps for my baby sister."

"I bet they're all beautiful. With heart-stopping faces and killer smiles." She turned her head, let herself trace his mouth with her fingertip. "And between the looks and the breeding, they're a confident bunch. The kind who walk into a room, take one slow glance around and know exactly where they stand. I always envied that innate sense of self."

"I thought the word was *arrogance*."

"It is, but it's not always a criticism. Did you argue all the time?"

"As often as humanly possible."

"No one argued in my house. They reasoned. At least in an argument you have a chance to win."

"I've noticed you hold your own in that area."

"Beginner's luck," she claimed. "Wait until I'm seasoned a bit. I'll be a terror." She grinned. "Then I'll learn how to punch, in case arguing doesn't work."

Her lips were still curved when his lowered to them. The easy kiss turned dark quickly, began to heat rapidly around the edges. They both shifted, moving into it, into each other.

Emotion surged through him so powerfully, so violently that fury sprang up to tangle with need. "I shouldn't want you this much." He dragged her head back to try to clear his own. But all he could see were those dark gold eyes, and what was the shadow of himself drowning in them. "It's too damn much."

She remembered his words of the night before and gave them back to him. "Take what you need."

"I've been trying to. It doesn't stop."

The words sent a wild thrill soaring through her. Recklessly she knelt on the seat beside him, watched his gaze lower and follow the movement of her fingers as she unbuttoned her blouse. "Try again," she murmured.

He should never have touched her, was all he could think, because now he couldn't seem to stop. He drove the long, straight road back to Vegas at a fast clip, with Darcy sleeping like a child beside him, her head on his shoulder.

He'd taken her in the front seat of the car like a hormone-rattled teenager. He'd driven himself into her with a blind desperation, as though his life had depended on it.

And Lord help him, he wanted to do it again.

He'd broken all the rules with her. A man who made his living with games knew the rules, and when they could and should be ignored. He'd had no right to ignore them with her.

She'd been innocent and alone, and had trusted him.

He'd let his needs, and hers, step ahead of that. Now he was so tangled up in her, in what he wanted, in what was right, that nothing was clear.

He was going to have to step back. There was no

question of it. She needed room, and the chance to test those wings of hers. No one had ever given her that chance, including himself.

He could keep her, he knew it. She thought she loved him, and he could make her go on thinking it. Until eventually, he thought with an inner lurch, that glow of hers began to fade against the neon and glitter, and that light of fascinated joy dulled in her eyes.

Keeping her would ruin her, change her and eventually break her. That was one gamble he wouldn't take.

Caring for her left him only one answer. He had to back away and give her a nudge in the opposite direction. In the direction that was right for her.

He should do it quickly for her sake, and yes, for his own.

She was the only woman who'd ever slipped uninvited into his mind at odd hours of the day and night. He wanted to resent it but found that he was already afraid of the time that would come when she would fade into a memory.

And he was already furious thinking of the time when he would become little more than that to her.

She'd think of him now and then, he reflected, when she was tucked into some pretty home in a green-lawned suburbia. Children playing at her feet, a dog sleeping in the yard and a husband who wouldn't appreciate the magic of her nearly enough on his way home for dinner.

It was exactly where she belonged, exactly where she would go once he worked up the courage to cut the ties that bound her to him. Ties of gratitude, excitement and sex, he thought and despised himself for wanting to hold her with them.

He'd spoken no less than the truth when he'd told her

she didn't belong in the world he lived in. He believed that absolutely. She would come to the same truth once the gloss had dulled a bit.

Virtue and sin didn't mate comfortably.

He glanced down as he drove along the Strip and watched the carnival lights from the neon splash over her face. He would have to let her go, he told himself. But not yet.

Not quite yet.

the ocean looking out at a world built of sky and ocean. Then she'd stop... Stop and come to the same conclusion. The place was called a lie.

...that gesture stayed with her intently.

He glanced at her as he drove along the street and wondered briefly whether it was a mistake, whether just— if the price would be worth it to him, to sell him?

Little Liar

Nora Roberts
192

Chapter 11

The house grew up out of the sand like a little castle fashioned of soft colors and magic shapes. Darcy's first sight of it shot an arrow of love and longing into her heart.

It was tucked among palms, and desert plants were scattered near the wide sunny deck. The soft red of the tile roof accented the cool ivory and buffed browns of the exterior. The multilevels gave it a variety of charming rooflines and made her think of artistically placed building blocks.

It had a tower, a canny little spear that had her romantic heart picturing princesses and knights, even while the practical part of her nature snagged it greedily as the perfect writing space.

It was already hers, even before she stepped inside. She barely heard the Realtor's professional chatter.

Only three years old. Custom-built. The family moved back East. It's just come on the market. Bound to be a quick mover.

"Hmm." Darcy responded simply as they started up the brick walkway to the door flanked by glass etched with stars.

Stars had been lucky for her, she thought.

She stepped into the entrance onto the sand-colored tiles, let her gaze travel up to the lofty ceiling. Skylights. Perfect. It was an airy space with walls painted a cool, soft yellow. She would leave them alone, she decided, listening to her heels click on the tile as she wandered.

Another deck stretched along the back, accessed by atrium doors in a quiet blond wood. No dark colors here, she thought. Everything would be light, fresh. Her eyes gleamed with pleasure as she looked beyond the deck to the sparkling waters of the swimming pool.

She let the Realtor expound on the wonders of the kitchen, the subzero refrigerator, the custom-made cabinets, the granite counters. And was charmed by the cozy breakfast area tucked into a bay window. That was for family, she thought. For lazy Sunday mornings, and rushed school days, for quiet late nights and cups of tea.

She would enjoy cooking here, she thought, studying the range, the double ovens, the mirror black cooktop. She'd always been a plain and pedestrian cook, but she thought she would like experimenting with recipes, with herbs, sauces.

The maid's room and laundry area off the kitchen were easily as big as her entire apartment in Kansas. Darcy didn't miss the irony, or the wonder of it.

She'd put a trestle table in the dining room, she mused. That would suit the tone and go well with the small tiled fireplace for chilly desert nights. Watercolors for the walls, soft bleeding tones.

She'd learn how to entertain, have intimate, casual dinner parties as well as sparkling, sophisticated ones. Loud, bawdy, backyard barbecues. Yes, she thought she could be a good, and what was better, an interesting hostess.

She toured each of the four bedrooms, checking views, space, approving the builder's choice of random-width pine for the floors, and the bright jazz of contrast tiles scattered in amusing patterns among the neutral colors of the baths.

She knew she goggled at the master suite, and didn't care. The two-level area boasted its own private deck, fireplace, an enormous dressing area with closets large enough to live in and a bath that rivaled the one at The Comanche with a lagoon-sized motorized tub in an unexpected clay color.

The treated skylight above it cut the glare while offering a dazzling view of desert blue sky.

Ferns, she imagined, in copper and brass pots, crowded together, all lush and green. She would jumble them on the wide ledge behind the tub and every bath would be like swimming in a secluded oasis.

The tower was octagon shaped, generous with windows. The walls were cream, the floor tiles the color of stone. Her workstation would go there, she decided, facing the desert. Not a desk, but a long counter, perhaps in a sharp, deep blue for contrast. It would have dozens of drawers and cubbyholes.

She needed to go shopping for a computer system—a fax, a desktop copier. Reams of paper, she thought with a giddy burst of joy.

She would put a love seat on the other side of the room and create a small seating area, and she'd want shelves there, floor to ceiling, for books and small treasures.

She would sit there, writing hour after hour, and know she was a part of everything around her.

The Realtor had been silent for the past several minutes. She'd been in the game long enough to know when to sell, and when to step back. The potential buyer didn't have much of a poker face, she mused, already imagining the tidy commission.

"It's a lovely property," the Realtor said now. "A quiet, settled neighborhood, convenient for shopping but tucked just far away enough from the city to offer a sense of solitude." She offered Darcy a bright smile. "So, what do you think?"

Darcy pulled herself back and focused on the woman. "I'm so sorry, I've forgotten your name."

"It's Marion. Marion Baines."

"Oh, yes, Ms. Baines—"

"Marion."

"Marion. I appreciate you taking the time to show me through."

"Happy to do it." But she felt a little hitch in her stomach, a sign of a sale slipping away. "It might feel a little large for your needs. You did say you were single."

"Yes, I'm single."

"It might seem a bit overwhelming, but empty houses often do. You'd be amazed how it all comes together when it's furnished."

Darcy had already seen it come together as she could picture it furnished, perfectly, in her mind. "I'll take it."

"Oh." Marion's smile faltered, then spread. "Wonder-

ful. I'm so pleased you want to make an offer. If you like
we can use the kitchen to fill out the paperwork, and
I can present your offer to the sellers this afternoon."

"I said I'd take it. I'll pay the asking price."

"You—well." Something in that fresh face and
youthful eyes had her hesitating. Even as she ordered
herself to keep her mouth shut and close the deal, she
found herself speaking. "Ms. Wallace, Darcy... I'm con-
tracted to represent the sellers, but I realize this is the
first time you've bought property. I feel obligated to
mention that it's usual to make an offer of...somewhat
less than the asking price. The sellers may accept it,
or counter."

"Yes, I know. But why shouldn't they get what they
want?" She smiled and turned back to gaze out the window. "I'm going to."

It was so simple really, she discovered. A few forms
to be filled out, papers to be signed, a check to be written. Earnest money, it was called. Darcy liked the sound
of it. She was very earnest about the house.

She listened as home loans were explained to her,
fixed interest rates, balloon payments, mortgage insurance. Then decided to keep it simple and pay cash.

When the settlement date was set, she breezed out to
her rented car, thrilled by the knowledge that in thirty
short days she would have a home.

The minute she was back in her suite, she grabbed
the phone. She knew she had to call Caine, ask him to
represent her interests in the settlement or recommend
a local real estate lawyer. She needed to choose an insurance company and take out a home owner's policy.

She wanted to shop for furniture, to pick out dishes and linens.

And oh, she'd forgotten to measure the windows for the plantation blinds she wanted.

But first she wanted to share her news and excitement.

"Is Mac—Mr. Blade available?" she asked when Mac's assistant answered the phone. "It's Darcy Wallace."

"Hello, Ms. Wallace. I'm sorry, Mr. Blade's in a meeting. May I take a message?"

"Oh…no, thank you. If you could just tell him I called."

She hung up, deflated as the image in her head of driving him out to the house and telling him it was hers faded. It would have to wait.

She buried herself in work instead, pushing herself toward the end of the book. If her luck held and the agent she'd contacted wanted to see more, she intended to be ready.

When two hours had passed and he hadn't returned her call, she resisted the urge to pick up the phone again. She made herself coffee, then spent another hour tweaking an earlier chapter.

When the phone rang, she pounced. "Hello."

"Darcy. Deb said you called earlier."

"Yes. I wondered if you could spare an hour. There's something I want to show you."

There was a hesitation, a humming kind of silence that had her shifting in her chair.

"I'm sorry. I'm tied up here." In his office Mac sat at his desk and realized the first step away was the hardest. "I'm not going to have any time for you."

"Oh. You must be busy."

"I am. If anything's wrong I can send the hotel manager or the concierge up."

"No, nothing's wrong." The cool formality of his voice made her shudder. "Nothing at all. It can wait. If you have time tomorrow…"

"I'll let you know."

"All right."

"I have to go. Talk to you later."

She stared at the phone in her hand for several seconds before replacing it slowly on the hook. He'd seemed so distant, so different. Hadn't that been mild irritation in his voice, an underlying impatience?

No, she was imagining things. Finding her hands gripped tightly together, she swore at herself and separated them.

He was just busy, she told herself. She'd interrupted his work. People hated to be interrupted. It was her own sense of disappointment—which was foolish—that was making her overreact to a very natural incident.

He'd spent the whole of last evening with her, she remembered, had made wild, almost desperate love to her under the stars. No one could need a woman so much in the night then flick her off like a pesky gnat the next day.

Of course they could, she admitted and pressed her fingers to her eyes. It was naive, even stupid to pretend it couldn't and didn't happen.

But not with Mac. He was too kind, too honest.

And she loved him far, far too much.

He was just busy, she insisted. She'd taken up huge amounts of his time over the past two weeks. Naturally he would need to catch up, to concentrate on business, to take some breathing room.

She wasn't going to sulk about it. Darcy straightened her shoulders, tucked the chair back in place. She would concentrate on work herself, and take advantage of what was going to be a long, solitary evening.

She worked for another six hours, remembering to turn on the lights only when she realized she was working in the dark. She drained the pot of coffee and found herself stunned when she came to the end of her book.

Finished. Beginning, middle and end. It was all there now, she thought giddily, all inside this clever little machine and copied onto a small slim disc.

To celebrate she opened a bottle of champagne, though it was a bit of a struggle, and drank an entire glass. With reckless abandon she poured a second and took it to the desk with her to start refining the draft.

She put in twelve hours and went through half a bottle of the wine, which she counteracted with more coffee. It was hardly a wonder that when she finally tumbled into bed she was chased by odd and jumbled dreams.

She saw herself in the tower of her new house, alone. All alone and crowded there by mountains of paper and an enormous computer. Through the window she could see dozens of scenes flip by, like a fast-forward through a movie. Parties and people, children playing, couples embracing. The noise—laughter and music— was muffled by the glass that surrounded her.

When she pounded on it, no one heard her. No one saw her. No one cared.

She was in the casino, sitting at the blackjack table.

But she couldn't add up her cards, couldn't calculate the math. Didn't know what to do.

Hit or stand. Serena, elegant in a mannish tux, watched her impassively. *Hit or stand,* she repeated. *You have to make the choice, then deal with it.*

She doesn't know how to play. Mac stepped up beside her, gave her a brotherly pat on the head. *You don't know the rules, do you?*

But she did, she did. It was just that she couldn't seem to add the cards. There was so much at stake. Didn't they understand how much was at stake?

Never bet more than you can afford to lose, Mac told her with a cool smile. *The house always has the edge.*

Then she was alone again, stumbling along the arrow-straight road through the desert and the lights and colors of Vegas were trapped behind the rippling waves of heat, floating there. No matter how far she walked she couldn't get any closer.

Dust rose in a cloud as Mac drove up, his hair streaming in the wind. *You're going in the wrong direction.*

But she wasn't. She was going home.

He reached out, touched her cheek in an absent, avuncular gesture that made her cringe. *You don't belong here.*

"Yes, I do." Her own furious shout woke her. Sitting up in bed she was stunned by the raw and genuine extent of her anger. She seethed with it, forced herself to take deep, calming breaths.

The sun was bright on her face because she'd forgotten to draw the drapes the night before.

"No more bedtime champagne for you, Darcy," she muttered, rubbing her face as if to rub away the edges of the dreams.

Noting it was already nine, she gave in to impulse and grabbed the phone. Serena answered on the second ring.

"It's Darcy. I hope I'm not calling too early."

"No. Justin and I are just having our first cup of coffee."

"Are you busy today?"

"I don't have to be. What did you have in mind?"

Darcy stood back, nervously twisting her fingers as Serena walked through the first floor of the house.

"I know this might seem sudden," Darcy began. "It's the only one I looked at. But I had a picture in my head of what I wanted, and this…this was even better than that."

"It's…" Serena turned a last circle, then smiled. "Beautiful. It suits you so well. I think you've made a perfect choice."

"Really? Really?" Swamped with joy, Darcy steepled her hands at her mouth. "I was afraid you'd think I was crazy."

"There's nothing crazy about wanting a home of your own, or investing in excellent property."

"Oh, I wanted to show someone so badly. I raced back yesterday as soon as I'd signed the contract. I wanted to show Mac, but he was busy, and well…"

She moved her shoulders and stepped away before she could see Serena's troubled frown. As far as Serena knew, her son hadn't been any busier the day before than normal.

"You told him you bought a house, but he didn't have time to come out and take a look?"

"No, I just told him there was something I wanted

him to see. I guess it's silly, but I wanted him to see it first. Please don't tell him about it."

"No, I won't. Darcy, why did you decide to buy a house here, in Vegas?"

"That." Her response was instant as she walked over to the doorway to gaze out at the desert. "It pulls at me. For some people it's water, for some it's mountains, or it's big, bustling cities. For me it's the desert. I had no idea until I got here, and then I knew."

Glowing with pleasure, she turned back. "And I love the Strip, the fantasy of it, the magic and the snap in the air that says anything can happen. Everything does happen. Everybody needs a place, don't you think, that makes them believe they could accomplish something there? Even if it's nothing more than being happy."

"Yes, I do think that, and I'm glad you found it." Still she crossed the room, brushed a hand over Darcy's hair. "But it has to do with Mac, too, doesn't it?" When Darcy didn't answer, Serena smiled softly. "Darling. I can see how you feel about him."

"I can't help being in love with him."

"Of course, you can't. Why should you? But is the house for him, Darcy?"

"It could be," she murmured. "But it's for me first. It has to be. I need a home. I need a place. That's what I'm doing here. I know I can't expect him to feel about me the way I do about him. But I'm willing to gamble. If I lose, at least I'll know I played the game. No more watching from behind the window," she murmured.

"My money's on you."

Darcy's grin flashed like sunlight. "I ought to tell you that I've fallen in love with Mac's family, too."

"Oh, baby." Serena wrapped her close, rubbing

cheeks, and reminded herself she hadn't raised any id-
iots. Mac would come to his senses soon. "Show me
the rest of the house."

"Yes, and I was hoping you could go with me to look
at furniture."

"I thought you'd never ask."

Darcy was glad to be busy, to have so many details
juggling for space in her mind. Colors, fabrics, lamps.
Should she convert the smallest bedroom into a library
or would the downstairs den suit that purpose best?

Did she want ficus trees flanking the doorway on
the main level, or palms?

Every decision was monumentally important to her,
and a giddy delight.

Though she yearned to share them all with Mac,
they'd had no time alone together for two days.

He was putting all his efforts into keeping his mind
occupied and off her. Time, he'd decided, and space,
were what both of them needed to ease back far enough
and analyze their relationship.

He missed her miserably.

Freedom was undoubtedly what she needed, he told
himself. He paced his office, giving up on the idea of
work. She hadn't called him again, and from the information he'd discreetly drawn from the staff, she'd been
spending nearly as much time out of the hotel as in it.

Flexing those fairy wings, he imagined.

He hadn't let her do that, not really. He'd carried her
along, deluding himself initially that he was helping
her, then justifying the rest because he'd wanted her.

And still wanted her.

She'd come into his life lost and wounded and desperate for affection. He'd taken advantage of that. It hardly mattered what his motives were, the results were the same.

He imagined she believed herself in love with him. The idea had crossed his mind more than once to take advantage of that as well. To keep her for himself. To see that she went on believing it as long as possible.

After all, she had no experience. No man had touched her before he had touched her. She'd tumbled from a sheltered existence into a dazzling fantasy world. He could sweep her along in that world, keep her dazzled. And his.

It would be easy. And unforgivable.

He cared far too much to trap her, to clip those wings and watch the innocence tarnish. Her life was just beginning, he reminded himself. And his was already set.

Then she burst into his office, her eyes huge, her cheeks wax pale. "I'm sorry. I'm sorry, I know you're busy. I know I shouldn't disturb you, but—but—"

"What is it? Are you hurt?" He had his hands on her in one thumping heartbeat.

"No, no." She shook her head frantically, clutched at his shirt. "I'm okay. No, I'm not okay. I don't know what I am. I sold my book. I sold my book. Sold it. Oh, God, I'm dizzy."

"Sold it? Take slow breaths, come on, slow and deep. That's it. I thought the book wasn't finished."

"The other one. The one—last year. She said the new one, too. Both of them." Giving up, she dropped her forehead to his chest. "I need a minute. I can't think straight." Then she jerked her head up again, laughing wildly. "It's like sex. Maybe I should have a cigarette."

"Have a seat instead."

"No, I can't sit down. I'd bounce right off the chair. They bought the book, no, the books. Two-book contract. Can you imagine? I beat the odds. Again."

"Who bought the book, Darcy? And how?"

"Oh, okay." She gulped in another breath. "A few days ago I got a call from an editor in New York. Eminence Publishing. She'd seen me on the news, and she asked me to send her some of my work."

"A few days ago?" The stab of disappointment was sharp and sudden. "You never mentioned it."

"I wanted to wait until I had an answer. Boy, have I got one now." She pressed her fingers to her eyes as tears swam close. "I'm not going to cry, not yet. I picked an agent off my list. I knew the publisher only wanted to see my work because of the publicity, but there was a chance they'd like it. So I hired an agent."

"Over the phone."

"Yes." The obvious disapproval in his tone made her sigh. "I know it was risky, but I didn't want to wait. The agent called this morning and said they'd made an offer, a very decent offer. Then she advised me to turn it down."

As if that part were just sinking in, Darcy pressed a hand to her stomach. "I couldn't believe it. I had a chance like this, what I've wanted all my life, and she said to say no."

"Why?"

"That's what I asked her. She said…" Darcy closed her eyes, reliving the moment. "She said I had a strong talent, that I told a powerful story, and they were going to have to pay more for it. If they balked, she told me she would take the book to auction. She believed in me. So

I took the chance. Ten minutes ago, they bought them both. Now I think I'll sit down."

She all but slid into a chair.

"I'm so happy for you, Darcy." He crouched in front of her. "So proud of you."

"All my life I wanted this. No one ever believed in me." She let the tears come now. "'Be sensible, Darcy. Keep your feet on the ground.' And I always was. I always did because I never thought I was good enough for more."

"You're good enough for anything," he murmured. "More than good enough."

She shook her head. "I always wanted to be. When I was in school, I worked so hard. Both my parents were teachers, and I knew how important it was to them. But no matter how much I put into it, I brought home B's instead of A's. They'd look at my report card, and there'd be this silent little sigh. They'd tell me I'd done well, but I could do better if I just worked harder. I couldn't do better. Just couldn't. It was the best I could do, but it was never good enough."

"They were wrong."

"They didn't mean to be so critical. They just didn't understand." Wanting the anchor, she held tight to his hands. "I used to show them the stories I'd write, just once wanting them to be impressed, enthusiastic. It just wasn't in them, so I stopped showing them. And I stopped looking for their approval, at least outwardly."

She sighed, wiped at her face with her fingers. "I never sent off the first book. Couldn't find the courage to. I suppose inside I was always hoping, waiting for someone to tell me I was good enough. Now I've done it, and someone has."

"Here." He pulled a handkerchief out of his pocket and pressed it into her hands.

"I'm not sad." She sniffled, mopped at her face. "There's just so much going on inside me. So many things have been happening. I had to tell you."

"I'm glad you did. News like this can't wait." He framed her face in his hands, and after a brief internal struggle, pressed his lips to her forehead rather than her mouth. "We'll have to celebrate." He let his hands linger on her face a moment, then dropped them and rose. "We'll get together for drinks and you can tell me your plans."

"Plans?"

"You'll want to fly into New York for a few days, I imagine. Meet your publisher, your agent."

"Yes, maybe next week."

So soon, he thought and suffered as he looked down at her tear-streaked face and made the break. "You'll be missed around here," he said lightly. "I hope you'll keep in touch, let us know where you settle."

"Settle. But... I'm coming back here."

"Here?" He lifted a brow, then smiled. "Darcy, as delighted as we've been to have you, you can't keep living in a high roller's suite." He laughed a little and sat on the edge of his desk. "A high roller, you're not. You're more than welcome to stay until you finalize your travel plans."

He was running a business, she thought frantically. She'd been taking advantage of his generosity, occupying an expensive suite for two weeks. "I hadn't thought. I'm sorry. I'll book another room when I get back until—"

"Darcy, there's no reason for you to come back here."

"Of course there is." Her heart began to flutter hard in her throat. "I live here."

"The Comanche's not your home. It's mine." He wasn't smiling now, and his eyes had gone cool and hard. It was the only way he could face the stunned hurt on her face. "It's time for you to start your own life, and you can't do that here. You've accomplished something really extraordinary. Now enjoy it."

"You don't want me anymore. You're not just kicking me out of your hotel. You're kicking me out of your life."

"No one's kicking you out of anything."

"No?" She managed a half laugh and balled the handkerchief in her fist. "How stupid do you think I am? You've been avoiding me for days. You've barely touched me since I came in the room. Now you're giving me a little pat on the head and telling me to run along and have a nice life."

"I do want you to have a nice life," he began.

"As long as it's somewhere else," she retorted. "Well, that's too bad, because I'm having my life here. I bought a house."

He'd prepared himself for a miserable scene, for tears, for recriminations. But he was stunned speechless. "What? You bought what?"

"I bought a house."

"Have you lost your mind? A house? Here? What were you thinking of?"

"Myself. It's a new concept for me and I like it."

"You don't buy a damn house the way you do a new dress."

"I'm not the bubble-brain you apparently think I am. I know how to buy a house, and I've done it."

"You have no business buying a house in Vegas."

"Oh really?" Her emotions were careering so fast she didn't know how her words could keep pace. "Do you own the entire city and its environs now? Well, I seem to have found the one little spot you don't have control over. I like it here, and I'm staying."

"Life is not an endless cruise down the Strip."

"And Vegas is not only the Strip. It's the fastest growing city in the country, and one of the most livable. It has an excellent school system, job opportunities abound and the housing is very affordable. Water's a problem, and that's an issue that's going to have to be seriously addressed in the near future. However, the crime rate is markedly low in comparison with other major cities and the area's continuing ability to reinvent itself gives it high marks for potential into the next century."

She paused, her eyes glittering when he said nothing. "I'm a writer. I was a librarian. I damn well know how to research."

"Did your research mention how many pawnshops are in Vegas per square mile? Did it touch on prostitution, corruption, money laundering, gambling addictions?"

"Actually, it did," she said evenly now. "Sin exists. It may shock you to know I was aware of it before I came here."

"You simply haven't thought this through."

"You're wrong. Absolutely wrong. I didn't buy this house blind, and I didn't buy it so I could keep falling at your feet. I bought it for me," she said fiercely. "Because I found something I always wanted and never expected to have. But don't worry, Vegas is big enough so that I won't get in your way."

"Wait a minute. Damn it," he muttered, and put a

hand on her shoulder to turn her. But she spun around, lifting both hands with a look in her eye that warned him to keep his distance.

"Don't. I don't need placating, and I don't intend to cause a scene. I'm grateful to you, and I don't want to forget that. I fully intend to have a relationship with your parents, your family and don't want to put them, or you, in a position that makes that difficult. But you hurt me," she said quietly. "And you didn't have to."

She walked to the door, shut it firmly behind her.

Chapter 12

"So we agree to forgive two million of Harisuki and Tanaka's baccarat losses." Justin lounged in the wide leather chair, pretending he didn't notice his son's in-attention. "That puts them into the casino for ten and twelve million respectively. We comp the rooms, the meals, the bar bills and cover their wives' spending spree in the boutique. They'll be back," he said, drawing idly on his cigar. "And they'll drop the next several million right here instead of across the street. You arranged for the limo for them tomorrow?" He waited a beat. "Mac?"

"What? Yes. It's taken care of."

"Good. Now that we've finished all that up, you can tell me what's on your mind."

"Nothing in particular. Do you want a beer?"

Justin indicated assent with a wave of his hand. "We

always had to pry problems out of you. Your determination to handle everything yourself is admirable, but it's annoying." He smiled cheerfully at his son and accepted the cold brown bottle. "However, in this case, prying isn't necessary—trouble with Darcy."

"No. Yes. No," Mac repeated, and blew out a breath. "She sold her book. Actually she sold two books."

"That's wonderful. She must be thrilled. Why aren't you?"

"I am. I'm happy for her. It's what she's always wanted. I don't think I realized how much she wanted it. This will give her a whole new direction."

"Is that what's worrying you? She won't need you anymore?"

"No. The whole issue is for her to move ahead with her life. This was just some breathing space for her."

"Was it? Mac, are you in love with her?"

"That's not the point."

"It's the only point that counts."

"I'm wrong for her. This place is wrong for her." Restless, he stalked to the window, staring out at the carnival of neon and colored fountains. "Once she focuses she'll see that."

"Why are you wrong for her? It seemed to me you complemented each other very well."

"I run a casino. My peak hours are when sensible people are tucked into their beds." He jammed his hands into his pockets. "She's lived a sheltered life. More, a repressed one where she's been held back, held down. She's just starting to realize what she can do and be and have. I don't have any right to interfere with that."

"You're making this black-and-white, sinner and saint. I don't think either of you qualify. You're a businessman, and a good one. She's an interesting, refreshingly enthusiastic young woman."

"Who walked in here a few weeks ago," Mac reminded him. "A few weeks ago and at a turning point in her life. She can't possibly know what her feelings are."

"You underestimate her. But regardless, aren't your own feelings important?"

"I've already let my feelings take over more than once. She walked in here untouched." Mac turned back, his eyes swirling and dark. "I changed that. I should have kept my hands off her, but I didn't. I couldn't."

"Now you're going to punish yourself for being human," Justin concluded. "You're going to deny yourself a relationship that makes you happy, and your reasoning is she'll be better off."

"She's dazzled," Mac insisted, wondering why saying it all out loud this way made it sound so wrong and so foolish. "And only seeing what she wants to see. She bought a house, for God's sake."

"Yes, I know."

"And—you know." Mac stared at his father.

"She took your mother to see it the day after she signed the contract. I went to see it myself. It's a fine piece of property, an intriguing, attractive home."

"It's ludicrous to buy a house in a place you've only been for a few weeks, and when you've spent most of that time in a hotel casino. She's living in a fantasy land."

"No, she's not. She knows exactly what she wants, and I'm surprised you don't realize that. If you don't want her, that's a different matter."

"I can't stop wanting her." It was like an ache that couldn't be eased. "I was sure I could."

"Wanting's easy. The first time I saw your mother I wanted her. That was as natural as breathing. But loving her terrified me. Sometimes it still does."

Surprised, Mac lowered to a chair. "You make that part look easy, too. You always have. You're so... matched," he decided.

"Is that the problem?" Justin leaned over, put his hand over Mac's.

"No, not a problem. It's just that marriages work in our family. The odds are against it, but they work for us." He studied the gold band on his father's finger. Thirty years, he thought, and it still fit. That was a kind of miracle. "I figure they work because we're careful to find a mate—in the literal sense of the word. A match."

"You're seeing your mother and I as a set, something that came that way. It's not true. We were a half-breed ex-con who'd gotten lucky and the privileged daughter of wealthy, indulgent parents. Long odds, Mac, on a pair like that."

"But you were heading in the same direction."

Justin leaned back again, eyes sharp. "The hell we were. What we did was beat a new path, and there were plenty of bumps along the way."

"You're telling me I've made a mistake," Mac murmured. "And maybe you're right." He ran his hand over his face. "I'm not sure anymore."

"You want guarantees? There aren't any. Loving a woman's the riskiest game in town. You either put up your stake, or you back away from the table. But if you back away, you never win. Is she the woman you want?"

"Yes."

"I'll ask you again. Are you in love with her?"

"Yes." Admitting it intensified the ache. "And yes, it's terrifying."

Sympathizing, Justin smiled. "What do you want to do about it?"

"I want her back." He let out a long breath. "I've got to get her back."

"How bad have you screwed it up?"

"Pretty bad." It made him slightly ill to realize just how poorly he'd played his hand. "I all but shoved her out the door."

"It may take some fast talk to get her to open her side of that door again."

"So I'll talk fast." Misery vanished in a spurt of reckless energy. It was a new hand, he thought, fresh cards. And everything he had was going into the pot. "I'd better go down and try to work this out with her. She must be sitting in her room, miserable, when she should be out celebrating."

"I think you lose on that one," Justin murmured, studying the screens.

"There's a pair of star-shaped diamond earrings in the jewelry store downstairs." Mac checked his pocket to make certain he had his passkey for the elevator. Just in case. "She should have something special to celebrate selling her book."

He was suddenly nervous, a sensation he wasn't accustomed to. "Do you think the earrings and flowers are overkill?"

Justin ran his tongue around his teeth. "I don't think you can ever overkill in a situation like this. But...you're not going to find Darcy in her room."

"Hmm?"

"You better take a look. Screen three, second craps table from the left."

Anxious to be on his way, Mac glanced absently at the screen. Then looked again. His wounded fairy was decked out in that little killer of a red dress with spiked heels to match, and was blowing on a pair of dice.

"What the hell is she doing?"

"Going for an eight. That's her point. Five and a three," he said, and grinned when he heard his son slam the door on his way out. "The lady wins."

"Come on, baby. Come on, doll. Bring it home."

The man cheering beside Darcy was old enough to be her father, so she didn't mind the little pat he gave her butt. She took it as a good-luck wish.

She shook the dice in her hand, leaned over the long table and let them fly. Cheers roared out, and money and chips changed hands too quickly for her to follow.

"Seven! All right." She pumped a fist in the air. After raking in her pile of chips, she began recklessly distributing them again. "This on the point, and this, um, behind. Five's my point."

"Roll 'em, blondie." The man on the other side of her plunked a hundred-dollar bill on the table. "You're hot."

"Damn right I am." She sent the dice tumbling, squinting through the smoke, and howled with triumph when the ivories came up three and two.

"I don't know why I thought this game was so hard." She grinned then gulped from the fresh glass of champagne someone handed her. "Hold this, will you?" She shoved the glass at the butt-patter and picked up the dice. "Let mine ride," she told the croupier. "God, I *love* saying that!" She tossed the dice, then danced on three-inch heels.

Mac had to elbow his way through a crowd gathered four deep. His first sight of her was a tight little butt molded into clinging red. He caught her elbow just after her toss, and his words were swallowed by the roar of players and onlookers.

"What the hell do you think you're doing?"

She tossed back her head, drunk on victory. "I'm kicking your ass. Back up and give me room so I can kick it some more."

He snagged her wrist as she leaned over to scoop up the dice. "Cash in."

"The hell I will. I'm smoking."

"Come on, pal, let the lady roll."

Mac merely turned his head and iced down the eager player on the corner of the table with a look. "Cash her in," he ordered the croupier, then dragged Darcy through the bitter complaints of the crowd.

"You can't make me stop playing when I'm on a streak."

"You're wrong. This is my place, and I can make anybody stop playing anytime. The house has the edge."

"Fine." She jerked her arm free. "I'll take my business elsewhere, and I'm let them know the management at The Comanche can't hold up under a run of honest luck."

"Darcy, come upstairs. We need to talk."

"Don't tell me what I need to do." She pulled away again sharply, almost pleased when heads turned and attention zeroed in on them. "I told you I wouldn't cause a scene, but I will if you push me. You can kick me out of your casino, and you can kick me out of your hotel, but you can't tell me what I need to do."

"I'm asking you," he said with what he considered amazing patience, "to come with me so we can discuss this privately."

"And I'm telling you, I'm not interested."

"Okay, the hard way." He scooped her up and over his shoulder. He'd taken ten strides before she broke through the shock and began to struggle.

"Let go of me. You can't treat me this way."

"You made your choice," he said grimly, and ignored the stunned looks of guests and staff as he carted her to the elevator.

"I don't want to talk to you. I'm already packed. I'm leaving in the morning. Just let me go."

"The hell I will." He keyed in her floor, then dumped her back on her feet. "You've got a stubborn streak in you, and I'm—" He broke off when her fist punched into his stomach. It didn't do much more than bounce off and cause him to lift a coolly amused brow.

"We'll have to work on that."

Conceding that she was outgunned, Darcy folded her arms. When the doors opened into her suite, she sailed out. "This may be your place, but this is my room until morning, and I don't want you in it."

"We need to straighten things out."

"Things are perfectly straight, thank you just the same."

"Darcy, you don't understand."

She shoved away the hands he'd laid on her shoulders. "That's just it, isn't it? You don't think I understand anything. You think I'm a fluff-brained idiot who doesn't know how to take care of herself."

"I don't think you're an idiot."

"But fluff-brained just the same," she countered. "Well, I'm sharp enough to know that you got tired of me and your solution was to brush me off like an irritating child."

"Tired of you?" At the end of his rope, he dragged his hands through his hair. "I know I made a mess of it. Let me explain."

"There's nothing to explain. You don't want me. Fine. I'm not going to jump off a roof over it." She jerked a shoulder and turned away. "I'm young, I'm rich, I have my career to think of. And you're not the only man in the world."

"Just a damn minute."

"You were the first." She shot a searing look over her shoulder. "That doesn't mean you have to be the last."

Which had been one of his points. Exactly one of the reasons he'd been so determined to step away. But hearing it from her, seeing that hot, female look in her eyes had a rage bubbling up in him so violently it hazed his vision.

"Watch your step, Darcy."

"I've watched it all my life, and I'm finished. I like leaping before I look. And so far I'm landing on my feet. If and when I fall it'll be my problem and no one else's."

Panic skidded up his spine because he could see she meant it. She could do it, would do it. "You know damn well you're in love with me."

Her heart toppled and cracked. "Because I slept with you? Please."

However derisive her words, her fingers had linked together and twisted. It was just enough of a tell for him to call her bluff. "You wouldn't have slept with me if you hadn't been in love with me. If I held you right now. If I put my mouth on yours, you'd tell me without saying a word."

Every defense crumbled. "You knew, and you used it."

"Maybe I did. I've had a hard time with that, and made more mistakes because I couldn't get past it."

"Are you guilty or angry, Mac?" Wearily she turned away again. "You broke my heart. I'd have given it to you on a platter. It wasn't even enough for you not to want it, you ignored it."

"I told myself I was doing it for you."

"For me." A laugh choked out. "Well, that was considerate of you."

"Darcy." He reached out, but her shoulders rounded as she cringed away. An ache sliced through him as he dropped his hands again. "I won't touch you, but at least look at me."

"What do you want from me? Do you want me to say it's all right? That I understand. I won't hold it against you. It's not all right." Her breath hitched in a sob that was brutal to control. "I don't understand, and I'm trying not to hold it against you. You weren't obligated to feel what I felt—that was my gamble. But in the end you could have been kind."

"If I'd trusted my feelings, we wouldn't be having this conversation. And I don't want to have it here." When a hunch came this sudden and strong, he knew to ride it out. "I want to see your house."

"What?"

"I'd like very much to see your house. Now."

"Now?" She passed a hand over her eyes. "It's late. I'm tired. I don't have the keys."

"What's the name of the Realtor? Do you have a card?"

"Yes, on the desk. But—"

"Good."

To her confusion he walked to the phone, dialed the number and in less than two minutes was on a first-name basis with Marion Baines and jotting down her address.

"She'll give us the keys," Mac told Darcy when he hung up. "Shouldn't take more than twenty minutes to get to her place."

"You're a powerful man," she said dryly. "What's the point of this?"

"Take a chance." He smiled in challenge. "Leap before you look. Do you want a jacket?"

She refused one, and would have refused to go with him if she hadn't wanted one scrap of pride to take with her. They didn't speak. She thought that was best. Perhaps, somehow, this quiet drive would settle the nerves and let them part—if not as friends—with some respect for each other.

He seemed to know his way. He picked up the keys without incident, then easily wove toward the outskirts where her house stood, a soft silhouette under the slowly waning moon.

"Trust you," he murmured, scanning the shape. "You found a castle, after all."

It nearly made her smile. "That's what I thought when I saw it. That's how I knew it was mine."

"Ask me in."

"You've got the keys," she noted, and opened her door.

He waited until she'd rounded the hood, then held the keys out to her. "Ask me in, Darcy."

She fought the urge to snatch the keys from him, telling herself he was trying to do what he could to make the situation less miserable. She accepted the keys and started up the walk.

"I've never been in it at night. There are floodlights in both the house and yard."

He thought about her out there, alone, at night. "Is there a security system?"

"Yes, I have the code." She unlocked the door and turned directly to a small box beside it. She disengaged the alarm, then switched on the lights.

He said nothing, but walked through much as his mother had done. But in this case, the silence unnerved her. "I've been looking at furniture, found many pieces that I like."

"It's a lot of space."

"I've discovered I like a lot of space."

She'd put plants on the decks, he imagined. Cheerful pots full of lush green and delicate blossoms she'd baby. She'd want soft colors inside, cool and soothing, with the occasional flash to shake things up.

It amazed him how clearly he could imagine it, and how easy it was to know her after so little time.

He switched on the outside lights and watched them flood the blue water of the pool and the rippling sea of the desert beyond.

It was stunning, powerful, and in its own way calm as the night sky. Maybe he'd lost sight of this, he mused, this other side of the world from where he'd chosen to live. And because of that, had refused to accept her place there.

"This is what you want."

"Yes. This is what I want."

"The tower. You'll write there."

She ached a little, because he would know. "Yes."

"We never celebrated." He turned back. She was standing in the center of the empty room, her hands linked, her eyes shadowed. "My fault. I need you to know, Darcy, how happy I am for you, and how sorry I am I spoiled the moment."

Guilt, she thought. He was too kind a man not to feel it. "It doesn't matter."

"It matters," he corrected. "A great deal. I'd like to try to explain. I'd like you to try to see it from my viewpoint. You fell into my arms, literally, the first time I saw you. You were alone, lonely, a little desperate, completely vulnerable and impossibly appealing. I wanted you too much, too quickly. I'm good at resisting temptation, that's why I'm good at what I do. But I couldn't resist you."

"You didn't seduce me, you didn't force me. It was a mutual attraction."

"But it wasn't an even hand." He stepped toward her, relieved when she didn't back away. "I took you because I wanted you, because I could, because I needed to, knowing you'd want and need more. Deserved more. But I didn't intend to give it to you."

"It was a chance I took. You told me flat out, before we were lovers, you didn't have marriage on your mind. I didn't fall in bed with you blindly."

He paused a moment, surprised. "You gambled on me changing my mind?"

"The odds might have been long that you'd fall in love with me, but they weren't infinitesimal." The edge had come back into her voice. "Your grandfather thinks I'm perfect for you. So does your mother."

He very nearly choked. "You talked to my mother?"

"I love your mother," she said passionately. "And I have a perfect right to have someone to talk to."

"I didn't mean it that way. I'm getting off the track," he said with a sigh. "The way I saw it, you needed a little time to settle, to explore the possibilities, to have some fun and indulge yourself. So you'd gamble a little, spend some money, take a few rides. Discover sex."

"So you were what, tutoring me? How much more insulting can you possibly be?"

"I'm not trying to insult you. I'm trying to tell you what I believed, and that I was wrong."

"You haven't begun to say you were wrong yet. Maybe you should get started."

"You've got a nasty streak." He dipped his hands into his pockets. "I never noticed it before."

"I've been saving it up. So the little country mouse comes to the big city and the clever city mouse lets her taste a bit of sin, then shows her the door before she damns her soul to perdition? Is that close enough?"

"A long, wide nasty streak. You were alone and afraid and over your head."

"And you tossed me a float."

"Shut up." Patience straining, he gripped her arms. "Nobody ever gave you a choice. You said so yourself. No one gave you a chance. No one let you bloom. God, Darcy, you've done nothing but bloom since you got here, since you had that chance, that choice. How was I supposed to take that choice away from you? You've never been anywhere else. You've never been with anyone else. I wasn't going to watch you living in a hotel, wandering through a casino, locking yourself to me because you didn't know any better."

"And that's your way of giving me a choice. Funny, that's just the kind of choice people have been giving me all my life."

"I know. I'm sorry."

"So am I." She lifted her hands to his arms and pushed until he released her. "Are we finished?"

"No. Not yet."

"Oh, what's the point of this?" She strode away from him, her sassy shoes clicking on the tiles. "Why do you want a tour of the place now? Do we pretend we're pals? What are we doing here?"

"I wanted to finish this here because it's not my place. It's yours." He waited until she turned back. "The house always has the advantage."

"I don't know what you're talking about."

"My father told me something tonight I'd never considered. He said wanting is easy, but loving is terrifying." His eyes stayed locked on hers. "You terrify me, Darcy, right down to the bone." He watched as she wrapped her arms tight around her body. "When I look at you, I'm scared senseless."

"Don't do this. It's not fair."

"I tried to be fair, and all I did was hurt you, and make myself miserable. I'm playing a new hand now, and when the house has the edge, I can't afford to play fair. There's no point in backing away," he said when she did just that. "I'll only keep coming after you. You brought this on yourself. I'd have let you go."

He caught her, ran his hands from her shoulders to her wrists then back again. "You're trembling. Scared?" He touched his lips to the corner of hers. "That must mean you still love me."

Her breath was hot in her chest, tangling in her throat. "I won't have you feeling sorry for me. I don't—"

The kiss was sudden and violent. Her heart slammed once, twice, hard against her ribs then began a wild and unsteady beat.

"Is that what you think this is? This feels like pity to you?" He took her mouth again, diving deep. "Damn, this dress drives me crazy. I could have killed every man at that table tonight just for looking at you. I'll have to buy you a dozen more like it."

"You're not making sense. I don't know what you're saying."

"I love you."

This time her heart took one high, joyful leap. "You do?"

"I love everything about you." He lifted her hands, pressed them to his lips, then gently untangled her fingers. "And I'm asking you to buck the odds and give me another chance."

Her lips trembled, then curved. "I'm a big believer in another chance."

"I was counting on it." This time he kissed her gently, easing her into his arms. "But you're going to have to let me move in here."

"Here?" She was floating, drifting, close to dreaming. "You want to live here?"

"Well, I figure this is where you'll want to raise the kids."

"Kids?" Her dazzled eyes flew open again.

"You want kids, don't you?" He smiled when her head bobbed up and down. "I like big families—and coming from one, I'm a traditionalist. If we're going to make kids together, you have to marry me."

"Mac." It was all she could say, just his name. Nothing else would get through.

"Willing to risk it, Darcy?" He lifted her hands again, pressed them to his heart. "Want to take a gamble on us?"

His heart beat under her hands, and was no steadier than hers. "It so happens," she said with a brilliant smile, "I'm on a hot streak."

He laughed, scooped her off her feet in one wide, dizzying circle. "So I've heard."

* * * * *

THE PERFECT NEIGHBOR

To all my cyberpals
who've touched my heart with so many smiles.

Chapter 1

"So...have you talked to him yet?"

"Hmm?" Cybil Campbell continued to work at her drawing board, diligently sectioning off the paper with the skill of long habit. "Who am I talking to?"

There was a long and gusty sigh—one that had Cybil fighting to keep her lips from twitching. She knew her first-floor neighbor Jody Myers well—and understood exactly what *him* she was referring to.

"The gorgeous Mr. Mysterious in 3B, Cyb. Come on, he moved in a week ago and hasn't said a word to anyone. But you're right across the hall. We need some details here."

"I've been pretty busy." Cybil flicked a glance up, watching Jody, with her expressive brown eyes and mop of dusky-blond hair, energetically pace around the studio. "Hardly noticed him."

Jody's first response was a snort. "Get real. You notice everything."

Jody wandered to the drawing board, hung over Cybil's shoulder, then wrinkled her nose. Nothing much interesting about a bunch of blue lines. She liked it better when Cybil started sketching in the sections.

"He doesn't even have a name on the mailbox yet. And nobody ever sees him leave the building during the day. Not even Mrs. Wolinsky, and nobody gets by her."

"Maybe he's a vampire."

"Wow." Intrigued with the idea, Jody pursed her pretty lips. "Would that be cool or what?"

"Too cool," Cybil agreed, and continued to prep her drawing, as Jody danced around the studio and chattered like a magpie.

It never bothered Cybil to have company while she worked. The fact was, she enjoyed it. She'd never been one for isolation and quiet. It was the reason she was happy living in New York, happy to be settled into a small building with a handful of unapologetically nosy neighbors.

Such things not only satisfied her on a personal level, they were grist for her professional mill.

And of all the occupants of the old, converted warehouse, Jody Myers was Cybil's favorite. Three years earlier when Cybil had moved in, Jody had been an energetic newlywed who fervently believed that everyone should be as blissfully happy as she herself was.

Meaning, Cybil mused, married.

Now the mother of the seriously adorable eight-month-old Charlie, Jody was only more committed to her cause. And Cybil knew she herself was Jody's primary objective.

"Haven't you even run into him in the hall?" Jody wanted to know.

"Not yet." Idly, Cybil picked up a pencil, tapped it against her full-to-pouty bottom lip. Her long-lidded eyes were the green of a clear sea at twilight, and might have been exotic or sultry if they weren't almost always shimmering with humor.

"Actually, Mrs. Wolinsky's losing her touch. I have seen him leave the building during the day—which rules out vampire status."

"You have?" Instantly caught, Jody dragged a rolling stool over to the drawing board. "When? Where? How?"

"When—dawn. Where? Heading east on Grand. How? Insomnia." Getting into the spirit, Cybil swiveled on her stool. Her eyes danced with amusement. "Woke up early, and I kept thinking about the brownies left over from the party the other night."

"Atomic brownies," Jody agreed.

"Yeah, so I couldn't get back to sleep until I ate one. Since I was up anyhow, I came in here to work awhile and ended up just standing at the window. I saw him go out. You can't miss him. He must be six-four. And those shoulders…"

Both women rolled their eyes in appreciation.

"Anyway, he was carrying a gym bag and wearing black jeans and a black sweatshirt, so my deduction was he was heading to the gym to work out. You don't get those shoulders by lying around eating chips and drinking beer all day."

"Aha!" Jody speared a finger in the air. "You *are* interested."

"I'm not dead, Jody. The man is dangerously gorgeous, and you add that air of mystery along with a tight butt…" Her hands, rarely still, spread wide. "What's a girl to do but wonder?"

"Why wonder? Why don't you go knock on his door, take him some cookies or something. Welcome him to the neighborhood. Then you can find out what he does in there all day, if he's single, what he does for a living. If he's single. What—" She broke off, head lifting in alert. "That's Charlie waking up."

"I didn't hear a thing." Cybil turned her head, aiming an ear toward the doorway, listened, shrugged. "I swear, Jody, since you gave birth you have ears like a bat."

"I'm going to change him and take him for a walk. Want to come?"

"No, can't. I've got to work."

"I'll see you tonight, then. Dinner's at seven."

"Right." Cybil managed to smile as Jody dashed off to retrieve Charlie from the bedroom where she'd put him down for a nap.

Dinner at seven. With Jody's tedious and annoying cousin Frank. When, Cybil asked herself, was she going to develop a backbone and tell Jody to stop trying to fix her up?

Probably, she decided, about the same time she told Mrs. Wolinsky the same thing. And Mr. Peebles on the first floor, and her dry cleaner. What was this obsession with the people in her life to find her a man?

She was twenty-four, single and happy. Not that she didn't want a family one day. And maybe a nice house out in the burbs somewhere with a yard for the kids. And the dog. There'd have to be a dog. But that was for some time or other. She liked her life right now very much, thanks.

Resting her elbows on her drawing board, she

propped her chin on her fists and gave in enough to stare out the window and allow herself to daydream. Must be spring, she mused, that was making her feel so restless and full of nervous energy.

She reconsidered going for that walk with Jody and Charlie, after all, but then heard her friend call out a goodbye and slam the door behind her.

So much for that.

Work, she reminded herself, and swiveled back to begin sketching in the first section of her comic strip, "Friends and Neighbors."

She had a steady and clever hand for drawing and had come by it naturally. Her mother was a successful, internationally respected artist; her father, the reclusive genius behind the long-running "Macintosh" comic strip. Together, they had given her and her siblings a love of art, a sense of the ridiculous and a solid foundation.

Cybil had known, even when she'd left the security of their home in Maine, she'd be welcomed back if New York rejected her.

But it hadn't.

For over three years now her strip had grown in popularity. She was proud of it, proud of the simplicity, warmth and humor she was able to create with everyday characters in everyday situations. She didn't attempt to mimic her father's irony or his often sharp political satires. For her, it was life that made her laugh. Being stuck in line at the movies, finding the right pair of shoes, surviving yet another blind date.

While many saw her Emily as autobiographical, Cybil saw her as a marvelous well of ideas but never recognized the reflection. After all, Emily was a statuesque blonde who had miserable luck holding a job and worse luck with men.

Cybil herself was a brunette of average height with a successful career. As for men, well, they weren't enough of a priority for her to worry about luck one way or the other.

A scowl marred her expression, narrowing her light-green eyes as she caught herself tapping her pencil rather than using it. She just couldn't seem to concentrate. She scooped her fingers through her short cap of brandy-brown hair, pursed her softly sculpted mouth and shrugged. Maybe what she needed was a short break, a snack. Perhaps a little chocolate would get the juices flowing.

She pushed back, tucking her pencil behind her ear in an absentminded habit she'd been trying to break since childhood, left the sun-drenched studio and headed downstairs.

Her apartment was wonderfully open; aside from the studio space, that had been the main reason she'd snapped it up so quickly. A long service bar separated the kitchen from the living area, leaving the lower level all one area. Tall windows let in light and the street noises that had kept her awake and thrilled for weeks after her arrival in the city.

She moved well, another trait inherited from her mother. What her father called the Grandeau Grace. She had long limbs that had been suited to the ballet lessons she'd begged for as a child—then grown tired of. Barefoot, she padded into the kitchen, opened the refrigerator and considered.

She could whip something interesting up, she mused. She'd had cooking lessons, too—and hadn't become bored with them until she'd outdistanced her instructor in creativity.

Then she heard it and sighed. The music carried through the old walls, across the short hallway outside her door. Sad and sexy, she mused, the quiet sob of the alto sax. Mr. Mysterious in 3B didn't play every day, but she'd come to wish he would.

It always stirred her, those long liquid notes and the swirl of emotion behind them.

A struggling musician? she wondered. Hoping to find his break in New York. Brokenhearted, no doubt, she continued, weaving one of her scenarios for him as she began to take out ingredients. A woman behind it, of course. Some cold-blooded redhead who'd caught him under her spell, stripped his soul, then crushed his still-throbbing heart under her four-inch Italian heel.

A few days before, she'd invented a different lifestyle for him, one where he'd run away from his filthy rich and abusive family as a boy of sixteen. Had survived on the streets by playing on street corners in New Orleans—one of her favorite cities—then had worked his way north as that same vicious family—headed by an insane uncle—scoured the country for him.

She hadn't quite worked out why they were scouring, but it wasn't really important. He was on the run and comforted only by his music.

Or he was a government agent working undercover.

An international jewel thief, hiding from a government agent.

A serial killer trolling for his next victim.

She laughed at herself, then looked down at the ingredients she'd lined up without thinking. Whatever he was, she realized with another laugh, apparently it looked like she was making him those cookies.

His name was Preston McQuinn. He wouldn't have considered himself particularly mysterious. Just private. It was that ingrained need for privacy that had plopped him down in the heart of one of the world's busiest cities.

Temporarily, he mused, as he slipped his sax back into its case. Just temporarily. In another couple of months, the rehab would be completed on his house on Connecticut's rocky coast. Some called it his fortress, and that was fine with him. A man could be blissfully alone for weeks at a time in a fortress. And no one got in unless the gates were lifted.

He started back upstairs, leaving behind the nearly empty living room. He only used it to play—the acoustics were dandy—or to work out if he didn't feel like going to the gym a couple of blocks away.

The second floor was where he lived—temporarily, he thought again. And all he needed in this way station was a bed, a dresser, the right lighting and a desk sturdy enough to hold his laptop, monitor and the paperwork that they often generated.

He wouldn't have had a phone, but his agent had forced a cell phone on him and had pleaded with him to keep it on.

He did—unless he didn't feel like it.

Preston sat at the desk, pleased that the little turn with his sax had cleared out the cobwebs. Mandy, his agent, was busy chewing on her inch-long nails over the progress of his latest play. He could have told her to spare the enamel. It would be done when it was done, and not a minute before.

The trouble with success, he thought, was that it became its own entity. Once you did something people liked, they wanted you to do it again—only faster and bigger. Preston didn't give a damn about what people wanted. They could break down the doors of the theater to see his next play, give him another Pulitzer, toss him another Tony and bring him money by the truckloads. Or they could stay away in droves, critically bomb the work and demand their money back.

It was the work that mattered. And it only had to matter to him.

Financially, he was secure, always had been. Mandy said that was part of his problem. Without the need or desire for money to keep him hungry, he was arrogant and aloof from his audience. Then again, she also said that was what made him a genius. Because he simply didn't give a damn.

He sat in the big room, a tall, muscular man with disordered hair the color of a well-fed mink's pelt. Eyes of cool blue scanned the words already typed. His mouth was firm and unsmiling, his face narrow, rawboned and carelessly handsome.

He tuned out the street sounds that seemed to batter against the windows day and night, and let himself slip back into the soul of the man he'd created inside the clever little computer. A man struggling desperately to survive his own desires.

The harsh sound of his buzzer made him swear as he felt himself sucked back into that empty room. He considered snarling and waiting it out, then weighed in human nature and decided the intruder would probably keep coming back until he dispatched them once and for all.

Probably the eagle-eyed old woman from the ground floor, Preston decided as he started down. She'd already tried to snag him twice when he'd headed out to the club in the evening. He was good at evading, but it was becoming a nuisance. Smarter to hit her face-on with a few rude remarks and let her huff away to gossip about him.

But when he checked the peephole, he didn't see the tidy woman with her bright bird's eyes, but a pretty brunette with hair short as a boy's and big green eyes.

From across the hall, he realized, and wondered what the hell she could want. He'd figured since she'd left him alone for nearly a week, she intended to keep right on doing so. Which made her, in his mind, the perfect neighbor.

Annoyed that she'd spoiled it, he opened the door, leaned against it. "Yeah?"

"Hi." Oh, yes, indeed, Cybil thought, he was even better when you got a good close-up look at the face. "I'm Cybil Campbell. 3A?" She offered a bright, friendly smile and gestured to her own door.

He only lifted an intriguingly winged eyebrow. "Yeah?"

A man of few words, she decided and continued to smile—though she wished his eyes would flicker away just long enough for her to crane her neck and see beyond him into the apartment. She couldn't very well try it when he was focused on her, without appearing to be prying. Which, of course, she wasn't. Really.

"I heard you playing a while ago. I work at home and sound travels."

If she was here to bitch about the noise, she was out of luck, Preston mused. He played when he felt like playing. He continued to study her coolly—the pert, slightly turned-up nose; the sensuously ripe mouth; the long narrow feet with sassily painted pink toes.

"I usually forget to turn the stereo on while I'm working," she went on cheerfully, making him notice a tiny dimple that winked off and on beside her mouth. "So it's nice to hear you play. Ralph and Sissy were into Vivaldi big-time. Which is fine, really, but monotonous when that's all you hear. They used to live in your place, Ralph and Sissy," she explained, waving a hand toward his apartment. "They moved to White Plains after Ralph had an affair with a clerk at Saks. Well, he didn't really have an affair, but he was thinking about it, and Sissy said it was move out of the city or she'd scalp him in a divorce. Mrs. Wolinsky gives them six months, but I don't know, I think they might make it. Anyway…"

She held out the pretty yellow plate with a small mountain of chocolate-chip cookies heaped on it, covered by clear pink plastic wrap. "I brought you some cookies."

He glanced down at them, giving her a very brief window of opportunity to sneak a peek around him and see his empty living room.

The poor guy couldn't even afford a couch, she thought. Then his unsmiling blue eyes flicked back to hers.

"Why?"

"Why what?"

"Why did you bring me cookies?"

"Oh, well, I was baking them. Sometimes I cook to clear out my head when I can't seem to concentrate on work. Most often it's baking that does it for me. And if I keep them all, I'll just eat them all and hate myself." The dimple kept fluttering. "Don't you like cookies?"

"I've got nothing against them."

"Well then, enjoy." She pushed them into his hands. "And welcome to the building. If you need anything I'm usually around." Again she gestured vaguely with pretty, slim-fingered hands. "And if you want to find out who's who around here, I can fill you in. I've lived here a few years now, and I know everybody."

"I won't." He stepped back and shut the door in her face.

Cybil stood where she was a moment, stunned speechless by the abrupt dismissal. She was fairly certain that she'd lived for twenty-four years without ever having had a door shut in her face, and now that she'd had the experience, she decided she didn't care for it.

She caught herself before she could pound on his door and demand her cookies back. She wouldn't sink that low, she told herself, turning sharply on her heel and marching back to her own door.

Now she knew the mysterious Mr. Mysterious was insanely attractive, built like a god and as rude as a cranky two-year-old who needed a swat on the butt and a nap. Well, that was fine, just fine. She could stay out of his way.

She didn't slam her door—figuring he'd hear it and smirk with that go-to-hell mouth of his. But when she was safely inside, she turned to the door and indulged in a juvenile exhibition of making faces, sticking out her tongue and wagging her fingers from her ears.

It made her feel marginally better.

But the bottom line was the man had her cookies,

her favorite dessert plate, her very rare animosity. And she still didn't know his name.

Preston didn't regret his actions. Not for a minute. He calculated his studied rudeness would keep his terminally pert neighbor with the turned-up nose and sexy pink toenails out of his hair during his stay across the hall. The last thing he needed was the local welcoming committee rolling up at his door, especially when it was led by a bubbly motormouth brunette with eyes like a fairy.

Damn it, in New York, people were supposed to ignore their neighbors. He was pretty sure it was a city ordinance, and if not, it should be.

Just his luck, he thought, that she was single—he had no doubt that if she'd had a husband she'd have poured out all his virtues and delights. That she worked at home and would therefore be easy to trip over whenever he headed out was just another black mark.

And that she made, hands-down, the best chocolate-chip cookies in the known universe was close to unforgivable.

He'd managed to ignore them while he worked. Preston McQuinn could ignore a nuclear holocaust if the words were pumping. But when he surfaced, he started to think about them lying in his kitchen on their chirpy yellow plate.

He thought about them while he showered, while he dressed, while he eased out the kinks brought on by hours sitting in one spot with posture his third-grade teacher, Sister Mary Joseph, had termed deplorable.

So when he went down for what he considered a well-earned beer, he eyed the plate on the counter. He'd popped the top, took a thoughtful drink. So what if he had a couple? he mused. Tossing them in the trash wasn't necessary—he'd given perky Cybil the heave-ho.

She was going to want her party plate back, he imagined. He might as well sample the wares before he dumped the plate outside her door.

So he ate one. Grunted in approval. Ate a second and blew out a breath of pure appreciation.

And when he'd consumed nearly two dozen, he cursed.

Like a damn drug, he thought, feeling slightly ill and definitely sluggish. He stared at the near-empty plate with a combination of self-disgust and greed. With what scraps of willpower he had left, he dumped the remaining cookies in a plastic bowl, then crossed the room to get his sax.

He was going to walk around the block a few times before he headed to the club.

When he opened the door he heard her stomping up the stairs. Wincing, he drew back, leaving his door open only a crack. He could hear that mile-a-minute voice of hers going, which had him lifting a brow when he saw she was alone.

"Never again," she muttered. "I don't care if she sticks bamboo shoots under my nails, holds a hot poker to my eye. I will never, ever, go through that torture again in this lifetime. That's it. Over, done."

She'd changed her clothes, Preston noted, and was wearing snug black pants with a tailored black blazer, offsetting them with a shirt the color of ripe strawberries and long dangles at her ears.

She kept talking to herself as she opened a purse the size of a postage stamp. "Life's too short to be bored witless for two precious hours of it. She will not do this to me again. I know how to say no. I just have to practice, that's all. Where the bloody hell are my keys?"

The sound of the door opening behind her made her jump, spin around. Preston noted that the dangles in her ears didn't match and wondered if it was a fashion statement or carelessness. Since she apparently couldn't find her keys in a bag smaller than the palm of his hand, he opted for the latter.

She looked flushed, flustered and fresh. And smelled even better than her cookies. And because he noticed, she only irritated him more.

"Hold on," he said simply, then turned back into his apartment to get her plate.

Cybil had no intention of holding on, and finally found her key where it had decided to hide in the narrow inner pocket of the bag—where she'd put it so she'd know just where it was when she needed it.

But he beat her. He strode out of his apartment, letting the door slam at his back. He carried his saxophone case in one hand and her plate in the other.

"Here." He wasn't going to ask her what had put that sulky look on her sea-fairy face. He had no doubt that she'd tell him, for the next half hour.

"You're welcome," she snapped, snatching it from him. Because her head was throbbing after two hours of listening to Jody's cousin Frank's monotone account of the vagaries of the stock market, she decided she'd give Mr. Mysterious a piece of her mind while the mood was on her.

"Look, buddy, you don't want to be friends, that's just fine. I don't need any more friends," she said, swinging the plate for emphasis. "I have so many now

I can't take another on until one moves out of the country. But there's no excuse for behaving like a snot, either. All I did was introduce myself and give you some damn cookies."

His lips wanted to twitch, but he controlled it. "Damn good cookies," he said before he could stop himself, then immediately regretted it as the temper in her eyes switched to amusement.

"Oh, really?"

"Yeah." He walked away, leaving her reluctantly intrigued and completely baffled.

So she followed impulse, one of her favorite hobbies. After unlocking her door quickly, she stuck the plate on the table inside, locked up again, then, trying to keep her footsteps muffled, set off to follow him.

It would be a great strip gag for Emily, she thought, and handled right could play out for weeks.

Of course she'd have to make Emily wild about the guy, Cybil decided as she tried to tiptoe and race down the steps at the same time. It wouldn't just be normal, perfectly acceptable curiosity but dreamy-eyed obsession.

Breathless with the excitement of the chase, her mind whirling with possibilities, Cybil rushed out the front door, looked quickly right and left.

He was already halfway down the block. Long stride, she thought, and, grinning, started after him.

Emily, of course, would be sort of skulking, then jumping behind lampposts; or flattening herself against walls in case he turned around and—

Nearly yelping, Cybil jumped behind a lamppost as the object of the chase sent an absent glance over his shoulder. With a hand over her heart, Cybil dared a peek and watched him turn the corner.

Annoyed that she'd worn heels instead of flats to dinner, she sucked in a breath and made the dash to the corner.

He walked for twenty minutes, until her feet were screaming and her initial rush of excitement was draining fast. Did the man just wander the streets with his saxophone every night? she wondered.

Maybe he wasn't just rude. Maybe he was crazy. He'd been recently released from the asylum—that's why he didn't know how to relate to people in the normal way.

His filthy rich and abusive family had caught him, locked him up so that he couldn't claim his rightful inheritance from his beloved grandmother—who had died under suspicious circumstances and had left him her entire fortune. And all those years of being imprisoned by the corrupt psychiatrist had warped his mind.

Yes, that would be exactly what Emily would cook up in her head—and she'd be certain her tender care, her unqualified love, would cure him. Then all the friends and neighbors would try to talk her out of it—even as she dragged them into her schemes.

And before it was over Mr. Mysterious would—

She pulled up short as he walked into a small, dingy club called Delta's.

Finally, she thought, and skimmed back her hair. Now all she had to do was slip inside, find a dark corner and see what happened next.

Chapter 2

The place smelled of whiskey and smoke. Not really offensive, Cybil thought. More…atmospheric. It was dimly lit, with a pale-blue light illuminating a stingy stage. Round tables hardly bigger than pie plates were crammed together, and though most of them were occupied, the noise level was muted.

She decided people talked in whispers in such places, planning liaisons, affairs, or enjoying those already made.

At a thick wooden bar on the side wall, patrons loitered on stools and huddled over their drinks as if protecting the contents from invaders.

It was, she decided, the kind of club that belonged in a black-and-white movie from the forties. The kind where the heroine wore long, slinky dresses, dark-red lipstick with a sweep of her platinum hair falling sulkily over her left eye as she stood on the stage under a single key light, torching her way through songs about the men who'd done her wrong.

And while she did, the man who wanted her, and had done her wrong, brooded into his whiskey with his world-weary eyes shadowed by the brim of his fedora.

In other words, she thought with a smile, it was perfect.

Hoping to go unnoticed, she scooted along the rear wall and found a table and, sitting, watched him through a haze of smoke and whiskey fumes.

He wore black. Jeans with a T-shirt tucked into the waistband. He'd already taken off the leather jacket he'd put on against the evening chill. The woman he was speaking with was gorgeous, black and outfitted in a hot red jumpsuit that hugged every curvaceous inch. She had to be six feet tall, Cybil mused, and when she threw back her beautiful head and laughed, the full rich sound rocked through the room.

For the first time Cybil saw him smile. No, not just smile, she thought, transfixed by the lightning transformation of that stern and handsome face. That hot punch of grin, the hammer-blow power of it, couldn't be called anything as tame as a smile.

It was full of fun and affection and sly humor. It made her rest her chin on her fisted hands and grin in response.

She imagined he and the beautiful Amazon were lovers, was certain of it when the woman grabbed his face in her hands and kissed him lavishly. Of course, Cybil thought, a man like that—with all those secrets and heartaches—would have an exotic lover, and they would meet in a dim, smoky bar where the music was dreamy and sad.

Finding it wonderfully romantic, she sighed.

Onstage, Delta gave Preston's cheeks an affectionate pinch. "So now you got women following you, sugar lips?"

"She's a lunatic."

"You want me to bounce her out?"

"No." He didn't glance back but could feel those big green eyes on him. "I'm pretty sure she's a harmless lunatic."

Delta's tawny eyes glittered with amusement. "Then I'll just check her out. Woman starts stalking my sugar lips, I gotta see what's she made of, right, André?"

The skinny black man at the piano stopped noodling keys long enough to smile up at her out of a face as battered and worn as the old spinet he played. "That you do, Delta. Don't hurt her, now—she's just a little thing. You ready to blow?" he asked Preston.

"You start. I'll catch up."

As Delta glided offstage, André's long, narrow fingers began to make magic. Preston let the mood of it slide into him; then, closing his eyes, let the music come.

It took him away. It cleared his head of the words and the people and the scenes that often crowded his head. When he played like this, there was nothing but the music, and the aching pleasure of making it.

He'd once told Delta it was like sex. It dragged something out of you, put something back. And when it was over, it was always too soon.

In the back, Cybil drifted into it, slid down into those

low, bluesy notes, rose up with the sudden wailing sobs. It was different, she thought, watching him play than just hearing it through the walls. Watching him, there was more power, more heartbreak, more of that subtle sexual pull.

It was music to weep by. To make love to. To dream on.

It caught her, focused her on the stage so she didn't see Delta moving toward her table.

"What's your pleasure, little sister?"

"Hmm." Distracted, Cybil glanced up, smiled vaguely. "It's wonderful. The music. It makes my heart hurt."

Delta lifted a brow. The girl had a bright and pretty face, she mused. Didn't look much like a lunatic with that tipped nose and those long-lidded eyes. "You drinking or just taking up space?"

"Oh." Of course, Cybil realized, a place like this needed to sell drinks. "It's whiskey music," she said with another smile. "I'll have a whiskey."

Delta's brow only arched higher. "You don't look old enough to be ordering whiskey, little sister."

Cybil didn't bother to sigh. It was an opinion she heard constantly. She flipped open her purse, pulled out her driver's license.

Delta took it, studied it. "All right, Cybil Angela Campbell, I'll get your whiskey."

"Thanks." Content, Cybil rested her chin on her fists again and just listened. It surprised her when Delta came back not with one glass of whiskey but two, then folded that glamorous body into the chair next to her.

"So, what are you doing in a place like this, young Cybil? You got a Rainbow Room face."

Cybil opened her mouth, then realized she could hardly say she'd followed her mysterious neighbor all over Soho. "I don't live far from here. I suppose I just followed an impulse." She lifted the whiskey, gestured with it to the stage. "I'm glad I did," she said, then drank.

Delta's lips pursed. The girl might look like a varsity cheerleader, but she drank her whiskey like a man. "You go wandering around the streets alone at night, somebody's going to eat you up, little sister."

Cybil's eyes gleamed over the rim of her glass. "Oh, I don't think so. Big sister."

Considering, Delta nodded. "Maybe, maybe not. Delta Pardue." She touched her glass to Cybil's. "This is my place."

"I like your place, Delta."

"Maybe, maybe not." Delta let loose that rich laugh again. "But you sure like my man there. You've had your pretty cat's-eyes on him since you came in."

Thoughtfully, Cybil swirled her whiskey while she debated how to play it. Though she had no doubt she could handle herself on the streets—or anywhere else, for that matter—Delta outweighed her by at least thirty pounds. And as she'd said, it was her place. Her man. No point in making a potential new friend want to rip out her lungs at their first meeting.

"He's very attractive," Cybil said casually. "It's hard not to look. So I'll keep looking if it's all the same to you. I doubt his eyes are going to wander when he's got someone like you in focus."

Delta's teeth flashed in a brilliant grin. "Maybe you can take care of yourself, after all. You're a smart girl, aren't you?"

Cybil chuckled into her whiskey. "Oh, yeah. I am. And I do like your place. I like it a lot. How long have you owned it, Delta?"

"This? Two years here."

"And before? It's New Orleans I'm hearing in your voice, isn't it?"

Delta inclined her head. "You got good ears."

"I do, actually, for dialects, but yours is one I couldn't miss. I have family in New Orleans. My mother grew up there."

"I don't know any Campbells—what's your mama's maiden name?"

"Grandeau."

Delta eased back. "I know Grandeaus, many Grandeaus. Are you kin to Miss Adelaide?"

"Great-aunt."

"Grand lady."

Cybil snorted, drank. "Stuffy, irritating and cold as winter. The twins and I—my brother and sister—used to think she was a witch of the wicked sort."

"She has power, but it only comes from money and a name. Grandeau, eh? Who's your mama?"

"Geneviève Grandeau Campbell, the artist."

"Miss Gennie." Delta set her whiskey down so that she could rear back and thump a hand to her heart as she rocked with laughter. "Miss Gennie's little girl comes into my place. Oh, the world is a wonderful thing."

"You know my mother?"

"My mama cleaned house for your *grandmère,* little sister."

"Mazie? You're Mazie's daughter? Oh." Instantly bonded, Cybil grabbed Delta's hand. "My mother talked about Mazie all the time. We visited her once when I

was a little girl. She gave us beignets, fresh and wonderful. We sat on the front porch and had lemonade,
and my father did a sketch of her."

"She put it in her parlor and was very proud. I was
in the city when your family came. I was working. My
mama, she talked of that visit for weeks after. She had
a place deep in her heart for Miss Gennie."

"Wait until I tell them I met you. How is your mother,
Delta?"

"She died last year."

"Oh." Cybil laid her other hand over Delta's, cupping
it warmly. "I'm so sorry."

"She lived a good life, died sleeping, so died a good
death. Your mama and your daddy, they came to the fu-
neral. They sat in the church. They stood at the grave.
You come from good people, young Cybil."

"Yes, I do. So do you."

Preston didn't know how to figure it. There was
Delta, a woman he considered the most sane of anyone
he knew, huddled together with the pretty crazy woman,
apparently already the fastest of friends. Sharing whiskey, laughs. Holding hands the way women do.

For more than an hour they sat together in the back
of the room. Now and then, Cybil would begin what
could only have been one of her chattering monologues,
her hands gesturing, her face mobile. Delta would lean
back and laugh, or lean forward, shaking her head in
amazement.

"Look at that, André." Preston leaned on the piano.

André wiggled his fingers loose, then lit a cigarette.
"Like a couple of hens in the coop. That's a pretty girl
there, my man. Got sparkle to her."

"I hate sparkle," Preston muttered, and no longer in the mood to play, tucked his sax in the case. "Catch you next time."

"I'll be here."

He thought he should just walk out, but he was just a little irritated to have his good friend getting chummy with his lunatic. Besides, it would give him some satisfaction to let his nosy neighbor know he was onto her.

But when he stopped by the table, Cybil only glanced up and smiled at him. "Hi. Aren't you going to play anymore? It was wonderful."

"You followed me."

"I know. It was rude. But I'm so glad I did. I loved listening, and I might never have met Delta otherwise. We were just—"

"Don't do it again," he said shortly, and stalked to the door.

"Ooooh, he's plenty pissed off," Delta said with a chuckle. "Got that ice in his eyes, chills down to the bone."

"I should apologize," Cybil said as she bolted to her feet. "I don't want him angry with you."

"Me? He's—"

"I'll come back soon." She dropped a kiss on Delta's cheek, making the woman blink in surprise. "Don't worry, I'll smooth things over."

When she dashed out, Delta simply stared after her, then let out one of her long laughs. "Little sister, you got no idea what you're in for. Then again," she mused, "neither does sugar lips."

Outside, Cybil dashed down the sidewalk. "Hey!" she shouted at his retreating back, then cursed herself for not having the sense to ask Delta what the man's name was. "Hey!" Risking a twisted ankle, she switched from jog to run and managed to catch up.

"I'm sorry," she began, tugging on the sleeve of his jacket. "Really. It's completely my fault."

"Who said it wasn't?"

"I shouldn't have followed you. It was impulse. I have such a problem resisting impulse—always have—and I was irritated because of that idiot Frank and…well, that doesn't matter. I only wanted to—could you slow down a little?"

"No."

Cybil rolled her eyes. "All right, all right, you wish I'd get run over by a truck, but there's no need to be upset with Delta. We just started talking and we found out that her mother used to work for my grandmother, and she—Delta, I mean—knows my parents and some of my Grandeau cousins, so we hit it off."

He did stop now, to simply stare at her. "Of all the gin joints in all the towns in all the world," he muttered, and made her laugh.

"I had to follow you into that one and make pals with your girlfriend. Sorry."

"My girlfriend? Delta?"

And to Cybil's amazement, the man could laugh. Really laugh, with a wonderful baritone rumble that melted all the ice and made her sigh in delight.

"Does Delta look like anyone's *girl*friend? Man, you are from Mars."

"It's just an expression. I didn't want to be presumptive and call her your lover."

His eyes were still warm with amusement as he stared down at her. "That's a happy thought, kid, but the guy I was just jamming with happens to be her husband, and a friend of mine."

"The skinny man at the piano? Really?" Pursing her lips, Cybil thought about it, found it charming and romantic. "Isn't that lovely?"

Preston only shook his head and started walking again.

"What I meant was," Cybil continued—he'd just known she couldn't possibly be finished—as she hurried along beside him, "I'm sure she came back to check me out, you know? To make sure I wasn't going to hassle you, and then, well, one thing led to another. I don't want you to be annoyed with her."

"I'm not annoyed with her. You, on the other hand, have gone so far beyond being an annoyance I can't find the word."

Her mouth fell into a pout. "Well, I'm sorry, and I'll certainly make it a point to leave you alone, since that's apparently what you like best."

Her perky nose went up in the air, and she sailed across the street in the opposite direction from their building.

Preston stood there a moment, watching her scissor those very pretty legs down the opposite sidewalk. Then, with a shrug, he turned the corner, telling himself he was glad to be rid of her. It wasn't his concern if she wandered around alone at night. She wouldn't have been out walking around on those silly, skinny heels if she hadn't followed him in the first place.

He wasn't going to worry about it.

And swearing, he turned around, headed back. He was going to make sure she got home, that was all. Back inside, where he could wash any responsibility for her welfare off his hands and forget her.

He was still the best part of a crosstown block away when he saw it happen. The man slid out of the shadows, made his grab and had Cybil letting out an ear-piercing scream as she struggled. Preston dumped his case, sprinted forward with his fists already clenched.

Then skidded to an amazed halt as Cybil not only broke free but doubled her attacker over with a hard knee to the groin, knocked him flat with a perfect uppercut.

"I only had ten lousy dollars in here. Ten lousy dollars, you jerk!" She was shouting by the time Preston gathered his wits and rushed up beside her. "If you'd needed money, why didn't you just ask!"

"You hurt?"

"Yes, damn it. And it's your fault. I wouldn't have hit him so hard if I hadn't been mad at you."

Noting that she was nursing the knuckles on her right hand, Preston grabbed it by the wrist. "Let's see. Wiggle your fingers."

"Go away."

"Come on, wiggle."

"Hey!" The shout came from a woman hanging out an open window across the street. "You want I should call the cops?"

"Yes." Cybil snapped the word back as she wiggled her fingers and Preston probed, then blew out a steadying breath. "Yes, please. Thanks."

"Polite little victim, aren't you?" Preston muttered. "Nothing's broken. You might want to get it X-rayed anyway."

"Thanks so much, Dr. Doom." She jerked her hand

away, kept her chin lifted and gestured with her unin-jured hand in what Preston thought of as a grandly regal gesture. "You can go. I'm just fine."

As the man sprawled on the sidewalk began to moan and stir, Preston set a foot on his throat. "I think I'll just stick around. Why don't you go get my sax for me. I dropped it back there when I still believed the Big Bad Wolf ate Red Riding Hood."

She nearly told him to go get it himself, then de-cided if she had to hit the jerk on the sidewalk again, she'd hurt herself as much as him. With stiff dignity, she walked down the block, picked up the case and car-ried it back.

"Thank you," she said.

"For what?"

"For the thought."

"Don't mention it." Preston added a bit more weight when the man on the ground began to curse.

When the squad car pulled up ten minutes later, he stepped back. Cybil wasn't having any trouble giving the cops the details, and Preston harbored the hope that he could just slide away and stay out of it. The hope died as one of the uniforms turned to him.

"Did you see what happened here?"

Preston sighed. "Yeah."

And that was why it was nearly 2:00 a.m. before he trooped up the steps with Cybil toward their respective apartments. He still had the unappealing taste of po-lice station coffee in his mouth and a low-grade head-ache on the brew.

"It was kind of exciting, wasn't it? All those cops and bad guys. It was hard to tell one from the other in the detective bureau. Well, you could because the detectives have to wear ties. I wonder why. It was nice of them to show me around. You should have come. The interrogation rooms look just the way you imagine they would. Dark and creepy."

He was certain she had to be the only person on the planet who could find a sunny side to being mugged.

"I'm wired," she announced. "Aren't you wired? Want some cookies? I still have plenty."

He nearly ignored her as he dug out his keys, then his stomach reminded him he hadn't eaten anything for the past eight hours. And her cookies were a minor miracle.

"Maybe."

"Great." She unlocked her door, left it open, stepping out of her shoes as she walked to the kitchen. "You can come in," she called out. "I'll put them on a plate for you so you can take them back and eat them in your own den, but there's no point in waiting in the hall."

He stepped in, leaving the door open behind him. He should have known her place would be bright and cheerful, full of cute and classy little accents. With his hands in his pockets, he wandered around, tuning out her bubbling chatter while she transferred cookies from a canister in the shape of a maniacally grinning cow to the same bright-yellow plate she'd used before.

"You talk too much."

"I know." She skimmed a hand over her spiky bangs. "Especially when I'm nervous or wired up."

"Are you ever otherwise?"

"Now and then."

He noted a scatter of framed photos, several pairs of earrings, another shoe, a romance novel and the scent of apple blossoms. Each suited her, he thought, as perfectly as the next. Then he paused in front of a framed copy of a comic strip on the wall.

"'Friends and Neighbors,'" he mused, then studied the signature under the last section. It read simply, Cybil. "This you?"

She glanced over. "Yes. That's my strip. I don't imagine you spend much time reading the comics, do you?"

Knowing a dig when he heard one, he looked back over his shoulder. It must have been the late hour, he decided, after a long day that made her look so fresh and pretty and appealing. "Grant Campbell—'Macintosh'— that your old man?"

"He's not old, but yes, he's my father."

The Campbells, Preston mused, meant the Mac-Gregors. And wasn't that a coincidence? He moved over to stand on the opposite side of the counter and help himself to the cookies she was arranging in a stylish circular pattern.

"I like the edge to his work."

"I'm sure he'll appreciate that." Because he was reaching for another cookie, Cybil smiled. "Want some milk?"

"No. Got a beer?"

"With cookies?" She grimaced but turned to her refrigerator. Preston had a chance to see it was well stocked as she bent down—which gave him a chance to appreciate just what snug black slacks could do for a perky woman's excellent butt—and retrieved a bottle of Beck's Dark.

"This do? It's what Chuck likes."

"Chuck has good taste. Boyfriend?"

She smirked, getting out a pilsner glass before he could tell her he'd just take the bottle. "I suppose that indicates that I'm the type to have *boy*friends, but no. He's Jody's husband. Jody and Chuck Myers, just below you in 2B. I was out to dinner with them tonight, and Jody's excessively boring cousin Frank."

"Is that what you were muttering about when you came home?"

"Was I muttering?" She frowned, then leaned on the counter and ate one of his cookies. Muttering was another habit she kept trying to break. "Probably. It's the third time Jody's roped me into a date with Frank. He's a stockbroker. Thirty-five, single, handsome if you like that lantern-jawed, chiseled-brow sort. He drives a BMW coupe, has an apartment on the Upper East Side, a summer place in the Hamptons, wears Armani suits, enjoys French-provincial cuisine and has perfect teeth."

Amused despite himself, Preston washed down cookies with cold beer. "So why aren't you married and looking for a nice split-level in Westchester?"

"Ah, you've just voiced my friend Jody's dream. And I'll tell you why." She wagged a cookie, then bit in. "One, I don't want to get married or move to Westchester. Two, and really more to the point, I would rather be strapped to an anthill than strapped to Frank."

"What's wrong with him?"

"He bores me," she said, then winced. "That's so unkind."

"Why? Sounds honest to me."

"It is honest." She picked up another cookie, ate it with only a little guilt. "He's really a very nice man, but I don't think he's read a book in the last five years or seen a movie. A few selected films, perhaps, but not a movie. Then he critiques them."

"I don't even know him, and I'm already bored."

That made her laugh and reach for another cookie. "He's been known to check out his grooming in the back of his spoon at the dinner table—just to make sure he's still perfect—and he can spend the rest of his life, and yours, talking about annuities and stock futures. And all that aside, he kisses like a fish."

"Really." He forgot he'd wanted to grab a handful of cookies and get out. "And how is that exactly?"

"You know." She made an *O* with her mouth, then laughed. "You can imagine how a fish kisses, which I suppose they don't, but if they did. I nearly escaped without having the experience tonight, then Jody got in the way."

"And it doesn't occur to you to say no?"

"Of course it occurs to me." Her grin was quick and completely self-deprecating. "I just can't seem to get it out in time. Jody loves me, and for reasons that continue to elude me, she loves Frank. She's sure we'd make a wonderful couple. You know how it is when someone you care about puts that kind of benign pressure on you."

"No. I don't."

She tilted her head. Remembering his empty living room. No furniture, and now no family. "That's too bad. As inconvenient as it may be from time to time, I wouldn't trade it for anything."

"How's the hand?" he asked when he saw her rubbing her knuckles.

"Oh. A little sore still. It'll probably give me some trouble working tomorrow. But I should be able to turn the experience into a good strip."

"I can't see Emily laying a mugger out on his ass."

Cybil's face glowed on a grin. "You *do* read it."

"Now and again." She was entirely too pretty, he thought suddenly. Entirely too bright. And it was abruptly too tempting to find out if she tasted the same way.

That's what happened, Preston supposed, when you hung around eating homemade cookies in the middle of the night with a woman who made her living looking at the light side of life.

"You don't have your father's edge or your mother's artistic genius, but you have a nice little talent for the absurd."

She let out a half laugh. "Well, thank you so much for that unsolicited critique."

"No problem." He picked up the plate. "Thanks for the cookies."

She narrowed her eyes as he headed for the door. Well, he was going to see just how much of a talent she had for the absurd in some upcoming strips, she decided.

"Hey."

He paused, glanced back. "Hey, what?"

"You got a name, apartment 3B?"

"Yeah, I've got a name, 3A. It's McQuinn." He balanced his beer and his plate, and shut the door between them.

Chapter 3

When scenes and people filled her head, Cybil could work until her fingers cramped and refused to hold pencil or brush.

She spent the next day fueled on cookies and the diet soft drinks she liked to pretend balanced out the cookie calories. On paper, section by section, Emily and her friend Cari—who over the last couple of years had taken on several Jody-like attributes—plotted and planned on how to discover the secrets of the Mr. Mysterious.

She was going to call him "Quinn," but not for several installments.

For three days she rarely left her drawing board. Jody had a key, so it wasn't necessary to run down and let her in every time she dropped over for a visit. And Jody was always happy enough to dash down to open the door for Mrs. Wolinsky or one of the other neighbors who stopped by.

At one point on the third evening, enough people were in the apartment to have put together a small, informal party while Cybil remained coloring in her big Sunday strip.

Someone had turned on the stereo. Music blared, but it didn't distract her. Laughter and conversation rose up the stairs, and there was a shout of greeting as someone else dropped in.

She smelled popcorn, and wondered idly if anyone would bring her some.

Leaning back, she studied her work. No, she didn't have her father's edge, she acknowledged, or her mother's genius. But all in all, she did indeed have a "nice little talent."

She had a quick and clever hand at drawing. She could paint—quite well, really, she mused—if the mood was right. The strip gave her an arena for her own brand of social commentary.

Perhaps she didn't dig into sore spots or turn a sarcastic pencil toward politics, but her work made people laugh. It gave them company in the morning over their hurried cup of coffee or along with a lazy Sunday breakfast.

More than anything, she thought as she signed her name, it made her happy.

If McQuinn in 3B thought his careless comment insulted her, he was wrong. She was more than content with her nice little talent.

Flushed with the success of three days' intense work, she picked up the phone as it rang and all but sang into it. "Hello?"

"Well, well, there's a cheery lass."

"Grandpa!" Cybil leaned back in her chair and

stretched cramped muscles. "Yes, I'm a cheery lass, and there's no one I'd rather talk to than you."

Technically, Daniel MacGregor wasn't her grand-father, but that had never stopped either of them from thinking of him as such. Love ignored technicalities.

"Is that so? Then why haven't you called me or your grandmother? You know how she worries about you down there in that big city all alone."

"Alone?" Amused, she held out the phone so the sounds of the party downstairs would travel through the receiver to Hyannis Port. "It doesn't feel as if I'm ever alone."

"You've got the place full of people again?"

"So it seems. How are you? How is everyone? Tell me everything."

She settled back, happy to chat with him about family, her aunts and uncles, her cousins, the babies.

She listened and laughed, added her own comments, and was pleased when he told her there was a family gathering in the works for the summer.

"Wonderful. I can't wait to see everyone again. It's been too long since Ian and Naomi's wedding last fall. I miss you."

"Well then, why do you have to wait until summer? We're right here, after all."

"Maybe I'll surprise you."

"I called with one for you. I'll wager you haven't heard as yet that little Naomi's expecting. We'll have another bairn under the Christmas tree this year."

"Oh, Grandpa, that's wonderful. I'll call them to-night. And with Darcy and Mac ready to have theirs any day, we'll have lots of babies to cuddle this Christmas."

"For a young woman so fond of babes, you ought to be busy making your own."

It was an old theme and made her grin. "But my cousins are doing such a fine job of it."

"Hah! That they are, but that doesn't mean you can shirk your duty, little girl. You may be a Campbell by birth, but you've got some MacGregor in your heart."

"Well, I could always give in and marry Frank."

"The one with the fish mouth?"

"No, he just kisses like a fish. Then again…yeah, the one with the fish mouth. We could make you some guppies."

"Bah. You need a man, not a trout in an Italian suit. A man with more on his mind than dollars and cents, with an understanding of art, with enough of a serious nature to keep you out of trouble."

"I keep myself out of trouble," she reminded him, but decided it was best not to mention the mugging incident. "Besides, Grandma won't let me have you, so I'll just have to pine away here in the big, bad city."

He let out a bark of a laugh. "All the men in that city, you ought to be able to find one to suit you. You get out and about, don't you? You're not sitting there all day writing your funny papers."

"Just lately, but I hit a hot streak here and needed to run with it. There's this new guy across the hall. Kind of surly and standoffish. No, actually, let's just say it straight. He's rude and abrupt. I think he's out of work, except he plays the sax sometimes in this little club a few blocks from here. He's just the perfect new neighbor for Emily."

"Is that so?"

"He stays inside his apartment all day, doesn't talk to anyone. His name's McQuinn."

"If he doesn't talk to anyone, how do you know his name?"

"Grandpa." She allowed herself a smug smile. "Have you ever known me to fail getting anyone to talk to me if I put my mind to it? Not that he's the chatty sort even when you prime his pump with cookies, but I wheedled his name out of him."

"And how does he look to you, little girl?"

"He looks good, very, very good. He's going to drive Emily crazy."

"Is he, now?" Daniel said, and laughed with delight.

When he'd gotten all that he needed to know out of his honorary granddaughter, Daniel made his next call. He hummed to himself, examined his nails, buffed them on his shirt, then grinned fiercely when Preston answered the phone with an impatient, "Yeah, what?"

"Ah, you've such a sweet nature to you, McQuinn. It warms my heart."

"Mr. MacGregor." There was no mistaking that booming Scottish burr. In an abrupt shift of mood, Preston smiled warmly and pushed away from his computer.

"Right you are. And how are you settling in to the apartment there?"

"Well enough. I have to thank you again for letting me use it while my house is a construction zone. I'd never have been able to work with all those people around." He scowled at the wall as the noise from across the hall battered against it. "Not that it's much better here tonight. My neighbor seems to be celebrating something."

"Cybil? She's my granddaughter, you know. Sociable child."

"You're telling me. I didn't realize she was your granddaughter."

"Well, in a roundabout way. You ought to shake yourself loose, boy, and join the party."

"No, thanks." He'd rather drink drain cleaner. "I think half the population of Soho's crammed in there. This building of yours, Mr. MacGregor, is full of people who'd rather talk than eat. Your granddaughter appears to be the leader."

"Friendly girl. It comforts me to know you're across the hall for a bit. You're a sensible sort, McQuinn. I don't mind imposing by asking you to keep an eye on her. She can be naive, if you get my meaning. I worry about her."

Preston had the image of her flattening a mugger with the speed and precision of a lightweight boxer and smiled to himself. "I wouldn't worry."

"Well, I won't knowing you're close by. Pretty young thing like Cybil...she is a pretty thing, isn't she?"

"Cute as a button."

"Smart, too. And responsible, for all it seems like she's fluttering through life. You can't be a dim-witted flutterer and produce a popular comic strip day after day, now can you? Got to be creative, artistic and practical enough to meet deadlines. But you know about that sort of business, don't you? Writing plays isn't an easy business."

"No." Preston rubbed his eyes, gritty from fighting with work that refused to run smooth. "It's not."

"But you've a gift, McQuinn, a rare one. I admire that."

"It's been feeling like a curse lately. But I appreciate it."

"You should get yourself out, take your mind off it. Kiss a pretty girl. Not that I know much about writing—though I've two grandchildren who make their living from it, and damn well, too. You should make the most of being right there in the city before you take yourself back and lock the doors on your house."

"Maybe I will."

"Oh, and McQuinn, you'll do me the favor of not mentioning to Cybil that I asked you to mind her a bit? She'd get huffy over it. But her grandmother worries herself sick over that girl."

"She won't hear it from me," Preston promised.

Since the noise was going to drive him crazy, Preston took himself off. He played at the club but found it didn't quite get him past the thoughts that jangled in his brain.

It was too easy to imagine Cybil sitting at the table in the back, her chin on her fists, her lips curved, her eyes dreamy.

She'd invaded one of his more well-guarded vaults, and he resented it bitterly.

Delta's was one of his escapes. There were times he'd drive into the city from Connecticut just to slip onto the stage with André and play until all the tension of the day dissolved into, then out of, the music.

He could drive home again or, if the hour grew too late, just drop down on the cot in Delta's back room and sleep until morning.

No one bothered him at the club or expected more than he wanted to give.

But now that Cybil had been here, he'd started to

look at that back table, and wondered if she'd slip in again. To watch him with those big green eyes.

"My man," André said as he stopped to take a long drink from the water glass he kept on his beloved piano. "You ain't just playing the blues tonight. You got 'em."

"Yeah. Looks like."

"Usually a woman tangled up there when a man's got that look about him."

Preston shook his head, scowling as he lifted the sax to his lips. "No. No woman. It's work."

André merely pursed his lips as Preston sent out music that throbbed like a pulse. "You say so, brother. If you say so."

He got home at three, prepared to beat on Cybil's door and demand quiet. It was a letdown to arrive and discover the party was over. There wasn't a sound coming from her apartment.

He let himself in, locked up, then told himself he'd take advantage of the peace. After brewing a pot of coffee strong enough to dance on, he settled back at his machine, back into his play, back into the minds of characters who were destroying their lives because they couldn't reach their own hearts.

The sun was up when he stopped, when the sudden rush of energy that had flooded him drained out again. He decided it was the first solid work he'd managed in nearly a week, and celebrated by falling facedown and fully dressed into bed.

And there he dreamed.

Of a pretty face framed by a fringe of glossy brown hair, offset by long-lidded and enormous eyes the color of willow fronds. Of a voice that bubbled like a brook.

Why does everything have to be so serious? she asked him, laughing as she slid her arms up his chest, linked them around his neck.

Because life's a serious business.

That's only one-half of one of the coins. There are lots and lots of coins. Aren't you going to dance with me?

He already was. They were in Delta's, and though it was empty, the music was playing, low and sultry.

I'm not going to keep my eye on you. I can't afford it.

But you already are.

The top of her head reached his chin. When she tilted her head back, flicked her tongue lazily over his jaw, he felt the rush of his own blood.

That's not all you want to keep on me, is it?

I don't want you.

There was that laugh, light as air, frothy as champagne. *What's the point of lying,* she asked him, *in your own dreams? You can do anything you want to me in dreams. It won't matter.*

I don't want you, he said again, even as he pulled her to the floor.

He awoke, sweating, tangled in sheets, appalled, amazed, and finally when his head started to clear, amused.

The woman was a menace, he decided, and the only thing that had reflected any sort of reality in the painfully erotic dream was that he didn't want her.

He rubbed his hands over his face, glanced at the watch still on his wrist. Since it was after four in the afternoon, he judged he'd gotten the first decent eight hours of sleep he'd had in nearly a week. So what if it was at the wrong end of the time scale?

He trooped down to the kitchen, drank the dregs of the coffee and rooted out the only bagel that still looked edible. He was going to have to break down and buy some food.

He spent an hour working out, mechanically lifting weights, reminding his body it wasn't built to simply sit at a keyboard. Pleased that the sweat he'd worked up this time had nothing to do with sexual fantasies, he spent another twenty minutes indulging in a hot shower, and shaved for the first time in three—or maybe it was four—days.

He thought he might take himself out for a decent meal—which would be a nice change of pace. Then he'd face the tedium and low-grade horror of going to the market. Dressed and feeling remarkably clearheaded and cheerful, he opened his door.

Cybil dropped the hand she'd lifted to ring his buzzer. "Thank God you're home."

His mood wavered as his thought zoomed right back to the dream, and the barroom floor. "What?"

"You have to do me a favor."

"No, I don't."

"It's an emergency." She grabbed his arm before he could walk by. "It's life and death. My life and very possibly Mrs. Wolinsky's nephew Johnny's death. Because one of us is going to die if I have to go out with him, which is why I told her I had a date tonight."

"And you think this interests me because…"

"Oh, don't be surly now, McQuinn, I'm a desperate woman. Look, she didn't give me time to think. I'm a terrible liar. I mean, I just don't lie very often, so I'm bad at it. She kept asking who I was going out with, and I couldn't think of anybody, so I said you."

Because she'd meant it when she'd told him she was desperate, she darted in front of him to block his path.

"Kid, let me point out one simple fact. This isn't my problem."

"No, it's mine, I know it, and I would have made something better up if she hadn't caught me when I was working and thinking of something else." She lifted her hands, pushed them through her hair and had it standing in spikes. "She's going to be watching, don't you see? She's going to know if we don't go out of here together."

She whirled away to pace and rap her knuckles against her temples as if to stimulate thought. "Look, all you have to do is walk out of here with me, give an appearance of a nice, casual date. We'll go have a cup of coffee or something, spend a couple of hours, then come back—because she'll know if we don't come back together, too. She knows everything. I'll give you a hundred dollars."

That stopped him. The basic absurdity of it pulled him up short at the head of the stairs. "You'll pay me to go out with you?"

"It's not exactly like that—but close enough. I know you can use the money, and it's only fair to compensate you for your time. A hundred dollars, McQuinn, for a couple hours, and I'll buy the coffee."

He leaned back against the wall, studying her. It was just ridiculous enough to appeal to a sense of the absurd he'd all but forgotten he had. "No pie?"

Her laugh erupted on a gush of relief. "Pie? You want pie? You got pie."

"Where's the C note?"

"The...oh, the money. Hold on."

She dashed back into her apartment. He could hear her running up the steps, slamming around.

"Just let me fix myself up a little," she called out.

"Meter's running, kid."

"Okay, okay. Where the hell is my...ah! Two minutes, two minutes. I don't want her to tell me I'd hold on to a man if I'd just put on lipstick."

He had to give her credit. When she said two minutes, she meant it. She ran back out, her feet in another pair of those skinny heels, her lips slicked with deep pink and earrings dangling. Mismatched again, he noted as she handed him a crisp hundred-dollar bill.

"I really appreciate this. I know how foolish it must seem. I can't stand to hurt her feelings, that's all."

"Her feelings are worth a hundred bucks to you, it's your business." Entertained, he stuffed the bill in his back pocket. "Let's go. I'm hungry."

"Oh, do you want dinner? I can spring for a meal. There's a diner just down the street. Good pasta. Okay, now. Pretend you don't know she's keeping her eye out for us," she murmured as they walked to the entrance. "Just look natural. Hold my hand, will you?"

"Why?"

"Oh, for heaven's sake." She snatched his hand, linked her fingers firmly with his, then shot him a bright smile. "We're going on a date, our first. Try to look like we're enjoying ourselves."

"You only gave me a hundred," he reminded her, surprised when she laughed.

"God, you're a hard man, 3B. A really hard man. Let's get you a hot meal and see if it improves your mood."

It did. But it would have taken a stronger man than

he to hold out against an enormous, family-style bowl of spaghetti and meatballs and Cybil's sunny disposition.

"It's great, isn't it?" She watched him plow through the food with pleasure. Poor man, she thought, probably hasn't had a decent meal in weeks. "I always eat too much when I come here. They give you enough for six starving teenagers with each serving. Then I end up taking home the rest and eating too much the next day. You can save me from that and take mine home with you."

"Fine." He topped off their glasses of Chianti.

"You know, I bet there are dozens of clubs downtown that would be thrilled to hire you to play."

"Huh?"

"Your sax."

She smiled at him, luring him to look at her mouth, that flickering dimple, and wonder again.

"You're so good. I can't imagine you won't find steady work really soon."

Amused, he lifted his wine. She thought he was an out-of-work musician. Fine, then. Why not? "Gigs come and they go."

"Do you work private parties?" Inspired, she leaned on the table. "I know a lot of people—someone's always having a party."

"I bet they are, in your little world."

"I could give your name out if you like. Do you mind traveling?"

"Where am I going?"

"Some of my relatives own hotels. Atlantic City's not far. I don't suppose you have a car."

He had a snazzy new Porsche stored in a downtown garage. "Not on me."

She laughed, nibbled on bread. "Well, it's not difficult to get from New York to Atlantic City."

As entertaining as it was, he thought it wise to steer off awhile. "Cybil, I don't need anyone to manage my life."

"Terrible habit of mine." Unoffended, she broke the bread in half and offered him part. "I get involved. Then I'm annoyed when other people do the same to me. Like Mrs. Wolinsky, the current president of Let's Find Cybil a Nice Young Man Club. It drives me crazy."

"Because you don't want a nice young man."

"Oh, I suppose I will, eventually. Coming from a big family sort of predisposes you—or me, anyway—into wanting one of your own. But there's lots of time for that. I like living in the city, doing what I want when I want. I'd hate to keep regular hours, which is why nothing ever stuck before cartooning. Not that it isn't work or doesn't take discipline, but it's my work and my time. Like your music, I guess."

"I guess." His work was very rarely a pleasure—as hers seemed to be. But his music was.

"McQuinn." Smiling, she nudged her bowl to the side, thinking it would make him a very nice meal later in the week. "How often do you really rip loose and come up with more than, oh, say, three declarative sentences in a row during a conversation?"

He ate the last half of his last meatball, studied her. "I like November. I talk a lot in November. It's the kind of transitory month that makes me feel philosophical."

"Three on the button, and clever, too." She laughed at him. "You have a sly sense of humor in there, don't you?" Sitting back, she sighed lustily. "Want dessert?"

"Damn right."

"Okay, but don't order the tiramisu, because then I'd be forced to beg you for a bite, then two, then I'd end up stealing half of it and go into a coma."

Keeping his eyes on hers, he signaled for the waitress with the casual authority of a man used to giving orders. It made Cybil's brow crease.

"Tiramisu," he told the waitress. "Two forks," and made Cybil weak with laughter. "I want to see if putting you into a coma actually shuts you up."

"Won't." She patted her chest as the last laugh bubbled out. "I even talk in my sleep. My sister used to threaten to put a pillow over my head."

"I think I'd like your sister."

"Adria's gorgeous—probably just your type, too. Cool and sophisticated and brilliant. She runs an art gallery in Portsmith."

Preston decided they might as well finish off the wine. It was a very nice Chianti, he mused, which probably explained why he was feeling more relaxed than he had in weeks. Months, he corrected. Maybe years. "So, are you going to fix me up with her?"

"She might go for you," Cybil considered, eyeing him over her glass and enjoying the happy little buzz the wine had given her. "You're great-looking in a sort of rough, I-don't-give-a-damn way. You play a musical instrument, which would appeal to her love and appreciation of the arts. And you're too nasty to treat her like royalty. Too many men do."

"Do they?" he murmured, realizing that his talkative dinner companion was well on her way to being plowed.

"She's so beautiful. They can't help it. Worse, she's irritated when they're dazzled by the way she looks, so she ends up tossing them back. She'd probably end up breaking your heart," she added, gesturing with her glass. "But it might be good for you."

"I don't have a heart," he said when the waitress brought their dessert. "I thought you'd figured that out."

"Sure you do." With a sigh of surrender, Cybil picked up her fork, scooped up the first bite and tasted with a long moan of pleasure. "You've just got it wrapped in armor so nobody can bayonet it again. God, isn't this wonderful? Don't let me eat any more than this one bite, okay?"

But he was staring at her, amazed that the little lunatic across the hall had zeroed in on him so accurately, so casually, when those who claimed to love him had never come close.

"Why do you say that?"

"Say what? Didn't I tell you not to let me eat any more of this. Are you a sadist?"

"Never mind." Deciding to let it go, he yanked the plate out of her reach. "Mine," he said simply. And proceeded to eat the rest.

He only had to poke her once with his fork to hold her off.

"Well, I had fun." Cybil tucked her arm through his as they walked back toward their building. "Really. That was so much more entertaining than an evening trying to keep Johnny from sliding his hand up my skirt."

For some reason, the image irritated him, but Preston merely glanced down. "You're not wearing a skirt."

"I know. I wasn't sure I could get out of the date, and this was my automatic defense system."

The breezy saffron-colored slacks struck him abruptly as more sexy than defensive. "So why don't you just break Johnny's face like you did the mugger's the other night?"

"Because Mrs. Wolinsky adores him, and I'd never be able to tell her that the apple of her eye has hands like an ape."

"I think that's a mixed metaphor, but I get the picture. You're a pushover."

"Am not."

"Are so," he said before he caught himself and fell too deeply into the childish game. "You let your friend Joanie—"

"Jody."

"Right, push her cousin on you, and the old lady downstairs sticks you with her nephew with the fast hands, and God knows how many other friends you have dumping their cast-off relatives in your lap. All because you can't just say butt out."

"They mean well."

"They're meddling with your life. It doesn't matter what they mean."

"Oh, I don't know." She blew out a breath and smiled at a young couple strolling on the opposite side of the street. "Take my grandfather. Well, he's not really my grandfather if you get picky, which we don't. He's my dad's sister Shelby's father-in-law. And on my mother's side, she's cousin to the spouses of his other two children. It's a little complicated, if you get picky."

"Which you don't."

"Exactly. There's all this convoluted family connection between Daniel and Anna MacGregor and my parents, so why niggle? My aunt Shelby married their son Alan MacGregor—you might have heard of him. He used to live in the White House."

"The name rings a distant bell."

"And my mother, the former Geneviève Grandeau, is a cousin of Justin and Diana Blade—siblings—who married, respectively, Daniel and Anna's other two children, Serena and Caine MacGregor. So Daniel and Anna are Grandpa and Grandma. Is that clear?"

"Yes, I can follow that, but I've forgotten the entire point of the exercise."

"Me, too." She laughed in delight, then had to tighten her grip before she overbalanced. "A little too much wine," she explained. "Anyway, let me think… Yes, I have it. Meddling. We were talking about meddling, which my grandfather—who would be Daniel MacGregor—is the uncontested world champ at. When it comes to matchmaking, he knows no peer. I'm telling you, McQuinn, the man is a wizard. I have…"

She had to stop, use her fingers to count. "Um, I think it's seven cousins so far he's managed to match up, marry off. He's terrifying."

"What do you mean 'match up'?"

"He just sort of finds the right person for them— don't ask me how—then he works out a way to put them together, let nature take its course, and before you know it, you've got wedding bells and bassinets. He just told me my cousin Ian and his wife are expecting their first. They were married last fall. The man's batting a thousand."

"Does anyone tell him to butt out?"

"Oh, constantly." She tipped up her head and grinned. "He just doesn't pay attention. I figure he's going to work on Adria or Mel next—give my brother, Matthew, time to season."

"What about you?"

"Oh, I'm too slick for him. I know his canny tricks, and I'm not going to fall in love for years. What about you? Ever been there?"

"Where would that be?"

"Love, McQuinn, don't be dense."

"It's not a place—it's a situation. And there's nothing there."

"Oh, I think there will be," she said dreamily. "Eventually."

For the second time, she pulled up short. "Oh, damn. That's Johnny's car. He's come in from New Jersey, after all. Damn, damn, damn. Okay, here's the plan."

She whirled around, shook her head clear when it spun. "I should never have had that last glass of wine, but I'm still master of my fate."

"You bet you are, kid."

"Enough to know you call me 'kid' so you can feel superior and aloof, but that's beside the point. We're just going to stroll on down a few more feet until we're right in front of her window. Very natural, okay?"

"That's a tough one, but I'll see what I can do."

"I just love that nasty streak of sarcasm. Okay, this is fine, this is good. Now, we're going to stand right here, because she's watching, I promise. Any minute you'll see her curtains twitch. Look for it."

Because it seemed harmless, and he was starting to enjoy the way she held on to him, he flicked a glance over her head. "Right on cue. So?"

"You're going to have to kiss me."

His gaze shot back to hers. "Am I?"

"And you're going to have to make it look good. If you do it right, she'll figure Johnny's a lost cause—for a while, anyway. And I'll give you another fifty."

He ran his tongue around his teeth. She had her face tipped back and looked as appealing as a single rosebud in a garden of thorns. "You're going to pay me fifty bucks to kiss you."

"Like a bonus. This could send Johnny back to Jersey for good. Just think of it as being onstage. Doesn't have to mean anything. Is she still watching?"

"Yeah." But he wasn't looking at the window now, and didn't have a clue.

"Great. Good. Make it count, okay. Romantic. Just slide your arms around me, then lean down and—"

"I know how to kiss a woman, Cybil."

"Of course you do. No offense meant whatsoever. But this should be choreographed so that—"

He decided the only way to shut her up was to get on with it, and to get on with it his way. He didn't slide his arms around her—he yanked her against him, and nearly off her feet. He had one glimpse of those big green eyes widening in shock, before his mouth crushed down on hers and sent the next babbling words sliding down her throat.

He was right. That was her last dizzy thought. He was absolutely right. He did know how to kiss a woman.

She had to grab on to his shoulders. Had to rise up to her toes.

She had to moan.

Her head was spinning in fast, giddy circles. Her heart had flipped straight into her throat to block any chance of air. It made her feel helpless, lost, shaky as his mouth pumped heat like a furnace into her body.

And his mouth was so hard, so hard, and stunningly hungry. What else could she do but let him feed?

It was like the dream, he thought. Only better. Much,

much better. Her taste hadn't been so unique in his imagination. Her body hadn't trembled with quick, hard little shock waves. Her hands hadn't clawed their way up into his hair to fist while she moaned pure pleasure into his mouth.

He yanked her back, but only to see if her eyes had gone dark, if heat had climbed into her cheeks the way he felt it climb through his system. She only stared at him, her breath coming short and fast through parted lips, her hands still clutched in his hair.

"Next one's on me," he murmured, and took her under again.

A horn blasted. Someone cursed. There was a rush of displaced air from a passing car. Someone shoved an apartment window open and let out a stream of blistering rock music and the acrid smell of burned dinner.

She might have been on a deserted island with crystal-blue waves crashing at her feet.

When he drew her away the second time, he did so slowly, with his hands skimming down from her shoulders to her elbows, then back in a gesture that stopped only a hint short of a caress. It gave her enough time to feel her head revolve once, like a slow-motion merry-go-round, before it settled weakly on her shoulders.

He wanted to lap her up on the spot, every inch of that flushed, lovely skin. To devour her innate—and, to him, misplaced—cheerfulness that shone out of her like sunlight. He wanted all that impossible, unflagging energy under him, over him, open to him.

And he had no doubt that once he had, he'd leave them both bitter.

Now the hands that lingered on her shoulders eased

her back off her toes. Steadied her. Released her. "I think that ought to do it."

"Do it?" she echoed, staring up at him.

"Satisfy Mrs. Wolinsky."

"Mrs. Wolinsky?" Absolutely blank, she shook her head. "Oh. Oh, yeah." She blew out a long breath and decided her system might settle sometime before the end of the next decade. "If it doesn't it's hopeless. You're awfully good at it, McQuinn."

A reluctant smile flitted around his mouth. The woman was damn near irresistible, he thought, and, taking her arm, turned her toward the front of the building. "You're not half-bad at it yourself, kid."

Chapter 4

Cybil sang as she worked, belting out a duet with Aretha Franklin. Behind her, the open window welcomed the cool April breeze and the amazing noise that was the downtown streets in brilliant sunshine.

The stream of light was no sunnier than her mood.

Turning to the mirror on the wall beside her, she tried to work her face into a state of shock to help her with a character expression. But all she could do was grin.

She'd been kissed before. She'd been held by and against a man before. As far as she was concerned comparing all her other experiences to that stunning sidewalk embrace with the man across the hall was like pitting a firecracker against a nuclear attack.

One hissed, popped and was momentarily entertaining. The other detonated and changed the landscape for centuries.

It had left her marvelously dizzy for hours.

She loved the sensation, adored every moment of that giddy, slack-muscled, purely feminine rush. Could there be anything more wonderful than feeling weak and strong, foolish and wise, confused and aware all at the same time?

And all she had to do was close her eyes, let her mind wander back, to feel it all over again.

She wondered what he was thinking, what he was feeling. No one could be unaffected by an experience of that...magnitude. And after all, he'd been right there with her at ground zero. A man couldn't kiss a woman like that and not suffer some potent residual effects.

Suffering, Cybil decided, as her body tingled, was highly underrated.

She chuckled; she sighed; then, bending over her work, sang with Aretha about the joys of feeling like a natural woman.

"God, Cyb, it's freezing in here!"

Cybil looked up, beamed. "Hi, Jody. Hi, sweet Charlie."

The baby gave her a sleepy-eyed smile as Jody strode to the window with him cocked on her hip. "You're sitting in front of an open window. It can't be more than sixty degrees out there." With a little grunt, Jody shoved the window closed.

"I was feeling kind of warm." Cybil set her pencil aside to stroke Charlie's pudgy cheek. "It's miraculous, isn't it, that men start out this way? As pretty little babies? Then they...wow, boy do they grow up into something else."

"Yeah." Puzzled, Jody frowned, examined her friend's somewhat glassy eyes. "You look funny. Are you okay?" Jody laid a maternal hand on Cybil's forehead. "No fever. Stick out your tongue."

Cybil obeyed, crossing her eyes as she did and making Charlie bubble with laughter. "I'm not sick. I'm fabulous. I feel like a million after taxes."

"Hmm." Unconvinced, Jody pursed her lips. "I'm going to put Charlie down for his morning nap. He's zonked. Then I'll get us some coffee and you can tell me what's going on."

"Sure. Um-hmm." Dreaming again, Cybil picked up a red pen and began to doodle pretty little hearts on scrap paper.

Since that was fun, she drew larger ones, sketching Preston's face inside one.

He had a great one, she mused. Hard mouth, cool eyes, very strong features set off by that thick, dark hair. But that mouth softened a bit when he smiled. And his eyes weren't cool when he laughed.

She loved making him laugh. He always sounded just a little out of practice. She could help him with that, she mused, drawing his face again with the warmth of laughter added. After all, one of her nice little talents was making people laugh.

And after she'd helped him find some steady work, he wouldn't have so much to worry about.

She'd get him some work, make certain that he ate regular meals—she was always cooking too much for one person anyway—and she was sure she could find someone who had a secondhand sofa they were willing to part with on the cheap.

She knew enough people to start the ball rolling here and there for him. He'd feel better, wouldn't he, once he was more settled in, more secure? It wouldn't be like meddling. That was her grandfather's territory. She would just be helping out a neighbor.

A gorgeous, sexy neighbor who could kiss a woman straight into the paradise of delirium.

Of course that wouldn't be why she was doing it. Cybil shook herself, turned the scraps of paper over a little guiltily. She'd helped Mr. Peebles find a good podiatrist, hadn't she? And nobody would consider him a cool-eyed Adonis with great hands, would they?

Of course not.

She was just being a good neighbor. And if there were any other…benefits, well, so what?

Satisfied with her plans, she folded her legs under her and got back to work.

Jody settled the baby, thinking as she always did when she tucked him in that he was the most beautiful child ever to grace the planet. When his heavy eyes shut, his blanket was smoothed and his favorite teddy bear left on guard, she trotted downstairs to turn down the music.

As at home in Cybil's kitchen as her own, she poured morning coffee into two thick yellow mugs, sniffed out a couple of cranberry muffins, then loaded up a tray.

The midmorning ritual was one of her favorite parts of the day.

In the past few years, Cybil had become as close as a sister to her. Closer, Jody thought, wrinkling her nose. Her own sisters were always bragging about their husbands, their kids, their houses—when anyone could see her Chuck and her Charlie were miles superior. But Cybil listened. Cybil had held her hand through the difficult decision to quit her job and stay home with the baby full-time. It had been Cybil who'd stood by during those early days when she and Chuck had been panicked over every burp and sniffle Charlie had made.

There was no better friend in the world. Which was why Jody was determined to see Cybil blissfully happy.

She carried the tray up, set it on the table, then handed Cybil her mug.

"Thanks, Jody."

"Great strip this morning. I can't believe Emily decking herself out in a trench coat and fedora and tailing Mr. Mysterious all over Soho. Where does she get this stuff?"

"She's a creature of impulse and drama." Cybil broke off a piece of a muffin. It was usual for them to discuss Emily and the other characters as separate people. "And she's nosy. She just has to know."

"What about you? Did you find out anything yet about our Mr. Mysterious?"

"Yeah." Cybil said it on a sigh. "His name's Mc-Quinn."

"I heard that." Instantly alert, Jody jabbed out a finger. "You sighed."

"No, I was just breathing."

"Uh-uh, you sighed. What gives?"

"Well, actually…" She was dying to talk about it. "We sort of went out last night."

"Went out? Like a date?" Quickly, Jody pulled over a chair, sat, leaned close. "Where, how, when? Details, Cyb."

"Okay. So." Cybil swiveled so they were face-to-face. "You know how Mrs. Wolinsky's always trying to fix me up with her nephew?"

"Not again?" Jody rolled her dark eyes. "Why can't she see you two are totally wrong for each other?"

Vast affection prevented Cybil from mentioning that it might be the same selective blindness that prevented Jody from seeing the flaws in the Cybil-Frank match.

"She just loves him. But anyway, she'd cooked up another date for me for last night, and I just couldn't face it. You have to swear you won't tell her—or anyone."

"Except Chuck."

"Husbands are excluded from the vow of silence in this case. I told her I already had a date—with McQuinn."

"You had a date with 3B?"

"No, I just told her I did because I was flustered. You know how I start babbling when I lie."

"You should practice." Nodding, Jody bit into a muffin. "You'd get better at it."

"Maybe. So after I tell her, I realize she's going to be looking for us to leave together, and I have to cut some kind of deal with McQuinn to go along with it. I gave him a hundred and bought him dinner."

"You paid him." Jody's eyes widened, then narrowed in speculation. "That's brilliant. The whole time I was dating—especially during that drought period I told you about my sophomore year in college? I never thought about just offering a guy some money to have dinner with me. How'd you settle on the hundred? Do you think that's, like, the going rate?"

"It seemed right. He's not working regularly, you know. And I figured he could use the money and a hot meal. We had a good time," she added with a new smile. "Really good. Just spaghetti and conversation. Well, mostly one-sided conversation, as McQuinn doesn't say a lot."

"McQuinn." Jody let the name roll over her tongue. "Still sounds mysterious. You don't know his first name."

"It never came up. Anyway, it gets better. We're walking back. I think I loosened him up, Jody. He really seemed relaxed, almost friendly. Then I see Johnny Wolinsky's car, and I panicked. I'm figuring she's not going to stop trying to shove him at me unless she thinks I've got a guy. So I cut another deal with McQuinn and offered him fifty bucks to kiss me."

Jody pursed her lips, then sipped coffee. "I think you should've said that was included in the hundred."

"No, we'd already defined terms, and there wasn't time to renegotiate. She was looking out the window. So he did, right there on the sidewalk."

"Wow." Jody grabbed the rest of her muffin. "What move did he use?"

"He just sort of *yanked* me against him."

"Oh, man. The yank. I really like the yank."

"Then I was plastered there, up on my toes because he's tall."

"Yeah." Jody chewed, licked crumbs off her lips. "He's tall. And built."

"Really built, Jody. I mean the man is like a rock."

"Oh, God." On the moan, Jody rubbed her stomach. "Wow. Okay, so you're plastered up there, on your toes. What next?"

"Then he just…swooped."

"Oh-oh, the yank and swoop." Crumbs scattered as Jody waved her hands. "It's a classic. Hardly any guy can really pull it off, though. Chuck did on date six.

That's how we ended up back at my apartment, eating Chinese in bed."

"McQuinn pulled it off. He really, really pulled it off. Then, while my head was exploding, he yanked me back, just looked at me."

"Man. Man."

"Then he just…did it all again."

"A double." Near tears with vicarious excitement, Jody gripped Cybil's hand. "You got a double. There are women who go all their lives without a double. Dreaming of, yes, but never achieving the double yank and swoop."

"It was my first," Cybil confessed. "It…was…*great!*"

"Okay, okay, just the kiss part, okay? Just the lips and tongues and teeth thing. How was that?"

"It was very hot."

"Oh… I'm going to have to open the window. I'm starting to sweat."

She jumped up, shoved up the window and took a deep gulp of air. "So, it was hot. Very hot. Keep going."

"It was like being, well, devoured. When your system just goes…" At a loss, she lifted her hands, wiggled them wildly. "And your head's circling around about a foot above your shoulders, and… I don't know how to describe it."

"You've got to." Desperate, Jody squeezed Cybil's shoulders. "I'm on the edge here. Try this—on the one-to-ten scale, where did it hit?"

Cybil closed her eyes. "There is no scale."

"There's always a scale—you can say off the scale, but there's always a scale."

"No, Jody, there is no scale."

Eyeing Cybil, Jody stepped back. "The no scale is an urban myth."

"It exists," Cybil said soberly. "The no scale exists, my friend, and has now been documented."

"Sweet Lord. I have to sit down." She did so, her eyes never leaving Cybil's face. "You experienced a no scale. I believe you, Cyb. Thousands wouldn't. Millions would scoff, but I believe you."

"I knew I could count on you."

"You know what this means, don't you? He's ruined you for anything less. Even a ten won't satisfy you now. You'll always be looking for the next no scale."

"I've thought of that." Considering, Cybil picked up her pencil to tap. "I believe it's possible to live a full and happy life, hitting with some regularity between seven and ten, even after this experience. Man goes to the moon, Jody. Travels through space and time, finds himself on another world, but only briefly. He must come back to earth and live."

"That's so wise," Jody murmured, and had to dig a tissue out of her pocket. "So brave."

"Thank you. But in the meantime," Cybil added with a grin, "there's no harm in knocking on the door across the hall from time to time."

Because she didn't want to appear overanxious, Cybil put in a full morning's work. She didn't break until after two, when she thought her neighbor might enjoy sharing a cup of coffee, maybe a nice walk in the April sunshine.

He really had to get out of that apartment more, she decided. Take advantage of all the city had to offer. She imagined him brooding behind his locked door, worried about his lack of employment, the bills.

She was certain she could help him with that. There was no reason she couldn't put a buzz in a few ears and get him a few gigs to tide him over.

She heard the sax begin to weep as she stood in her bedroom fussing with her makeup. It made her tingle again, the low, sexy throb of it.

He deserved a break, something to take that cynical gleam out of his eyes. Something that would prove to him life was full of surprises. She wanted to help him. There was a quality about him—an underlying unhappiness she was driven to smooth away.

After all, she'd made him laugh. She'd helped him relax. If she could do it once, she could do it again. She badly wanted to see him laugh again, to hear that sardonic edge to his voice when he made some pithy comment, to see that grin flash when she said or did something that got through his cynical shield.

And if they lit a few sexual sparks between them while she was at it, what was wrong with that?

She was on her way downstairs, and singing again, when the buzzer from the entrance door sounded on her intercom.

"Yes?"

"I'm looking for McQuinn. 3A?"

"No, he's 3B."

"Well, damn it. Why doesn't he answer?"

"Oh, he probably doesn't hear you. He's practicing."

"Buzz me in, will you, sweetie? I'm his agent and I'm running way behind."

"His agent." Cybil perked up. If he had an agent, Cybil wanted to meet her. She'd already thought of half a dozen names to pass on for possible jobs. "Sure. Come on up."

She released the door, then opened her own and waited.

The woman who stepped out of the little-used elevator looked very professional, very successful, Cybil noted with some surprise, in her snazzy power suit of drop-dead red. She was thin and wiry, with a sharp-featured face, dark-blue eyes that were snapping with annoyance and an incredibly fabulous mane of streaked blond hair.

She moved with the precision of a bullet and carried a leather briefcase that Cybil estimated cost the equivalent of a month's rent on a good uptown apartment.

So, she mused, why was her client scrambling for work if his agent could afford designer duds and pricey accessories?

"3A?"

"Yes, I'm Cybil."

"Amanda Dresher. Thanks, Cybil. Our boy here isn't answering his phone, and apparently forgot we had a one o'clock at the Four Seasons."

"The Four Seasons?" Baffled, Cybil stared. "On Park?"

"Is there another?" With a laugh, Mandy pressed the buzzer on 3B and—knowing her prey—held it down. "Our Preston's loaded with talent, but he's my biggest pain in the butt."

"Preston." It only took a minute for the confusion to form, settle, then clear away. "Preston McQuinn." She let out a shaky breath that was equal parts betrayal and mortification. *"A Tangle of Souls."*

"That's our boy," Mandy said cheerfully. "Come on,

come on, McQuinn, answer the damn door. I thought when he decided to stay in the city for a couple months I'd be able to keep better track of him. But it's still an obstacle course. Ah, here we go."

They both heard the bad-tempered snick of locks being turned. Then he yanked open the door. "What the hell do you... Mandy?"

"You missed lunch," she snapped. "You're not answering the phone."

"I forgot lunch. The phone didn't ring."

"Did you charge the battery?"

"Probably not." He stood where he was, staring across the hall to where Cybil watched him with wounded eyes in a pale face. "Come on in. Just give me a minute."

"I've already given you an hour." She tossed a glance over her shoulder as she walked inside. "Thanks for buzzing me up, sweetie."

"No problem. No problem at all." Then Cybil looked Preston dead in the eye. "You bastard," she said quietly, and closed her door.

"Don't you have any place to sit in here?" Mandy complained behind him.

"No. Yes. Upstairs. Damn it," he muttered, despising the slide of guilt. Doing his best to shrug it off, he closed his door. "I don't use the space down here much."

"No kidding. So who's the kid across the hall?" she asked as she set her briefcase on the kitchen counter.

"Nobody. Campbell, Cybil Campbell."

"I thought she looked familiar. 'Friends and Neighbors.' I know her agent. He's crazy about her. Claims she's the only ego-proof, neurosis-free client he's ever had. Never whines, doesn't miss deadlines, never demands coddling, and is currently making him a fat pile of money on the sales of her trade books and calendars, plus the merchandising tie-ins."

She sent Preston a baleful look. "I wonder what it's like to have a neurosis-free client who remembers lunch dates and sends me gifts on my birthday."

"The neuroses are part of the package, but I'm sorry about lunch."

Annoyance faded into concern. "What's up, Preston? You look ragged out. Is the play stalled?"

"No, it's moving. Better than I expected. I just didn't get a lot of sleep."

"Out playing your horn till all hours again?"

"No." Thinking of the woman in 3A, he thought. Pacing the floor. Wanting the woman in 3A. The woman who now, undoubtedly, considered him a slightly lower life-form than slime.

"Just a bad night, Mandy."

"Okay." Because as irritated as he could make her, she cared about him. She crossed the room to give his tensed shoulders a brisk rub. "But you owe me lunch. How about some coffee?"

"There's some on the stove. It was fresh at six this morning."

"Let's start over, then. I'll make it." She moved behind the counter. After she had the coffee going, she poked into the cupboards. She considered Preston's welfare part of her job.

"God, McQuinn, are you on a hunger strike? There's nothing in here but potato-chip crumbs and what once might have been cracked-wheat bread and is now a science project."

"I didn't make it to the market yesterday." Again his

gaze flicked to the door and his mind to Cybil. "Mostly I call in dinner."

"On the phone you don't answer?"

"I'll recharge the battery, Mandy."

"See that you do. If you'd remembered sooner, we'd be sitting in the Four Seasons right now, drinking Cristal to celebrate." She grinned as she leaned on the counter toward him. "I closed the deal, Preston. *A Tangle of Souls* is going to be a major motion picture. You got the producers you wanted, the director you wanted and the option to do the screenplay yourself. All that plus a tidy little fee."

She gave him an amount in seven figures.

"I don't want them to screw it up," was Preston's first reaction.

"Leave it to you." Mandy sighed. "If there's a downside, you find it. So do the screenplay."

"No." He shook his head, walking to the window to try to absorb the news. A film would change the intimacy the play had achieved in the theater. But it would also take his work to millions. And the work mattered to him.

"I don't want to go back there, Mandy. Not that deep."

She poured two cups of coffee and joined him at the window. "Supervisory capacity. Consultant?"

"Yeah, that works for me. Fix it, will you?"

"I can do that. Now, if you'll stop turning cartwheels and dancing on the ceiling, we can talk about your work in progress."

Her dry tone got through, made his lips twitch. He set his coffee on the windowsill, turned and took her sharp-boned face in his hands. "You're the best, and certainly the most patient agent in the business."

"You're so right. I hope you're as proud of yourself as I am. Are you going to call your family?"

"Let me sit on it a couple days."

"It's going to hit the trades, Preston. You don't want them to hear about it that way."

"No, you're right. I'll call them." Finally, he smiled. "After I charge the phone. Why don't I clean up and take you out for that champagne."

"Why don't you. Oh, one more thing," she added as he started for the stairs. "Pretty Miss 3A? Are you going to tell me what's going on between you?"

"I'm not sure there's anything to tell," he murmured.

He still wasn't sure when he knocked on her door later that evening. But he knew he had to answer for that look he'd put in her eyes.

Not that it had been any of her business in the first place, he reminded himself. He hadn't asked her to come nosing around. In fact he'd done everything to discourage her.

Until last night, he thought, and hissed out a breath.

Bad judgment, he decided. It had just been bad judgment. He shouldn't have followed impulse and gone along with her. Shouldn't have compounded the mistake by enjoying himself.

Or by kissing her.

Which he wouldn't have done, his mind circled back, if she hadn't asked him to.

When she pulled open the door, he was ready with an apology. "Look, I'm sorry," he began, delivering it with an impatient edge of annoyance. "But it was none of your business anyway. Let's just straighten this out."

He started to step in, coming up short when she slapped a hand on his chest.

"I don't want you in here."

"For God's sake. You started it. Maybe I let it get out of hand, but—"

"Started what?"

"This," he snapped, furious at the sudden lack of words, hating the kicked-puppy look in her eyes.

"All right, I started it. I should never have brought you cookies. That was devious of me. I shouldn't have worried that you didn't have a job, shouldn't have bought you a decent meal because I thought you couldn't afford it on your own."

"Damn it, Cybil."

"You let me think that. You let me believe you were some poor, out-of-work musician, and I'm sure you had a few private laughs over it. The brilliant, award-winning playwright Preston McQuinn, author of the stunning, emotionally wrenching *A Tangle of Souls*. But I bet you're surprised I even know your work. A bubble-head like me."

She shoved him back a step. "What would a fluffy comic-strip writer know about real art, after all? About serious theater, about *literature*? Why shouldn't you have a few laughs at my expense? You narrow-minded, arrogant creep." Her voice broke when she'd promised herself she wouldn't let it. "I was only trying to help you."

"I didn't ask for your help. I didn't want it." He could see she was close to tears. The closer she got, the more furious he became. He knew how women used tears to destroy a man. He wouldn't let it happen. "My work's my own business."

"Your work's produced on Broadway. That makes it public business," she shot back. "And that has nothing to do with pretending to be a sax player."

"I play the damn sax because I like to play the damn sax. I didn't pretend to be anything. You assumed."

"You let me assume."

"What if I did? I moved in here for a little peace and quiet. To be left alone. The next thing I know you're bringing me cookies, then you're following me and I'm spending half the night in the police station. Then you're asking me to go out so you can slip by a seventy-year-old woman because you don't have the guts to tell her to butt out of your personal life. And you top it off by offering me fifty dollars to kiss you."

Humiliation had the first tear spilling over, trailing slowly down her cheek and making his stomach clench. "Don't." The order whipped out of him. "Don't start that."

"Don't cry when you humiliate me? When you make me feel stupid and ridiculous and ashamed?" She didn't bother to dash the tears away but simply looked at him out of unapologetically drenched eyes. "Sorry, I don't work that way. I cry when someone hurts me."

"You brought it on yourself." He had to say it, was desperate to believe it. And escaped by stalking to his own door.

"You have the facts, Preston," she said quietly. "You have them all in an accurate row. But you've missed the feelings behind them. I brought you cookies because I thought you could use a friend. I've already apologized for following you, but I'll apologize again."

"I don't want—"

"I'm not finished," she said with such quiet dignity

he felt one more wave of guilt. "I took you to dinner because I didn't want to hurt a very nice woman, and I thought you might be hungry. I enjoyed being with you, and I felt something when you kissed me. I thought you did, too. So you're right." She nodded coolly, even as another tear slid down her cheek. "I did bring it all on myself. I suppose you save all your emotions for your work, and can't find the way to let them into your life. I'm sorry for you. And I'm sorry I trod on your sacred ground. I won't do it again."

Before he could think of how to respond, she shut her door. He heard her locks slide into place with quick, deliberate clicks. Turning, he let himself in to his own apartment, followed her example by closing, then locking, the door behind him.

He had what he wanted, he told himself. Solitude. Quiet. She wouldn't come knocking on his door again to interrupt his thoughts, to distract him, to tangle him up in feelings and conversations he didn't want. In feelings he didn't know what to do with.

And he stood, exhausted by the storm and sick of himself, staring at an empty room.

Chapter 5

He couldn't sleep, except in patches. And the patches were riddled with dreams. In them he would find himself wrapped around Cybil. His back in a corner, up against a wall, at the edge of a cliff.

It always seemed as if she'd maneuvered him there, where there was nowhere to go but to her.

And when he did, the dreams became brutally erotic, so that when he managed to rip himself from them, he found himself aroused, furious and filled with the memory, the taste, of her in his mouth.

He couldn't eat, found himself picking at food when he bothered with it at all. Nothing satisfied him; everything reminded him of that simple meal they'd shared a few nights before.

He lived on coffee until his nerves jangled and his stomach burned in protest.

But he could work. It seemed he could always flow into a story, into his people, when his emotions were pumped. It was painful to tear those feelings out of his own heart and have the characters he created gobble them greedily up. But he relished the exchange, even fed on it.

He remembered what Cybil had said before she'd closed the door on him—that he used all his emotions in his work and didn't know how to let them into his life.

She was right, and it was better that way. There were, to his mind, very few people he could trust with feelings. His parents, his sister—though his need to fulfill their expectations of and for him was a double-edged sword.

Then Delta and André, those rare friends he allowed himself and who expected no more from him than what he wanted himself.

Mandy, who pushed him when he needed pushing, listened when he needed to unburden and somehow managed to care about him even when he didn't.

He didn't want a woman digging her way into his heart. Not again. He'd learned his lesson there, and had kept any and all applicants since Pamela out of that vulnerable territory.

She'd cured him, he thought, with lies, deceptions, betrayals. A man could learn a good deal at the tender age of twenty-five that held him in good stead for the duration. Since he'd stopped believing in love, he never wasted time looking for it.

But he couldn't stop thinking of Cybil.

He'd heard her go out several times in the last three days. He'd been distracted more than once by the laughter and voices and music from her apartment.

She wasn't suffering, he reminded himself. So why was he?

It was guilt, he decided. He'd hurt her and it had been neither necessary nor intentional. He'd been charmed by her; reluctantly, but charmed nonetheless. He hadn't meant to make her feel foolish, to bruise her feelings. Tears could still rip at him, even knowing how false and sly they could be when they slid down a woman's cheek.

But they hadn't looked false or sly on Cybil, he remembered. They'd looked as natural as rain.

He wasn't going to resolve the problem—his problem, he thought—until he'd settled with her. He hadn't apologized well; he could admit that. So he'd apologize again now that she'd had some time to get those emotions of hers she was so free with under some control.

There was no reason for them to be enemies, after all. She was the granddaughter of a man he admired and respected. He doubted Daniel MacGregor would return the compliment if he learned that Preston McQuinn had made his little girl cry.

And, Preston realized, Daniel MacGregor's opinion mattered to him.

So, a little voice nagged at him, did Cybil's.

That was why he was pacing the living area of his apartment instead of working. He'd heard her go out, again, but hadn't been quite quick enough to get downstairs and into the hall before she'd gone.

He could wait her out, Preston thought. She had to come back sometime. And when she did, he'd head her off and offer her a very civilized apology. It was blatantly obvious the woman had a soft heart. She'd have to forgive him. Once she had, they could go back to being neighbors.

There was the matter of the hundred dollars, as well, which instead of amusing him as it had initially, now made him feel nasty.

He was sure she'd be ready to laugh the whole thing off now. How long could that kind of cheerful nature hold a grudge?

He would have been surprised to find out just how long, and how well, if he'd seen Cybil's face as she rode the elevator up to the third floor.

It annoyed her, outrageously, that she had to pass the man's door to get to her own. It infuriated her that doing so made her think of him, remember how stupid she'd been—and how much more stupid he'd made her feel.

She shifted the weight of the two bags of groceries she carried in either arm and tried to dig out her key so she wouldn't have to linger in the hallway a second longer than necessary.

The elevator gave its usual announcing thud when it reached her floor. She was still searching for the elusive key when she stepped off.

Her teeth set when she saw him, and her eyes went frosty.

"Cybil." He'd never seen her eyes cold, and the chill of them threw him off rhythm. "Ah, let me give you a hand with those."

"I don't need a hand, thank you." She could only pray to grow a third one, rapidly, that could find her bloody keys.

"Yes, you do, if you're going to keep rooting around in that purse."

He tried a smile, then scowled as they played tug-of-war with one of her bags. In the end he just wrenched it out of her grip. "Look, damn it, I said I was sorry.

How many times do I have to say it before you get out
of this snit you're in?"

"Go to hell," she shot back. "How many times do I
have to say it before you start to feel the heat?"

She finally snagged the key, jabbed it into the lock.
"Give me my groceries."

"I'll take them in for you."

"I said give me the damn bag." They were back to
tugging, until she hissed out a breath. "Keep them,
then."

She shoved open the door, but before she could slam
it in his face, he'd shoved it open again and pushed
his way inside. Their eyes met, both narrowed, and he
thought he caught a glint of violence in hers.

"Don't even think about it," he warned her. "I'm not
an underweight mugger."

She thought she could still do some damage but decided it would only make him seem more important
than she'd determined he would be. Instead, she turned
on the heel of her pink suede sneakers, dumped her
bag on the counter. When he did the same, she nodded briskly.

"Thanks. Now you've delivered them. Want a tip?"

"Very funny. Let's just settle this first." He reached
in his pocket, where he'd folded the hundred-dollar bill
she'd given him. "Here."

She flicked the money a disinterested glance. "I'm
not taking it back. You earned it."

"I'm not keeping your money over what turned out
to be a bad joke."

"Bad joke!" The ice in her eyes turned to sharp green
flames. "Is that what it was? Well, ha-ha. Now that you
bring it up, I owe you another fifty, don't I?"

That hit the mark, had his jaw clenching as she grabbed up her purse. "Don't push it, Cybil. Take the money back."

"No."

"I said take the damn money." He grabbed her wrist, yanked her around and crumpled the bill into her palm. "Now…" Then watched in astonishment as she ripped a hundred dollars into confetti.

"There, problem solved."

"That," he said on what he hoped was a calming breath, "was amazingly stupid."

"Stupid? Well, why break pattern? You can go now," she said.

Her voice was so suddenly regal, so completely princess to peon, he nearly blinked. "Very good, very effective," he murmured. "The lady-of-the-manor tone was so utterly unexpected."

Her next suggestion, delivered in the same haughty tone, was also utterly unexpected, to the point, and made him blink.

"That works, too," he acknowledged. "And I don't think you meant that in a romantic sense."

She simply turned, stalked around the counter and began to put away her groceries. If insults and swearing didn't work, perhaps ignoring him would.

It might have if he hadn't seen her fingers tremble as she pushed a box into the cupboard. And seeing it, he felt everything inside him fade but the guilt.

"Cybil, I'm sorry." He watched her hand hesitate, then grab a soup can and shove it away. "It took on a life of its own, and I didn't do anything to stop it. I should have."

"You didn't have to lie to me. I'd have left you alone."

"I didn't lie—or didn't start out to. But I let you assume something other than the truth. I want my privacy. I need it."

"You've got it. I'm not the one who just bullied his way into someone's apartment."

"No, you're not." He stuck his hands in his pockets, dragged them out again and laid them on the counter. "I hurt you, and I didn't have to. I'm sorry for it."

She closed her eyes as she felt the gate she'd sworn to keep locked on her heart creak open. "Why did you?"

"Because I thought it would keep you on your own side of the hall. Because you were a little too appealing for comfort. And because part of me got a kick out of you wanting to help me find work."

He saw her shoulders draw up at that and winced. "I didn't mean it that way. Cybil, how could I not be amused when you offered me a hundred dollars to have dinner with you? A hundred dollars so you could spare an old woman's feelings and get some out-of-work sax player a hot meal. It was…sweet. That's not a word that comes easy to me."

"It's humiliating," she muttered, and grabbed the second bag and began shoving produce into the fridge.

"Don't let it be." He took a chance and walked around the counter so they both stood in the kitchen. "It only backfired because the timing was off, and that's my fault. If I'd told you who I was over dinner, as I should have, you'd have laughed about it. Instead, I made you cry, and I can't stand knowing that."

She stood where she was, staring into the refrigerator. She hadn't expected him to care, for it to matter to him. But it did. She simply couldn't hold out against a caring heart.

Drawing a deep breath, she told herself they would start fresh. Try for casual friends. "Want a beer?"

Every knot in his shoulders loosened. "Oh, yeah."

"Figured." She reached in for a bottle, disposed of the top, reached for a glass. "I haven't heard you talk so much at one time since I met you." When she turned, offering the beer, her eyes were smiling. "You must be dry."

"Thanks."

Her dimple fluttered. "But I'm out of cookies."

"You could always make some more."

"Maybe." She turned away to deal with the groceries. "But I was thinking about baking a pie." Tossing a look over her shoulder, she lifted a brow. "We never did have that pie."

"No, we didn't."

Too appealing for comfort, he thought again. She was wearing an oversize cotton shirt, plain white. Leggings the color of summer skies, those silly shoes.

Since she'd been marketing, he doubted that the just-under-the-smoldering-point perfume had been dabbed on to please anyone but herself, and had no idea why she would wear two gold hoops in one ear and a single diamond stud in the other.

But it all combined into one fascinating package.

When she turned back to reach into the bag again, he took her wrist with his free hand. "Are we on level ground now?"

"Looks like."

"Then there's something else." He set the beer down. "I dream about you."

Now it was her mouth that went dry. And her stomach erupted with the crazed flapping of a hundred wings. "What?"

"I dream about you," he repeated, and stepped forward until her back was against the refrigerator. Her back against the wall this time, he thought. Not his. "About being with you, touching you." Watching her face, he skimmed his fingertips over the tops of her breasts. "And I wake up tasting you."

"Oh, God."

"You said you felt something when I kissed you, and thought I did, too." With his eyes still on hers, he ran his hands down her sides to her hips. "You were right."

Weak at the knees, she swallowed. Hard. "I was?"

"Yeah. And I want to feel it again."

She strained back as he leaned forward. "Wait!"

His mouth paused a breath from hers. "Why?"

And her mind went blank. "I don't know."

His lips curved in one of his rare smiles. "Stop me when you do," he suggested, then captured her.

It was the same. She was sure it wouldn't be, couldn't be the same fast, hot spin of heart and mind and body. But all those parts of her seemed to have been waiting, and poised to leap. Jody was right, she thought dimly. He'd ruined her.

Bright, fresh, soft as a sunbeam. She was all those things. Warm, sweet, generous. All the things he'd forgotten to need were trembling in his arms.

And he wanted them, wanted her with a quick punch of greed he hadn't expected.

On an oath, he savaged her throat. "Here. Right here."

"No." It was the last thing she'd expected to hear come out of her own mouth when his hands were making her ache for more. Even as the need roared in her blood she said it again. "No. Wait."

He lifted his head, kept eyes that had gone the color of a storm at sea on hers. "Why?"

"Because I..." Her head fell back on a moan when his hands, slow and firm, stroked up her body, awakening every pore.

"I want you." His thumbs circled her breasts, over them. "You want me."

"Yes, but—" Her hands opened and closed on his shoulders as she fought off a new spurt of longing. "There are a few things I don't let myself do on impulse. I'm really sorry to say this is one of them."

She opened her eyes again, let out one more shaky breath. How closely he watched her, she realized. How sharply, even with desire clouding his mind. He could step back from it, look through it, and measure.

"It's not a game, Preston."

He lifted a brow, surprised that she'd understood his thoughts so clearly. "No? No," he decided, because he believed her. "You wouldn't be good at that kind of game, would you?"

Someone had been, she thought, and was suddenly, brutally sorry for him. "I don't know. I've never played it."

He stepped back, shrugged and seemed completely in control again while her system continued to jangle. Unconsciously, she lifted her fingertips to her throat where his mouth had aroused dozens of raw nerves.

"I need time before I share myself that way. Making love is a gift and shouldn't be given thoughtlessly."

Her words touched him and, for reasons he couldn't understand, settled him. "It often is."

"Not for me." She shook her head. "Not from me."

Because he had a sudden urge to stroke her cheek, he hooked his thumbs in his front pockets. Better not to touch again, he reasoned. Not quite yet. "And telling me that is supposed to make me content to step back?"

"Telling you that is supposed to make you understand why I said no, when I want to say yes. When we both know you could make me say yes."

Heat flicked into his eyes. "That's a dangerous kind of honesty you have there."

"You need the truth." She didn't believe she'd ever known anyone who needed it more. "And I don't lie to men I'm planning to be intimate with."

He stepped forward again, watched her lips tremble on a strangled breath. He could make her say yes… and the power of that was heady. Using it, he realized, would damage something he wasn't completely sure he believed existed.

"You need time," he said. "You got an estimate on that?"

Her breath shuddered out again. "Right now it feels like five minutes ago. But…" She managed a weak laugh when his lips curved. "I can't really say, except you'll be the first to know."

"Maybe we could shave a couple of days off it," he murmured, and indulged himself by leaning down to rub his lips over hers.

Hoping it would focus her, she kept her eyes open. But her vision went blurry at the edges. "Um, yes, that's probably going to work."

"Let's shoot for a week," he murmured, deepening the kiss degree by degree until she went limp.

When he stepped back, she pressed a hand to her heart. "Fortnight. I've always liked that word, haven't you? We could try for a fortnight."

The last thing he'd expected to do when buffeted by desire was laugh. "I think we'll save that one for later."

"Right, good. Smart." She concentrated on breathing as he turned and picked up his beer. "Well, I have all this..." She gestured vaguely.

"Food?" he suggested. Delighted by her bewilderment.

"Food, yes. I have all this food. I thought I'd fix some..."

He waited a beat while she pressed her hand to her temple and frowned at the stove. "Dinner?"

"That's it. Ha. Dinner. Funny how words just skip out of reach sometimes. I'm going to fix dinner." She blew out a breath. "Would you like to stay for dinner?"

He sipped his beer, leaned back against the counter. "Can I watch you cook?"

"Sure. You can sit there and maybe slice vegetables or something."

"Okay." Because the idea had amazing appeal, he skirted the counter to sit on a stool. "You cook a lot?"

"Yes, I guess. I really like to cook. It's an adventurous process, all the ingredients, heat, timing, the mix of smells and textures and tastes."

"So...do you ever cook naked?"

She paused in the act of sniffing a glossy red pepper. Giggling, she set it on the counter between them. "McQuinn, you made a joke." She put a hand over his, squeezed. "I'm so proud."

"No, I didn't. That was a perfectly serious question."

When she laughed, leaned over to grab his face and kiss him noisily on the mouth, he wouldn't have recognized his own foolish grin. "So do you?"

"Never when I'm sautéing chicken. Which is what I'm about to do."

"That's all right. I have an excellent imagination."

She laughed again; then, catching the wicked gleam in his eyes, cleared her throat. "I think I want some wine. Do you want wine?" He only lifted his nearly full glass of beer. "Oh, yeah."

She took a bottle of white out of the refrigerator, then turned back, giggling again. "You're going to have to stop that."

"Stop what?"

"Stop making me think I'm naked. Go put on some music," she ordered, waving a hand toward the living area. "Maybe open a window, because it's really hot in here, and give me a minute to clear the lust out of my head so I can think of something else to talk about."

"You never have trouble talking."

"You consider that an insult," she said as he slid off the stool. "I don't. I'm a conversation connoisseur."

"Is that the current term for chatterbox?"

"Well, you're just full of wit and humor tonight, aren't you?" And nothing could have pleased her more.

"Must be the company," he murmured, then cocked a brow as he flipped through her CDs. "You have decent taste in music."

"You were expecting otherwise?"

"I wasn't expecting Fats Waller, Aretha, B.B. King. Of course, you've got plenty of chirpy stuff in here, too."

"What's wrong with chirpy music?"

In answer, he held up a CD of *The Partridge Family's Greatest Hits.* "I rest my case."

"Excuse me, but that was given to me by a very dear friend, and it happens to be a classic."

"A classic what?"

"Obviously, you have no appreciation for nostalgia and have failed to recognize the sly, underlying social commentary of David Cassidy's rendition of 'I Think I Love You,' or the desperate sexual motivation that permeates the mood of 'Doesn't Somebody Want To Be Wanted.' But I'd be happy to discuss them with you."

"I bet you actually know the lyrics."

She managed to swallow the chuckle and began to wash the vegetables. "Naturally. During a brief, shining period in my youth, *I* was in a band."

"Right." He settled on B.B.

"Lead vocals and rhythm guitar. The Turbos." She smiled as he walked back to the counter. "Jesse—lead guitar—was into cars."

"You play guitar."

"Yes. Well, I played the guitar. A hot red Fender, which I imagine my mother still has in my old room— along with my toe shoes, my chemistry set, the sketches I made when I was going to be a fashion designer and the books I collected on animal husbandry before I realized that if I became a vet, I'd have to euthanize animals as well as play with them."

She laid a cutting board on the counter, selected the proper knife from her block. "They were all quests."

Fascinating, he thought. The woman was absolutely fascinating. "Fender guitars and toe shoes were quests?"

"I couldn't make up my mind what I wanted to be. Everything I tried was so much fun at first, then it was just work. Do you know how to slice peppers?"

"No. Don't you consider what you do now work, of a sort?"

She sighed and began to slice the peppers herself. "Yes, and it's not of a sort, either. It's a lot of work, but it's still fun. Don't you enjoy writing?"

"Rarely."

She looked up again. "Then why do you do it?"

"It won't let me do anything else. It's my only quest."

She nodded, switching to fat, white mushrooms. "It's like that for my mother. She never wanted to do anything but paint. Sometimes, when I watch her working, I can see how painful it is for her to have a vision and to have to pull out all her skills to transfer what she wants to communicate to canvas. But when she's finished, when it's right, she glows. The satisfaction, maybe even the shock of seeing what she's capable of doing, I suppose. It would be like that for you."

She glanced up, saw him studying her speculatively. "It always surprises you when I understand something other than what's right on the surface, doesn't it?"

He grabbed her hand before she could turn away. "If it does, it only means I'm the one who doesn't understand you. I'm likely to keep offending you until I do."

"I'm ridiculously easy to understand."

"No, that's what I thought. I was wrong. You're a maze, Cybil. With dozens of twists and turns and unexpected angles."

Her smile bloomed slowly, beautifully. "That's the nicest thing you've ever said to me."

"I'm not a nice man. You'd be smart to boot me out, lock your door and keep it that way."

"Being smart, I've figured that out for myself already. However…" Gently, she laid a hand to his cheek. "You seem to be my new quest."

"Until it stops being fun and just becomes work?"

His eyes were so serious, she thought. And he was so ready to believe the worst. "McQuinn, you're already work, and you're still sitting in my kitchen." She smiled again. "Do you know how to slice carrots into pencil sticks?"

"I don't have a clue."

"Then watch and learn. Next time you're going to have to carry your weight." She peeled a carrot clean with a few quick, experienced strokes, then flicked a glance up at him. "Am I still naked?"

"Do you want to be?"

She laughed and picked up her neglected wine.

It took a long time to cook a simple meal when you were distracted by conversation, by lingering looks, by seductive touches.

It took a long time to eat a simple meal when you were sliding lazily into love with the man across from you.

She recognized the signs—the erratic beating of the heart, the bubbling in the blood that was desire. When those were tangled so silkily around dreamy smiles and soft sighs, love was definitely a short trip away.

She wondered what it would be like when she reached it.

It took a long time to say good-night when you were floating on deep, dark kisses in the doorway.

And longer still to sleep when your body ached and your mind was full of dreams.

When she heard the faint drift of his music, she smiled and let it lull her to sleep.

Chapter 6

With his hair still wet from his morning shower, Preston sat at his own kitchen counter on one of Cybil's stools she'd insisted he borrow. He scanned the paper as he ate cold cereal and bananas because Cybil had pushed both on him once she'd gotten a look at his cupboards.

Even a kitchen klutz—which apparently meant him—could manage to pour milk onto cold cereal and slice a banana, she'd told him.

He'd decided against taking offense, though he didn't think he was quite as clumsy in the kitchen as she did. He'd managed to put a salad together, hadn't he? While she'd done something incredible and marvelous to a couple of pork chops.

The woman was one hell of a cook, he mused, and was rapidly spoiling his appetite for the quick slap-together sandwiches he often lived on.

It didn't seem to bother her that they hadn't gone out to dinner since that first meal she'd cooked for him. He imagined she would, before much longer, tire of preparing the evening meal and demand a restaurant.

People generally got itchy for a change of pace when the novelty wore off and routines became ruts.

And he supposed they already had a kind of routine. They kept to their separate corners during the day. Well, except for the couple of times she'd dropped by and persuaded him to go out. To the market, just for a walk, to buy a lamp.

He glanced back toward his living room, frowning at the whimsical bronze frog holding up a triangular-shaped lamp shade. He still wasn't sure how she'd talked him into buying such a thing, or into paying Mrs. Wolinsky for a secondhand recliner she'd wanted to get rid of.

And rightfully so, he decided. Who the hell wanted a green-and-yellow plaid recliner in their living room?

But somehow he had one—which despite its hideous looks was amazingly comfortable.

Of course if you had a chair and a lamp you needed a table. His was a sturdy Chippendale in desperate need of refinishing—and as Cybil had pointed out—a bargain because of it.

She just happened to have a friend who refinished furniture as a hobby, and would put him in touch.

She also just happened to have a friend who was a florist, which explained why there was a vase of cheerful yellow daisies on Preston's kitchen counter.

Another friend—of which Preston had decided she had a legion—painted New York street scenes and sold them on the sidewalk, and couldn't he use a couple of paintings to brighten up the walls?

He'd told her he didn't want to brighten anything, but there were now three very decent original watercolors on his wall.

She was already making noises about rugs.

He didn't know how she worked it, Preston thought, shaking his head as he went back to his breakfast. She just kept talking until you were pulling out your wallet or holding out your hand.

But they kept out of each other's way.

Well, there had been Saturday afternoon, when she'd invaded with buckets and mops and brooms and God knows what. If he was going to live in a place, she'd told him, at least it could be clean. And somehow he'd ended up spending three hours of a rainy afternoon, when he should have been writing, scrubbing floors and chasing down dust.

Then again, he'd nearly gotten her into bed. Very nearly gotten her there, he remembered, when she'd stood in speechless shock at the state of his bedroom.

She'd gotten her voice back quickly enough and had launched into a lecture. He should have more respect for his workplace if not for his sleeping area, since they seemed to be one in the same. Why the hell did he keep the curtains drawn over the windows? Did he like caves? Did he have a religious objection to doing laundry?

He'd grabbed her out of self-defense and had stopped her mouth in the most satisfying of ways.

And if they hadn't tripped over a small mountain of laundry on the way to the bed, he doubted they'd have ended the afternoon with a trip to the cleaners.

Still, there were advantages, he thought. He appreciated a clean space, even though he rarely noticed a messy one. He liked tumbling into bed on freshly laundered sheets—though he would have preferred to tumble on them with Cybil. And it was hard to complain when you opened a cupboard and found actual food.

Even the sexual frustration was working for him. The writing was pouring out of it, and out of him. Maybe the play had taken a turn on him, focusing now more on a female character, one with a shining naiveté and enthusiasm. A woman alive with energy and optimism. And one who'd be seduced by and damaged by a man who had none of those things inside him. A man who wouldn't be able to stop himself from taking them from her, then leaving her shattered.

He saw the parallels well enough between what he created and what was, but he refused to worry about it.

He sipped his coffee, reminding himself to ask Cybil why his always tasted faintly of swamp water, and turned to the comic section to see what she'd been up to.

He skimmed it, frowned, then went back to the first section and read it again.

She was already at work, her window open, because spring had decided to be kind. A lovely warm breeze wafted through along with the chaos of street noise.

After her sheet of paper was set and scaled, she set her T-square back in its place in the custom-built tool area she'd designed to suit herself. She tilted her head, facing the first blank section. It was double the size of what would appear in the dailies in a couple of weeks. She already had it in her mind—the setup, the situation and the punch line that would comprise those five windows and give the readership their morning chuckle over coffee.

The elusive Mr. Mysterious, now known as Quinn, huddled in his dim cave, writing the Great American Novel. Sexy, cranky, irresistible Quinn, so serious, so intense in his own little world he was completely unaware that Emily was crouched on his fire escape, peering through the narrow chink of his perpetually drawn curtains, struggling to read his work in progress through a pair of binoculars.

Amused at herself—because in her own way Cybil knew her subtle little probes and questions on how his play was going were the more civilized version of her counterpart's voyeurism—she settled down to lightly sketch her professional interpretation of the man across the hall.

She exaggerated ruthlessly, his good points and his bad. The tall, muscular body, the ruggedly chiseled looks, the cool eyes. His rudeness, his humor and his perpetual bafflement with the world Emily lived in.

Poor guy, she thought, he doesn't have a clue what to do with her.

When the buzzer sounded, she tucked her pencil behind her ear, thinking Jody had forgotten her key.

She stopped to top off her coffee cup on the way. "Just hang on. Coming."

Then she opened the door and experienced one more rapid meltdown. His hair was just a little damp and he wasn't wearing a shirt. Boy, oh, boy, just look at those pecs, she thought, and barely resisted licking her lips.

His jeans were faded, his feet bare, and his face—his face was so wonderfully serious and sober.

"Hi." She managed to make it sound bright and easy

while she pictured herself biting him. "You run out of soap in the shower? Need to borrow some?"

"What? No." He'd forgotten he was only half-dressed. "I want to ask you about this," he continued, lifting the paper.

"Sure, come on in." It would be safe, she told herself. Jody would be there any minute and stop her from jumping Preston. "Why don't you get some coffee and come up? I'm working and it's rolling pretty well."

"I don't want to interrupt, but—"

"Not much does," she said cheerfully over her shoulder as she started up the stairs. "There's cinnamon bagels if you want one."

"No." Hell, he thought, and ended up pouring a cup of coffee and taking a bagel, after all.

He hadn't been upstairs before, since he'd never come over when she was working. He tormented himself by glancing into her bedroom, studying the big bed with its bold blue cover and sumptuous mountain of jewel-toned pillows, the slim rods of the white iron headboard where he could imagine trapping her hands under his as he finally did everything he wanted with her. To her.

It smelled of her, fresh, female, with seductive undertones of vanilla.

She kept rose petals in a bowl, a book beside the bed and candles in the window.

"Find everything?" she called out.

He shook himself. "Yeah. Listen, Cybil..." He stepped into her studio. "God, how do you work with all that noise?"

She barely glanced up. "What noise? Oh, that." She continued to sketch, using a new pencil, as she'd forgotten the one behind her ear. "Sort of like background music. Half the time I don't hear it."

The room looked efficient and creative with its neat shelves holding both supplies and clever tchotchkes. He recognized the work of the sidewalk artist in one of the paintings on her wall, and the genius of her mother in two others.

There was a complex and fascinating metal sculpture in the corner, a little clutch of violets tucked into a glass inkwell and a cozy divan heaped with more pillows against the wall.

But she didn't look efficient, bent over the big slanted board with her legs folded up under her, the toenails of her bare feet painted pink, a pencil behind one ear and a gold hoop in the other.

She looked scattered, and sexy.

Curious, he walked around to peer over her shoulder. An act that, he admitted, had anyone dared to try on him would have earned the offender a quick and painful death.

"What are all the blue lines for?"

"Scaling, perspective. Takes a little math before you can get down to business. I work in five windows for the dailies," she continued, sketching easily. "I have to set them on paper like this, work out the theme, the gag, the hit, so that the strip can move from start to finish in five connected beats."

Satisfied, she moved to the next section. "I sketch it in first, just need to see how it hangs—you'd say a draft, where you get the story line down, then decide where it needs to be punched up. I'll give it more details, fiddle a bit before I switch to pen and ink."

He frowned, focusing on the first sketch. "Is that supposed to be me?"

"Hmm. Why don't you pull up a stool. You're blocking the light."

"What is she doing there?" Ignoring the suggestion, he tapped a finger on the second window. "Spying on me. You're spying on me?"

"Don't be ridiculous—you don't even have a fire escape outside your bedroom." She looked into her mirror, made several faces that left him staring at her, then started on the third section.

"What about this?" he demanded, rapping the paper on her shoulder.

"What about it? God, you smell fabulous." Pleasing herself, she turned and sniffed him. "What kind of soap is that?"

"Are you going to have this guy take a shower next?" When she pursed her lips in obvious consideration, Preston shook his head. "No. There has to be a line. I was oddly amused when you introduced this parody of me into the script, but—"

He broke off as he heard her front door open and slam shut. "Who's that?"

"That would be Jody and Charlie. So you've gotten a kick out of the new guy?" She stopped sketching and shifted to smile up at him. "I wondered, because you hadn't mentioned it before. You know, some people don't even recognize themselves. They just have no self-awareness, I suppose, but I thought you'd see it if you happened to read the strip. Hi, Jody. There's Charlie."

"Hi." It wasn't an easy matter, even for a happily married woman, to keep her tongue from falling out when she was so suddenly and unexpectedly faced with a well-muscled, naked male chest. "Uh, hi. Are we interrupting?"

"No, Preston just had some questions about the strip."

"I love the new guy. He's really got Emily in a spin. I can't wait to see what happens next." She broke into a wide grin as Charlie exploded out a "Da!" and reached for Preston.

"He calls every man he sees 'Da.' Chuck's a little put out by it, but Charlie's just a guy's guy, you know."

"Right." Absently, Preston ran a hand over Charlie's downy brown hair. "I just want to get something straight about how this thing is going," he began, turning back to Cybil.

"Da!" Charlie said again, arms extended hopefully, smile sleepy.

"Just how close to reality do you work?" Preston asked, automatically taking the baby and settling him on his shoulder.

Cybil's heart simply melted. "You like babies."

"No, I toss them out of third-story windows at every opportunity," he said impatiently, then shook his head when Jody squeaked. "Relax. He's fine. What I want to know is this business here." Shifting the baby, he dropped the comic section on her board.

"Oh, the 'no scale' bit. This is really part one. They'll run the second half of it tomorrow. I think it works."

"Chuck and I fell over laughing when we read it this morning," Jody put in, relaxed again as she watched Preston absently patting the now-sleeping baby.

"You've got these two women here—"

"Emily and Cari."

"I know who they are by now," Preston muttered,

narrowing his eyes at both women. "They're discussing—they're rating, for God's sake—the way Quinn kissed Emily a couple days ago."

"Uh-huh. Chuck laughed?" Cybil wanted to know. "I wondered if men would get it or if it would just hit with women."

"Oh, yeah, he died over it."

"Pardon me." With what he considered admirable restraint, Preston held up a hand. "I'd like to know if the two of you sit around here discussing your various sexual encounters and then rating them on a scale of one to ten before you then give the American public a good chuckle over it with their corn flakes."

"Discussing them?" Eyes wide and innocent, Cybil stared up at Preston. "Honestly, McQuinn, this is a comic strip. You're taking it too seriously."

"So all this about the no scale is just a bit?"

"What else?"

He studied her face. "I wouldn't like to think that when I finally get you into bed, I'm going to read about my performance in five sections in the morning paper."

"Oh, my. Oh, well." Jody patted a hand on her heart. "I think I'll just take Charlie and go put him down for his nap." She eased him out of Preston's arms and hurried out.

"McQuinn." Cybil smiled, tapped her pencil. "I have a feeling that event would be worth the full Sunday spread."

"Is that a threat or a joke?"

When she only laughed, he spun her stool around, then knocked the air out of her lungs with a fierce and demanding kiss. "Tell your friend to go away, and we'll find out."

"No, I'm keeping her. She's all that stopped me from biting your throat when you came in."

"Are you trying to drive me crazy?"

"Not really. It's kind of a side effect." Her pulse had gone from slow shuffle to manic tap dance. "You've got to go. I've finally found a distraction I can't work through. And you're it."

Seeing no reason he should go crazy alone, he leaned down one last time and took her mouth. "When you speak of this—" he caught her bottom lip between his teeth, drawing it erotically through them "—and I expect you will, be accurate."

He walked to the doorway, turning back in time to see her shudder. "No scale?" he said, realizing he suddenly found it not just amusing but gratifying.

When she managed to do nothing more than make one helpless gesture with her hands, he laughed. And was still grinning when he jogged down her steps and out the door.

"Safe?" Jody whispered, poking her head into the doorway.

"Oh, God, God, Jody, what am I going to do here?" Shaken, Cybil stabbed the second pencil behind her ear, knocked the first out of place, and didn't even bother to curse. "I thought I had it all figured out. I mean what's wrong with easing yourself into what promises to be a blistering, roof-raising affair with an incredibly intense, gorgeous, interesting man?"

"Let me think." Holding up a finger, Jody strolled in and picked up the coffee Preston had never touched. "Okay, I've got it. Nothing. The answer to that question is nothing."

"And if you're a little bit in love with him, that only sweetens the deal, right?"

"Absolutely. Otherwise it's fun but sort of like eating too much chocolate at one sitting. You enjoy it when it's going on, then you feel a little queasy and ashamed."

"But what if you went all the way in. What do you do when you've gone over the brink?"

Jody set down the coffee. "You went over the brink?"

"Just now."

"Oh, honey." All sympathy, Jody wrapped her arms around Cybil and rocked. "It's all right. It had to happen sooner or later."

"I know, but I always thought it would be later."

"We all do."

"He won't want me to be in love with him. It'll just annoy him." Turning her face to Jody's shoulder, she let out a shaky breath. "I'm not too happy about it myself, but I'll get used to it."

"Sure you will. Poor Frank." With a sigh, Jody patted Cybil's shoulder, then stepped back. "He never really had a shot, did he?"

"Sorry."

"Oh, well." Jody dismissed her favorite cousin with an absent flick of the wrist. "What are you going to do?"

"I don't know. I guess running and hiding's out."

"That's for wimps."

"Yeah. Wimps. How about pretending it'll go away?"

"That's for morons."

Cybil drew a bracing breath. "How about shopping?"

"Now you're talking." On a quick salute, Jody headed for the door. "I'll see if Mrs. Wolinsky will watch Charlie, then we'll handle this problem like real women."

* * *

She bought a new dress. A slinky length of black sin that made Jody roll her eyes and declare, "The man's a goner," when Cybil tried it on.

She bought new shoes. Mile-high heels as thin as honed scalpels.

She bought new lingerie. The kind women wear when they expect it to be seen by a man who'll then be compelled to rip it off.

And she imagined Preston's wide hands and long fingers peeling the silky-as-cobwebs hose down her legs.

Then there were flowers to choose, candles, wine.

Marketing for a meal she would design to tease the senses and whet the palate for a more primitive kind of appetite.

By the time she got home she was loaded down, and she was calm.

There was a scene to be set, and doing so gave her focus. Because she wanted to take the rest of the day to prepare, because she needed it to be perfect, she wrote a note to Preston and stuck it to her door.

Then she locked herself in, drew a deep breath and took everything up to the bedroom.

She arranged tender lilies and fragrant rosebuds in vases, in bowls, and set them on tables, the dresser, the windowsills. Then she grouped candles, all white, a trio here, a single there, a half-dozen scented tealights on a circle of mirrored glass.

Some she lit so the room would fill with soft light and gentle fragrance while she worked.

She unwrapped two slender-stemmed wineglasses, placed them just so on the low table in front of the curved wicker chaise. Reminded herself to chill the wine.

Facing the bed, she stopped, considered. Would turning down the duvet and sheets be too obvious? Then she laughed at herself. Why stop now?

When it was done, when she could look around the room and see there was nothing that wasn't as she needed it to be, she went down to make the early preparations for the meal she intended to cook.

She listened, hoping he'd begin to play so that some of him would come inside her rooms with her. But his apartment remained silent.

With careful deliberation she chose music for mood, arranging CDs in her changer.

Satisfied, she went back up, laid her new dress on the bed, shivered in anticipation as she set the black lace bra and the blatantly provocative matching garter belt beside it and imagined what it would feel like to wear them.

Powerful, she decided. Secretive and certain.

She shivered again, thrilling to the clutch of lust deep in her center, then went to draw a hot, frothy bath.

She poured wine, lit more candles to promote the mood, before she slipped into the tub. And closing her eyes, she imagined Preston's hands, rather than the frothy water, on her.

Nearly an hour later, she was slathering every inch of her body with cream, sliding her fingers along to make certain her skin was silky and scented, when Preston tugged her note off the front door:

McQuinn, I've got plans. I'll see you later. Cybil

Plans? Plans? She had plans when he'd worked himself into a turmoil over her all day? He read the note again, furious with both of them, as he hadn't been able to get the image of spending yet another foolish evening with her out of his head.

For God's sake, he'd gone out and bought her flowers. He hadn't bought flowers for a woman since...

He crumpled the note in his hand. What else could he expect? Women were, first and foremost, tuned to their own agenda. He'd known it, accepted it, and if he'd let himself forget that single relevant detail with Cybil, he had no one to blame but himself.

She'd see him later?

It appeared she was a game player, after all. But he didn't have to step up to bat.

He turned, marched back into his apartment, where he tossed the lilacs that had inexplicably reminded him of her on the kitchen counter. He flipped her balled note across the room, picked up his sax and stalked out to work off his temper at Delta's.

At exactly seven-thirty, Cybil took the stuffed mushrooms she'd slaved over out of the oven. The table was set for two, with more candles, more flowers precisely arranged. There was a wonderfully colorful avocado-and-tomato salad chilling along with the wine.

Once they'd enjoyed their appetizers and first course, she intended to destroy him with her seafood crepes.

If all went according to plan, they'd polish off the meal with icy champagne and fresh raspberries and cream. In bed.

"Okay, Cybil."

She took off her apron, marched to the mirror to check the fit and line of the dress. She slipped on her heels, added another dash of perfume, then gave her reflection a bracing smile.

"Let's go get him."

She sauntered across the hall, pressed his buzzer, then waited with her heart hammering. Shifting from foot to foot, she buzzed again.

"How could you not be home? How *could* you? Didn't you get the note? You must have. It's not on the door, is it? Didn't I specifically say I'd see you later?"

Groaning, she thumped her fist against the door. Then she jerked upright and blinked.

"I said I had plans. Oh, my God, you didn't get it, did you, you thick-headed jerk? *You're* the plans. Oh, hell." She made a dash back through her open door for her key, realized she didn't have anywhere to put it. With a shrug, she stuck it into her bra rather than waste time running upstairs for a bag.

In thirty seconds flat, she was risking a broken neck by running down the stairs.

"Woman trouble, sugar lips?"

Preston looked over at Delta as he took a break to wet his throat. "No woman. No trouble."

"This is Delta." She tapped a finger to his cheek. "Every night this week you come in here late and you play like a man who's got a woman on his mind. And this man doesn't much mind having her there. Now tonight, you come in early and you're playing like a man who's got trouble with the woman. Did you have a fight with that pretty little girl?"

"No. We've both got other things to do."

"Still holding you off, is she?" She laughed, but not without sympathy. "Some women take more romance than others."

"It has nothing to do with romance."

"Maybe that's your problem." Delta wrapped an arm around his shoulders and squeezed. "Do you ever buy her flowers? Tell her she has beautiful eyes."

"No." Damn it, he had brought her flowers. She hadn't bothered to stick around to take them. "It's sex, not a courtship."

"Oh, sweetheart. You want one, you better do the other with a woman like that."

"That's why I'm better off without a woman like that. I want it simple." He picked up the sax, lifted a brow. "Now, are you going to let me play, or do you want to give me more advice on my love life?"

With a shake of her head, she stepped back. "When you have a love life, *cher,* I'll have advice."

He blew off a riff, listening to the music inside his head. Inside his blood. He let the notes come, but the music didn't take his mind off her. He could use that, as well, he told himself. Here, where sharing was a pleasure. Not with words, where it was often pain.

The notes slipped out, throbbed in the air, sobbed into a wail.

And she walked in the door.

Her eyes, full of secrets, met his through the haze of smoke, held. And the smile she sent him as she slid into a chair made his palms go damp. She moistened her lips, trailed a finger up from the center of the low bodice of the slinky black dress to the base of her throat. And back again.

He watched, his blood swimming, as she crossed long, long legs with a movement so slow, so studied, it had to be deliberate. Surely the way she ran her hand from calf to knee to thigh was designed to make a man's gaze follow the movement.

His did, and his pulse leaped like a wolf on the hunt.

She sat through the song, leaning back in the chair, hooking one arm provocatively over the back. When the notes faded, she traced the tip of her tongue lazily over those hot red lips.

Then she rose, her gaze still locked with his as the music pumped. She ran a hand down her hip, turned on those man-killer heels and started back out. She glanced over her shoulder, sent him a sultry invitation with no more than a lift of eyebrow and left the door swinging behind her.

The oath that came out of his mouth when he lowered the sax was absolutely reverent.

"You going after that, brother?"

Preston crouched to push his sax into its case. "Do I look stupid, André?"

"No." André chuckled and kept on playing. "No, you don't."

Chapter 7

She was waiting on the sidewalk when he came out, standing in the white wash of a streetlight with one hand resting on a cocked hip, her head angled, her lips curved in the barest hint of a smile. It made him think of a photograph, some arty shot perfectly framed and cropped for a classy magazine.

Sex in black and white.

He started toward her, taking more in the closer he came. The short, whiskey-colored hair sleeked to frame her face. The short black dress sleeked to frame her body.

No jewelry to distract the eye.

Mile-high heels designed to showcase mile-long legs.

The only color was on those huge green eyes under sooty lashes and the siren red of her mouth. A mouth, he noted, that was curved in smug, female satisfaction.

He was three steps away when her scent reached out like a crooked finger and beckoned him the rest of the way.

"Hello, neighbor." She purred it—one more hot bullet to his loins.

He tilted his head, lifted a brow. "Change of plans... neighbor?"

"I hope not." She took the last step, moving into him, deliberately sliding her hands up his sides, over his shoulders, around his neck. Her body fit suggestively to his as she purred again.

Then she laughed, shook her head. "You were the plans, you knothead."

She wondered if it was the announcement or the mild insult that had his eyes narrowing in speculation.

"Is that so?"

"McQuinn." She tilted her head, brought her mouth a whisper from his. Then, with her eyes on his, slowly licked. "Didn't I tell you you'd be the first to know?"

"Yeah." With his free hand he cupped her neck, keeping that wet red mouth tantalizingly close to his. "How fast can you walk in those heels?"

She laughed again, just a little breathlessly now. "Not very. But we've got all night, don't we?"

"It might just take longer than that." He stepped back, and after a moment, held out a hand for hers. "Where did you get the lethal weapon? The dress," he added when she gave him a blank look.

"Oh, this old thing." This time her laugh was warm and rich. "I bought it today, thinking of you. And when I put it on tonight, I was thinking of what it was going to be like when you took it off me."

"You must have been practicing," he said when he

could manage to form words again. "Because you're damn good at this."

"Actually, I'm making it up as I go along."

"Don't stop on my account."

It was amazing, she thought, that a balmy spring evening could suddenly seem as sultry as summer in the Tropics. "Sorry I wasn't more specific in my note. I had a lot on my mind." She turned, delighted that the heels brought her eye level with his mouth. "A lot of you on my mind."

"It pissed me off." It didn't seem so hard to admit it.

"Pardon me if I find that very flattering. When I knocked on your door and you didn't answer, I had essentially the same reaction. I spent a lot of time getting ready for you. You can be flattered."

"It must have taken a while to paint on what there is of that dress."

"Not just that." She'd managed to keep her heartbeat fairly steady, but as she paused at the entrance to their building, it began to plunge and kick. "I made dinner."

"You did?" He wasn't just flattered, he realized. He wasn't just aroused. He was touched.

"A fairly fabulous one, if I do say so myself," she added, backing into the building. "With a sassy little white wine to set it off—and an elegant and icy champagne to go with dessert."

She led the way into the elevator, pushed the button for three, then leaned back against the wall. "Which I thought we could enjoy in bed."

He kept a step away, knowing if he touched her they wouldn't be leaving the elevator for a very long time. "Anything else I should know about these plans of yours?"

"Oh, I don't think you're going to need me to write anything down." She stepped off the elevator, tossed one of those slow smiles over her shoulder and strolled to her door.

He thought if he managed to get inside without exploding, he'd show her he could make plans of his own. "Key?"

"Hmm." Keeping her eyes on his, she slid a finger under the deep scoop of her bodice, touched metal and watched his gaze drop, heat, linger. "Gee." She slid her finger up again, circled it lazily at the base of her throat. "I can't seem to find it. Maybe you can get it for me."

He decided he had news for medical science. It was possible to remain conscious and upright after all the blood had drained out of your head.

He trailed his finger along the inviting swell above the black silk—felt her shiver, heard the catchy intake of her breath. Then dipped down, taking his time, gliding his finger lazily over heated flesh, gently abrading her nipple until her eyes clouded and closed.

"I'd say you're the one who's been practicing," she managed, and made him smile.

"I'm just making it up as I go along."

"Mmm-hmm. Don't stop on my account."

He didn't intend to. Not for hours. "Looks like I found it," he murmured, hooking the key.

"Yeah." She let out a long, long breath. "I just knew you would."

He slid the key home, released locks. "Ask me in, Cybil."

"Come in."

He pushed open the door, backed her inside. Reaching behind, he locked the door. Clamping his hands on her hips, he kept walking.

"Dinner?"

"Can wait." He lifted the phone off the hook as they passed it.

"The wine?"

"Later. Much later." Her heels bumped into the bottom step. This time he smiled. "Keep going."

On legs that had gone weak, she moved up the stairs with her hands braced on his shoulders.

"Ask me to touch you."

"Touch me." She sighed as his hands traveled up.

"Ask me to taste you."

"Taste me." And moaned as his mouth brushed over the rise of her breasts.

When they reached the bedroom door, his teeth scraped along her throat, her jaw, and left her mouth aching for attention.

"Kiss me."

"I will." But he only teased the corners of her lips with the tip of his tongue. "I want the light."

"No, I have candles. They're everywhere." She broke free to grab a matchbook, then fumbled. "I can't. I'm shaking. Isn't that ridiculous?"

He took the matches from her and danced his fingertips along her thigh. "I want you to. Don't move," he ordered, then worked his way around the room setting the candles alight.

The glow shimmered. The scent whispered.

Tossing the matches aside, he moved back to where she stood, her eyes huge and full of nerves, needs and candlelight.

"Now." His hands slid around her waist, down. "Ask me to take you."

She kept her eyes on his. "Take me."

His mouth captured hers, plundered, rocking her with the first punch of the power they'd built between them. She grabbed on, as much to add to the storm as ride it. This was what she wanted, this bold, blistering, battering heat. The crash of senses, the war of needs.

"I want you." She raced wild kisses over his face. "I want you in bed."

Then she gasped as he whirled her around, dragged her back against him. It stunned her to see them reflected in the mirror, to see the gleam of desire in his gaze as it traveled down her body.

"We have all night," he reminded her. "Watch."

He dipped his head to the curve of her neck and shoulder, sharp little bites that had the first helpless sounds catching in her throat.

She watched his hands travel up, saw them, felt them cup her breasts, squeeze, release, slide over silk, his fingers sliding under it, tugging the material. She braced for him to rip.

Then shuddered as he simply let his hands glide over her again, then down. She cried out in aroused shock as he pressed against her center.

His head lifted, his teeth catching the lobe of her ear as their gazes met in the mirror. She'd driven him crazy when she'd walked into the club. He intended to return the favor.

"Tell me you want more."

Her muscles had gone lax, her bones to jelly. "Preston."

He traced his fingers up and down her thighs, felt

the muscles quiver and the flesh heat. "Tell me you want more."

"God." Her head fell back on his shoulder as she fought for air. "I want more."

"So do I."

He moved from silky hose to silky flesh, torturing himself. Her scent was destroying him, the feel of her urging him to take all of her. But he drew it out, even as his own breath became labored; he held back the animal pacing inside him.

Because when he let it go, he knew it would devour them both.

He nipped his way around the back of her neck, her shoulders, while he tugged down the zipper of her dress. He peeled it off her, then bit back a groan.

Sex in black and white, he thought again.

Even through the haze of desire she saw his eyes change. Saw something dangerous flash into them. It shocked her to realize that was what she wanted. The danger, the risk, the glory of breaking whatever choke chain he had on his control.

Power swirled into her as she covered his hands with hers and guided them over her. "I bought this today," she whispered, holding his hands to her breasts. "So you could rip it off me tonight."

She curled her fingers with his, nudged them over the thin silk connecting the lace. And let out one sharp gasp when he yanked the dress apart.

And with that single movement, he broke.

He spun her around, his mouth ravishing hers now, his hands close to brutal as he dragged her to the bed.

He was going to eat her alive, and couldn't stop it. He felt her arch and buck when his hand covered her.

Heard her choked scream as he drove her over the first ragged edge. Then he was tearing at silk and lace, desperate for more.

He feasted on her breasts, the firm fragrant swell of them, while her heart hammered against his mouth. Her hands drove him wild as they pulled at his shirt, as her nails scraped down his back.

Her mouth was as greedy as his, her hands as rough and impatient as they tugged and dragged at his jeans. And when they closed around him, fire burst in his blood.

She rolled with him, tangling in the sheets she'd so carefully smoothed. Panting, shuddering, she wrapped herself around him, bowed up in urgent demand.

When he drove into her, heat into heat, the explosion of pleasure was huge, a fast, hard, turbulent wave that drenched the skin and swamped the soul. With one throaty moan, she matched him for speed and fury.

More was all he could think. He had to have more of her. Clamping her hands on the slim iron poles of the headboard, he plunged deeper. She arched, accepted. Mad on the pleasure of her, he watched her face, absorbing every flicker of shock and delight as he took her higher, and faster, then over so that she sobbed out his name, so that her eyes went dark and blind.

As her body melted under his, he let himself pour into her. Surrendered himself.

His hands continued to hold hers on the rungs, though her fingers had gone limp. His body continued to cover hers while she quaked. He stayed inside her. Mated.

"Are we still breathing?"

He turned his head, felt the pulse in her throat scrambling. "Your heart's still beating."

"Good, that's good. Is yours?"

"Seems to be."

"Okay, then it's probably safe for us to stay here like this for the next five or ten years. I'm pretty sure I'll be able to move by then."

He lifted his head. Though she kept her eyes closed, Cybil was aware she was being studied, imagined that clear blue and focused gaze. And smiled. "I seduced the hell out of you, McQuinn. It was awfully nice of you to return the favor."

"No problem. It was the least I could do."

"Nobody ever made me feel like this before." She opened her eyes. "No one ever touched me this way."

She saw her mistake immediately. The way his eyes shuttered, the way he retreated from the intimacy. If it was light, if it was sexy, if it was dangerous, he was with her. But there was to be no tenderness, no heart, no slippery sentiment, to change the balance.

It made her ache for both of them.

"You've got great hands." She made her smile sassy as she wiggled her fingers under his. "Definitely major-league hands."

"You've got some real contenders yourself." He rolled onto his back, relieved and annoyed with himself for feeling that deep inner jolt when she'd looked at him with so much dazzled emotion in her eyes.

He wasn't going to let things shift into that area between them. Because once it did, it was over. That part of him that was hope and heart had long ago been calcified.

She wanted to curl into him, to curve her body into

the warmth of his, but imagined that was another taboo. *Keep it simple,* she warned herself, *or he'll walk right out the door.*

So she sat up, instead, flicked her fingers through her disordered hair. "I think that wine would go down well right now, don't you?"

"Oh, yeah." He skimmed his fingers along her calf, because he had to touch, had to keep that connection. "You mentioned something about dinner."

"McQuinn, I have an amazing meal in store for you." She leaned down to give him a careless kiss. "Everything's done but the crepes—seafood crepes, which I will whip up in front of your astonished eyes."

"You're going to cook?"

"Mmm-hmm."

He watched her slide out of bed, walk to the closet on legs that had his blood stirring again. "What's that for?"

"This? It's called a robe," she said with a laugh as she slipped into it. "It's often used to cover nakedness."

He got up, crossed to her and tugged the belt loose again. "Take it off."

A quick thrill shimmied down her spine. "I thought you wanted dinner."

"I do. And I want to watch you cook it."

"Then—oh." She laughed again and pulled the robe together. "I am not cooking crepes naked. That little fantasy of yours is doomed."

He didn't think so. "Actually, I was wondering if you had any more of…" He turned to the bed, found what was left of the lacy black garter belt. "This sort of thing."

Surprised, then intrigued, she lifted her eyebrows.

"No intelligent shopper buys only one. I have another little ensemble in red. Break-your-heart, tart red."

His smile spread slowly as he tossed the black lace aside. "Why don't you put it on? I'm really hungry."

Preparing crepes in sexy underwear was not without its risks. Cybil discovered just what it was like to be ravished against the pantry door.

Amazing.

And plundered on the living-room rug.

Incredible.

And being savaged under the hot, beating spray of the shower was an experience she would be more than willing to repeat.

Through the hours of the night he'd reached for her, thrilled her, had never seemed quite able to get enough of her. Or she of him. They'd been so completely in tune, so utterly together, that at times it had seemed his heart had beat inside hers.

The candles had gutted out in their own fragrant pools, and light had been seeping softly through the windows when she'd fallen into an exhausted sleep.

Only to wake alone.

She knew it shouldn't hurt her that he hadn't slept with her, hadn't woken with her. It wasn't to be like that between them. She knew that, accepted that. There would be no soft and foolish words between them, no baring of souls.

The border of intimacy stopped at the physical, with his side of it walled thick. Her heart was her own problem, not his.

How could he know she'd never given herself so absolutely to any other man? Why should he be expected to know that the primitive power of their desire for each other was driven by love on her side?

She rubbed her tired eyes and ordered herself up and out of bed.

She'd walked into the relationship with her eyes open, she thought as she tidied up the bedroom. She'd known its limitations. His limitations. They could be together, enjoy each other, as long as certain lines weren't crossed.

Well, that was fine. She wasn't going to pine and sigh over it. She was in charge of her own emotions; she was responsible for her own actions; and she was hardly going to mope around because she was involved with an exciting, fascinating, interesting man.

"Damn it!" She hurled her shoes into the closet. "Damn it, damn it, damn it!"

Cybil leaped on the bed, grabbed the phone. She had to tell someone, talk to someone. And when it was this vital, there was really only one someone.

"Mama? Mama, I'm in love," she said, then burst into wild tears.

Preston's fingers flew over the keyboard. He'd had less than three hours' sleep, but his system was revved, his mind clear as crystal. His first major play had been wrenched out of him, every word a wound. But this was pouring out, streaming like wine out of a magic bottle that had only been waiting to be decanted.

It was so fully alive. And for the first time in longer than he could remember, so was he.

He could see it all perfectly, the sets, the staging, the characters and everything inside them. The doomed, the damned, the triumphant.

A world in three acts.

There was an energy here, inside these people who formed on the page and lived on the stage already set inside his head. He knew them, knew how their hearts would leap and how they would break.

The thread of hope that ran through their lives hadn't been planned, but it was there, woven through and tangled so that he found himself riding on it with them.

He wrote until he ran dry; then, disoriented, glanced around the room. It was dark but for the lamp he'd switched on and the steady glow from his computer screen. He hadn't a clue what time it was—what day, for that matter. But his neck and shoulders were stiff, his stomach empty, and the coffee in the cup on his desk looked faintly revolting.

Standing, he worked out the worst of the kinks, then walked to the window, pushed open the curtains. There was a hell of a spring storm going on. He hadn't noticed. Now he watched the flashing of lightning, the scurry of desperate pedestrians rushing to appointments or shelter.

The entrepreneur on the corner was doing a brisk business in the umbrellas, which no one in New York seemed to own for longer than it took the pavement to dry.

He wondered if Cybil was looking out her window, watching the same scene. What she would think of it, how she would turn something so simple and ordinary as a thunderstorm in the city into the bright and ridiculous.

She'd use the Umbrella Man, he decided, work up an entire biography for him, give the figure in black slicker and hood a name, a background, a personality full of quirks. And the anonymous street vendor would become part of her world.

She had such a gift for drawing people into her world.

He was in it now, Preston mused. He hadn't been able to stop himself from opening that colorful door and stepping inside the confusion, the delights, the energy.

She didn't seem to understand he didn't belong there.

When he was inside, when he was surrounded by her, it seemed as though he could stay. That if he let it, life could be just that simple and extraordinary.

Like a storm in the city, he thought. But storms pass.

He'd nearly let himself sink into it that morning. Nearly let himself sink in and stay in that warm bed, with that warm body that had turned to curl around him in sleep.

She'd looked so...soft, he thought now. So welcoming. What had moved through him as he'd watched her in that fragile light had been a different kind of hunger. One that yearned to hold, to sigh out all the troubles and doubts and hold on to dreams.

It had been safer for both of them to leave her sleeping.

He flicked the curtains closed and walked downstairs.

He started fresh coffee, foraged for food, toyed with the idea of a nap.

But he thought of her, and of the night, and knew the restlessness inside him wouldn't allow him to rest.

What was she doing over there?

He had no business knocking on her door, interrupting her work just because his was finished for now. Just because the drum of rain made him feel edgy and alone. Just because he wanted her.

He liked being alone, he reminded himself as he prowled the living area. He needed the edge for his work.

He wanted to sit with her and watch the rain. To make slow, lazy love with her while it pounded the streets and sidewalks and cocooned them from everything but each other.

Wanted her, he admitted, just a little too much for comfort.

He told himself it was safe enough to want. It was crossing the line from want to need that was dangerous. Just how close, he wondered, was he already skirting that very thin, very shaky line?

When a woman got inside a man this way, it changed him, left him wide-open so that he made mistakes and exposed pieces of himself better left alone.

She wasn't Pamela. He wasn't so blind he believed every woman was a liar and a cheat and cold as stone. If he'd ever known anyone with less potential for cruelty and deceit, it was Cybil Campbell.

But that didn't change the bottom line.

From want to need to love were short, skidding steps. Once a man had taken the fall and ended up broken, he learned to keep his balance at all costs. He didn't want the desperation, the vulnerability, the loss of self that went hand in hand with genuine intimacy. And he'd stopped believing himself capable of those things.

Which meant there was nothing to worry about, he told himself, sipping his coffee and staring at his door as if he could see through it and through the one across the hall. She wasn't asking for anything more than passion, companionship, enjoyment.

Exactly as he was.

She was perfectly aware the arrangement was temporary.

He'd be gone in a few weeks, and their lives would go comfortably in other directions. She with her crowds of friends, he with his contented solitude.

He'd set his cup down with a violent snap before he realized the idea annoyed him.

They could still see each other from time to time, he told himself as he began to pace again. His house in Connecticut was a reasonable commute from the city. Isn't that why he'd chosen it in the first place?

He came into the city often enough. There was no reason he couldn't make it more often.

Until she got involved with someone else, he thought, jamming his hands in his pockets. Why should a woman like that wait around for him to breeze in and out of her life?

And that was fine, too, he decided as his temper began to rumble like the thunder outside. Who was asking her to wait around? She could damn well hook herself up with any idiot her interfering friends tossed at her.

But not, by God, while he was still across the hall.

He strode to her door, intending to make a few things clear. And opened it just in time to watch Cybil launch herself joyfully into the arms of a tall man with sun-streaked brown hair.

"Still the prettiest girl in New York," he said in a voice that hinted of beignets and chicory. "Give me a kiss."

And as she did, lavishly, Preston wondered which method of murder would be most satisfying.

Chapter 8

"Matthew! Why didn't you tell me you were coming? When did you get in? How long are you staying? Oh, I'm so happy to see you! You're all wet. Come inside, take off your jacket—when are you going to buy a new one? This one looks like it's been through a war."

He only laughed, hefted her off her feet and kissed her again. "You still never shut up."

"I babble when I'm happy. When are you—oh, Preston." She beamed at him out of eyes shining with joy. "I didn't see you there."

"Obviously." Bare hands, he thought, would be the most satisfying. He would simply take the guy with the smug brown eyes and the scarred leather jacket apart piece by piece. And feed each one to Cybil. "Don't let me interrupt the reunion."

"It's great, isn't it? Matthew, this is Preston McQuinn."

"McQuinn?" Matthew ran his tongue around his teeth. He was fairly sure the man braced in the hallway wanted to break them. "The playwright. I caught your work the last time I was in the city. Cyb cried buckets. I practically had to carry her out of the theater."

"I wasn't that bad."

"Yes, you were. Of course, you used to tear up during greeting-card commercials, so you're an easy mark."

"That's ridiculous, and—oh, my phone. Hang on a minute." She darted inside, leaving the men eyeing each other narrowly.

"I'm a sculptor," Matthew said in the same lazy drawl. "And since I really need my hands to work, I'll tell you I'm Cybil's brother before I offer to shake."

"Brother?" The murderous gleam shifted but didn't quite fade. "Not much family resemblance."

"Not especially. Want to see my ID, McQuinn?"

"That was Mrs. Wolinsky," Cybil announced as she dashed back. "She saw you come in but couldn't get to her door in time to waylay you. I'm supposed to tell you she thinks you're more handsome than ever." Chuckling, Cybil grabbed both his cheeks. "Isn't he pretty?"

"Don't start."

"Oh, but you are. Such a pretty face. All the female hearts flutter." She laughed again, then snagged Preston's hand. "Come on, let's have a drink to celebrate."

He started to refuse, then shrugged. It wouldn't do any harm to take a few minutes to size up Cybil's brother.

"What kind of sculptor?"

"I work in metal primarily." Matthew peeled off his jacket, tossed it carelessly over the arm of a chair. It barely had time to land before Cybil snatched it off.

"I'll just hang this in the bathroom to dry. Preston, pour us some wine, will you?"

"Sure."

"She have any beer?" Matthew wanted to know and sauntered over to lean on the counter while Preston moved through the kitchen with a familiarity that had the big brother arching a brow.

"Yeah." He plucked out two, popped the tops, then took out the wine for Cybil. "You work in the South?"

"That's right. New Orleans suits me better than New England. Weather-wise, it gives me more room to work outside if I want. Cyb hasn't mentioned you. When did you move in?"

Preston lifted his beer, noted Matthew's eyes were nearly the exact color of Cybil's hair. Like good aged whiskey. "Not long ago."

"Work fast, do you?"

"Depends."

"Preston." Cybil heaved a sigh as she came back. "Couldn't you have used glasses?"

"We don't need glasses." Matthew grinned, keeping a challenging eye on Preston. "We'll just drink our beer like real men, then chew up the bottle."

"Then you probably don't want any dainty cheese and crackers, or girlie pâté to go with it."

"Says who?" Matthew demanded, and slid onto a stool. "You used to have four of these, didn't you?"

"Oh, Preston borrowed one. What are you doing in New York, Matthew?" She stuck her head in the fridge.

"Just some quick preliminary business for my show this fall. I'm only here for a couple days."

"And you checked into a hotel, didn't you?"

"Your revolving-door policy drives me crazy." Matthew gestured toward Preston with his beer. "You've lived across the hall for a bit, right? So you know what goes on in here. It's terrifying. She lets..." He shuddered dramatically. "People in here."

"Matthew is a professional recluse," Cybil said dryly as she began preparing a small feast. "You two should get along famously. Preston doesn't like people, either."

"Ah, finally. A man of sense." Matthew aimed one of his quick, crooked smiles at Preston and decided he might like him, after all. "I let her talk me into staying here once," Matthew continued, stealing a cracker. "Oh, the horror. Three days, people dropping in, talking, eating, drinking, standing around, bringing their relatives and pets."

"It was only one little dog."

"Who insisted on sitting in my lap, without invitation, then ate my socks."

"If you hadn't left them lying on the floor, he wouldn't have eaten them. Besides, he only chewed them a bit."

"It's all a matter of perspective," Matthew concluded. "And you see, in a civilized hotel, the only people who drop in are housekeeping and room service—and they knock first and very rarely bring along small, toothy dogs." He reached over, pinched her chin. "But I'll let you cook me dinner, darling."

"You're so good to me."

"You ever had Cyb's homemade chicken potpie, Mc-Quinn?"

"Can't say I have."

"Well, watch me sweet-talk us into some."

It was an interesting way to spend the evening, Preston thought later, watching Cybil relate to her brother.

The ease of affection, humor, occasional exasperation. He remembered it had been like that between him and his sister. Before Pamela.

After that, there had still been affection, but the ease of it had vanished. All too often he had felt an awkwardness that had never been there before.

But awkwardness wasn't a problem with the Campbells. They cheerfully told embarrassing stories about each other, and when that paled ganged up to tell him about their absent and therefore defenseless sister and any number of cousins.

By the time he left, he was wondering if he could work bits of them into act 2, for a little comic relief.

Work, Preston decided, since Cybil was likely to be occupied with family for quite some time yet, was his best hope for the rest of the night.

"I like your friend." Matthew stretched out his legs and swirled the brandy Cybil had opened in his honor.

"That's handy—so do I."

"A little on the sober side for you."

"Ah, well." She settled in beside him on the sofa. "A little change of pace now and again can't hurt."

"Is that what he is?" Matthew gave her earlobe a tug. "I noticed you two didn't waste any time getting locked together when I so accommodatingly strolled upstairs to make a phone call."

"If you were making a phone call, how do you know what we were doing down here? Unless you were spying." She smiled sweetly, fluttered her lashes and got another jerk on the ear.

"I wasn't spying. I just happened to glance down the stairs at one very strategic moment. And since he looked at you any number of times during the evening like he knew you'd be a lot more tasty than your chicken pot-pie—which was great, by the way—I cleverly put two and two together."

"You were always bright, Matthew. I suppose it's reasonable to say, since you're being nosy, that Preston and I are together."

"You're sleeping with him."

Deliberately, Cybil widened her eyes. "Why, no—we've decided to be canasta partners. We realize it's a big commitment, but we think we can handle it."

"You always were a smart-ass," he muttered.

"That's how I make my fame and fortune."

"Now you're making it turning McQuinn across the hall into Emily's elusive and irritable Quinn."

"How could I resist?"

Matthew drummed his fingers, shifted. "Emily thinks she's in love with him."

Cybil said nothing for a moment, then shook her head. "Emily is a cartoon character who pretty much does what I tell her to do. She's not me."

"She has pieces of you—some of your most endearing and annoying pieces."

"True. That's why I like her."

Matthew blew out a breath, frowned into his brandy. "Look, Cyb, I don't want to horn into your personal life, but I'm still your big brother."

"And you're so good at it, Matthew." She leaned over to kiss his cheek. "You don't have to worry about this. Preston didn't and isn't taking advantage of your baby sister." She took Matthew's brandy, sipped, handed it back. "I took advantage of him. I baked him cookies, and ever since he's been my love slave."

"There's that mouth again." Uncomfortable, he pushed off the sofa, paced a bit. "Okay, I don't want the details, but—"

"Oh, and I was so looking forward to sharing all of them with you, especially the home videos."

"Shut up, Cybil." Working his way from uncomfortable to embarrassed, Matthew dragged a hand through his hair. "I know you're grown-up, and you're seriously cute in spite of that nose."

"My nose is very attractive." She sniffed with it.

"We all worked hard to make you believe that, and you've overcome that little deformity so well."

She had to laugh. "Shut up, Matthew."

"All I want to say is…be careful. You know? Careful."

Her eyes went soft as she rose. "I love you, Matthew. In spite of that annoying facial tic."

"I don't have a facial tic."

"We worked hard to make you believe that." Laughing again, she slipped her arms around him for a fierce hug. "It's so nice to have you here. Can't you stay longer?"

"Can't." He rested his cheek on the top of her head. "I'm going up to Hyannis for a couple days. I'll hang out, do some sketching. Grandpa wheedled."

"He's the champ. Is Grandma pining for you?" Cybil asked, leaning back to grin.

"Fretting herself down to skin and bones. Why don't you come up? Give him a bonus. And that way we can spot each other when he starts on why we're not settled down and raising a pack of little people."

"Hmm. Well, he has called here a couple times in the last few weeks—hasn't given me a chance to call first." She considered, juggling time and duties in her head. "I'm enough strips ahead to take a couple of days. I do have a meeting day after tomorrow, though, that I shouldn't break."

"Come up afterward." He angled his head when he saw her mull it over, hesitate. "You can ask your canasta partner to drive up with you. We'll have a tournament."

"He might enjoy that," she murmured. "I'll check with him. Either way, I'll come."

"Good." And, Matthew thought, he hoped Preston accepted the invitation. He would love to see Daniel MacGregor work him over.

Since it was after midnight when Matthew went off to his hotel, Cybil told herself to go upstairs to bed. She hadn't gotten much sleep the night before—and neither had Preston. The reasonable, the practical, the thing to do was climb into bed, shut off the light and get some much-needed rest.

So she walked across the hall and pushed his buzzer.

She was beginning to think he'd gone to bed, or down to the club, when she heard the rattle of locks.

"Hi. I never offered you a nightcap."

He glanced over her shoulder, back at her face. "Where's your brother?"

"On his way to his hotel. I opened some brandy, and—"

She didn't manage the rest, or even much of a squeak of surprise as he yanked her inside, kicked the door closed and shoved her against it. Her mouth was much too busy being assaulted by his.

When he switched to her neck, she managed to suck in a breath. "I guess you don't want any brandy." Since he was already dragging off her shirt, she returned the favor. "Or after-dinner mints."

The force of need that had slammed into him the moment he'd seen her was outrageous. He couldn't stem it, even with his hands rushing over her to take. Greedy, his mouth crushed back on hers while he pulled her head back to dive yet deeper.

And she strained against him, just as urgently, just as desperately, groaning in pleasure as he tugged her trousers down her hips.

Whatever she had was his.

He filled his hands with her breasts, then his mouth descended, sucking, nipping while her nails bit, arousing points of pain, into his back. Her skin, like warmed silk, drove him to possess. Desire, a freshly whetted blade, twisted as he moved down her until her hands vised on his shoulder and her breath was only gasping sobs.

Not possible, not possible to feel so much and survive, was her last coherent thought. Then he used his mouth on her, his fingernails raking lightly down her body as with lips and teeth and tongue he drove her beyond reason.

She heard her own cry of shocked release dimly, struggling for air as her system rocked from the hot explosion of pleasure. Destroyed, she sagged against the door, utterly open to him.

Surrender only fanned the flames.

His hands slipped, slid, over her damp skin. His mouth continued its relentless assault, demanding more, still more, until her body began to quiver again. Until he felt her begin to heat and move and stretch toward the next peak.

He left her groaning, traveling back up her body, slicking his tongue over flesh that tasted erotically of salt and woman. His hands were rougher than he intended as he dragged her to the chair, pulled her down on him, lifted her hips.

His eyes met hers, watching, watching as that soft, clouded green darkened and blurred, watching as those long lids flickered, watching still as he lowered her.

Now, as she closed around him, surrounded him in hot, slippery heat, their groans mixed. Her head fell back, exposing that lovely white arch of throat where a pulse beat in wild hammer blows.

And she began to ride.

The pace was hers now, and it was fast and fierce. Each thrust of hips slapped them both toward the dark swirl of delirium. He craved it, that moment when sanity ripped away.

Bright arrows of sensation, each separate and sharp, stabbed through him. The sumptuous taste of her flesh in his mouth, the wet silk texture of it as his hands sought more of her, those low, animal sounds in her throat and the sheer wonder of her face flushed with pleasure and purpose.

He teetered on the edge, struggling to hold on another instant, just one more instant where he could no longer tell where she began and he left off. But she closed around him, a glorious fist of triumph, and, breathing his name, dragged him over with her.

Then, as she had before, she melted onto him. The sensation of having her head lie on his shoulder, her lips against his throat, spread a hazy glow through him. Closing his eyes, he held on to it, and to her.

He remembered what she had said to him before. No one had ever touched her as he had.

No one, he thought, had ever reached him as she had. But, however clever he was with words on paper, he didn't know how to begin to tell her.

"I wanted to get my hands on you all evening." That, at least, he could say without risking either of them.

"Mmm. And to think I nearly went up to bed." With a long, contented sigh, she nuzzled his hair. "I knew this chair was perfect for you."

A chuckle rumbled in his chest. "I was thinking of having it recovered. But now I'm having it bronzed."

She leaned back, cupping her hands on his face. "I love those little unexpected pockets of humor in you."

"It's not funny," he said in serious tones. "It's going to cost me a fortune."

He expected her to laugh, a sound he'd grown to depend on. But her smile was wistful, her eyes soft. "Preston." She murmured it, then lowered her mouth to his.

The slow, deep, gentle kiss stirred the soul rather than the blood. It reached into him, brushed hesitant fingers over his heart and made him yearn for something he refused to believe in.

Something struggled to shift inside him, made his hands tremble with the effort to hold it still and steady. But the sweetness of it seeped in, left him reeling.

He crossed over that thin line between want and need, and felt himself stumble terrifyingly close to the edge of love.

She sighed, pressed her cheek to his. And wished.

"You're cold," he murmured, feeling her skin chill.

"A little." She kept her eyes squeezed tight another

moment, reminding herself you couldn't always have everything you wished for. "Thirsty. Want some water?"

"Yeah, I'll get it."

"No, that's all right." She slid off him, leaving him slightly baffled by the sense of loss. "Do you have a robe?"

He worked up a smile again. "What is this obsession you have with robes?"

"Never mind." She snatched up his shirt and pulled it on. "Matthew likes you," she commented as she walked into the kitchen.

"I like him." He could take a deep breath now. Could, he told himself, regain his balance now. "The piece up in your studio. That's his work?"

"Yeah. Terrific, isn't it? He's got such a unique vision of things. And watching him work—if he doesn't murder you—is an amazing experience."

She opened a bottle of water, poured a tall glass to the rim, then drank down nearly a third before moving back to Preston. She didn't notice his blink of surprise when she settled, cozy as a cat, into his lap.

"So anyway," she began, offering him the glass, "how do you feel about taking a little trip?"

"A trip?"

"A couple of days in Hyannis Port. Matthew's going up to see our grandparents—the MacGregors—and I thought I might do the same. Grandpa loves to complain that we don't visit enough. It's a great place. The house is…well, I can't describe it. But you'd like it. You'd like them. Want to get out of Dodge for a bit, McQuinn?"

"It sounds like a family thing." It struck him as odd, and totally out of character, that he should feel so unhappy with the idea of her being away for a couple of days.

"With The MacGregor, everything is a family thing. Grandpa loves people. He's over ninety, and has the most amazing energy."

"I know. He's fascinating. They both are." He glanced back as she frowned at him. "I know them. Slightly. They're acquaintances of my parents."

"Oh? I didn't realize. I told you the rather convoluted family connection, didn't I? MacGregor to Blade. Blade to Grandeau. Grandeau to Campbell. Campbell to Mac-Gregor, not necessarily in that order."

"Don't start. It makes my ears ring."

She laughed, dutifully kissed them. "Well, since you know them and you've met Matthew, it wouldn't be like dropping yourself in on a group of strangers. Come with me." She ran her lips from his ear to his neck. "It'll be fun."

"We could stay right here in this chair and have even more fun."

She chuckled warmly. "There are dozens and dozens of rooms in Castle MacGregor," she murmured. "And in many of them, there are big…soft…beds."

"When do we leave?"

"Really?" Thrilled at the idea, she leaned back. "Day after tomorrow? I have a meeting midmorning. We can leave right after. I can rent a car."

"I have a car."

"Oh." She cocked her head. "Hmm. Is it a sexy car?"

"How do you feel about four-door sedans?"

"It's probably very sturdy, very reliable. I appreciate a sensible car."

"Then you're not going to like my Porsche."

"A Porsche?" She giggled in delight. "Oh, tell me it's a convertible."

"What else?"

"Oh, yeah. Tell me it's a five-speed."

"Sorry, it's a six-speed."

Her eyes widened. "Really? *Really?* Can I drive?"

"Of course. If by the day after tomorrow the icicles have finished forming in Hell, you're at the wheel."

Pouting only a little, she began to play with his hair. "I'm an excellent driver."

"I'm sure you are." He decided it would be much more productive to distract her than to listen to her try to change his mind. He rolled the cold glass over her naked back, making her gasp and arch so that her breasts flattened delightfully against his chest.

"Now...what do you think we could accomplish if we laid this recliner back?"

"All manner of amazing things," she murmured, turning her neck to give his teeth better access. "Did you know my grandfather owns this building?"

"Sure. He told me about the apartment when I was looking for a place. Turn like...yeah, that's the way."

"He told you about the apartment?" Somehow he'd managed to shift so that his body covered hers, distracting her from a niggling thought just beginning to form in her mind. "When did he... Oh, God, you're so awfully good at that."

"Thank you. But I'm about to get much better."

Chapter 9

The house The MacGregor built stood arrogantly on the cliffs above a surging sea. Nothing about the old gray stone was sober. Everything about it, from its spearing towers and jutting turrets, to the snapping flag that carried the crest of the clan, shouted pride.

He had built as he'd intended to, on a sturdy foundation, with grandiose vision. And he had built to last.

The wild and rambling roses that would bloom brilliantly come summer did nothing to soften the effect but only added to that sense of magic.

"Stop," Preston murmured, and laid a hand on Cybil's arm. "Stop the car."

Because she understood, and was pleased to see the sight of that fanciful structure affect him as it always did her, she braked gently.

"It's like a fairy tale, isn't it?" She leaned on the steering wheel to study the house through a driving curtain of rain. "Not one of the wimpy G-rated versions, but one with blood and guts."

"I've seen photographs. They don't come close."

"It's not just a house. It's the most generous of homes. Whenever we visited we'd always find something new. Something marvelous."

As she would this time, she thought. With Preston. "It shows well in the rain, doesn't it?" she commented.

"I imagine it always shows well."

"You're right. You should see it in the winter. We always come up during Christmas. The snow and the wind turn it into something frozen out of time. And last year, just at the end of summer when the roses were tumbling and the sky was so hard and blue you waited for it to crack like an egg, my cousin Duncan got married here. But in the rain…" She smiled dreamily, leaning on the wheel. "It feels like Scotland."

"Have you ever been?"

"Mmm. Twice. Have you?"

"No."

"You should. It's your roots. You'll be surprised how much they tug at you when you breathe the air in the highlands or look out at a lowland loch."

"Maybe I will. I might want a couple of weeks to decompress when the play's finished." He turned his head, lifted his eyebrows. "How's the car handling for you?"

"Since you've only let me drive it for approximately forty-five seconds, it's difficult to be sure. Now, if you let me take it out for a spin tomorrow…"

"Even your powers of persuasion aren't going to get you behind the wheel longer than it takes to go up the drive."

Cybil shrugged carelessly, thought, *We'll see about*

that, and drove decorously up the hill, parked. "Thank you very much." She gave him a light kiss, and the keys.

"You're welcome."

"Let's not worry about the bags now. We'll make a dash for it and see how long it takes to have whiskey and scones by the fire."

She pushed open the car door, ran like a bullet through the rain, then stopped on the covered porch to shake her head like a wet dog and laugh.

For ten full seconds, he couldn't move. He could only stare at her, through the shimmering curtain of rain, her cap of hair sleek and soaked, her face alive with the delight of it. He wanted to think it was desire, straight and uncomplicated. But desire rarely struck so deeply or had fingers of fear clawing at the gut.

If he couldn't ignore it, he'd deny it. He stepped into the rain, let the wind slap at his cheeks like a teasing woman as he walked to her. And while she laughed, he yanked her hard against him and took her mouth with a kind of violent possession.

For once her hands only fluttered helplessly as the sudden, almost brutal, kiss staggered her. But she tasted the desperation on his mouth, felt the barely restrained fury in the body that pressed to hers. And her hands reached for him, stroked once, then held.

"Preston."

He heard her murmur through the roaring in his brain that was like the rain and the sea battering against him. The soft sound of her voice had him gentling his hold, then the kiss, before he forced himself to draw back.

"With all your family around," he managed, and skimmed her dripping hair behind her ear in an absent gesture that made her heart flutter foolishly, "I might not be able to do that for a while."

"Well." She breathed deep, hoping to settle herself. "That ought to hold me." And smiling, she took his hand and pulled him inside.

There was warmth, immediate and welcoming.

Bright swords and shields glowed on the walls. It was, after all, the home of a warrior and one who had never forgotten it. There was the scent of flowers and wood, and of age that speaks of dignity rather than dust.

"Cybil!" Anna MacGregor came down the wide stairs, her soft face aglow with pleasure. Her sable hair was swept back, her deep-brown eyes clear and smiling as she held out her arms to take Cybil into them.

"Grandma." She breathed deep, exhaled lavishly. "How can you always be so beautiful?"

With a laugh, Anna squeezed tighter. "At my age the best you can hope for is presentable."

"Not you. You're always beautiful. Isn't she, Preston?"

"Very."

"You're never too old to appreciate a considerate lie from a handsome young man." Anna shifted, keeping one arm around Cybil's waist as she held out a hand. "Hello, Preston. I doubt you'll remember me. You couldn't have been more than sixteen the last I saw you."

"About," he agreed, taking her hand. "But I remember you very well, Mrs. MacGregor. It was at the Spring Ball in Newport, and you were very kind to a young boy who wanted to be anywhere else."

"You remember. Now I am flattered. Come, let's get you warmed up. Rain's cold this time of year."

"Where are Grandpa and Matthew?"

"Oh." Anna laughed lightly as she led them down the hall into what the family called the Throne Room. "Daniel's got poor Matthew hammering on the pump for the pool. He says it's acting up, and you know how your grandfather is about his daily swim. Claims it keeps him young."

"Everything keeps him young."

The term for the room was apt, with Daniel's regal high-back chair dominating a great space carpeted in scarlet. The furnishings were old and massive, the carvings deep. Lamps were already lit against the gloom, and a fire blazed boldly in the big hearth.

"We'll have tea. I imagine Daniel will insist we add whiskey to that and use company as an excuse for it. Sit, be comfortable," she invited. "If I don't let him know you're here, I'll never hear the end of it."

"You sit," Cybil insisted. "I'll go. I'll have the tea sent along on the way."

"You're a good girl." Anna patted Cybil's hand as she sat by the fire. "You always were." Anna gestured to the chair beside hers. "Preston, Daniel and I saw your play in Boston some months ago. It was powerful, and wrenching. Your family must be so proud of what you've accomplished."

"Actually, I think they were more surprised."

"Sometimes that amounts to the same thing. We never really expect our children or our siblings, no matter how we admire them, to exhibit real genius. It brings us a jolt, and we think—how could I have missed that all those years?"

"You know my family," he said quietly. "So you'd know the play cut very close to home."

"Yes, I know. Sometimes a wound needs to be lanced or it festers. Is your sister well?"

"Yes, she has the children. They center her."

"And you, Preston? Is it your work that centers you?"

"Apparently."

"I'm sorry." Annoyed with herself, Anna lifted her hands. "I'm prying—and I usually leave that to my husband. I'm interested because I remember that young boy at the Spring Ball and the way he looked after his sister. It reminded me of the way Alan and Caine always looked after Serena—and how it irritated her as it appeared to irritate…it's Jenna, isn't it?"

"Yes." He smiled now. "It used to drive her crazy." But the smile soon faded. "If I'd done a better job of it years later, she'd never have been hurt."

"Preston, you didn't hurt her," Anna reminded him. "And, truly, I didn't mean to take you back there. Will you tell me about what you're working on now, or do you keep such matters secret?"

"It's a love story, set in New York. At least, that's the way it's turning out."

His gaze flicked past her shoulder when he heard laughter rolling down the hall. Yes, Anna thought, that seemed to be the way it was turning out.

"Haven't you given the man a whiskey yet, Anna?"

Daniel stepped into the room and simply dominated it. Size, presence and that great booming voice that refused to thin with age. His eyes glittered blue as the lochs of his homeland; his hair and rich full beard were stunningly white.

"Is that any way to welcome a man after he's come in out of the rain and brought up my favorite grandchild from the city?"

"Oh, fine," Matthew muttered, trailing in behind him. "When you wanted your pool fixed *I* was your favorite grandchild."

"Well, it's fixed now, isn't it?" Daniel said, and with a bark of laughter slapped Matthew on the back with the affection a father grizzly might show to his cub.

"It's good to see you, Mr. MacGregor." Preston crossed the room, hand extended to shake. But for Daniel this was rarely sufficient when he'd taken an interest in a man. He clapped Preston into a hug with the force of a steel trap biting closed.

"You're looking fit, McQuinn, and a good drink of whiskey always makes a Scotsman fitter."

"You'll have a drop in your tea, Daniel," Anna warned him as she rose to fetch the decanter.

"A drop." For a big man, he could still manage to sulk like a child. "Anna."

"Two drops," she conceded with a smile tugging at her mouth. "Tell me, Preston, do you smoke cigars?"

"Not as a rule, no."

Anna turned, angled her head in warning at Daniel. "Then if I come across you with one in your hand, I'll know who stuck it there before he dashed out of the room."

"The woman'll nag you to death," Daniel muttered. "Well, sit down, boy, and tell me how you and Cybil are getting on."

Little alarm bells sounded in Preston's head. "Getting on?"

"Neighbors, aren't you?"

"Yeah." Relieved, Preston sat. "Across-the-hall neighbors."

"Pretty as a primrose, isn't she?"

"Grandpa." Cybil sighed as she wheeled in a loaded tea tray. "Don't start on McQuinn. He hasn't even been here ten minutes."

"Start what?" Daniel narrowed his eyes at her. "Are you pretty or not?"

"I'm adorable." She laughed and kissed his nose. While she was close, she whispered in his ear. "Behave and I might tip a bit of my whiskey into your tea while she's not looking."

Daniel's teeth flashed in a grin; his eyebrows wiggled. "There's a lass."

"You won't believe these scones, McQuinn." Satisfied she'd bribed The MacGregor, Cybil loaded a small plate. "I can't quite pull them off. Mine are close, but not quite there."

"Cybil's a fine cook," Daniel agreed, scowling when he watched his wife measure a measly two drops of whiskey into a cup for him. "You've been feeding the man a bit from time to time, haven't you, lass? Like a proper neighbor."

"She made us all a potpie last night." Matthew loaded a scone with strawberry jam. He'd promised to be a buffer, he remembered. "Preston, you want whiskey or are you making do with tea?"

"I'll take the whiskey, thanks. Neat."

"And how else would a man drink it?" Daniel muttered, pouting into his teacup. "So you've had a taste of our Cybil," he added, and watched with a barely suppressed grin as Preston nearly bobbled a scone.

"Excuse me?"

"Her cooking." Daniel's eyes radiated innocence. *Oh, aye,* he thought, *I've got you on the reel, laddie.*

"Woman who can cook like my darling here ought to have a family to feed."

"Grandpa." Cybil tapped her finger on her whiskey glass.

When a man was torn between his drink of choice and his granddaughter's future, what choice did he have? Sacrifices, Daniel mused, had to be made. "What man doesn't appreciate a hot meal well made, I'd like to know? You can't disagree with that, can you, lad?"

Somehow, somewhere, there was dangerous ground, was all Preston could think. "No."

"There!" Daniel pounded a fist, made plates rattle. "Hah! McQuinn's a good and honorable name. You've done proud by it."

"Thanks," Preston said cautiously.

"But a man your age should be thinking of what comes after him. You must be thirty by now."

"That's right." *And how the hell do you know that?* Preston wondered.

"A man gets to be thirty, it's time to take stock, to consider his duties to name and family."

"I've got a few years left," Matthew whispered to Cybil.

She merely elbowed him. "Do something," she hissed.

"If he turns it on me, it's gonna cost you."

"Name your price."

"Oh, I will." And cheerfully throwing himself on the sword, Matthew dropped into a chair. "Grandpa, I haven't told you about this woman I've been seeing lately."

"Woman?" Distracted, Daniel blinked, then zeroed in on his grandson. "What woman would that be? I thought you were too busy building your big metal toys to pay any mind to women."

"I pay them plenty of mind." Matthew grinned, lifted his whiskey in salute. "This one's something special."

"Is she, now?" Shifting gears, Daniel settled back. "Well, it would take a special lass to catch your eye for more than a blink."

"Oh, I've been looking at this one for a while. Name's Lulu," Matthew decided on the spot. "Lulu LaRue, though I think that's her stage name. She's a table dancer."

"Dances on tables!" Daniel roared as his wife choked back a laugh, then continued to drink her tea. "Naked on tables?"

"Of course naked. What's the point otherwise? She's got the most amazing tattoo on her—"

"Naked, tattooed dancing girls! I'll be damned, Matthew Campbell. You want to break your dear mother's heart? Anna, are you listening to this?"

"Yes, of course I am, Daniel. Matthew, stop teasing your grandfather."

"Yes, ma'am." Matthew shrugged, grinned and watched Daniel's eyes narrow into blue slits. "But I don't see why I can't have a naked, tattooed dancing girl if I want."

Much later, after the rain had passed and night had fallen and Preston had slipped into her room to take advantage of her and the big four-poster bed, Cybil hummed in contentment.

It had been a near perfect day.

Perfect enough that she let herself curl up against the man she loved and pretend, in this fairy tale world, that he had scaled the walls of the castle to find her. And love her. And stay with her for always.

"Tell me something," he murmured, too relaxed to worry about how soothing it was to lie there with her arm draped over him, her head in the curve of his shoulder and their bodies sharing a lazy, intimate warmth.

"Okay. Despite exhaustive research, the exact number of angels who can dance on the head of a pin has never been fully documented."

"I thought it was 634."

"That's mere speculation. Nor in related studies has it ever been fully discovered precisely how many frogs one must kiss before finding the prince."

"That goes without saying. But…" He loved the way she chuckled as she shifted closer. "What I really wanted to know—and you would be the handiest authority on the subject—is what the hell was all that with your grandfather at tea?"

"Which all?" She lifted her head, skimmed her hair back from her brow, then rolled her eyes. "Oh, that all. I didn't warn you because I had the pathetic hope that it wouldn't be necessary. The fault is entirely mine."

She shifted, rolling over so that her body lounged cozily over his. "Do you know you have wonderful eyes, McQuinn? They're almost translucent, like I could dive right into that moonlight blue and just disappear."

"Is that a genuine comment or an evasion of the subject at hand?"

"Both." But since it had to be dealt with, she sat up, kissed him, then reached for the robe she'd tossed at the foot of the bed earlier.

"Why do you have to cover up whenever you talk to me?"

She glanced over, and to his surprise, flushed a little. "A latent puritanical streak?"

"Incredibly latent," he noted, but only smiled as she belted the robe. "Now, about your grandfather and his sudden interest in my family name—or as he put it during dinner—the good blood, strong stock in my ancestry."

"Well, McQuinn, you're a Scotsman."

"Third-generation Rhode Islander."

"Hardly matters in the vast and historic scheme of things."

She rose and poured them a glass to share from the pitcher of ice water that had been placed on the bedside table. "I'll apologize first," she said, without looking at him. "But hope you'll understand Grandpa means well. It's all out of love, and he wouldn't have done it if he didn't like you."

Something much too akin to nerves moved into Preston's stomach. "Done what, exactly?"

"I didn't realize it—or it didn't sink in fully until we got here. It should have," she murmured, sitting on the bed and handing him the glass before she'd sipped herself. "The other night when you mentioned how you knew each other and he'd put you onto the apartment across from mine, I should have latched on to it. Well." She jerked her shoulders. "It wouldn't have mattered anyway."

"What, Cybil?"

She blew out a breath, lifted her lashes and looked directly into his eyes. "He's picked you out for me. It's just that he loves me," she said quickly. "And he wants what he thinks is best for me—that's marriage, a family, a home. And that appears to be you."

It wasn't nerves, Preston discovered. It was outright

terror. "How the hell did he come to that conclusion?" he demanded, and set his water back on the table with a hard click of glass on wood.

"It's not an insult, McQuinn." Her voice chilled several frigid degrees. "It's a compliment. As I said, he loves me very much, so he obviously thinks a great deal of you if he believes you'd make me a proper husband and be a good father for the many great-grandchildren he hopes I'll give him."

"I thought you didn't want marriage."

"I didn't say I did. I said he wanted it for me." Her chin jerked up before she got out of bed again, stalking to the bureau to snatch up her brush and drag it over her hair. "And the fact that you're so obviously appalled is incredibly insulting."

"I suppose you think it's amusing."

"I think it's sweet."

"You think it's sweet for your ninety-something grandfather to pick out men for you?"

"He isn't grabbing them off the street corner for me to audition." Ridiculously hurt, she slammed down the brush. "You needn't panic, McQuinn. I'm not buying my trousseau or booking chapels. I'm perfectly capable of finding my own husband when and if I want one. Which I've already said I don't."

She tossed her head and, for lack of something better to do with her hands, wrenched open a jar of cream and began to slather it on her hands.

"Now, I'm tired, and I'd like to go to bed. And since you don't care to sleep with me after sex, you should go."

Was it just temper, he wondered, or was there something more in the reflection of her eyes in the mirror? "Why are you angry?"

"Why am I angry?" she said quietly, unsure if she wanted to weep or scream. "How can someone who writes about what's inside people with such insight, such sensitivity, ask a question like that? Why am I angry, Preston?"

She turned then because it was best to face the issue head-on. "Because you're sitting there in the bed we just shared, still warm from me and utterly baffled, completely shocked that someone who loves me thinks there could or should be something more between us than sex."

"Of course there's more between us than sex." His own temper started to twitch as he grabbed his jeans and tugged them on.

"Is there? Is there really?"

The cool, flat tone had him looking over, had the sneaky worm of guilt sliding into him. "I care about you, Cybil. You know I do."

"You find me amusing. That's not the same thing."

Yes, there was more than temper, he realized before she turned away. There was hurt. Somehow he'd hurt her again without plan or purpose. He took her arm, firmly turned her back. "I care about you."

Her heart, already too much his, softened. "All right." She touched a hand to his, squeezed, released. "Let's forget about it."

He wanted to agree, to keep it simple. But the smile she'd tossed him before she'd walked to the window hadn't reached her eyes. And those eyes had been wounded. "Cybil, I don't have more than that."

"I didn't ask for more than that. The moon's come out. All the clouds have been blown away. We can walk the cliffs tomorrow. It's a little chilly, though." Absently, her heart weeping in her breast, she rubbed her arms. "I think we need another log on the fire."

"I'll do it."

The fire in the fieldstone hearth still burned bright and cheerful. But he took a log from the carved box, sat it on the flames, then watched them rise up, lick, curve greedily around it.

For a time the only sound in the room was the crack and the hiss of wood being consumed.

Maybe it was because she didn't ask, so deliberately didn't ask, that he was compelled to tell her. "Would you sit down?"

"I like standing here looking at the stars. You can't see the stars in New York. It's all the lights. You forget to look up, much less wonder where the stars are. In Maine, where I grew up, they filled the sky. I never realize I miss them until I see them again. You can get along, very well, for long periods, without a lot of things. Hardly even noticing you're missing them."

When his hands came to her shoulders, she tensed, an instinctive movement it took concentrated effort to undo. But she smiled when she turned. "Why don't we go out and get a better look at them while they're there."

"I want you to sit down and listen to me."

"All right." Struggling to be casual, she walked to one of the deep chairs in front of the fire. "I'm listening."

He sat beside her, leaned forward in his chair and kept his eyes on her face. "I always wanted to write. I can't remember otherwise. Not the novels my father had hoped for. It was always plays. Everything was very clear in my head. The stage, each set, the movement of the actors, the precise angle and quality of the lights. Often, maybe too often, that was the world I lived in.

You come from a prominent family, one with a lot of social obligations and demands."

"I suppose that's true."

"So do I. I tolerated that end of it, enjoyed it occasionally, but for the most part just tolerated or eluded it."

"You value your privacy," she said. "I understand that. My father's the same, and Matthew."

"I valued it. I needed it." Too restless to sit, he rose to wander the room. "I love my parents, my sister, no matter how little we sometimes understand one another. I'm sure I hurt them countless times with small acts of carelessness, but I do love them, Cybil."

"Of course you do," she began, but said nothing more when he shook his head.

"My sister, Jenna, she was always so outgoing, so easy with people. She's a lovely woman. She wasn't quite twenty-one when she married. Married my best friend from college. I introduced them."

It still scraped him raw to think of that. The first step in the whole miserable journey had been his. Glancing at the water, he wished it were whiskey.

"They were great together," he murmured. "Shining with love, full to bursting with hope and plans. Jacob came along just over a year later. And less than a year after that she was pregnant again and glowing with it."

He stuck his hands in his pockets, moved to the window. But he didn't see the stars. "About that time, my first play was being produced. Locally, just a small theater group, but a place with cachet. My father's an important writer, so that made his son's work of some interest."

"It's of interest on its own," Cybil declared, and he glanced back, grateful to her for understanding his need for that separate legitimacy. But she would, he thought, because of who she was and from what she'd come.

"Now I certainly hope so. But not then, not right at the start. And it was vital to me that my work stand on its own and not lean on his. Part of that was pride," he continued thoughtfully. "But part of it was respect. Whatever the reason, this play, this first of mine to be produced, was incredibly important to me."

Because he turned away, seemed to need a moment to gather himself, she spoke again. "I didn't sleep at all the night before my first strip came out. However much I loved the work, I couldn't have stood it if people thought I was using my father's accomplishments as a stepping stone."

"Some always will," Preston murmured. "You can't let it matter. The work has to matter most, and this play did to me. There wasn't any aspect of it I wasn't involved in—the set designs, the staging, the casting, the rehearsals, lighting cues. All of it."

She smiled a little. "I imagine you drove everyone, including yourself, insane."

"I'm sure I did. The company had a lot of talent. The actress who played the lead was stunning, certainly the most beautiful woman I'd ever seen. She dazzled me."

He faced her. "I'd just turned twenty-five, and I was hopelessly in love with her. Every minute I spent with her was a gift. Just to watch her onstage, saying lines I'd written, that had come from me. Having her look at me and smile and ask me if that was how I meant it to be. The more I became involved with her, the less the play meant to me."

Even now it burned inside him, what he'd tossed aside. And what he'd had stolen. "She was gentle. Oh, and sweet. Even a little shy when she wasn't onstage. I made excuses to be with her, then began to realize she was making them to be with me. We became lovers on a Sunday afternoon, in her bed, and afterward, she cried on my shoulder and told me she loved me. I think I would have cut off my arm for her at that moment."

Cybil folded her hands in her lap and wondered what it would be like to be loved like that by a man like him. She didn't speak because she could see there was more. And what was left still caused him pain.

"For weeks," he continued, "my world revolved around her. The play opened, garnered very decent reviews. All I could think was that the play had been the vehicle that had given her to me. That was all that mattered."

"Love should matter most."

"Should it?" He laughed shortly and the cynical light was back in his eyes. "But words last, Cybil. That's why a writer should take care with them."

Love lasts. She wanted to say it, nearly did, but she could already see his hadn't.

"I bought her gifts," he continued, "because they made her happy, took her dancing or to the club because she loved to be with people. She was so beautiful I thought she deserved to be showcased. She needed the right clothes, the right jewelry, to be showcased in, didn't she? So why not buy them for her? And if she needed a little to tide her over, why not write her a check? It was only money, and I had more than enough."

Cybil could see where it was going, or thought she could. She wanted, so badly, to go to him, to slip her arms around him in comfort. But it wasn't unhappiness in his voice, in his eyes; it was bitterness.

"She had talent, and I wanted to help her become an

important actress. Why not use my influence—or my father's, my family's—to boost her career?"

"You loved her," Cybil said quietly, already hurting for him. "What you wouldn't have used for yourself, you would use for someone you loved."

"And that makes it right?" He shook his head. "No, it's never right to use someone else. But I did. She talked about marriage, shyly again, almost wistfully. I hesitated there. Her career needed her attention. We could wait to settle down. After the play, I told her, after she began to move up, we'd go to New York and we'd both *own* theater. We'd own it together."

Together, he thought, was all too often a word that didn't hold true. "Then one day she came to me, weeping, shaking, so pale you could almost see through that beautiful skin. She told me she was pregnant, and lovely, terrified tears slipped out of her eyes and down her cheeks. She blamed herself, begged me not to abandon her. Where would she go, what would she do? She had little money. She was afraid. She thought I would hate her."

"No," Cybil whispered. "You wouldn't hate her."

"Of course I didn't. I didn't hate her, I didn't blame her. I was afraid, I was shaken, but part of me was thrilled. The decision had been taken out of my hands. I didn't need to be practical now but could marry her, start a life with her."

He prowled now, restless in the cage of his own past. "Money was no problem. I'd come into a large part of my inheritance at twenty-five, would come into more at thirty. Money wasn't a problem," he said again, then lifted the poker and jabbed viciously at the logs blazing.

"I dried her tears, and I held her, told her everything would be fine. It would be wonderful. We'd be married right away. We'd stay in Newport until the baby was born, then we'd go to New York just as we'd planned. It would be three of us instead of two, but we'd be happy. We had a touching parting scene as she left to go back to her little apartment—to rest and call her family and tell them the wonderful news. We agreed to go to my parents after the show that evening and tell them.

"I started making plans almost immediately. Imagined myself as her husband, as the father of the child we'd made together."

"You wanted the baby," Cybil said, remembering the ease with which he'd held little Charlie.

"Yes, I did."

He turned to her then, his back to the fire. But the heat that pumped from the flames couldn't reach the cold memories left inside him. "I wanted her, and the child, and the life I imagined we could make together. And while I was floating on that particular cloud my sister came to my door."

He could still see it, still bring it back. Every movement, every gesture. Another play on another stage. "Like Pamela, she was weeping, she was trembling, she was pale. And like Pamela, she was pregnant. Further along, just showing, so I was worried at the state she was in. She clung to me, sobbing and sobbing, and finally managed to tell me her husband was having an affair."

His voice changed now, darkened, flattened, as did his eyes. "She told me that she'd dashed back home, leaving Jacob with my mother, because she'd forgotten something. They were to be out all day, so she wasn't expected back only an hour after she'd left. Wasn't expected to walk in and find her husband scrambling back into his trousers and a woman in her bed. Her own bed."

"Oh, Preston, how horrible for her." She rose then, wanting to comfort. "How awful for your family. She must have…" She trailed off as it clicked. The scenes he'd been painting for her, the scenes he'd painted in his play. "Oh, no. Oh, God."

He stepped back from the sympathy she offered. "Her name was Leanna in *A Tangle of Souls,* but she was pure Pamela. Beautiful and clever and cold. A woman who could act without rehearsing the lines. Who could play a man brilliantly, all for money, for power, for the possibilities. She would have married me for those things, and to give a socially prominent name to the baby my closest friend, my sister's husband, had planted in her. But I was no longer in the mood."

"You loved her, and she hurt you. Hurt all of you. I'm so sorry."

"Yes, I loved her, but she taught me. You can't trust the heart. My sister trusted hers, and it almost destroyed her. If she hadn't had Jacob and the baby on the way, I think it would have. They needed her, and that's what got her through."

"But you didn't have that."

"I had my work, and the satisfaction of facing the woman who'd cut through our lives. She wept and she swore it was all a lie. Some terrible mistake. She begged me to believe her, and I very nearly did. She was that good."

"No," Cybil murmured. "You were in love. You'd have wanted to believe her."

"Either way. We argued, and some of the layers on that perfectly presented mask of hers fell away. I saw her for what she was. A schemer, a liar, a cheat. A woman who thought nothing of seducing and sleeping with another's husband for pleasure and going from him to another man for gain. But she finished the run of the play." He smiled thinly. "The show must go on."

"How did you stand it?"

"She was good, and it was only a matter of reminding myself the work was more important than she was, more important than anything else." He arched a brow. "You think that was a cold decision on my part?"

"No." She laid her hands on his shoulders, then on his cheeks, wondering that he couldn't see the hurt was still there. "No, I think it was brave." Then she leaned into him, held him, sighing when his arms finally came around her. "She didn't deserve even the smallest piece of your heart, Preston. Then or now."

"Now she's only an interesting character in a play. I won't give anyone that much ever again. I don't have it to give."

"If you believe that, you've let her take more." She lifted her head, and her eyes were drenched. "You've let her win."

"Nobody won, my sister, my friend, me. Three lives damaged, and all she got from it was a few auditions. Nobody won," he murmured, and brushed a tear from her cheek with his thumb. "Don't cry. I didn't tell you to make you cry, just to help you understand who I am."

"I know who you are, and I can't help hurting for you."

"Cybil." He brought her close again. "If you keep wearing your heart that close to the surface, someone's going to come along and break it."

She closed her eyes but didn't tell him someone already had.

Chapter 10

It was time, Daniel decided, to have a private little chat with young Preston McQuinn. It was simple enough to lure the man up into his tower office while Cybil was busy with Anna in another part of the house. And Matthew—well, the boy was likely off somewhere or other looking for inspiration for one of his metal toys.

Matthew's sculptures invariably brought Daniel both puzzlement and pride.

"Have a seat, lad. Stretch out your legs." Daniel walked to the bookshelf, took out a copy of *War and Peace* and chose a cigar out of the hollow. "Will you have one?"

Preston only lifted a brow. "No, thanks. Interesting literature, Mr. MacGregor."

"Well, a man does what he can to keep his woman off his back." Daniel ran the length of the cigar under his nose, sniffing in appreciation, sighed in anticipation as he sat, then took his time lighting it. Part of the pleasure was in the small and delightful steps.

He unlocked the bottom drawer in his huge oak desk, took out a large carved shell and set it in the center of his blotter as an ashtray. Following that came a tiny battery-operated fan. It was the newest of Daniel's attempts to keep Anna from sniffing him out.

"Wife doesn't want me smoking." The pity of it had Daniel shaking his head. "And the older she gets, the sharper her nose. Got one like a bloodhound," he muttered, then settled back, sighed. "Now, then."

"What if she comes up?" Preston wanted to know.

"We worry about that if and when, boy, if and when." But his healthy fear of his wife's wrath had him nudging the little fan closer. "So tell me, your play's going well for you?"

"Yes, it is."

"I'm not only asking as an investor, I want you to know. I'm interested in you."

"Mmm-hmm."

"Admire your father's work. Got some of his books around here." Daniel leaned back in the enormous leather chair, puffed out smoke. "A bird tells me that Hollywood's taken quite an interest in your work, McQuinn."

"You've got a good ear for birds."

"I do indeed. How does it sit with you, this movie business?"

"Well enough."

"You play poker, don't you, McQuinn?"

"I've been known to ante up occasionally."

"I'll wager you play a fine game of it. You're not one

to give your hand away. I like that." Contemplatively, Daniel tapped his cigar on the shell. "You'll be in New York a few more weeks?"

"Another month, anyway. Most of the work on the house should be done by then."

"A fine big house, too, by the sea." Daniel smiled as Preston narrowed his eyes. "The birds tell me all manner of things. It's good for a man to have a house of his own. Some of us aren't meant to live in a hive, with people buzzing through the next wall. We need our own space, for ourselves, for our family. Room to spread out," he continued, gesturing. "A place where a man can go to have a damn cigar in his own house without being nagged half to death."

As Daniel scowled, took another puff, Preston's lips twitched.

"True enough," Preston agreed. "Though I wouldn't say my house is anywhere near the scale of yours."

"Young yet, aren't you? You build as you go. And you'd need the sea, as I did, having grown up with it outside your door."

"I prefer it to the city." Since he wasn't quite sure where the conversation was headed, Preston didn't relax quite yet. "And if I had to live in a suburban development I'd likely slit my throat in a week."

Daniel laughed, puffed and eyed Preston through the cloud of smoke. "You're a man who needs his privacy, and that's a reasonable thing. But when solitude and privacy become isolation, it's not always healthy, is it?"

Preston angled his head. "I don't see any neighbors mowing their yards and trimming their hedges when I look out the windows of Castle MacGregor."

Daniel's grin flashed in his beard. "That you don't,

McQuinn. But while private we are, isolated we aren't. You know Cybil grew up by the sea, as well." He clamped the cigar between his teeth. "Along the coast of Maine, where her father guarded his privacy like a pit bull."

"So I've heard," Preston said mildly.

"Her father's a good man for all he's a Campbell." Idly, Daniel drummed his fingers on the edge of his desk. "Time was a highlander'd sooner bed down with rats and weasels than let a Campbell through the front door. You don't hold the '45 against him and his, do you, McQuinn?"

It took him a minute, possibly longer, to realize Daniel referred to the Jacobite Rebellion over two hundred years before. Thinking a laugh would be out of place, he disguised it with a cough. "No," he said, very seriously. "Times change. We have to move on."

"Right enough." Pleased, Daniel thumped a fist on the desk. "And as I said, he's a good man, and his wife's a fine woman. Comes from good stock herself. Their children do them proud."

At sea, Preston merely nodded. "I'm sure you're right."

"Of course I'm right. You've seen for yourself, haven't you? She's a bright and lovely woman, my Cybil. A heart big as the moon, warm as the sun. She draws people to her just by being. There's a light about her, don't you think?"

"I think she's unique."

"That she is. There's no deceit in her, or guile," Daniel continued, his blue eyes sharp and focused. "Too often she puts her own feelings aside to spare another's. Not that she's a doormat, not with that good Scots' blood in her. She'll spit when she's cornered, but she's more likely to hurt herself before she'd hurt another. Causes me some worry."

Though he was hearing no more than he'd seen for himself, Daniel's words had Preston shifting uncomfortably in the chair. "I don't think you have to worry about Cybil."

"It's a grandparent's right, duty, and pleasure if it comes down to it, to worry about his chicks. She wants a place to put all the love she holds inside her. The man who engages that heart of hers will live his life lucky."

"Yes, he will."

"You've had your eye on her, McQuinn." Daniel leaned forward now. "I don't need birds to tell me that."

More than my eye, Preston thought with an inward wince. "As you said, she's a lovely woman."

"And you're a single man of thirty. What are your intentions?"

Well, Preston thought, that was cutting straight to the core. "I don't have any."

"Then it's time you got some." To punctuate, Daniel banged his fist on the desk. "You're not blind or stupid, are you?"

"No."

"Well then, what's stopping you? The girl's exactly what you need to lighten up that serious nature of yours, to keep you from burrowing into a cave like a bear with indigestion." Eyes narrowed, he jabbed out with the cigar. "And if I didn't know you were just what's best for her, you wouldn't be within arm's reach, I can tell you that."

"You put me in arm's reach, Mr. MacGregor." Feeling trapped, and furious because of it, Preston pushed out of his chair. "You dumped me on her doorstep, under the guise of doing me a favor."

"I did you the finest favor of your life, lad, and you should be thanking me for it, instead of looking murderous."

"I don't know how the rest of the family and acquaintances handle your button pushing, but I can tell you I don't appreciate or need it."

"If you didn't need it," Daniel disagreed in a roar, "why are you still moping about something that's gone—and never really was—instead of taking hold of what is?"

The temper that had been heating Preston's eyes turned to ice. "That's my business."

"It's your flaw," Daniel disagreed, more pleased than not to watch the anger, and the control. "And a man's entitled to one or two. I've had over ninety years in this world to watch people, to measure them, to see them as they are. I'll tell you something, McQuinn, that you're either too young or too stubborn to see for yourself— you match, the pair of you. One balancing the other."

"You're wrong."

"Hah! Damned if I am. The lass wouldn't have asked you to this house if she wasn't already in love with you. And you'd not have come unless you were already in love with her."

So he goes pale at that, Daniel thought, sitting back again with satisfaction. Love, for some, was a scary business.

"You've miscalculated." Preston spoke softly as his stomach clenched into a dozen tight fists. "Love has nothing to do with what's between Cybil and me. And if I hurt her. When I hurt her," Preston corrected, "you'll own part of the blame for it."

He stalked out, leaving Daniel puffing on his cigar. Hurt was part of love, he acknowledged. Though he'd suffer for knowing his precious girl would ache a bit along the way. And yes, he'd own part of the blame for it. But when the man stopped wriggling like a stubborn trout on the line and made her happy... Well then, who would own the credit, he'd like to know, if it wasn't Daniel MacGregor?

And laughing, he finished his cigar in secret delight.

Cybil was sorry the trip to Hyannis had put Preston in a prickly mood. One, she thought, that hadn't completely reversed itself after a week back in New York.

He was a difficult man. She accepted that. Now that she knew the full story of what he'd been through, what had been done to him, she didn't see how he could be otherwise.

It would take him, a man with that much sensitivity, that much heart, a long time to trust again. A long time to allow himself to feel again.

She could wait.

But it hurt. She couldn't stop it from hurting when he turned away from her just a little too quickly, or barricaded himself against her with his work, his music or the long, solitary walks he'd begun to take at odd hours.

Walks where he made it clear he wanted to be alone, that he didn't want to share with her.

She told herself his work was giving him trouble— though he never talked about his play with her any longer. She imagined he didn't think she could understand the pain, the joy, the frustration of his work or what parts of himself it could swallow. That stung, but she told herself she accepted it.

She'd always been able to lie to herself more easily than she had to others.

Her own work had taken a new turn and was involving more of her time and energy. The meeting she'd had just before leaving for Hyannis had been a vital one. But she'd told no one. Not family, not friends, not her lover.

Superstitious, she supposed, as she climbed out of a cab in front of her building. She'd been afraid to say it out loud and jinx it before it was real.

Now it was.

She pressed a hand to her heart, felt it thud in hard, excited beats. Heard herself giggle. Now it was very real, and she couldn't wait to tell everyone.

Maybe she'd have a party to celebrate. A loud, silly, joyful bash of a party.

Champagne and balloons. Pizza and caviar.

As if preparing for it, she danced up the steps. She had to call her parents, her family, to grab Jody so they could squeal at each other.

But first, she had to tell Preston.

She used the knuckles of both fists, rapping a cheerful tattoo on his door. He'd be working, she thought, but this couldn't wait. He'd understand.

They had to celebrate. Glug champagne in the middle of the afternoon, get a little drunk and stupid and make crazy love.

When he opened the door she was shining like a sunbeam.

"Hi! I just got back. You won't believe it."

He was rumpled, unshaven, and resented the fact

that one look at her could yank his mind right out of his play. Just one look. "I'm working, Cybil."

"I know. I'm sorry. But I'm going to burst if I don't tell somebody." She lifted her hands to his face, rubbed them over the stubble. "You look like you could use a quick break anyway."

"I'm in the middle of things," he began, but she was already breezing in.

"I bet you haven't eaten lunch. I just had the most incredible lunch at this new hot spot uptown. Why don't I fix you a sandwich and we'll—"

"I don't want a sandwich." He heard the edgy snap to his voice, didn't bother to soften it as he stalked to the stove to pour coffee that had been ripening for hours. "And I don't have time for one. I want to work."

"You have to eat." She had her head inside his fridge, then brought it out again when she heard him go upstairs. "Oh, for heaven's sake." She blew out a breath, rolled her eyes and started up after him.

"Okay, forget the sandwich. I just have to tell you how I spent my day. God, McQuinn, it's dark as a tomb in here." Instinctively, she marched to the window, started to throw open the drapes.

"Leave them alone. Damn it, Cybil."

Her hand froze, then dropped away, as slowly, as completely, as her mood. He was already at the keyboard, she noted, already closed off from her, just as he closed himself off from the life that surged and pulsed outside his curtained window.

He worked with lamplight and stale coffee. And with his back to her.

Nothing that was inside her, that had been bubbling like a geyser, mattered to him.

"It's so easy for you to ignore me," she murmured. "To dismiss me."

There was no mistaking the hurt in her voice. He braced himself against it, refused to feel guilty. "It's not easy, but right now it's necessary."

"Yes, you're working, and I've got some nerve, don't I, interrupting genius, interfering with such a grand enterprise. One I couldn't possibly understand."

Irritated, he flicked a glance at her. "You can work with people hovering. I can't."

"Then again," she continued, "it's easy for you to ignore and dismiss me at other times, too, when work has nothing to do with it."

He pushed away from the keyboard, shifted toward her. "I'm not in the mood to argue with you."

"And, of course, it always comes down to your moods. If you're in the mood to be with me or be alone. To talk to me or be quiet. To touch me or turn away."

There was a hint of finality in her tone that had panic skating up his spine. "If that didn't suit you, you should have said so."

"You're right. Absolutely. Exactly right. And just now it doesn't suit me, Preston, to be treated like a mild annoyance easily swatted aside, then picked up again when you have a moment. It doesn't suit me to have what matters to me shrugged off as unimportant."

"You want me to stop work and listen to how you spent the day shopping and having lunch?"

She opened her mouth, closed it again, but not before one small sound of hurt had escaped.

"I'm sorry." Furious with himself, he got to his feet. She looked as if he'd slapped her. "I'm streaming toward the end of this, and I'm distracted, nasty." He dragged his hands through his hair because she hadn't moved, hadn't stopped staring at him with those wide, wounded eyes. "Let's go downstairs."

"No, I have to go." Because she could feel ridiculous tears stirring in her throat, burning there. "I have some calls to make, and I have a headache," she said, lifting a hand to rub at her throbbing temple. "It makes me irritable. I think I need some aspirin and a nap."

She started out, stopping when he laid a hand on her arm. He felt her tremble and absorbed a hard wash of shame. "Cybil—"

"I don't feel well, Preston. I'm going home to lie down."

She broke free, rushed out. He winced as he heard the slam of the door. "You stupid son of a bitch," he muttered, rubbing his fingers against his eyes. "Why didn't you just kick her a couple of times while you were at it?"

Disgusted with himself, he paced the room, shoving his hands in his pocket, then pulling them out again to yank at the drapes.

The sun was brilliant, streaming through the glass, making him narrow his eyes in defense. Maybe he did close himself off from what was on the other side, he thought. He worked better that way. And he didn't have to justify or explain his work habits to anyone.

He didn't have to hurt her that way.

But damn it, she'd burst in on him at the worst possible time. He was entitled to his privacy, to his space when the work and the words were racing through him.

He didn't dismiss her. He didn't ignore her. How the hell did you ignore someone who wouldn't get out of your mind no matter what else was sharing the space with her?

But he'd been trying to, hadn't he? Very deliberately trying to do both, ever since the little session with Daniel MacGregor in his tower office in Hyannis Port.

Because the clever, canny, meddling old man was right.

He was already in love with her.

If he ignored it, dismissed it, kept pushing it just a little further out of reach, it might go away before it got a good, firm grip on him.

He wasn't risking love again, not when he knew exactly what it could do to twist heart and soul, to wring every drop of blood out of them. He wasn't going to allow himself to become that vulnerable to her.

He'd get over it, he told himself, and pulled the curtains shut again. He'd put things back on balance and they'd both be happier.

And as far as his insufferable behavior of the last few days, he'd make it up to her. She hadn't done anything to deserve it, except exist. She'd done nothing but give, he thought. He'd done nothing but take.

Knowing work was out of the question, he went downstairs. He considered going across the hall, knocking, leading in with the apology he owed her. But she was entitled to her privacy, as well, he decided. He'd give it to her and take a walk.

He didn't think about buying her flowers until he saw them, bright and sunny in an outdoor cart. Not roses, he mused. Too formal. Not the daisies—they were cheerful but ordinary. He settled on tulips in butter yellow and creamy white.

The minute they were in his hand, he felt lighter.

He kept walking, realizing he'd gone on too long without taking the time to really let his mind clear. As it did, he thought more about what she'd said in that brief, dark scene in his room.

Just how often had she nudged aside her own moods, her own needs, to accommodate his? The MacGregor had hit that one, as well. It was her nature to think about the needs of those she cared about before her own.

He'd never known anyone as selfless, generous or unfailingly happy in her own skin. He'd stopped being all those things, except when he was with her. When he let himself really *be* with her.

She'd been so excited when she'd burst into his apartment. He'd become so used to seeing her that way he hadn't considered it might have been something special that had put that shine in her eyes.

He'd taken care of that quickly enough, he thought viciously.

And he'd taken her for granted, he realized, almost from the first moment.

He could change that. And would. He'd give her back as much as he took, put them on equal ground. So when the time came to step back from each other— and it would—they might have a chance to do so as friends.

He simply couldn't imagine his life without her as part of it any longer.

He stayed out the rest of the afternoon, into early evening. When he went to her door with flowers, he didn't feel foolish. He felt settled. And when she opened it, he felt right.

"Did you get some rest?"

"Yes." She'd dived into sleep the way a rabbit dives into a thicket. To hide. "Thanks."

"Feel like company?" He brought the tulips up into

her line of sight. And when she stared at them, he recognized simple shock. "And tulips?"

"Ah...sure. They're wonderful. I'll get a vase."

Just how much had he left out, he wondered, if his bringing her a handful of flowers stunned her? "I'm sorry about this afternoon."

"Oh." So the flowers were an apology, she thought, as she took a blue glass vase from a cupboard. She shook off the vague disappointment that they hadn't been for no reason at all and turned to smile. "It doesn't matter. It's what you get when you disturb a bear in his den."

"It matters." He laid a hand on hers over the tulips. "And I'm sorry."

"All right."

"That's it? A lot of women would make a man grovel a little."

"I don't care for groveling much. Aren't you lucky?"

He lifted her hand, turning it over to press his lips to the palm. "Yes. I am." And for the second time he saw blank shock on her face.

He'd never given her tenderness, he realized, amazed at his own stupidity. Never given her the simple glow of romance. "I thought, if you're feeling better, you might like to go out to dinner."

She blinked. "Out?"

"If you like. Or if you're not feeling up to it," he continued, coming around the counter, "we can have a quiet dinner in. Whatever you want," he murmured, cupping her face to brush his lips over her forehead.

"Who are you? And what are you doing in Preston's body?"

He chuckled, then kissed her cheeks, one, the other. "Tell me what you want, Cybil."

To be touched like this. Looked at like this. "I... I can just fix something here."

"If you want to stay in, I'll take care of dinner."

"You? *You?* All right, that's it. I'm calling the cops."

He drew her into his arms, held her. "I'm not threatening to cook. We'd never survive the night that way." He nuzzled her hair, stroked it. "I'll order in."

"Oh, well, all right." He was holding her, she thought dizzily. Just holding her, as if that was enough, as if that was everything.

"You're tight." He murmured it, sliding his hands up to rub at the tension in her shoulders. "I don't think I've ever known you to be knotted up. The headache still bothering you?"

"No, not much."

"Why don't you go up. Soak in the tub until you're relaxed. Then you can put on one of those robes you're so fond of and we'll have a quiet dinner."

"I'm fine. I can..." She trailed off as his mouth skimmed hers, retreated, then returned, softly, gently, sweetly enough to dissolve her knees.

"Go on up." He drew her away, smiling as she stared up at him with slumberous, confused eyes. "I'll take care of everything."

"All right. I guess I'm a little unsteady yet." Which might explain why she wasn't entirely sure how to get upstairs in her own apartment. "The, ah, number for the pizza place is on the phone."

"I'll take care of it." He gave her a nudge toward the steps. "Go relax."

"Okay." She started to the steps, up, then stopped and turned back to study him. "Preston?"

"Yeah?"

"Are you…" With a half laugh she shook her head. "Nothing. Never mind. I won't be long."

"Take your time," he told her. It was going to require a bit of his to make certain everything was ready for her when she came back down.

If the hint of romance nearly shocked her speechless, he thought she'd have a hard time forming a single word by the time the evening he was planning was over.

He picked up the phone, punched the button on memory next to Jody's name. "Jody? Preston McQuinn. Yeah. Listen, does Cybil have a favorite restaurant around here? No, not the diner," he said with a laugh. "We're moving upscale. Let's try French and fancy."

He had to grin at Jody's long, three-toned "Oh," then scribbled down the name she gave him. "I don't suppose you'd have the number handy. You do, huh? You're a genius. Now, let's see if you can hit three for three. Which dessert on their menu sends her into a coma? Got it, thanks. Special?" He glanced upstairs, grinned. "No, nothing special. Just a quiet dinner in. Thanks for the tip."

He laughed again as Jody continued to shoot out questions. "Hey, we both know she'll tell you all about it tomorrow."

He hung up, dialed the restaurant and outlined his needs. Then, metaphorically pushing up his sleeves, got down to work.

Chapter 11

She did as he'd suggested and took her time. She needed it to adjust to this strange new mood of his. Or was it a side of him, she wondered, he just hadn't shown her before?

How could she have known he had such sweetness in him? And how could she have predicted that his showing her, giving her that sweetness, would make it so much more difficult for her to stay in control of her own feelings?

She loved him when he was careless and cross, when he was amused and amusing, when he was hot and hungry. How much more could she love him when he was kind and caring?

He was making an effort, she thought, to apologize to her for hurting her. And he didn't even know, not really, just what he'd done. But it mattered enough—she mattered enough—for him to want to make it right again.

How could she say no?

A quiet, casual evening at home would be good for both of them. He didn't like crowds, and at the moment, she didn't have the energy for them herself. So they'd eat pizza in front of the TV, be easy with each other again. They'd laugh, talk about something unimportant and make love on the sofa while an old movie flickered on the screen.

They'd make things simple again. Because simple was really what was best for both of them.

Steadier, she belted a long, silky blue robe, flicked her fingers through her nearly dry hair, and started downstairs.

She heard the music first. Low, dreamy. The kind that set the pulse for seduction. It didn't puzzle her for long. After all, the man liked his music. But when she was halfway down the steps, she saw the candles burning. Dozens of them, with pinpoint flames that flickered and swayed.

He was standing in that shimmering light, waiting for her.

He'd changed into trousers and a black shirt and had shaved off the two days' growth of beard. His hand was already held out for hers, and she stepped down to take it, more than a little dazzled at the way the light glinted on his hair and deepened the blue of his eyes.

"Feeling better?"

"I'm fine. What's going on here?"

"We're having dinner."

"The set's a little elaborate for..." He raised her hand to his lips, nibbled lightly at her knuckles, and had the breath strangling in her throat. "Pizza," she managed, and he only smiled.

"I like looking at you in candlelight. Seeing what it does to your eyes. Those exotic, enormous eyes," he murmured, and drew her close to kiss them gently closed. "And your skin." He trailed his lips over her cheek. "That impossibly soft skin. I'm afraid I've put bruises on it forgetting just how soft it is."

"What?" Her head seemed to be circling slowly.

"I've been careless with you, Cybil. I won't be tonight." He lifted her hands again, kissed them again, and had her heart stumbling.

"I have something for you," he told her, and picked up a small square box with an elaborate pink bow from the counter.

Instantly, she whipped her hands behind her back. "I don't need gifts. I don't want them."

He frowned, puzzled at the shaky edge in her voice. Then realized she was thinking of Pamela. "It's not because you need them, or ask for them, or anything else for that matter. It's because they made me think of you." He held the box out. "Open it before you decide. Please."

Feeling foolish, she took the box, gently removed the bow. "Well, who doesn't like presents?" she said lightly. "And you missed my birthday."

"I did?"

He said it with such guilty surprise she laughed. "Yes, it was in January, and just because you didn't know me is really no excuse for not giving me a present. So this will…" She stopped, stared into the box at the earrings, two long dangles of hematite in the shape of a dozen tiny, foolish fish. Like minnows on the line.

She laughed, rolled with it as she took them out, held them up and shook so they would clack together. "They're ridiculous."

"I know."

"I love them."

"I figured you would."

Eyes sparkling, she slipped the thin wire backs through her ears. "Well, what do you think?"

"They're you. Definitely."

"It's such a sweet thing to do."

She tossed her arms around him, kissed him lavishly enough to have his blood heating. Then he heard the sniffle.

"Oh, God, don't. Don't do that."

"Sorry." She pressed her face to his throat. "It's just—flowers and candles and silly fish all in one night. It's so thoughtful." But she drew a long breath, blew it out, stepped back. "There, all clear."

"Thank God." He brushed his thumb over her lashes where a tiny tear clung. "Ready for champagne?"

"Champagne?" Baffled, she lifted her hands. "Well, it's tough not to be ready for champagne."

She watched as he stepped into the kitchen, took a bottle from her own crystal ice bucket and began to open it. What in the world had gotten into him? she wondered. Suddenly, he was relaxed, happy, romantic...

"You finished your play! Oh, Preston, you finished it."

"No, I didn't. Not quite." He popped the cork, poured the wine.

"Oh." Trying to puzzle it out, she angled her head as he turned, handed her a glass full of straw-colored, bubbling wine. "Then what are we celebrating?"

"You." He touched his glass to hers. "Just you." He laid a hand on her cheek, then lifted his own glass to her lips.

She tasted the wine, a froth on the tongue, silk in the throat. But it was the way he looked at her that made her head spin. "I don't know what to say to you."

"Well, there's an unprecedented event." Smiling, he brought the wine to his own lips, tasted it. Tasted her.

"Ah, so this is all a ploy to shut me up." Chuckling, relaxed again, she enjoyed the champagne. "Very clever, aren't you?"

"I haven't even started." He took the glass from her, set it aside, then drew her into his arms. Even as she lifted her mouth, expecting the kiss—expecting, he was sure, demand and heat—he skimmed his cheek over hers and began to move to the rhythm of the music. "I've never asked you to dance."

"No." Her eyes drifted closed. "You haven't."

"Dance with me, Cybil."

She ran her hands up his back, laid her head on his shoulder and fell into the music and him. They danced, swaying together in the kitchen washed with candle glow.

When his lips grazed her jaw, she turned her head so that his mouth cruised over hers. Her pulse was slow, slow and thick, her limbs weak as water.

"Preston." She murmured it, rising on her toes to give him more.

"That must be dinner," he said against her lips.

"What?"

"Dinner. The buzzer."

"Oh." She'd thought the buzzing was in her head, and had to brace a hand on the counter for balance when he left her to release the outer door.

"I hope you're not disappointed," he commented, unlocking her door. "It isn't pizza."

"Oh, that's all right. Anything's fine." How was a woman supposed to eat when her stomach was full of tiny, energetic butterflies?

But her eyes widened when, rather than a delivery boy, two tuxedoed waiters appeared at the door.

She watched, astonished, as with discretion and efficiency they arranged food on the table Preston had already set with her best dishes. In less than ten minutes, they were gone, and she'd yet to find her voice.

"Hungry?"

"I… It looks wonderful."

"Come, sit down." He took her hand again, led her to the table in front of the window, then bent to brush a kiss at her nape.

She must have eaten. She would never be able to remember what, or how it had tasted. Her innate powers of observation had deserted her. All she could see was Preston. All she would remember was the way his fingers had brushed hers, how his mouth had skimmed over her knuckles. How he had smiled and poured more wine, until her head was swimming with it.

How he had looked at her when he'd risen and held out a hand for hers to bring her to her feet. The way her heart had tripped when he'd lifted her right off them and into his arms.

She suddenly seemed so delicate. So vulnerable when she trembled. Even if he'd wished it otherwise, he couldn't have been anything but gentle.

He carried her up the steps, into the bedroom, and laid her on the pillows. He lit the candles as he had once before, but this time when he turned to her, when he came to her, his touch was feather soft.

And he took her, dreaming, into the kiss.

He gave more than he'd thought he had left in him. Found more in her open response than he'd believed possible. If she trembled, it wasn't triumph he felt but tenderness.

And he gave it back to her.

Slow, silky, sumptuous kisses. Long, liquid, lingering caresses. He had her floating on some high, lace-edged cloud where the air was full of perfume and the world beyond it insignificant.

Gently, he slipped the robe from her, the glide of his hands sending silvery shivers along her skin and shimmering warmth beneath it. Through dazed eyes she watched as he drew back, as his gaze followed the lazy trail of a single fingertip over her body.

"You're so lovely, Cybil." Those suddenly intense blue eyes met hers. "How many times have I forgotten to tell you? To show you?"

"Preston—"

"No. Let me do both. Let me watch you enjoy being touched as I should have touched you before. Like this," he murmured, skimming his fingertips over her.

Her breath caught, and the cloud beneath her began to rock. Then he lowered his head and let his mouth follow the path his fingertips had blazed.

Now she was drowning, slowly floating beneath the surface of a warm dark sea. Helpless there, drifting with only his hands and lips to anchor her. And that first wave came in a long, liquid crest that washed through her system to leave it weak and heavy with pleasure.

He wanted to have her steep in it, sate her with it. No sharp flash this time but a slow burn. He explored and exploited every inch of her, lingering when her breath quickened, savoring when her body arched on each steadily building delight.

And his blood swam with it; his heart jolted until he was as lost and open as she.

He murmured her name as he slipped into her, moaned it as she wrapped around him in welcome.

With long, deep thrusts, he moved in her while their mouths met in a soft and stirring kiss. In a slow, sleek rhythm, she moved under him while their hands met to complete yet another link.

They swallowed each other's sighs, gripped each other's hands as they let themselves shatter.

And he was there when she awoke, holding her, as he'd held her while they slept.

"It's definitely number one of the modern-day Top Ten Most Romantic Evenings." Jody expertly changed Charlie's diaper, cooing at him between commentary. "It knocks that Valentine's Day carriage ride around the park and dozen white roses with diamond-chip earrings attached that my cousin Sharon experienced down to a poor second place. She's going to be peeved."

"No one's ever paid that much attention," Cybil murmured, hugging one of the teddy bears in Charlie's vast collection. "Not just the you-know."

"But the you-know." Jody cocked her eyebrows as she fastened Charlie's fresh diaper. "That was excellent, right?"

"It was spectacular. You know that scene in *Through the Mist,* where Dorian and Alessa find each other after being cruelly separated by her evil, ambitious uncle?"

"Oh." Jody rolled her eyes, lifting Charlie up to bounce him. "Do I ever. I was up till two reading that book, then I woke up Chuck." She smiled reminiscently. "We were both a little tired the next day but very, very loose. Anyway—" she shook herself, before carrying Charlie into the living room so he could practice his crawling "—it was that good?"

"It was better."

"No way."

"It was like having him take my heart out and hold it, then give it back to me."

"Oh, man." Weak-kneed, Jody slipped into a chair. "That's beautiful, Cyb. Just beautiful. You ought to write a romance novel yourself."

"But it wasn't just that. It was all of it. Everything." Still giddy, she threw her arms out and twirled in a circle, making Charlie rock back on his butt and clap in delight.

"I'm so in love with him, Jody. I didn't think you could be this much in love and not have it all just come steaming out of you. There shouldn't be room inside for it all."

"Oh." Jody's sigh was long and loud. "When are you going to tell him?"

"I can't." With a sigh of her own, Cybil picked up Charlie's red plastic hammer and tapped the oversize head on her palm. "I'm not brave enough to tell him something he doesn't want to hear."

"Cyb, the guy's crazy about you."

"He's got feelings for me, and maybe, maybe if I can wait, if he realizes I'm not going to let him down, he'll let himself feel more."

"Let him down?" The very idea ruffled Jody's feathers. "You never let anyone down. But maybe this time you're letting Cybil down."

"He's got reasons to be careful," she said, then shook her head before Jody could speak. "I can't tell you about it. They're his own."

"Okay."

"Thanks. I've got to go. I have a million errands to run. Need anything?"

"Actually, I do. If you're going out anyway."

"I'll just add it to the list. I've got a few things to pick up for Mrs. Wolinsky, and I told Mr. Peebles I'd see if the green grapes looked good at the market. Just let me find my shopping list."

"I'm only asking because you're going out anyway and because it's you." Jody bit her lip, then grinned. "Don't tell anybody what you're getting for me, okay?"

"I won't." Absently, Cybil dug through her purse. "I know that list is in here somewhere."

It took longer than she'd expected—but Cybil found shopping usually did. Then, by the time she'd delivered the goods to Mrs. Wolinsky, the grapes—which had looked appetizing enough for her to buy a pound of her own—to Mr. Peebles and knocked on Jody's door, it was after five o'clock.

She hissed in frustration when Jody didn't answer. It appeared her friend could stand the suspense, though Cybil herself wanted instant gratification. But either Jody had taken Charlie out for a little walk or she was visiting one of the other neighbors and they'd both just have to wait.

Arms loaded, Cybil took the elevator up.

And grinned like a fool when she saw Preston waiting for her in the hall. "Hi."

"Hi, neighbor." He scooped the bags out of her arms,

then bent down and kissed her. "Hold it," he said when she dropped back from her toes to the balls of her feet. "Let's do that again."

"Okay." Laughing, she wound her arms around his neck, shifted back to her toes and put a great deal more energy into the greeting. "How's that?"

"That was fine. What have you got in here? Bricks?"

Searching for her ever-elusive key, she laughed again. "Food mostly, and some cleaning supplies. Some this and some that. I picked up a few things for you. The apples looked very good, and they're better for you to snack on while you're working than candy bars or stale bagels."

She found her key with a little *aha!* and unlocked the door. "Oh, and I got you some ammonia—it'll take care of that grime you're letting build up on your windows."

"Apples and ammonia." He set the bags on the counter. "What else could a man ask for?"

"Cheesecake, straight from the deli. It was irresistible."

"It'll have to wait." He spun her around, off her feet, and began to twirl with her.

"Well, you're in a mood, aren't you?" Grinning, she bent down to kiss him. "If your smile got any bigger, I might fall in."

"You'd be better than cheesecake. I finished the play."

"You did?" The hands that were braced on his shoulders slid around to hug his neck. "That's wonderful. That's great."

"I've never had anything move so fast. It still needs work, but it's there. All there. You had a lot to do with it."

"Me?"

"So much of you kept jumping into it. Once I stopped trying to push you back out, it just raced."

"I'm speechless. What did you write about me? What was I like? What did I do in it? Can I read it?"

"So much for speechless," he noted, and set her back on her feet. "After I fiddle with it a bit more you can read it. Let's go to the diner and celebrate."

"The diner? You want to go celebrate something like this with spaghetti and meatballs?"

"Exactly." And he didn't give a damn if it was sentimental. "With you, where you once took a struggling musician out for a hot meal."

"Did you put that in there? About me paying you? God."

"You'll like it, don't worry."

"What's my name—in the play, what's my name?"

"Zoe."

"Zoe." She pursed her lips, considered, then the dimple fluttered at the corner of her mouth. "I like it."

"Nothing ordinary quite fit. She kept tossing them back at me." He laughed a little, shook it off.

"You look so happy." She reached up, brushing at his hair. "It's nice to see you look so happy."

"I've been doing a lot of that lately. Come on. Let's go."

"I have to put the groceries away, fix my face. Then we'll go."

"Go fix whatever you think's wrong with your face. I'll put them away."

"All right. They actually have places," she called out as she ran up the stairs. "They don't just get tossed into cupboards."

"Just make it fast," he told her, and started pulling things out of the first bag.

He'd been going crazy for the past hour, just waiting for her to get back so he could tell her. Tell her first. And to tell her, to find a way to tell her, that somehow, somewhere, over the last few weeks, everything had changed for him.

And though he'd fought it, ignored it, denied it, it had changed nonetheless. He realized that for the first time in much, much too long, the sensation he continued to feel was simple happiness.

She was right. He looked happy. He was happy. But it wasn't just the play. It was Cybil, and it had been all along.

She made him happy.

It had come out in his work. There was an underlying glow of hope in this play he hadn't intended to put there when he'd begun. But it was just there—shimmering and impossible to resist. The way she was.

It had come out in his life when she had come into his life. With cookies and chatter and compassion. With generosity and laughter and verve.

What he felt for her—what she, being who she was, had given him no choice but to feel—filled him, completed him and, he thought, in a very real sense saved him.

The last line of his play said it, he mused.

Love heals.

With a little time, a little effort, he thought, he had a chance of making the kind of life with her he'd stopped believing really existed.

He reached in the second bag, pulled out a box. And

felt the world that had so recently gone rock steady, waver, shake and fall away under his feet.

"I was going to change, but I decided not to waste the time when we could be celebrating." She clattered down the steps at a dead run, the foolish earrings he'd given her swinging. "I just have to call Jody, see if she's back yet. Then we're out of here."

"What the hell is this, Cybil?" Pale, coldly furious, he tossed the home pregnancy test kit on the counter. "Are you pregnant?"

"I—"

"You think you're pregnant, but you don't tell me. What? Were you going to pick your time, your place, your *mood,* then let me in on it?"

The color of excitement and pleasure that had been glowing in her cheeks drained so that she was as pale as he now. "Is that what you think, Preston?"

"What the hell am I supposed to think? You waltz in, all smiles, not a care in the world, and there's this." He rapped a finger on the box. "And you're the one who claims she doesn't play games, doesn't tell lies. What else is keeping this from me but both of those?"

"And that makes me like Pamela, doesn't it?" All the joy that had shimmered in her heart throughout the day turned to ashes, cold and gray. "Calculating, deceitful. Just one more user."

He had to steady himself, to calm, but the slash of betrayal where he had finally, finally, decided to trust was ripping through him. "This is you and me, no one else. I want an explanation."

"I wonder if there's ever really been a you and me and no one else," she murmured. "I'll give you an explanation, Preston. I picked up apples for you, grapes for 1B and several small items for Mrs. Wolinsky. And I picked up that handy little will-it-be-pink-or-blue kit for Jody. She and Chuck are hoping they're expecting a baby brother or sister for Charlie."

"Jody?"

"That's right." Every word she spoke hurt her throat. "I'm not pregnant, so you can relax on that score."

"I'm sorry."

"Oh, so am I. I'm terribly sorry." Her eyes ached as she picked up the box, examined it. "Jody was so excited when she asked me to buy this. So hopeful. For some people the idea of making a child is a joyful one. But for you," she went on, putting the box down, making herself look at him, "it's a threat, just a bad memory of a bad time."

"It was a poor reaction, Cybil. Knee-jerk."

"You could say instinctive, I suppose. What would you have done, Preston, if it had been mine? If I'd been pregnant? Would you have thought I'd tricked you, trapped you, done it on purpose to ruin your life? Or maybe you'd have wondered if I'd been with another man and was laughing at you behind your back."

"No, I wouldn't have thought that." The very idea shocked him. "Don't be ridiculous. Of course I wouldn't have thought that."

"What's ridiculous about it? She did it—why not me? Why the hell not me? You let her jump right back in here. You're the one who left the door open for her."

"You're right. Cybil—"

She stepped back sharply when he reached for her. "Oh, don't. I can't quite figure out if you think I'm just another calculating bitch or pathetically malleable. But I'm neither. I'm just me, and I've been nothing but honest with you. You had no right to hurt me like this, and I had no right to let you. But that stops now. I want you to go."

"I'm not going until we settle this."

"It's settled. I don't blame you for it. I'm just as much at fault. I gave too much and expected too little. You were honest with me. 'This is all I have. Don't ask for more,' you said. 'This is what I am. Take it or leave it.' It's my own fault that's what I did. But I won't be doing it anymore. I need someone in my life who respects me, who trusts me. I'm not settling for less. So I want you out."

She strode to the door, flung it open. "Get the hell out."

Because in spite of the fire in her eyes, they were swimming with tears; despite the fists her hands were clenched in, they were shaking. He went to the door, but he stopped, looked at her.

"I was wrong. Completely wrong. Cybil, I'm sorry."

"So am I." She started to slam the door, then drew a deep breath. "I lied. I haven't always been honest with you, but now I will be. I'm in love with you, Preston. And that's the pity of it."

He said her name, started toward her, but she shut the door. He heard the locks snap into place.

He pounded on the door, cursed through it. He paced the hallway, then stalked into his own apartment to call her. But she wouldn't answer.

He tried pounding again, and finally feeling that everything he'd begun to treasure in his life was slipping away, he tried begging. But she was upstairs, with that door closed, as well, and couldn't hear him as she wept in the dark.

Chapter 12

"**I** ought to go find the son of a bitch and break his legs, his arms. Then his neck." Grant Campbell paced the kitchen of the home he'd built with his wife, his mood as dark and rough as the sea that thrashed outside.

"That wouldn't stop her from hurting." Gennie turned from the window where she'd been watching for her daughter and studied her husband.

Long and lean, she mused, and still just a bit dangerous. So much the man she'd fallen in love with all those years ago. And so much more.

"It'd make me feel a hell of a lot better," Grant muttered. "I'm going out to get her."

"No, don't." Gennie laid a hand on his arm before he could storm out the door. "Let her be awhile."

"It's dark," he said, and felt helpless.

"She'll come in when she's ready."

"I can't stand it. I can't stand the look he put in her eyes."

"She has to hurt before she can heal. We both know that." Because they both needed it, Gennie slipped into his arms, rested her head on his shoulder. "She knows we're here."

"It was easier when one of them would fall down. Scrape or break something."

"You didn't think so then." Her laugh was as warm as it had been when he'd first met her; her voice was rich and recalled the scent of magnolias in full bloom. She tipped back her head, cupped his face. "You always hurt more than they did."

"I just want to put her on my lap, make it go away." He lowered his brow to Gennie's. "Then I want to rip the bastard's lungs out."

"Me, too," she said, pleased when he chuckled.

That was how Cybil saw them when she came in the room. The two of them standing in the kitchen, standing close, their eyes on each other's.

And that, she decided, that bond, that intimacy, was what she wanted. What she'd been willing to give.

She walked to them, slipped an arm around each to make a circle. "Do you know how many times in my life I've come in here and seen the two of you just like this? And how lovely it is?"

"Your hair's wet." Grant rubbed his cheek over it.

"I was watching the waves crash." She tilted her head to kiss him. "Stop worrying so, Daddy."

"I will. When you're fifty. Maybe." He patted her cheek. "Want some coffee?"

"Mmm, no. Nothing really. I think I'll take a hot bath, then snuggle into bed with a book. It always worked for me when I was a teenager working off a crush."

"During those crises, I ran your bath," her mother reminded her. "Why break tradition?"

"You don't have to do that, Mama."

"Let me fuss." Gennie slipped an arm around her shoulders.

With a sigh, Cybil let herself be guided out. "I was sort of hoping you would."

"Your father needs to be alone to pace and curse your young man."

"He's not my 'young man,'" Cybil muttered as they started up the wide, circular stairs Grant had designed to echo the narrow, metal ones in the lighthouse just beyond the house. "He never was."

"But you're not a teenager now." Gently, Gennie turned Cybil as they moved into the bedroom where Cybil had dreamed her young-girl dreams. "And this isn't a crush."

The tears came again, spurting out of her center, flooding her heart, throat, eyes, as she shook her head. "Oh, Mama."

"There, baby." She led Cybil to the bed, still covered with its colorful quilt, and, sitting beside her, opened her arms.

"I want to hate him." Burrowing into the comfort, Cybil wept and clung. "I want to hate him. If I could, for just a little while, I'd stop loving him."

"I wish I could tell you that you would. I wish I knew. Some men are so hard, so baffling." Gennie rocked her daughter as she spoke. "I know you, sweet baby. I know if you love him there's something in him that makes him worthy of it."

"He's wonderful. He's horrible. Oh, Mama." Cybil leaned back, weeping still. "He's just like Daddy."

"Oh, God help you." With a half laugh, Gennie gathered her close again.

"I always loved the story." Her breath hitched, and she gratefully took the tissue Gennie snagged from the box near the bed. "The story about how you met—when your car broke down in the storm and you were lost, and you stumbled on the lighthouse where he was living like a hermit. And he was so cranky and rude."

She paused to blow her nose, while Gennie stroked her hair and added, "He couldn't wait to get rid of me."

"The way he tells it, you burst in on him. And he was annoyed because you were wet and beautiful." Cybil sighed and studied her mother's face with its honey-toned skin, its strong bones, the lovely fall of dark hair that framed it. "You're so beautiful, Mama."

"You have my eyes," Gennie said softly. "That makes me feel beautiful."

Tired after the storm of tears, Cybil wiped them dry. "We're just wrong for each other," she said at length. "Preston and I. He's so fiercely private, so absorbed in his work. But it's not that he doesn't have humor."

She sighed, rose, walked to the window so that she could see the moon on the water. "Sometimes he can be incredibly charming, unexpected, delightful. He's so moody you never know what's going to pop up. And there's this amazing sensitivity, and you realize he's almost afraid to trust, to feel. Then he touches you, and you're lost. All the things that he is, all of those complicated things he is, are there when he touches you. But he still doesn't quite let you in."

"Good Lord. He *is* like your father. Cybil, you have

to do what's right for you. But if you love him this much, you may never be happy unless you at least try to work things out with him."

"He thinks I'm frivolous." The fighting edge came back in her voice, pleasing Gennie enormously. "And that my work is less important than his just because it's different. He doesn't trust me. He thinks he can flick me off like a gnat one minute, and he can't keep his hands off me the next."

She whirled around, ready to spew out more complaints, and saw her mother smiling. "What?"

"How did you find another? I thought I had the only one."

"Grandpa found him."

Gennie's smile sharpened, her aristocratic eyebrows arched. "Oh," she said in the regal tone Cybil recognized as dangerous. "Oh, really."

For the first time in more than twenty-four hours, Cybil smiled.

Preston scowled and shoved his sax back in his case. Damn the woman. He couldn't even play out his frustration. He certainly couldn't work, which he'd proven after spending most of a miserable day between staring at his screen and going across the hall to bang on Cybil's door.

That was before he'd finally realized she wasn't inside anymore.

She'd left him. Which he decided was the smartest thing she'd done since she'd met him. And after brooding over it, he'd figured out the best thing he could do for both of them was to be gone when she got back. From wherever the hell she'd gone.

He was going back to Connecticut in the morning. He could tolerate construction workers, plumbers, electricians and whoever else would descend on him on a daily basis for the next few weeks. But he couldn't tolerate living across the hall from a woman he loved and couldn't have due to his own stupidity.

Everything she'd said to him had been completely true. He had no defense.

"I won't be around for a while, André."

The piano player looked up through the haze of smoke from the cigarette between his lips. "That so?"

"I'm heading back to Connecticut tomorrow."

"Uh-huh. Woman chase you away?" Brow cocked, André stretched back. "That your tail I see between your legs, brother?"

With a short, humorless laugh, Preston picked up his case. "See you around."

"I'll be right here." When Preston's back was turned, André jerked up his chin, signaling his wife, then stabbed a thumb in Preston's direction.

With a nod, she glided over to block Preston's exit. "Leaving early tonight, sugar lips."

"I haven't got anything in me. And I want an early start in the morning. I'm going back to Connecticut."

"Back to the boonies?" She smiled, hooked her arm around his shoulders. "Well, let's have us a goodbye drink, 'cause I'm gonna miss your pretty face."

"I'll miss yours, too."

"Not just mine," she said, then held up two fingers to the bartender. "That little girl put the blues into you, and you can't put them all in your sax. Not this time. Not with her."

"No, not with her." He lifted his glass. "That's over."

"Why's that?"

"Because she said it is." He drank, let the fire course through him, but found it didn't quite warm his insides.

Delta let out a short laugh. "When did a man take that for an answer?"

"When the woman means it, this man takes it."

"McQuinn." Delta patted his cheek. "You sure are a fool."

"No argument. That's why it's over. I ruined it—I have to live with it."

"You ruin it—you have to fix it."

"When you hurt someone that much, they've got the right to lock you out."

"Honey, when you love someone that much, you've got the right to pick that lock, then do a lot of crawling on your hands and knees." She turned, studied him eye to eye. "You love her that much?"

He turned his glass, watched the whiskey through the smoke. "I didn't know there was this much. That there could be."

"Sugar lips." She kissed him. "Go pick yourself a lock."

He shook his head, tossed back the rest of his drink, then started the walk home.

Delta was wrong, he told himself. Sometimes you couldn't fix it. You couldn't pick the lock, and you were better off not trying. Why should she let him back in? He carried the image of how her face had paled, how her eyes had gone huge and hollow—and how the tears had swirled in them over the heat of anger.

He didn't have any right to ask her to listen. To let him crawl or beg or play on her sympathies.

And he didn't realize he'd started to run until he'd

reached Jody's door, out of breath, and was pounding on it.

"For God's sake." After checking the peep, Jody wrenched open the door and hitched her robe closed. If Chuck didn't sleep like a rock, she wouldn't have had to race out of bed before the noise woke the baby. "It's after midnight. Are you crazy?"

"Where is she, Jody? Where did she go?"

She wrinkled her nose, lifting her chin with a dignity that was difficult to maintain in a robe covered with pink kittens. "Are you drunk?"

"I had one drink. No, I'm not drunk." He'd never felt more sober, or more desperate. "Where's Cybil?"

"Like I'd tell you after you broke her heart. Go back up to your hole," she ordered, pointing dramatically. "Before I wake up Chuck and some of the other people around here. They might just lynch you on the spot." Her bottom lip trembled. "Everyone loves Cybil."

"So do I."

"Right. That's why you made her cry her eyes out." As her own threatened to fill, Jody dug a ratty tissue out of the pocket of her robe.

All Preston could do was close his eyes against the vicious guilt. "Please tell me where she is."

"Why should I?"

"So I can crawl, and give her a chance to kick me while I'm down. So I can beg. For God's sake, Jody, tell me where she is. I have to see her."

Jody sniffled into the tissue, but the eyes over it had cleared. And now they narrowed as they studied Preston's face and saw pale desperation. "You really love her?"

"Enough to let her send me away if that's what she wants. But I have to see her first."

What could a romantic heart do but sigh? "She's at her parents' in Maine. I'll write it down for you."

Rocked with relief, stunned with gratitude, he had to close his eyes again. "Thanks."

"If you hurt her again," she muttered as she scribbled on the back of an envelope, "I'll hunt you down and kill you with my bare hands."

"I won't even put up a fight." He blew out a breath. "Are you, ah…"

She glanced over, then smiled and laid a hand on her belly. "Yeah, I'm 'ah.' I'm due on Valentine's Day. Isn't that perfect?"

"It's great. Congratulations." He took the envelope she handed him. Then stuffed it into his pocket, framed her face in his hands and kissed her. "Thank you."

She waited until he'd dashed out, then exhaled, long and sharp. "Oh, yeah," she murmured as she closed and locked the door. "I can see how that could work into a no scale. Definitely no-scale potential." Then she closed her eyes, crossed the fingers of both hands. "Good luck, Cybil."

"The MacGregor." Grant said the words through clenched teeth, his dark-brown eyes snapping as visions of murder and mayhem danced through his mind. "Interfering old goat."

Because it was a sentiment Grant had expressed in various terms any number of times since she'd told him the night before of Daniel's matchmaking plot, Gennie didn't bother to suppress the grin. Her husband adored Daniel MacGregor.

"I thought it was 'meddling old blockhead.'"

"That, too. If he wasn't six hundred years old, I'd kick his butt."

"Grant." Gennie set down her sketch pad, deciding the lovely old maple she'd been sketching would be in full leaf rather than tender bud before her husband stopped pacing. "You know he did it out of love."

"Didn't work, did it?"

Gennie started to speak; then, hearing the sound of a car, turned, shielding her eyes against the slant of the midmorning sun. She felt a little ripple go through her heart. "I'm not so sure of that," she murmured.

"Who the hell is that?" It was Grant's usual sentiment when someone dared to trespass on his staunchly guarded privacy. "If that's another tourist, I'm getting the gun."

"You don't have a gun."

"I'm buying one."

She couldn't help it. Gennie sprang to her feet, tossed the sketchbook down on the glider and threw her arms around him. "Oh, Grant, I love you."

The feel of her broke through his darkening mood like sun through storm clouds. "Genviève." He lowered his head, took her mouth. His blood stirred and his heart warmed. "Tell whoever that is to go away and never come back."

Gennie kept her arms around him, laid her head on his shoulder and watched the gorgeous little car fight its way down the narrow, rutted road Grant refused to have repaired. "I think that's going to be up to Cybil."

"What?" Grant's eyes narrowed as he shifted his gaze to watch the car's progress. "You figure that's him? Well, well," he said, and would have pushed his way clear if his wife's arms hadn't tightened around him. "I'm going to be able to kick some butt, after all."

"Behave."

"The hell I will."

Preston spotted them as a particularly nasty bump snapped his teeth together. He'd been too busy cursing whoever considered this ditch in the middle of nowhere a road to notice much more than the next rut, but as his gaze was drawn up, he saw the couple standing in the yard of a rambling white farmhouse.

Not really standing, he thought. Embracing. There on the grass just greening with spring, beside an old-fashioned glider positioned to nestle between graceful shrubs, were the parents of the woman he loved.

He wondered which one of them would kill him first.

Resigned, he muscled the car down the lane and scanned the place where he would likely be buried in a shallow grave.

He'd seen it before, he realized, in the work of Geneviève Campbell. She'd painted here, he thought, with love and with brilliance. The romantic old whitewashed lighthouse that loomed over the cliff, the tumbling rocks that showed color and age in the morning light, the bent and twisted trees—all had been pulled together to form a place and a painting of wild beauty.

The house, with its gleaming white paint, its many windows and cozily covered porch, the tidy flower beds waiting for the spring that would come late to this part of the world, offered simple comfort.

Cybil had grown up here, he thought, in this wild and wonderful place.

He stopped the car, but the sense of relief that his bones could now stop rattling couldn't compete against nerves. The couple on the lawn had turned to watch him. Even at a distance, Preston could see the sentiment on the rugged face of Cybil's father.

And the sentiment wasn't *welcome*.

He stepped out of the car, determined to live long enough to see Cybil and say his piece. After that, he supposed, all bets were off.

No wonder, Gennie thought, as she watched Preston cross the yard. No wonder she'd fallen so hard. Feeling Grant tense, she dug her fingers into his waist in warning. He vibrated like a pit bull on a choke chain.

"Mrs. Campbell. Mr. Campbell." Preston nodded but knew better than to offer his hand. It would be very hard to type with a stub. "I'm Preston McQuinn. I need Cybil—need to see Cybil," he corrected, flustered.

"How old are you, McQuinn?"

Preston's brows knit at the unexpected question delivered in slow, measured tones that didn't dilute the threat. "Thirty."

Grant inclined his head. "You want to live to see thirty-one you get back in that car, put it in reverse and just keep going."

Preston kept his eyes level, unconsciously rolling his shoulders like a boxer preparing for a bout. "Not until I've seen Cybil. After that, you can take me apart. Or try to."

"You're not getting within ten feet of her." Grant set Gennie aside as if she weighed little more than a child's doll.

As he took a menacing step forward, Preston kept his hands at his sides. Cybil's father could have first blood, he decided. He'd earned it.

"Stop it!" Gennie dashed between them, slapped a

hand on each of their chests. She sent her husband one withering look, then offered Preston the same.

He had a moment to think he'd just been chastised by a queen, then his heart stumbled. "She has your eyes." He had to swallow. "Cybil. She has your eyes."

And the soft green of them warmed. "Yes, she does. She's on the cliff, behind the lighthouse."

"Damn it, Gennie."

Before he could stop himself, Preston lifted a hand to the one she pressed to his heart. He could feel his own thundering beat. "Thank you."

He lifted his gaze to Grant's, held it. "I won't hurt her. Not ever again."

"Damn it," Grant muttered again when Preston started for the cliffs in long, determined strides. "Why did you do that?"

With a sigh, Gennie turned back, took her husband's face in her hands. "Because he reminded me of someone."

"Like hell."

She laughed. "And I think our daughter's going to be a very happy woman very shortly."

He let out one exasperated sigh. "I should've gotten just one punch in, on principle. Damn, if he wasn't going to let me."

Then Grant glanced over, watched Preston disappear behind the wide white base of the tower. "I might've been able to do it if one look at your eyes hadn't cut him off at the knees. He's stupid in love with her."

"I know. Remember how scary that is?"

"It's still scary." With a laugh, he pulled her against him again. "The boy's got guts," Grant mused. "And being your daughter, Cybil will twist them into knots for a while before she forgives him."

"Of course she will. He deserves it. Daniel was right about them," she added.

"I know." Grant grinned down at his wife. "But let's not tell him for a while and make him suffer."

She was sketching, sitting on a rock with the wind ruffling through her dark hair, her head bent over the pad, her pencil flying.

The sight of her stole his breath. He'd driven through the night, through the morning, all the while trying to imagine how he would feel when he saw her again. For once his imagination had fallen far short.

He said her name, then realized his shaky whisper wouldn't carry over the sounds of wind and water. He started down the narrow beaten path toward the sea.

Maybe she heard him, or perhaps his shadow changed her light. Or maybe she simply sensed him. But her head came up, and her eyes whipped to him. Emotions stormed through them before they turned the chilly green of a winter sea.

Then, as if his presence didn't matter in the least, she began to sketch again. "You're a long way from home, McQuinn."

"Cybil." His throat felt rusty.

"We're not much on visitors around here. My father often talks about mining the road. Too bad he hasn't gotten around to it."

"Cybil," he said again, while his fingers itched to touch her.

"If I'd had any more to say to you, I'd have said it

in New York." *Go away!* her mind screamed. *Go away before the tears come back.*

"I have something to say to you."

She flicked him a disinterested glance. "If I'd wanted to hear it...same goes." She closed her sketchbook, rose. "Now—"

"Please." He lifted a hand, but when her eyes flared in warning dropped it again. "Hear me out. Then if you want me to go, I'll go. You're too...fair," he said for a lack of a better word, "not to listen."

"All right." She sat back on the rock, opened her sketchbook again. "I'll just keep working, if you don't mind."

"I—" He didn't know where to begin. All the speeches he'd rehearsed, all the pleas and promises, deserted him. "My agent ran into yours yesterday."

"Really? What a small, insular world we live in."

He might have winced at that biting tone, but he was too busy looking at her. "He told her about the series— the television series they're going to do based on your strip. She said it was a major deal."

"For some."

"You didn't tell me."

She spared him another glance. "You're not interested in my work."

"That's not true, but I can't blame you for thinking it. I worked it out, time-wise. The day you came to see me, almost bursting with excitement. You'd come to tell me, and I ruined it for you. I—" He broke off, had to turn away and stare out over the green and restless sea. "I was distracted by the play, and more, what I was feeling for you. What I didn't want to feel for you."

Her fingers tightened and she broke the tip of her

pencil. Furious with herself, she stuck it behind her ear and dug in her small tool bag for another. "If that's what you came to say, you've said it. Now you can go."

"No, that's not what I came to say, but I'll apologize for it, and tell you I'm happy for you."

"Whoopee."

He shut his eyes, fisted his hands. So, she could be cruel, he thought, when it was deserved. "Everything you said to me the night you threw me out of your life was right. I let something that had happened a long time ago stand in front of now. I used it to cut myself off from the best thing that's ever happened to me. I watched my sister's world shatter, saw her struggle to function over the betrayal and the pain, to raise her son alone and give birth to another before the ink was dry on her divorce papers."

How could she hold herself aloof from that, Cybil thought, as she closed her book again? How could she be unmoved? "I know it was hell for her, for both of you. No one should have gone through what your sister did, Preston."

"No, they shouldn't. But people do."

He turned back, met her eyes. Already, he thought in wonder, already there was sympathy in them. "It would work, wouldn't it, if I used my sister to play on your compassion? That's not what I want to do. Not what I'm going to do."

He walked to where the land fell off, where it seemed to have been hacked by an ax to form a wall that faced the churning sea. Gulls screamed overhead, swooping down with flashes of white wings, then rising up again to soar.

She came here, he thought, here to this place whenever she visited her childhood home. Came here on those rare times when she needed to be alone with her thoughts.

It was only right, he supposed, that he finally gave her his thoughts, and the feelings behind them, in a place that was hers.

"I loved Pamela. What happened between us changed me."

"I know." She would have to forgive him, Cybil realized as she could feel her heart softening. Before she let him go.

"I loved her," he repeated, turning toward her again, stepping forward. "But what I felt for her isn't a shadow, isn't even a pale substitute, for what I feel for you. What I feel when I think of you, when I look at you. It overwhelms me, Cybil. It makes me ache. It makes me hope."

Her lips trembled open. Her heart began to beat in a quick, almost painful rhythm she recognized as joy. She saw on his face what she'd never really believed she would see. Struggling to absorb it, she looked away, down the long, rocky coast that seemed to stretch into forever.

"For what?" she managed. "What does it make you hope for?"

"Miracles. I hurt you. I've no excuse for it." He spoke quickly, terrified she would tell him it no longer mattered, that it was too late. "I attacked when I thought you might be pregnant because I was angry at myself. Angry that part of me was thinking that having a baby with you would be a way I could keep you."

When her head whipped around, her eyes wide with shock, he dragged his hands through his hair. "I knew you didn't want marriage, but if you'd been... I could have pushed you into it. And my only defense against that kind of thinking, against using something like that, was to turn on you."

"Pushed me into marriage?" was all she could say. Staggered, she rose, walked a few feet away to stare blindly down into the thrashing waves. How was she supposed to keep up with this? she wondered. How had it all changed so fast?

"It's no excuse, but you have a right to know I never thought you'd planned it or tricked me. I've never known anyone less calculating than you. Cybil, you're a warm, generous woman, with a capacity for joy unlike anyone else I've ever known. Having you in my life...you made me happy, and I think I'd forgotten how to be."

"Preston." She turned back, her vision blurry with tears.

"Please, let me finish. Just hear me out." He grabbed her hands now, gripping hard. "I love you. Everything about you staggers me. You said you loved me. You don't lie."

"No." She saw him clearly now. The exhaustion in his eyes, the tension in his face. If he hadn't been holding her hands so tightly she would have tried to smooth it all away. "I don't lie."

"I need you, so much more than you need me. I know you can get over me and move on. You're too resilient, too open to life, not to. Nothing would stop you from being what you are. You can tell me to go. You'll forget me. Whatever part I played in your life won't keep you from being happy."

He kept his eyes on her face, surrendering everything to the desperate whirl of emotion inside him.

"And I'll never in my life get over you. I'll never stop loving you or stop regretting everything I did to push you away from me. You can tell me to go," he said in a voice strained taut with emotion. "And I will. Please God." Helpless, he lowered his brow to hers. "Please don't tell me to go."

"Do you believe that?" she said quietly. "Do you really believe I could forget you?" Amazed at how steady her voice, and her heart was, she waited until he lifted his head and looked down at her. "Maybe I could get over you and be happy. But why should I risk it? Why should I tell you to go when I want you to stay?"

He let out the air clogging his lungs. Even as her lips began to curve, he pulled her against him, kept her there, swaying with relief. She felt him shudder once as he pressed his face to her shoulder.

"You didn't let me ruin it." His voice was raw, and his heart seemed to batter against hers until it moved inside her.

"No, I didn't." She held on, rocked with the knowledge that he had so much feeling for her in him. This strong, stubborn, serious man was weak for love of her. "I couldn't. I need you, too."

He held her away from him, his heart in his eyes as he skimmed his thumbs over her cheeks. "I love this face. I thought I lost it." He brushed his lips over her brow, her eyelids. "I thought I lost you, Cybil. I can't…"

His mouth covered hers. He meant to be gentle, to show her she would be cherished, but emotion raged through him, wild and strong as the sea below them. All of it poured into the kiss.

When he drew back, her eyes were wet. "Don't cry."

"You're going to have to get used to it. We Campbells are an emotional lot."

"I figured that out. Your father wants to break me into very small pieces."

"When he sees you make me happy, he'll let you live." She grinned, and laughter bubbled out. "He'll love you, Preston, and so will my mother. First because I do, then because of who you are."

"Moody, rude, short-tempered?"

"Yes." She laughed again when he winced. "I could deny it, but I'm such a lousy liar. She took his hand in hers and began to walk. "I love it here. This is where my parents met and fell in love. He lived in the lighthouse then, like a hermit, guarding his work, irritated that a woman had come along to distract him."

She shot him a sidelong look. "He's moody, rude, short-tempered."

The similarity had him grinning. "Sounds like a very sensible man." He brought their joined hands to his lips. "Cybil, will you go to Newport with me and meet my family?"

"I'd like that." She glanced up, her head angling when she saw that familiar intense expression in his eyes. "What?"

He stopped, turned to her in the shadow of the great light with the water warring against the rocks below. "I know you don't want marriage or a house in the country. You like living in New York in the center of things, and I don't expect—you'd like the house," he said, interrupting his own thoughts. "It's a great old place, near the coast like this. Anyway," he continued, shaking his head as she remained silent, just looking at him, "I don't expect you to change your lifestyle. But if you decide, later on, that you want to marry me, make a home and a family with me, will you tell me?"

Her heart did three wonderful and stylish handsprings, but she only nodded. "You'll be the first to know."

Telling himself to be content with that, he gave her hand a quick squeeze. "Okay."

He started to walk again, surprised when she stopped, pulling back so that both their arms were extended, linked only by warm fingers. "Preston?"

"Yeah?"

"I want to marry you, make a home and a family with you." The smile lit up her face as he gaped at her. "See, you're the first to know."

Hope spun cheerfully into bliss. "Sure." He brought her stumbling into him with one quick jerk. "But did you have to keep me dangling for so long?"

Then she was laughing as he swung her off her feet, spinning her in dizzy circles.

* * * * *